Golden Angel

CLAIRE HOGAN

Copyright © 2024 by Claire Hogan

Paperback: 978-1-963050-57-8
eBook: 978-1-963050-58-5
Library of Congress Control Number: 2023923560

All rights reserved. No part of this publication may be reproduced, distributed, or transmitted in any form or by any electronic or mechanical means, without the prior written permission of the publisher, except in the case of brief quotations embodied in critical reviews and certain other noncommercial uses permitted by copyright law.

This Book is a work of fiction. Names, characters, places, and incidents either are the product of the author's imagination or are used fictitiously. Any resemblance to actual persons, living or dead, events, or locales is entirely coincidental.

Ordering Information:

Prime Seven Media
518 Landmann St.
Tomah City, WI 54660

Printed in the United States of America

NOTE TO READER

All my love,

Claire

Xoxo

Thank you so much for reading

Truly appreciated

X

TABLE OF CONTENTS

1	1
2	5
3	19
4	26
5	39
6	49
7	55
8	63
9	71
10	85
11	106
12	118
13	131
14	142
15	160
16	182
17	196

18	202
19	220
20	230
21	243
22	255
23	270
24	284
25	297
26	310
27	322
28	334
29	354
30	362
31	379
32	401
33	418
34	434
35	448
Epilogue	462

1

Two months earlier I was working for An Garda Síochána and had been for six years. However, I did not risk my life patrolling the streets of Dublin. Fully trained with honours, I sat behind a damn desk! I love my job immensely, but it didn't fulfil me and always left me wondering if something was missing.

Evee, my best friend, works in an orphanage in China and has done so for several years now, returning home for holidays or special occasions. Unfortunately, that was the only time I got to see her. She'd come to life talking about her job, the babies and youngsters she helped care for and said it was one of the most rewarding experiences of her life. I always wanted to go back with her but instead settled for full-time employment, happy to know I had security if things didn't work out. Evee was lucky coming from a very wealthy family who supported her choices wholeheartedly and would do anything for her.

So, after serious thought and heartfelt deliberation, I decided to apply for a three-year career break which was worth up to €36,000 – €12,000 annually. It wasn't great but it was something and kept my job open. Where else can you do that? Officers could apply for a variety of reasons, including foreign travel, further education or other employment opportunities. Being just a pencil pusher, with no particular skills, my application had no chance of being refused entry to the scheme. My parents of course, particularly my dad, would go ballistic. Which is why I decided not to say anything until it had been approved. I've since heard they had changed it to a year and almost impossible to get approved because recruitment is so low. I was lucky I applied at the right time.

One evening over dinner I casually revealed my intentions and the proverbial shit hit the fan. The dramatics from my mother, a grown woman, in tears and wailing like a Banshee. "There were plenty of children in Ireland who needed love and affection, why did I have to go to the other side of the world to give it? Look after your own first?" she cried. As dad's brother was a high-up commissioner, I was conveniently placed behind a desk instead of where I wanted to be, interacting with the community and their needs out on the streets. If dad had even a sniff of my intentions, my application would have conveniently disappeared! You could say, I was wrapped in cotton wool from the day I was born.

I didn't have a boyfriend and being quite shy hasn't helped. I didn't mind though. I loved my own company much to the detriment of my mother who wanted lots of grandchildren to spoil. She said I'd end up an old spinster with a hundred cats, alone on my rocking chair! I was already looking forward to it. As a result of an incident, I had stopped going to staff parties and this pretty much cut off any chance of meeting anyone through work. The night in question was a birthday celebration for Andy, one of the male officers. It started well and was looking like it was going to be a good night even though I wasn't much of a drinker. Maybe the odd cocktail if I couldn't taste the alcohol. I found it entertaining, sitting back and watching people getting plastered. Don't get me wrong, I wasn't a party pooper. I let my hair down and joined in the fun and games, singing and dancing with the best of them. They were just too drunk to know I was still sober.

Anyway, I was sitting there watching the dance floor and all the shapes they were throwing, laughing silently to myself. It was just too funny. One of the officers from another station sat down beside me. Oh, here we go. He was broad and quite good-looking with a mop of curly hair which baffled me. How on earth did he get his hat on? The look on my face must have given me away. "The power of shit loads of hair gel," he laughed introducing himself. He seemed really nice and very entertaining, but of course, he was pissed as a fart. Staggering to the bar he asked if I'd like a drink, calling me by my nickname, wiggling his eyebrows. When he returned, he was all over me. "So shaggy, would you like to split from here and have a quiet drink somewhere else?" "Em no thanks," I sighed, "I'm staying for one more then going home, ALONE!"

"Ahh sure don't be like that now," he slurred, "I'd love you to show me how you got your nickname," he said, wiggling those stupid fucking eyebrows again. I just wanted to rip them off his stupid-looking face!

"Sorry, have I missed something? What's so interesting about the name 'shaggy' all of a sudden? They call me that because I have curly hair, right?" Saying it out loud made me doubtful and I could feel my eyes widen with fright as I waited. He spit his drink across the table and I was ever so grateful he hadn't sat opposite me.

"Ah, Jesus no! Seriously, is that what you thought? Come on now, has any female officer ever once called you shaggy?" Come to think of it, they hadn't. "So, Donal, why do they call me shaggy, I know you're itching to tell me?" He shifted uncomfortably and looked from left to right like he was about to reveal something juicy. "Well, apparently you love doggy. Face down, on the shag pile, hence shaggy. Shaggy as in the carpet."

"Jesus Christ, I know what a fucking shag pile is!" I blink. My eyes widened in shocked disbelief. I could have fucking died of embarrassment. All those years thinking they had accepted me. Stupidly giggling because I thought it was so cute that they called me 'shaggy'. Oh God, I was mortified. None of the female officers had the decency to tell me. It upset me knowing I didn't have a friend amongst them after all. "Who on earth started that degrading rumour?" I hissed, fuming.

He sobered up quickly enough when he saw the look on my face. "I'm sorry Rhylee, it's obvious you didn't know."

I stood, throwing my coat on, bending so we were eye to eye. "You let everyone with a dick big or small, know that I now consider that nickname sexual harassment. If I ever hear as much of a whisper, they will be standing in front of HR. Do I make myself clear?"

He nodded his head, sitting up straight, repeating he was so sorry. I walked away with a heavy heart and never socialised with them again.

2

As Evee worked full-time, she was able to get my CV to the top of the list through the agency she was registered with and it helped that I had a degree in child development. It took eight weeks for approval, allowing me to fly back with her after the Christmas holidays. I was moving in with her and insisted on paying half the rent which fell upon deaf ears because her parents had paid the lease for a year. I wasn't keen, so we agreed I'd do the weekly shop. It was a relief knowing I was contributing even though it seemed small.

My new job in Shanghai was five days a week, Monday to Friday, six hours a day for six months to a year, leaving the weekends free. I didn't need much experience as long as I could provide love and care. Help was needed to make their lives at the orphanage as happy as possible and to assist the permanent staff. The children were infants and toddlers, three months to six years. I could give them as much love as they needed. I loved children and loved making them happy. I applied for a one-year contract which would be reviewed after ten months and if I worked out, would hopefully be invited to stay for another if I was still interested. My heart was in my mouth as I approached my first day but it felt less nerve-wracking knowing Evee was by my side. She had enough confidence for both of us. I'd never in a million years do anything like this on my own.

I settled in nicely and loved the job. It was a great challenge, but nothing I couldn't handle. However, I was sometimes sad and teary-eyed when my shift ended. Never got that kind of satisfaction or fulfilment in my other job. All the children were wonderful and I particularly loved looking after the babies, wishing I could get them all forever homes.

It was the weekend and because it was the closest, I decided to do some shopping at the Yuyuan Market in the Old Shanghai City. It was also beside the Old City God Temple which we were going to visit next time. Evee was doing an extra shift so couldn't join me. I planned to head off early to the city on the Shanghai Metro and be home at six to meet her for dinner. I loved the city and everything about it was vibrant and full of energy, just like the people. However, on this particular occasion, I found the train ride a little daunting. Everyone just stared at me and when I caught them, they just continued. At least in Ireland, if you were caught staring at someone, you'd look away embarrassed. I mentioned it to Evee and she said it was because I was so fair and blonde. Suppose I stuck out like a sore thumb.

I was tempted to stop at the numerous street vendors to try the Nan Xiang steamed stuffed buns or crispy fried cake. Or to taste the local traditional snacks, Yangchun noodles, fried stuffed buns and chop rice cakes. I only managed a slice of toast before setting off on my adventure, eager to be on my way. Sure, I was here for a year and could come back anytime with Evee to sample the local and regional specialities. She knew all the best places for tasty nibbles and I didn't know enough. I heard so many horror stories of people eager to try every delicacy. Paying for it afterwards camped on the toilet with a jumbo pack of loo rolls. No thanks! I was immersed in the lively atmosphere of the bustling streets exploring the famous markets and stalls, where locals stocked up on everything from electronics to fish. Certainly not a place for the fainthearted. The one thing I didn't like was the fish markets. It was unreal seeing live fish for sale, hundreds to choose from but knowing that you picked what you wanted and they'd prepare it in front of you. Eek!! Eh no, I don't think so. I've always been quite happy getting the frozen stuff from the supermarket. Too many fish piled into small tanks, not having enough room to swim about, and poor little turtles climbing on top of each other trying to make their escape. I wanted to set them free. Not only that, but they had fish from all parts of the world and surprisingly, fresh oysters from Ireland! Who would believe it? No, it wasn't a landmark I'd recommend to anyone who cared to ask my opinion.

However, the outdoor bird market was a kaleidoscope of colour with a variety of species chirping and singing away. It wasn't uncommon to find parrot owners stopping by to chat with each other carrying exotic birds on their shoulders and happy for you to take photos. The loud grumbling noises coming from my tummy told me it was time to make my way back and as I was close to a train station, headed that way. The maps were easy enough to understand and I knew exactly where I was, even though I had travelled further than I should have. Easy to do in a place like this, wandering from one wonderful street to the next because every turn had something new and interesting. Treasure troves around every corner. The hardest thing is stopping yourself from buying everything. Especially gold jewellery. Everything was so cheap.

The station platform was quite packed and everyone seemed to have their heads down not interested in the bustling mania around them. I reckoned they were used to it, just another ordinary day to them but it wasn't. Only for it was getting late, I would have walked to the next Metro station because this one looked a little downtrodden. It was after five when I noticed a gang of kids all dressed in black rushing through the ticket lobby. I thought they were on a school tour, dashing to catch the train home, but none of them swiped tickets. On closer inspection, they varied in age and as they headed in my direction, people darted out of their way. Like they knew something awful was about to happen without the slightest outward show of surprise. Standing a few metres away I noticed a well-to-do elderly lady. I thought she looked out of place in her expensive clothes, perfect make-up and Chanel handbag. Everyone else seemed less well-off and it looked like she wasn't meant to be there.

In a split second, the tiny aggressors had confronted her and, in a blink, a knife was held close to her face. Was this really happening? Why wasn't anyone stepping in to help?? I looked around in disbelief. Surely this can't be happening in broad daylight. With my adrenaline pumping and my heart racing, I dropped my shopping and ran headfirst into the altercation screaming like a demented lunatic. The child criminals got such a fright they pushed the woman to the ground with violence, before dispersing like lightning over the train tracks. Apart from the little one now pointing a knife at me. Shockingly, he must have only been about five or six. He jabbed the air and before I caught my breath, he forcibly slid the pointed blade under the strap of my bag and in one slick move cut it free. I swung him round sending both him and my bag flying but not before the knife pierced my arm sending bolts of pain searing through my body. He looked at me, I think with regret before picking up my bag and running away. I fucking loved that bag and it had cost me two weeks' wages. I looked around for help, seeing the lady lifeless on the ground. I knelt beside her and gently rested her head on my lap. Thankfully, she was conscious and there wasn't any sign of blood. She cried gently as I tried to comfort her and screamed for someone to fucking help. I couldn't believe what just happened, a mugging by an army of pint-sized children. In ten minutes, we were surrounded by police and medics, then brought separately to hospital.

I didn't realise how bad the wound was until the nurse tried to peel my blood-soaked top off me. She gathered up my hair which was tinged with blood and piled it in a bun on the top of my head. I sat on the bed in my bra with my top hanging around my waist. What a time to be grateful I'd put some decent underwear on. Well, what did they care? I was just another number in this overpopulated metropolis! I heard a commotion outside and raised voices, someone sounded angry. The curtain to my cubicle ripped open. I gasped. Standing there was the most handsome, distinguished-looking doctor I could have wished for. He possessed the kind of beauty that would stop you in your tracks. Only for the fact that I was sitting, I'd be weak in the knees. His face was handsome and well-defined, his features carved from marble. His blue eyes scorched me, burning right through my skin. He would still be beautiful had they been any other colour. Lashes we girls pay a fortune for and lips full and perfectly symmetrical made me wonder how they would feel against mine. Lustrous shiny black hair to his jawline. Slim yet muscular. Hey, who wants a boyfriend with a smaller waist than yours? Perfection personified, hot as fuck or as Evee would say, a fuckin ride. I could see him gracing the front covers of all the top magazines. My cheeks heated as I straightened up and smiled shyly, obviously forgetting my state of undress. I was shy when it came to things like that. He strode in with masculinity and confidence, like a BOSS. That's how a man is supposed to walk. The kind of man I want. Enough confidence for both of us and then some. Doctor GQ looked towards the ground and in a deep gravelly voice, introduced himself as Gui Lee. Omg, that voice. Was it an American accent? It did things to my insides. He spoke like someone who spent a considerable time being educated in the English-speaking world. He takes my hand and gently shakes it, his thumb lightly circles the back of my hand as he maintains eye contact. Oh holy crap. Not surprising at all, his hands were the softest and of course, he had the best-shaped cuticles

I'd ever seen on a man. I noticed too, that he never said doctor. He was accompanied by several suited men whom I thought were interns. Looking back, how stupid. What intern could afford such expensive suits, and wouldn't they be wearing white overcoats? Duh!! He took one look at my state of undress and in one angry sentence, the room cleared immediately. He circled me slowly, his gaze moving casually over my body. Oh my God, he was gorgeous and smelled divine. My mother always taught me not to stare. She hasn't met Gui Lee. He just stood there, silently watching, unnerving me, giving me goosebumps and I could have sworn he sniffed my hair. I turned to see what he was doing and was told to look straight ahead. "Oh." I fall silent.

"Does it hurt?" he asked gently. Giving me a slow sexy smile. Or was I imagining he was flirting with me. I nodded. Swallowing the lump in my throat. I couldn't talk. For the first time in my life, I was stuck for words. He stepped forward, blue eyes on mine, gently tracing his index finger slowly up my arm circling the incision. I get goosebumps

No, no, don't make eye contact.

Shy should have been my middle name. I looked away holding my breath. "Such perfect white skin not a blemish, until now," he murmured while staring at my heaving chest. His finger travelled slowly to my collarbone when I smacked it away and winced, a painful reminder why I was there in the first place. His eyebrow raised in surprise. "Am I making you uncomfortable?" Slowly lifting my eyes to meet his I answered, "Please tell me you're a fucking doctor before I scream the place down!" He looks smug. Prick!

"No, I'm not actually," he smirks. "I'm here to thank you for saving my mother's life," he says eloquently.

I raised a brow. "Oh."

When I realised, he wasn't a doctor my face flushed hot with embarrassment. I felt unnecessarily exposed in front of this beautiful stranger who exudes power from every pore. I tried frantically to cover myself up.

"Leave it, the doctor will be here presently."

"Well, would you mind leaving and let the real doctors do their job," I fumed.

He opened the curtain and in Chinese called for one. Chinese or English, his voice was so sexy. While waiting I asked after his mother. "She sustained mild bruising and a broken wrist but it could have been worse. Thankfully with rest, she'll be fine but keeps asking after her 'Jīnsè de tiānsh."

"I'm sorry, I don't speak Chinese."

"She's asking for the 'Golden angel'."

I stared blankly at him. "Oh no, did they steal that too?"

He roared out laughing and holy crap he was even more handsome, that jaw … dimples and those intense eyes.

"I'm glad I amuse you, Mr. Gui."

He laughed again which pissed me off even more.

Absolute prick!

"It's Mr Lee, but please call me Gui. My mother calls you a golden angel and I can see why."

"Golden?"

He reached out and touched my hair. "She's right. Your hair is like spun gold," he says, his eyes still locked on mine.

"My hair? Oh. I wouldn't go that far. More candy floss than gold. But thank you."

Please shut up! You're talking shite!

I don't know why I blushed when he said that. Maybe it was his tone or the way his eyes pierced through my very soul. Holy crap, was I going into shock?

"That's very sweet, I hope your mother makes a speedy recovery," I murmured trying to keep my eyes off his full mouth. As if reading my mind, he teasingly licked his lips as his eyes dropped to my breasts and then back up to my mouth. I watched mesmerised until he coughed loudly. His eyes lingered on my mouth.

"Oh, umm, I thought it strange she was unaccompanied, especially in such a rough area?"

"The same could be said about you, Miss ...... I didn't catch your name. Well?" he prompts me.

I fake a smile. "I didn't offer it. Oh Jesus, I don't feel very well, would you mind calling a bloody doctor. I need to get my arm sorted so I can leave this place and go home." He poked his head impatiently through the curtain and shouted something in Chinese. Two minutes later, the tiny cubicle was stuffed to capacity with several doctors and nurses. The doctor spoke briefly with him and he translated. "The wound is deep. You need stitches." He said without any emotion. He leaned back on the windowsill, both arms stretched wide like he owned the bloody place, eyes locked on mine as they stitched me up.

Overconfident prick!

I wanted to scream in pain every time the needle punctured my arm, twenty times, ten stitches. But for some reason I didn't want to utter a whimper in front of this Mr. Gui Lee in his expensive designer suit and handmade shoes, which screamed yes, I'm very successful and can afford nothing but the best. I never felt like this. I didn't know what was happening between us. Did he feel it too? Both of us were caught in a staring match, his eyes refusing to break the deadlock. The doctor spoke to him and all the while he kept his eyes pinned firmly on mine. He did his job, bowed his head to Mr Lee and left us alone, pulling the curtain tightly behind him. I think Mr Gui Lee was a force to be reckoned with. He walked towards me as I tried in a panic to pull my top on.

"Allow me, Miss …?"

"It's okay, I can dress myself, thank you."

Without hesitation, he was anchored between my thighs gently lifting my arm and sliding it through the sleeve. A man between my thighs, it felt good. Unfamiliar feelings shot through my body as little bolts of electricity pulsed between my legs. I wanted to slide to the edge just so I could feel him, his heat. I wanted more. Oh God I was attracted to him, shockingly attracted to this stranger. His confidence and authority turned me on. Like what the hell. I needed to leave before I made a show of myself. "Is there any point putting that back on, it's ripped to shreds."

His eyes flick to my breasts again. "Eh hellooo, my eyes are up here." I pointed to my head. He wasn't one bit embarrassed either. "Would you have me walk about like that?" I sighed, looking everywhere but at him, trying to stop my face from burning. He put his finger under my chin raising it so our eyes locked. Oh, God. I look away and gaze dreamily at his beautiful mouth, mesmerised as he runs his tongue over his plump bottom lip again.

Seriously, does he know what he's doing to me? Is he purposely teasing me?

He asked again, his tone authoritative now. "So? Your name," he commanded!

I frown. Fucking cheek. "Rhylee M… oh my God I'm going to puke." Quite unladylike, I slide off the bed right down his body, my legs almost buckling beneath me as I frantically dashed towards the bin. Mortified, I made the most horrendous gagging sound as I projectile vomited while he gently rubbed my back. Like it was the most natural thing in the world.

"Fuck, are you okay?" He sounded concerned. I looked up to find him watching me closely.

"I'm grand." I was uneasy with the closeness.

His eyes widened a little. "Clearly not," he mutters impatiently, running his eyes all over my face, touching the side of my cheek. He handed me a beautiful handkerchief with his name embroidered in the corner which I was half afraid to use. He noticed my hesitation.

"It's fine. Go ahead. Thanks to my mother I have quite a collection. She's managed to stitch my initials onto everything she could get her hands on, nothing is safe."

I giggled. He helped me up and motioned for me to sit down while he dispensed a cup of water. As he bent over, I shamefully stared at his tight arse.

Bless me, Father…

"My name is Rhylee Murphy."

Standing before me now, he was far taller than I thought, at least six foot five inches.

"That's a lovely name. Irish, isn't it?" He patted the bed like he was calling a puppy. Which I ignore.

"Yeah, how'd you know that?"

"I think Murphy gave it away. Very unusual spelling too, Rhylee."

"How do you know how I spell my name?"

"I looked at your chart."

I climbed on the bed as elegantly as I possibly could with one functioning arm and gladly accepted the water. The taste and smell of vomit was nauseating and I certainly didn't want him getting too close to find out!

"Why keep asking my name then?"

"I assumed it was misspelt, language barrier?"

"My mother likes to be controversial, with everything. Well, Mr Lee, I must bid you farewell. May I say goodbye to your mother?"

"She's left already."

"Oh, but didn't she break some bones?"

"This is not a suitable environment for her. She'll get the best care and attention she needs with me while she recuperates."

"Oh, I see, they do say the healing process is quicker when in the care of loved ones, physically and emotionally. Just keep a close eye on her, she's had a very traumatic experience and may go through a range of emotions. Then again, she might be a tough one."

"And who will be looking after you during your recovery, family, friends, or a boyfriend perhaps? Are you in a relationship, Miss Murphy?"

"Oh my God, what time is it? I forgot about Evee, she'll be up the wall with worry if she's not already at the police station chewing some poor fella's ear off."

"It's eight-thirty."

"Oh Christ, she'll be on to the Irish embassy if I don't get back. I couldn't phone because they snatched my bag."

He dug in his pocket and took out his. "Here use mine."

I stared at the screen blankly and looked perplexed. "You know you just type in the numbers, they're not in Chinese."

I wanted to say, 'No shit Sherlock,' but thought it rude and he didn't seem like the type of man who would find sarcasm funny. Or anything funny for that matter. "I've always had my phone so don't know her number."

"No worries. I'll drive you home, I insist. What's the address?"

My eyes popped and I looked startled realising the predicament I was in. I felt like a fucking idiot. I frowned. "I don't know, I've only been here a while, going to work and straight back to the apartment, this was my first day out on my own."

"So, you're living and working here."

"Yes, I work at the orphanage."

"Are you crazy going out alone when you're not familiar with your surroundings? That's exactly why things like this happen to people like you."

I shoved his phone into his chest and pushed past him. Stopping I turned to face him, trying to stop the tears from falling and whispered gently, "Only for people like me, your mother would probably be dead, because nobody else gave a fuck! Have a nice day Mr. Lee!"

I turned and stormed dramatically down the hall searching for the damn exit. I kicked myself for being so rude. At least I had an excuse. I'd just been stabbed and my emotions were all over the place. It didn't help matters that the man I left back there completely unnerved me.

Damn, I'll never see him again.

It was dark when I finally found my way outside, the overwhelming heat making my head spin. I vaguely remember strong arms circling my waist and being lifted effortlessly before passing out. I don't know how long I was unconscious but when I woke, a nurse was tending to my bandage. She smiled as I blinked awake taking in the luxury of my unfamiliar surroundings.

3

"Where am I, what kind of hospital is this?" The nurse didn't answer and just smiled.

"You are in my home Miss Murphy."

"Your house."

"A skyscraper to be precise."

"Where exactly?"

"Lujiazui, the financial district." Which meant nothing to me. Obviously the posh part. He owns a skyscraper. Wow! Like what the hell did he do? "Please abide by my rules while you are here." I sat up and watched him move with athletic grace across the room. Like he just stepped off a catwalk. Naked from the waist up in a pair of lounge bottoms, barely hanging on his toned hips as he ran a towel through his hair. Mesmerised. I gulped and stared. Jesus, he was a fine thing. I had never seen a man in that state of undress before except on tv. Which was always switched to another channel by my old fashioned dad.

At home, he controlled the tv and almost everything we watched. If the actors started kissing, he would cover my eyes with his hand until it was over, making me blush even more. My mother wasn't fussed about what we watched and was happy to leave the channel on when they were getting up to all sorts. Once dad walked in while mam and I were glued to Fifty Shades Of Grey. We had turned the sound right down so he wouldn't hear the moans and groans. We discovered that man would hear a pin drop. "Jesus Christ Patsy, what the hell are you watching?" he roared, swiping the remote from my hand in disgust.

Mam would calmly say, "Sure Patrick, it's only natural! How do you think Rhylee got here?"

I gave her a Jesus Christ don't you get me involved look. "Mr Lee, I would happily abide by your rules if indeed I was a guest, but seeing as I'm here against my will, I'll do no such thing!"

He stopped drying his hair and stared straight at me. His eyebrows raised in a, you going to argue with me look. I waited for a confrontation but none came. Instead, his eyes travelled from my mouth all the way down to my chest and rested there. I looked down and Holy God, my boobs were out for everyone to see, hard nipples giving away my arousal. I frantically grabbed the sheet almost covering my head to hide my embarrassment.

"Why am I naked," I screamed. "Where the fuck are my clothes, you sick bastard. What kind of dirty perv are you, putting me to bed naked," I shrieked from behind the sheet. I felt the bed dip beside me as he gently tugged the sheet down just enough to cover my modesty.

"Don't fucking touch me or I'll scream the place down."

"A perverted one Miss Murphy."

"Oh." I gulp. What do you even say to that?

"How old are you?" His steely gaze drags slowly down my body before reverting to my eyes. I got the chills.

"I asked you a question." I wanted to tell him to fuck right off and mind his own bloody business. "I thought you'd have a complete dossier on me by now?" Noticing his eyebrow slowly rising, I quickly added, "Twenty-seven and you?" He ignored my question. Not fair! His jet-black hair hung loose just below his jawline as I watched tiny droplets trickle down his sculpted biceps. Jesus, his chest was bigger than mine! And hairless. As were his arms and I bet his legs too? It was such a turn on and I found myself wondering if his balls were just as smooth. I blushed at the thought. My ick was hairy men. I knew my face was beetroot but I couldn't stop it if I tried. I hated blushing even though it was a perfectly natural thing. I always said it was a bloody curse! But it was nature's way of disclosing our true feelings. The more tense or embarrassed I got, the redder my face went. It was such a hindrance going through college.

"You look like a deer caught in the headlights, my sincere apologies if I've embarrassed you, Miss Murphy?" he said sympathetically. I was willing to forgive him because he was drop dead gorgeous and smelled like heaven. I had to cross my legs in an attempt to stop the arousing tingling down below. Evee called it 'fanny flutters.' I was aroused but couldn't explain why. I was shy and embarrassed at the same time. I scooted back and pushed myself against the headboard, trying to pull the sheet from under him.

"Do you mind?" He shifted slightly, freeing the bedding and in return, I noticed his crotch. Boner alert! I was stunned to see the hugest bulge and shamefully couldn't take my eyes off it. Holy fuck I'm going to hell!

He hooked a finger under my chin bringing my gaze up to meet his. Which was becoming a habit of his.

"Now I know how women must feel being stared at in an objectified way, as a sex object!"

"I'm sorry, I've never been in a situation like this." I blush. His interest piqued and he moved closer. "Like what exactly?"

I turned my head. "A huge boner." I covered my mouth. "Oh God! Can't believe I just said that out loud either. It's my nerves, I talk utter shite when I'm nervous. Can I go now?"

He smiled and I got that feeling again down below.

"I see," he answered, standing to fix himself. "Are you involved with anyone?"

"You go first. Men always come first anyway." I let out a huge guffaw. Delighted with my quick-witted anecdote.

"I would offer to disprove that theory if you weren't so shy."

I gulped. That was sexy as fuck. Looking nervously at his eyebrow, I immediately answered, "Not at the moment."

He nodded thoughtfully and I noticed his mood change.

"So why am I here exactly and where are my clothes?"

"I followed you after you left abruptly and luckily, I did because you fainted, either from the humidity or hunger?"

"All I remember was the extreme heat and feeling dizzy."

"You were unable to furnish me with an address, so that is why you are here now. As for your clothes, they were unwearable."

"What about my underwear," I asked shyly.

"Everything was discarded. My housekeeper kindly left something for you to wear which will suffice until we get you some clothes."

"I will not wear someone else's clothes."

"Fine, I'd be only too happy to see you walk around here naked. You saw how hard I was from just seeing your tits, completely naked I'd blow like a blocked steam pipe."

"Oh my God, that's disgusting, who even talks like that? You wouldn't use that kind of filthy language in front of your mother, huh?"

He tilts his head to the sky, pissed off. "You said you don't have a boyfriend, Miss Murphy? Makes sense now."

"No, I don't and what's that got to do with your lack of manners?"

He paused and looked at me in wonderment. "You're right, I have overstepped the mark. Forgive me, I lost myself for a moment, it will not happen again."

With that, he abruptly left the room. I groaned into the sheet. What the hell just happened?

I eyed the piece of clothing draped over the chair. I wrapped the sheet tightly about me and dragged myself out of bed. I picked it up and the tag was still on it. One hundred percent pure silk and 8,500 HKD. Holy crap! That's about a thousand euro. I held it up and it was just a plain boring nightdress, nothing sexy. It slipped smoothly over my body and felt lovely and cool against my skin covering me in all the right places and stopping just short of my knee.

I walked over to the full-length mirror and almost died. OMFG!! I looked like shite! I don't wear much makeup going to work, a touch of tinted moisturiser, a dab of blush, mascara and my hair in a ponytail. There wasn't any point in making an effort. If you didn't tie your hair up, the babies would pull the head off you or you'd end up with bits of food or God forbid, poo in it. One time I was grocery shopping and as I am paying, the shop assistant pointed to his cheek, then mine saying I had chocolate on my face. I hadn't eaten chocolate since I left Ireland!! Ughh. How on earth hadn't I smelled it? Well, what can I say? Must have just gotten used to it??

I honestly don't know why he didn't run screaming from the room and kick me out of his stunning home. I was totally out of place. The state of me. Oh yeah, I flashed my boobs. No man could resist a female exposing their breasts no matter how repulsive. He is a man after all. My hair, tinged with blood was like a dried-out sponge knotted and hanging off the side of my head, still in the elastic band. My face was blotchy with two unattractive panda eyes. I gulped in horror. I don't know what I was expecting to see, but it certainly wasn't the freak staring back at me now. I was mortified and couldn't shake the embarrassment.

What on earth must he be thinking? Him so perfect in every way, with beautiful women throwing themselves at him. In my deranged mind, I secretly imagined he was flirting with me. Hilarious. Now I was a fucking comedian. A fucking ugly one with bad hair. The shame of it. I looked again and cringed. I was fuming! It was obvious he only had me here out of respect for his mother. I wouldn't stay a minute longer.

Feeling stupid I barged out the door and opened everyone until I found him, storming into what must have been his office. I stopped in my tracks when I noticed he wasn't alone and heard the room come to a dead silence. Or had I come to my senses realising how rude and out of character I was behaving? I didn't have time to decide which one it was. He was seated casually in a large throne-like bamboo chair behind a huge desk. The room was decorated in rich tones of red, which is considered the luckiest colour in Chinese culture and black and gold. The entire room was bathed in oriental decor. From fabrics to the hand-painted Chinoiserie wallpaper which was jaw-droppingly stunning. I'd never seen anything like it. There was a sense of harmony where Asian and European design merged. It was lavish, luxurious and opulent all at once. Oh God, what have I done? So instead of looking like a very unattractive excuse for a woman, I now took centre stage in a roomful of spectators resembling a psychopath? I didn't look around knowing they were rendered speechless at the sorry sight shivering before them. It certainly sounded that way. I just stared at him as my heart pounded in my chest, right up to my ears. He didn't take his eyes off me as he spoke to someone at the back of the room. For all I know, he could have said, 'Nobody light a match, her hair looks highly flammable'! I giggled to myself and noticed his features change from annoyance to amusement.

4

"I apologise for interrupting your meeting, but I'd like to leave now. Can you please have someone drive me or if it's an inconvenience, give me appropriate clothing and I'll make my way home. I thank you for looking after me but I really must be getting back."

"Get back to what in particular, Miss Murphy. It seems to me you lead a rather boring life, would you agree?" I swallow the lump in my throat.

"Wait, what? How dare you. What's that got to do with you and NO, I don't. I have a wonderful life and I'm very happy with everything. Anyway, I don't need to convince you or anyone else for that matter."

"Indeed, you don't but I'm just at a loss as to why you would read such fiction if your life were as perfect as you say?" With that he held up a book like it was evidence in a courtroom and turned it around so I could see the cover – *The Wait*.

I blushed and tried not to show how embarrassed I was but knew my blushed cheeks gave me away. "Have you read it to make such a valid statement, or has the cover made you jump to conclusions? Who cares anyway what you think! Where did you find that, it was in my b...... bag?"

On cue, he held it up. He stood and moved from behind his desk sitting on the edge in front of me. He remained silent watching me, probably analysing my mental state. He was that close, all he had to do was stretch out his arm and touch my breast. Ooh, I wished everyone would disappear so he could.

Then my appearance brought me back to reality with a huge kick up the arse. As if! Get a grip darling, this man is gorgeous and powerful and has the likes of you mopping his floors. His housekeeper was very attractive, so you couldn't even be his cleaner. Scrubber comes to mind and would probably be more appropriate.

"Actually. That's not my book, it's my friend Evee's. So there!"

"Then why is your name written all over it in little red love hearts?"

"When I'm bored, I doodle. I had nothing to do on the train so I doodled."

"It's amazing how straight you can keep your face when you're lying, you would make a brilliant actress."

"How dare you." Why was he speaking to me with such contempt?

"Before you dig a bigger hole, I read the inscription inside, from Evee to you. Shall I remind you what she wrote? It might refresh your memory?"

Shit! I blushed, remembering how fierce dirty Evee's little message was. I knew she should have written it in Irish! I made a move to grab it, but he held it up high making me crash against him.

The only way I was getting it was to climb up his body. I made futile attempts to jump up and all I gained was sniggering from someone in the room while Gui ogled my bouncing boobs.

"What do you want, Gui?" I snap. "Who the hell cares who owns the damn book?" It took a minute for him to stop staring at my chest. "Seriously, haven't you seen a pair?" I crossed my arms, which pushed them up over the neckline. It's not like I had massive boobs or anything, just a perfect handful. Feeling dejected, I threw my clenched hands down by my sides, exhausted and ready to burst into tears. "I can't do this," I cried.

He peeled his jumper off and placed it over my head, gently encouraging me to put my arms through. "Best to stop any further distractions," he said kindly.

"Can you stop playing with me so I can just leave? I've had enough already. Some people are probably very worried about me right now. I bet my parents are flying over as we speak. My family have connections in high places back in Ireland and I'm probably on the news as missing!" I wouldn't be surprised. My mother loves drama. "Oh Miss Murphy, if only we were playing, I wouldn't be able to stop myself! We recovered your items two days ago while you were a sleeping beauty and contacted the relevant people. So, no need to worry about rushing home." He smirked.

"Why are you going out of your way to make me feel like shit? What, wait. I've been here for two whole days?? OMG! Look, I'm sure you're an extremely busy man and I've kept you away from running your little empire, or whatever it is you're doing here?"

"You're quite right. I do run an empire. I own one of the world's largest iron and steel manufacturing companies and one of two major banks. World domination can also be mastered from the comfort of one's home." I stared blankly at him. Is he for real? "Look, just keep the bloody things, I've had enough of your mind games." With that, I fearlessly turned and walked towards the door. I panicked, as I noticed so much muscle in one room, my bravery slowly depleting in a sigh. As I quickened my pace his voice boomed out around the room and two apes blocked my exit. Oh, Holy God, what now. I took a deep breath and turned around.

"Are you kidnapping me Mr. Gui?" Someone sniggered again.

Arsehole!

"Of course, not Rhylee." Oh God, I love how he says my name.

"I just thought you'd want to know we found most of the culprits responsible for attacking you."

"I wasn't attacked, your mother was, I just got in the way."

"I'm not going to argue with you, you were both hurt and there are consequences to pay."

Just then there was a shrill cry and a scuffle behind me. I looked over my shoulder and saw the little boy who had robbed me being held by the scruff of his neck. He had a look of sheer terror as we both eyed a sword lying on the table in front of him.

My host came up behind me, resting his hands on my shoulders, his warm breath tickling my neck, his scent enveloping me as he spoke in a gentle whisper, "The horse-chopping sword is from the Song dynasty during the reign of Emperor Shenzong. A rare piece measuring 1.2 metres and strong enough to chop through heavy armour or a child's arm in one clean swipe."

His tone was so pleasant he could almost be describing something beautiful and not a murderous weapon. He spoke in Chinese and the two men holding the child grabbed his arm while another picked up what looked like a wooden block and placed it on the table. The child screamed and cried trying to kick his way out of his hold. My hand went up to my throat when I realised what they were going to do.

"You see Miss Murphy, in this country, people like him are punished in a way that they will think twice about doing it again."

"Oh my God, no you can't," I screamed. Pushing as hard as I could against the monster holding the child. The tiny little human ran into my open arms tightly wrapping around me. "You've made a great mistake. It wasn't this child who did it. Imagine how you'd feel when you discover you punished the wrong person. It will send you to an early grave."

"Before you tell me another lie, know that I've watched the security footage over and over. By the way, what was the lullaby you sang to calm my mother? It was beautiful."

I gasp in horror. "It was eerily hypnotic." I screwed up my face.

"Oh please, you're taking the piss now!"

"I am not. I won't lie or take the piss, as you so eloquently put it."

I could feel my face turning red. I knew as well as anyone I hadn't a note in my head. Fucking comedian! No wonder someone kept sniggering, obviously watched the one-woman show too! I was even more annoyed.

"Look you twisted fuck, you just can't take the law into your own hands. No matter how wealthy you are." I couldn't stop the tears from falling. "I'll go straight to the authorities when I get out of here and contact every tv station that'll listen to me. I'm sure someone is willing to co-operate knowing who you are. I will do everything in my power to let everyone out there know what an animal you are. It's barbaric and I can't believe this is happening. You're not back in the Song Dynasty you know, where that kind of thing was acceptable! How can someone love and adore their mother as much as you and do something so unbelievingly inhumane at the same time?"

The little boy was hysterically crying now as I tried my best to calm him down.

"Do you think the authorities care about scum like him? They're quite happy to turn a blind eye if it means they don't have to deal with it themselves." He spoke in Chinese and the two men peeled the little one from me.

I was hysterical as I watched them place his tiny arm on the wooden block. I turned around and flung myself hard against him, falling to my knees inconsolably crying as I gripped the leg of his trousers. "Couldn't you be the better man? I wailed loudly. Let people know that you're not an animal. Give the boy a chance, take him in and educate him. I'm sure you were given loads of chances growing up. Imagine what people would say, that you are indeed an honourable person. Please, Mr Lee, I beg you."

I felt like I was going to cry myself into oblivion if he didn't stop. I was exhausted. I moved my hands up his thighs begging him not to harm the child. "Please, I'll do anything," I sobbed.

He nodded and the two heavies flanking the child released their grip dropping him to the ground. He ploughed straight into my arms, almost knocking me over planting his face tightly against me too terrified to look anywhere else. He was so tiny.

"What could you possibly *do* for me Miss Murphy," he said with a glint in his eye. Look around you?"

"I don't know, but it got your attention. Please, please, please, anything. I'll come every day after work and weekends and teach your mother English, or whatever."

"I am a very wealthy businessman with connections everywhere, globally in fact. If my mother wanted to learn another language, I would hire the top people to teach her. You shouldn't assume either that my mother can't speak English. She was educated in the finest university in America."

"I see, but I don't think your mother would have liked a teacher, she's different to you, more, em, down to earth, normal!"

"You got all that from your brief encounter considering the circumstances, how utterly observant of you. I'll ignore your insults, for now, Miss Murphy. I will give you one choice to save the child from becoming an outcast and it's non-negotiable. Do you understand what that means?"

My heart is pounding out of my chest. I know that I should run and get as far away as possible from this psycho. "Yes, yes, anything." Still sobbing, I refused to make eye contact knowing well I had an ugly crying face with bloodshot eyes and a puffy face. Not a pleasant sight at all.

"You will stay here, while you recuperate. The medical team looking after my mother can care for you too. You will remain in the room you occupy for now and will not leave the premises."

"But stay, for what, how long? I have a job to go to. I couldn't possibly do that. The orphanage is short-staffed as it is."

"It's all taken care of. They've been well-informed and wish you a speedy recovery. I've made a substantial donation so they can afford to hire someone in your absence if they so wish. Evee will pack a case for you and I will have it picked up."

"But I don't understand and how do you know where I work?"

"That bag of yours holds a wealth of information, including your security swipe card for the orphanage. Do you know it's not permitted to carry such things on your person when off work? If it got into the wrong hands, there would be catastrophic consequences. Orphanages and banks in China are somewhat alike, built like Fort Knox and both holding precious cargo as they like to say in the USA."

"I'm dumbfounded and find all this bizarre. You still haven't explained what I'll be doing while I'm locked up here."

"You don't need to know, yet."

"Eh yeah, I do. You're a fucking nut job! Who in their right mind would agree to something without knowing what it was? You are a businessman after all! I'm sure you go into every meeting with your eyes wide open after doing the necessary research?"

"Okay, I'll make this simple, you're an intelligent girl. The book you're reading should give you a fair idea of what I have in mind."

My cheeks burn and just as quickly turn pale with fright. It was a lot to take in as I tried to remember what the actual fuck was in it. "So, you want to adorn me with beautiful clothes and jewellery, give me mind-blowing orgasms and submit to you."

"Just the second half will suffice."

"Are you a Dominant? OMG! Are you out of your fucking mind?" I whisper. "I am not into kinky shit."

"No need to whisper, nobody speaks English."

"Then why does somebody keep sniggering?"

"Probably down to the provocative show you put on while trying to retrieve your bag. Even I was mesmerised watching your breasts bounce about under that nightie. It made me quite hard, indeed quite captivating."

I crossed my arms over my chest. "Oh, my God! You're all a bunch of deviant pricks who don't get out much?" I looked down at the little boy still clutching me tightly. "I am not into kink nor have I ever practised it. I am merely fascinated by it and have no intentions of ever partaking. I am not into physical pain or giving it nor would I like to be humiliated and I'm certainly not keen on taking orders."

"I would have believed otherwise."

"About what exactly?"

"Pain."

"Specifically?"

"As they stitched you up, you never once winced in pain. I'm sure it hurt like hell. I found it a little uncomfortable to watch."

"Of course, it hurt. What the hell do you think I am? I wasn't going to show you I was weak. Don't ask me why because I don't know myself. I wanted to scream the bloody place down, it hurt so much."

"Endorphins that are released in painful experiences are often perceived as pleasurable. The release of epinephrine and norepinephrine in pain can also cause a rush. So, I assumed you were a masochist and getting off on the pain being inflicted?"

"Jesus Christ, you are fucking insane. I was putting it down to just being stubborn. I'm certainly not into gratification by suffering physical pain. I'm the straightest vanilla pod on the tree!"

"It's not a tree."

"What's not a tree?"

"Where vanilla pods come from."

"Are you seriously trying to educate me right now on the origins of spices?"

"No, I just wouldn't want you going about your life thinking pods came from a tree."

"I see. Where DO they come from just in case, I was ever stopped by someone who actually cares."

"No need to be smart, it's from a tropical climbing orchid."

"I'll be sure to remember that for the next pub quiz.

To surmise, I don't think it's wrong or shameful if pain is someone else's cup of tea. Just not mine. I was always curious though, about the appeal and how they got off on it. Still, who's to say if pain and pleasure are right or wrong so long as it's practised safely and consensually."

"I'm sure you have specific fantasies and fetishes in mind and know what you DO want. You must be some way inclined, otherwise you'd be reading a book on 'How to knit,' or similar. Either way, don't deny it doesn't interest you. There are loads of people out there just like you."

"People like me?"

"Vanilla. Just waiting to fulfil their desires. I'm sure you've dreamt about it countless times and have a fair idea of what you'd like?"

"Look here, if I read about serial killers, would that make me want to be a murderer? NO!"

"Then answer me truthfully. Can you do that?"

"Of course, I can. I'm a practising Catholic!" I said, trying to keep a straight face.

"When you read these books, do they turn you on?"

"Yes," I answered shyly, looking around the room. "Good. Do they make you wet?"

I wanted to say, YOU make me wet in ways I never imagined possible and that I have never felt this way before. Of course, I wasn't going to admit that!

"Oh God, I'm not going to answer that." His demeanour changed.

"If I ask a question, I expect an answer! I won't accept rudeness. Do I make myself clear?" His eyes hold mine.

"Yes."

"Yes what?"

"Get lost. Don't think I'm calling you sir."

"Yes, what?"

"Jesus, all right. Keep your knickers on! Seriously, this is embarrassing. Are you sure nobody knows what I'm saying?" He saw my unease, nodded and the room immediately emptied. The heavies who remained attempted to peel the child off me as he kicked and screamed. He knew what they were going to do once they had left the room.

"Please, let him stay and I'll answer every question truthfully." Again, he nodded and they let him be.

"Do you mind if we sit down?"

"Are you okay, do you feel dizzy?" He looked genuinely concerned as he led us to one of four sofas.

"Jeez, how many sofas do you need?" Clenching his fists tightly and looking up at the ceiling, in obvious irritation, he muttered something inaudible and then pointed silently for me to sit. I snuggled into one of the corners as tightly as possible and pulled the shaking child onto my lap, wincing in pain.

"He's quite capable of climbing up there himself considering what he did to you. He's not as fragile as he looks."

"Look, you don't know how this is affecting him either? He's out of his comfort zone as much as I am. He's in a strange place not knowing what's going to happen next. Poor thing hasn't had a great start in life and he's probably wondering what the consequences of his actions are. So please, try your best to be one of the kind humans. At least for now anyway." The three of us sat in silence. "Please can you tell him it's going to be, okay?"

"That would be a lie, Miss Murphy. You haven't agreed to anything yet, therefore the child is not on safe ground."

"Can you at least get him something to eat and drink? How long has he been here?"

"I told you, they were caught while you were sleeping."

"But that's a long time to be fasting, he's only a baby, he must be so hungry. Please tell me you were decent enough to even throw him a piece of bread because that's how you treat people like him, isn't it, like animals!"

"Have you forgotten that *baby* took you down and almost killed you? Anyway, he's far from a baby."

"Don't be so dramatic. That child had to grow up fast in a life he didn't particularly want or ask for. He had to learn the hard way, skills to survive and stay safe. We don't know his circumstances and I'm amazed he's made it this far."

"I will have food served for you as you too have been fasting for quite some time. If you wish to share with this thief, by all means, do so."

"He may be a thief, but he's only a child. Please try to remember. But thank you."

5

He waited for me to finish then picked up the phone and barked orders down the line. Is he always like this I wondered. He certainly wasn't trying to harness his revulsion towards his tiny prisoner.

"So where were we, Miss Murphy?"

"Before I answer any more of your invasive questions, why me?"

"At the hospital when you realised, I wasn't a doctor your whole demeanour changed. Each time you blushed, my cock hurt. I found your shyness intriguing. But when you slapped my hand away, that's when I knew. You excited me in a way I never imagined. In my world, you would have been punished. Do you understand what I'm saying?"

"Yes. That's basically what's in the books I read."

"In my personal life, I have complete control over everything, especially sex. I'm the one who makes every decision. So, if you were mine, I would have not hesitated in spanking you. Do you understand?"

"I do and thought all that stuff about owning and submitting was a load of made-up crap."

"Ooh, that hurts. You see, I was already aroused seeing you half-naked, and then you went and slapped my hand away which made me harder. But for the fact that I can control my urges, you would certainly have noticed."

"Mr Lee, that kind of talk may appeal to other women, but it does nothing for me. Oh my God, I did feel something when I brushed against you before I threw up and assumed it was a gun?"

"A gun? Hahahaha! No. Perhaps the people who work for me though. I knew you were special even before I laid eyes on you. Saving my mother's life, putting her safety before your own when there was a shit load of men around who never stepped up to the mark and acted like they owned a pair! Then I saw you. Vulnerable and innocent with a brazen tongue. The complete opposite of what I imagined. Small and delicate with the most amazing blue eyes I had ever seen and as my mother said, spun gold for hair. For once I was stuck for words."

"As I remember you were more interested in my chest."

"Indeed, I was and then you shyly tried to cover yourself up. I was hooked, really bad. Other women would have used that to their advantage."

"Not all women are alike. I was embarrassed when I realised you weren't a doctor, but a stranger. That you had seen me in my underwear and touched me the way you did."

"I wanted to fuck you so much because I knew you weren't that kind of girl. It's not often, maybe rare, that I've met someone like you. Innocent."

"Maybe just shy and naive?"

"All of which I find intriguing. Tell me. Do I unnerve you?"

"I'm not afraid of you, I know you won't kill me or anything. Unless your patience runs out ha-ha. I lack experience. I've only read about these things."

"Have you fantasised about them?"

"Oh yes."

"Tell me."

"Do I have to?"

"Yes."

"It's embarrassing and too personal."

"I've already admitted I want to spank and fuck you. You should be well over it by now. Tell me how your books make you feel."

"Please don't ask me to explain my desires."

"I won't ask again." The look on his face changed to impatience very quickly. Confirming he was not a patient man and short-tempered when irritated. Something I'd have to remember if I was going to be living here for a while.

"I have always had a secret. A fantasy. I like when the man takes control. The idea of rough sex and being taken hard. Being spanked on bare skin and told you're going to be fucked hard. He gently pulls my hair, and lightly spanks my bottom as he fucks me. Oh Jesus, are you sure this little one doesn't understand English?"

"He can barely speak Chinese! Continue."

I couldn't look at him so I played with the child's hair, thinking it was very long for a boy.

"Do you masturbate afterwards?"

"Oh, for fuck's sake, really! Have you any idea how mortifying this is?"

"You made a promise!"

"I didn't make a promise." His face turned.

"Yes, yes I do. Most times," I quickly answered.

Knowing he wasn't someone to be trifled with.

"Do you come?"

"Sometimes." Turning away in discomfort I looked down at the contented child, pushed aside an unruly lock of hair then kissed the little one's forehead. He had fallen sound asleep. Poor thing must be exhausted and for the first time feels safe enough to do so.

"How?"

"I have a thingy." He raised an eyebrow.

"Explain."

"Dildo."

"Do you insert it to come?"

"No."

"I see. How do you know you're not kinky, maybe you just need to spice things up?"

"I'm not kinky and never said I was. You just assumed because of my literature. I like erotic books, they excite me.

"Have you ever been spanked?"

"Nope. I haven't done anything. As I said, I just like to fantasise."

"You're a very motherly person, just think of the consequences if you're not honest with me."

"Please don't use blackmail. I've already given my word."

"Forgive me."

"People are judged if spanking and hair pulling turns them on. That's why it's a secret."

"Thank you for your honesty, it's quite refreshing. Although your fantasies are very innocent. I'm sure there is lots more to those books you read?"

"You're right, most of them are BDSM but I'm not really into that. I like them because most times it leads to sex. It's just an exciting way to get from A to B. There's no harm in just reading and I don't have a problem with people who act out their fantasies. If both adults are consenting, then it makes for a happy fulfilled relationship."

"It looks like you've given this some thought?"

"I like to get lost in my books. As you said, I lead a very quiet life. I enjoy my books and the escapism."

"And here you are now, ready to partake in one or more of your fantasies." I looked down at the sleeping child in my arms. His cute chubby fingers scratching the hell out of his head. Peaceful and content, for the moment at least. Both our lives are about to change because of this one person.

"How do you propose we go about doing this?" I asked. My eyes not leaving the child, afraid of what I might see in his face if I looked up.

"This D/s relationship requires that both of us are physically, emotionally and psychologically healthy. I can account for myself one hundred percent. You on the other hand will have to be prepared of course."

"Prepared, like a lump of meat? Lovely."

"There is a ritual. It can take from one to two days, depending on the individual. In your case, it may take longer?"

"Rude!"

"As I was saying, it involves the submissive, YOU, preparing your body, bathing, shaving, then presenting yourself to me."

"What exactly does that mean, I don't think there's anything about rituals in anything I've read, so I'm at a loss."

"Surely, you're aware of the activities and if your energy is low or are unwell, you can't partake. So first on the list is good nutrition, appropriate sleeping hours and being stress-free."

"I think it's a bit late for that because my nerves are fried!"

"Also, it's quite common for slaves or submissives to shave parts of their bodies, usually the genitalia. One of the most intimate rituals shared in these relationships can be a shaving ritual."

"OMG, fuck right off. You are not shaving my bits. Absolutely No. Are you insane?"

He raised his hand, either to silence me from talking back or so I wouldn't wake the child. Quite sure it wasn't the latter! "You will be bathed, shaved, which I noticed, you drastically need."

That was embarrassing and I turned my face away with guilt. It was true, I hadn't bothered keeping up the maintenance down there since I relocated here. However, the thought of going to a beauty salon to be preened, primped and pampered was at least something to look forward to. "I thought you said I wasn't permitted to leave the building?"

"That's correct, they will come here and attend to you. There are beauty rooms on the third floor."

"Of course, there is!"

"Just so you know, every follicle will be removed from your body. I cannot abide bodily hair." This was something we both had in common but I wasn't going to say that. Nor was I ready to have every follicle ripped from my body.

"So, when will this happen?"

"When your arm is healed, can't be tying you up till then."

"I'm sorry, but I did mention I wasn't into that, only because I think it's dangerous."

"I don't dally in BDSM, Miss Murphy. I'm what you call a professional – in layman's terms and what you will be familiar with – I am a Dominant. I take this term very seriously. The safety of my sub is paramount."

"What if I said, I didn't like it."

"I would be very surprised indeed as my perception of you would change. I don't make mistakes. I'm a good judge of character."

"Oh no, I mean I don't like the idea of it. I've never done anything like that and it kind of scares me."

"I agree it's not for the faint-hearted. But know this, I will never hurt you. I will not go beyond your limits unless you beg me. Are you on the pill?"

"Yes."

"Great, one less thing for me to worry about. You'll see the doctor regardless for an examination. Hopefully, you'll pass with flying colours."

"What exactly does that entail?"

"He'll do blood work and test for STDs. I have a private doctor so the results will be confirmed that day. Once I get the go-ahead and your arm is healed, the pampering will begin."

"Seriously though. I'd hardly call it pampering. Having your private bits done is tolerable, but your whole body. Please don't tell me I have to have my arms waxed too?"

"Hairless!"

"Well, that's just weird."

"Not at all, only sounds weird. But the sensation of skin on skin is mind-blowing."

"I'll take your word for it."

"In about two weeks, you'll see for yourself."

"What on earth am I to do till then?"

"For now, rest. I've ordered you a Kindle so you can download as many dirty books as you like."

"Oh don't say that, it only makes what we're going to do, sound dirty."

"You really are innocent, aren't you?" I didn't answer. This was all mind-blowing and if you repeated everything that's happened so far, nobody would believe you. It's just totally bizarre. Any minute now I'm going to wake up and it would all be just a bad dream. I pinched myself. 'Ouch'! I wasn't dreaming. I looked up to find him staring at me. Then I remembered I resembled something out of a horror movie.

"Can this little one stay with me?"

"Definitely not!"

"But why, it makes no difference to you." As he looked at the child, I saw it on his face for a fleeting moment, repulsion.

"The child will have his room just as soon as he's scrubbed within an inch of his life."

"I'll do it. I'd love to."

"There's no point forming a bond with that child. Don't make this harder for yourself than it already is. One of you, if not both, is bound to get hurt."

"What do you care anyway once you see the back of us?"

"As much as you think I have no empathy, I'd prefer neither of you to get upset when this comes to an end."

"This is just fucked up, or maybe it's just you? In case you've forgotten, I work in an orphanage?"

"So, tell me, do you skip out the door when you clock out, leaving the events of the day behind you? I bet you hate when you close the door and head home alone. Wishing you could take them all with you?"

"That's different."

"I don't think so. Look, you have enough on your plate as it is. I can't have you being distracted."

"Well, I want to help look after him."

"I don't think you're in a position to make demands and this conversation has become tiresome. Believe me when I say, he will be looked after."

"You see, I don't know you well enough to believe you."

"Yet *you* have no issue staying here with a stranger. Who will be doing things to you, you can't even imagine."

"I believe you won't hurt me as you've said. But I know you have a revulsion towards him and his kind, as you put it."

"You will have long forgotten him once you're back to normality."

"I intend to take him with me to the orphanage." He sighed out loud.

"Christ!! You just won't let it go. At least when you're mine, you will not answer back!"

"I just want something to take my mind off, you know?? I can only read so many books and even then, I get bored. I'm a terrible worrier and will probably make myself sick. This is a huge thing for me and only for this child, we wouldn't be having this conversation. Please allow me some time with him, that's all I ask. The poor thing will be so lonely."

"Okay, let me think about it. Before you ask again, he will not share your bed."

"Just an odd night. Maybe?"

"I said NO!"

"Jesus, okay then!"

6

There was a tap on the door and it didn't open until he gave the word. The double doors to the adjoining room were opened. OMG! The table had been set in a whisper and fit for a king. Before me was a banquet, a feast of sorts. "Oh, are you having a dinner party?" It sat approximately twenty and half of the table was piled with copious amounts of food.

"I wasn't sure what you liked so had my chef make a selection. There's even Irish stew!"

I edged myself off the sofa gently holding the child, stopping mid-step as he tried to turn.

"You might as well wake him up."

"I will, you just don't shake a child from slumber. You probably would, or maybe one of your goons?"

"Those goons as you call them are not mine. They're my mother's security."

"Well, you should sack the whole lot of them after what happened to her. Why on earth are they still here?"

"And they think I'm a ball breaker," he laughed. "It's a long story."

"Well, I have plenty of time judging by the amount of food I have to get through." We both laughed. I sat down with the little one still on my lap.

"You won't be able to eat like that. Here, wake him up. I'm sure he can feed himself?"

I gently woke the sleeping mite and pointed to the food. He sat up like a rod, his eyes bulging. Before I could signal for him to eat, he was off my lap and sitting in the chair next to me, loading his hands with a little bit of everything. I put a plate in front of him and gently prised open his tiny fingers, dropping the food onto it. I don't think he knew what a plate was. No point in showing him a spoon or fork, it would have taken the enjoyment out of it. "No need to ask him twice," I giggled. "Please tell me you're going to join us?"

He leaned over and whispered in my ear, "The things I'm going to do to you now that you belong to me."

The smile drained from my face and I hid my emotions as best I could. But at what cost? I can't imagine what my parents or Evee would do if they ever found out. He sat opposite me and as far away from the child as possible, only looking at him with total disdain. What a fucking shit show!

He explained each dish as I loaded my plate with a sample of everything. "I thought you would have gone straight for the 'Irish' stew?

"I'm vegetarian and traditional stew is made with lamb. My mother uses beef."

"I should have known you'd be an animal lover too."

"I'm a pescetarian."

"What exactly does that mean?"

"It's just easier to say, vegetarian. It means being vegetarian while still including seafood in your diet. I haven't eaten meat or poultry since I turned eighteen when I was allowed to make the choice. I had never liked meat as a child and would throw it over the neighbour's back wall until they complained. Then it was a place of convenience, behind radiators, under furniture. Once I hid it in my doll's pram before we went on holiday only to arrive home to maggots. My mother was horrified and still insisted that I ate meat!"

"I don't think I could ever refrain from eating meat?"

"You wouldn't believe how your mind and body adapt. Over time, the craving for meat disappears. Evee, my best friend, has given it up since I got here and has been pleasantly surprised at how easy it's been. Considering she's been eating meat for the past twenty-five years. She said it was easy to switch because she can still eat fish and feels much healthier for it. I'm not making a speech here to convert you; those are her words."

"Maybe I'll give it a go, at least while you're here?"

"Maybe you should. It might be the only good thing that comes out of this?"

"Don't be such a pessimist. In a nanosecond, you've vaulted yourself into a worst-case scenario. I'm sure it must be frustrating and a time-consuming experience?"

"Puh-lease, I scoffed. Are you saying I should turn the negative into positive? Turn my frown upside down?"

He laughed. "Correct," he answered, unperturbed by my brattiness.

"Okay so, please explain to me how I can turn the following scenarios into positive experiences, and I will do my utmost to be an optimist!! Also, not in order of importance."

1. I've been robbed.
2. I've been stabbed.
3. I'm being held against my will.
4. I'm being emotionally blackmailed.
5. Almost a witness to child mutilation.
6. To be plucked/shaved/waxed within an inch of my life.
7. To live with a stranger.
8. To be an unwilling object for someone's sexual fantasies/gratification/desire.
9. To have sex with a stranger.
10. My freedom has been taken away.

He looked like the world was coming to an end. He slowly released his breath in a long-exaggerated sigh. "I'm speechless. I don't know what to say when you put it like that. All I can think of right now is your poor mother. I bet you were quite a handful?"

"How dare you! You don't know ME or my mother so are not in a position to make assumptions!"

"Touché."

Of course, he was right. Being an only child wasn't a walk in the park. I rebelled against my mother and everything she tried to do for me. Whether it was clothes or how she wanted to style my hair. It had to be my way or we weren't going anywhere. My dad always stuck up for me saying I was strong-willed and had my own little personality.

Apart from the agreeable noises coming from the little one, the rest of the meal passed in silence. That will give him something to think about, I thought to myself. I bet nobody has ever dared to answer him back let alone disagree with him, ever! I sat there with a hint of smug satisfaction, very pleased with myself. But the smug grin slowly evaporated in realisation, a fat lot of good it would do! Wasn't sure, but it looked like he now had a smug grin on his face. Prick! The food was amazing and it wouldn't take long to get used to dining like royalty.

"Would you like the leftovers to be packed up and handed out to the poor and homeless, perhaps the other thugs who tried to rob my mother would enjoy it?"

I looked at him with bewilderment. Maybe I had got through to him after all? "Really, oh that would be marvellous, I can help too."

He burst out laughing. "You're so gullible!"

"OMG! You're such a little shit! The poor and homeless are not something to joke about." Even now I couldn't find it in my heart to condemn them. He laughed even louder! "You have no heart," I screeched. God help the poor unfortunate eejit who marries you. Or maybe you are married, TO A DOORMAT?!! Oh, you're not married are you? I just couldn't go there and won't."

He didn't answer. Knowing he wouldn't stop me, I took the child's hand and walked back to my room, head held high and nose in the air. He laughed, a deep sexy sound. His laughter booming after me made me grin to myself. Ooh, he's such a knobhead. What the hell had I let myself in for? I closed the door gently, drowning out his laughter. I sat down and patted the bed for the tot to join me. He got all shy and it took forever to entice him up. There was a gentle tap on the door, followed by his knobhead peering in.

"I need a drink after that, would you like to join me?"

"Typical man, any excuse to get blotto!"

"I thought gender-specific comments such as that were infra dig! Good job I'm a man and don't get offended...!"

"Shut your face! I'm sure you're well used to your own company and love it!" Again, profuse laughter. "Ooh, just get lost!" I threw a cushion hitting the back of the door as his laughter faded into the distance. Prick. I smiled secretly to myself. Eventually, I was joined by my little friend.

"I know you don't understand me but would you like to get out of those dirty clothes?" I tried to show him what I meant but he got terribly upset. I snuggled under the covers and lifted them for him to join me. I lay there pondering. What is the nature of his business? He said he owned a bank. Was he a banker? More like a wanker. I giggled at my joke. Why is he a billionaire? At one point I was wondering if he was shady and if there was some sort of gangsterism involved in his wealth. He's wonderfully aloof and has an air of menace, of threat, about him. But he's also a controlling individual who is somewhat intimidating. I'm caught in a world that has assaulted my senses, challenging my understanding of right and wrong. I've been transplanted into an environment that is alien to me. This wouldn't have happened back in Ireland. Before long we were both snoring our heads off. Well, I hoped it was only him. It was comforting having him beside me apart from the odd elbow in the eye or kick to the ribs. At one stage he threw his little leg over me and squashed his little body tightly up against mine. It felt so nice. I'm not sure how long I slept but turned to find the space beside me empty.

7

My heart pounded as I thought the worst. He wouldn't have. We had an agreement. In a panic, I jumped up and searched the room, frantically looking under the bed. Fuck, they've taken him away. I ran out the door and down the hall to the dining room. Of course, it was empty. I was terrified. The images fleeting through my head made me cry out. In anger I opened every door on that floor. I couldn't even call out his name because I didn't bloody know it. Panting, I came to a halt. I listened carefully then slowly tiptoed until I reached the bottom. Bloody hell, how many doors did this place have? Edging towards the end I could hear running water. Like it was raining outside. Surprisingly, the door was ajar. I crossed to the other side so I could have a better view. I gulped at the sight before me. He was naked under the water which seemed to fall from the whole ceiling. Holy fuck. How was that even possible? Anything is possible I suppose when you're loaded. He wasn't alone.

Two girls dressed like me were smothering his body in silky suds and bathing him in silence. They were soaked through, revealing everything underneath. I didn't see why they were clothed, only that it looked very erotic. He lifted his arms as they poured oil from glass jugs, down his chest lathering him up with their hands. They moved in unison as they slid down his body until they were both on their knees. I looked straight at his penis almost gagging at the size of it. Fucking hell and it wasn't even hard? How was it possible he wasn't turned on? Even without an erection, he had the hugest dick ever. Hung like a horse comes to mind. Not that I was a judge of men's penises or anything. Lost in the moment and shutting out the absurd situation I found myself in, I moved my hands up to my now hard nipples running my palms over them as I watched him watching me. I was amazed at how quickly I was turned on and felt the wetness between my legs. Now I understood what Evee meant, a shower not a grower.

Holy fuck. This man is hot and huge! HUGE. His eyebrow rises in surprise. He just stares, an amused grin on his face. I look at him in awe.

My pussy starts to pulse and I can hear my heart beating in the quiet corridor. I scrape my nails over my nipples, gently groaning and notice his cock twitching. Just then his lips move and one of the girls elegantly stands and walks towards me. Oh God, was he inviting me to join him? I couldn't do that. My mind was a riot of what-if's. As she neared, I stood straight, hands by my side, heart pounding faster. Jesus? I wasn't ready for this. When she got to the door, I could scarcely believe how stunning she was up close. Her hair was silken black like his but longer down her back. Her eyes are black and enormous with bee-stung lips. Her breasts, though small, were beautifully formed, the contours peeking through the flimsy wet fabric. She smiled innocently as she slowly closed the door. Wait, what. Confused, I moved closer as the gap got smaller until it was closed shut in my face.

I stood there, looking at the door, shocked, scratching my head. What the fuck? Somewhat disappointed I slowly made my way back to my room recounting what I had just seen. Sitting on the bed I concluded that those two beautiful women did nothing for him but I made his cock twitch. It brought a smile to my face, knowing the power I had over him. Not sure why or how, but I did. How was I going to sleep after that little show? Between that and worrying about the child I was going to have a restless night.

There was a little tap on the door. Then a head popped in. In very good English she said, "The child is sleeping soundly, you need to rest."

That was all she said. Short and sweet. The thought of my little friend in danger left my mind. As soon as my head hit the pillow, I was out for the count. I woke to silence, stretching with a yawn and yelping as my stitches strained. "Ouch! Fuck's sake!" I peered over the covers remembering the shower scene. Oh, God. He watched me fondle myself. It hit me smack in the face with absolute horror. Oh nooo. I can't face him ever again. How could I? The embarrassment of it all! I sat there cringing. There was nothing else for me to do but stay in bed for the day, the week even, perhaps forever! I can't deny though, he's one hot fuck.

But what about the boy? I couldn't abandon him now and wouldn't. I'll act like nothing happened. I jumped out of bed and searched for a dressing gown. Of course, I didn't bloody find one. I tiptoed to the room I was familiar with and cautiously opened the door. He was there reading the newspaper as the child sat at the table eating breakfast. "OMFG!" I screamed at the top of my voice. They both looked up startled. "What the fuck have you done?" I ran and fell to my knees pulling him off the chair and into my arms. "How could you?" I yelled. "Tell me why you did it. You didn't get your way chopping his arm off so you thought you'd teach him a lesson by chopping all his beautiful hair off instead."

He peered over his paper and then very carefully and with great attention, folded it meticulously, placing it gently on the table, again, that smug look. "Pediculosis! And he is a she!" he said with a grin.

"Ped-a-what? Wait, What??"

"A parasite, commonly known as lice. Anyone who comes in close contact with someone who has the nasty fuckers, or even their clothing and belongings are at risk."

I took a deep intake of breath as my hands involuntarily shot up and scratched my head. "Oh sweet Jesus! NITS! Why didn't they just use nit lotion?"

"They did but she screamed the place down when they tried to get the knots out to comb the lotion through. For effective elimination of head lice, the infested individual, individuals in this case and the home must all be treated!" "So that's what was happening last night?" I blushed. "Not exactly, I didn't hug or sleep with 'Lan'. That's her name, it means Orchid."

"Oh, that's so sweet, such a pretty name. Her hair isn't that bad I suppose. It suits her. Nǐ hǎo Lan." She turned and smiled at me, then giggled as she laced her fingers through mine. "I suppose my pronunciation is a little funny?"

"I think it's just your accent, it is very cute."

"So, what's the plan, am I allowed to wash my hair or will you have your two minions, do it?"

"You read my mind, what a clever girl you are."

"I was taking the pi…., I was joking. I'm looking forward to having a bath, especially all by myself."

"NO!"

"No, what do you mean, NO?"

"I mean, you will not do anything yourself. This is the ideal time to have everything done. Those bugs couldn't have come at a better time."

"Are you kidding? I can't go through all that now. I'm supposed to be resting."

"Exactly, that's why you will have someone else do it for you. Please! Don't answer back, it's tiring! It is what it is. A very sensual and erotic way to start your experience and a wonderful way to unwind. It's a whole new level of sensory experience for your body and mind. Not to mention, the nits will be gone." His outburst of laughter brought me back to my senses.

"Jesus, you're so bloody infuriating!" I just wanted to slap that smirk right off his face.

"I could have you bound and blindfolded if it helped?"

"No, it wouldn't. Why even say that when I have told you I'll have nothing to do with the likes of that?"

"And I didn't agree either to it not happening!"

In quite an unflattering voice I repeated, "Well I didn't agree to it either!"

Sensing I was about to throw an apoplectic banana fit, Lan squeezed my hand and led me away to the safety of our bedroom. "Thank you for that Lan. You are a smart little girl." I sat on the bed and helped her up beside me. Her chubby little fingers are still in mine. Not content sitting on the lush bed, she scrambled onto my lap, kissed my cheek and snuggled tightly into me. "Oh dear, you're going to make it very difficult for me when this nightmare finally ends. I suppose there's absolutely nothing I can do about it, I'm stuck here, we both are. It seems the more irate I get, the more enjoyment he gets out of it and that pisses me off even more. Men, huh! Bunch of pricks! Thank goodness you don't understand what I'm saying."

She looked up at me and smiled, nodding her head. "Hey, seriously, you don't know what I'm saying, do you?" She smiled again and slid off my lap skipping over to the wardrobe. Being so tiny, she was barely able to open the huge doors. How did she attack me at the station? It just didn't seem possible that this little cherub had the strength of someone twice her age. She pointed to the rows and rows of hanging clothes.

"Wait, how did they get there, when? It was empty when I looked earlier!" I took each outfit down while she jumped up and down giggling with excitement. They were the most beautiful little girls' clothes I had ever seen. I fell to my knees and had a little cry. We spent a wonderful afternoon alone together. Lan trying on every single outfit with matching shoes. I couldn't make him out at all and wasn't going to try. It made me feel a little better and gave me some hope that what was about to happen over the next few weeks wouldn't be so bad after all. I could only hope.

It was late in the afternoon when Lan changed into her lovely new pj's and climbed into bed. The poor thing was exhausted after trying on hundreds of clothes. She whispered something, blew me a kiss before closing her eyes and within two seconds was out for the count. I giggled listening to her tiny snores and was thankful it wasn't me after all. Half excited, I walked across the room to the other set of matching doors. Maybe they were full of fabulous new clothes for me? Fuck it. They were still locked.

I opened the bedroom door and peered out. No sign of anyone and I couldn't hear anything. What was I going to do now? I thought for a minute then went to Lan's closet. I took one of her dresses and removed the outer plastic, tearing it in half and folding it several times until it fit into the palm of my hand. I headed for the bathroom where I had watched Gui's erotic shower scene. Jesus, my bloody nerves were gone as I closed the door behind me. Why did I feel like a criminal, breaking the law. Well, I suppose it's his law! I tutted. I was adamant nobody was going to bathe or remove hair from either my head or body! I looked at my hair in the mirror section by section and couldn't see any nits. I hadn't had head-to-head contact with Lan nor slept on the same pillow. That's how they spread. They climb from one head to another. Ughh! You'd think he'd be delighted I was going for a shower. The state of me!

Everything I needed was there and my only problem, I realised, was how to turn on the ultra-modern shower.

I wrapped the plastic sheet over my bandage and tucked the ends inside, hoping it wouldn't unravel. I fiddled and pressed every button and knob until the water poured from the ceiling. Thank goodness the hot and cold was obvious or I could have burned the head off myself.

I removed the elastic from my hair and slowly massaged my head. Oh God, it felt so good, especially after having the band in it for days. Immediately I felt the tension and stress slip away. It has been proven that the head is the centre of your entire nervous system, so a soothed head is a soothed body. According to *Lifestyle Health*. One of the many magazines I've read during my imprisonment, I mean, stay. I had no idea what I poured onto my hair because it was in Chinese only that it smelled divine. It wasn't lathering and my arms began to feel tired and heavy. Then my wound started aching. Holy fuck, what if it was for hair removal?? Oh, Jesus!! My heart jumped out of my chest. I screamed in horror, rinsing furiously. "FUCK, FUCK, FUCK!" Holding my hair, I ran to the mirror, checking it was still on my head and not falling in clumps to the floor. Oh my God, could you imagine? I think Mr Lee's interest in me would flow away just as quickly as the water down the plug hole.

8

A soft tap on the door interrupted thoughts of him rubbing my bald head before spanking me. I shivered at the image. Please don't let it be him. I'm sure he'd just barge through the door and throw me in his dungeon for disobeying his orders. I wrapped one of the enormous towels tightly around my body and walked slowly to the door. Passing the mirror, I checked my hair was still on my head. Phew. All good. To tell you the truth, I wasn't in the mood for arguing. Trying to lather my hair zapped all my energy. Taking a deep breath, I opened the door and closed my eyes waiting for the barrage of verbal diarrhoea. I waited and waited. Nothing, nada. Opening one eye and squinting through the other, I peered out the door. Strange, nobody was there? On the floor sat the most elegant Louis Vuitton travel case. I squealed with excitement as I picked it up and walked backwards into the room, shutting the door with my foot.

Oh my goodness, it even had a shoulder strap. I slowly opened the zip to reveal the mother lode of beauty products, IN ENGLISH! Hallelujah! Placing it on the vanity unit, I took everything out and read all the labels. I just couldn't stop smiling. It seems Mr High-and- Mighty caved in after all. I wasn't sure how long I had and figured as long as it took, otherwise, he wouldn't have left a shit load of stuff!

I washed my hair and then combed through a mask, leaving it on while I shaved my bits. I assumed that's why he included a razor. I had never shaved in my life, preferring to leave my hoo-ha to the professionals. Goodness, it was a challenging task, very fiddly. I would have been quite happy leaving it *au naturale* but unfortunately, a hairy bush isn't to Master's taste. It's true what they say, out of sight, out of mind so it kind of resembled a hairy man's beard and not for the faint hearted.

After that scary task was out of the way, I realised that monthly visits to the beauty salon were essential from now on. I rinsed off the mask, towel-dried my hair before combing through a leave-in conditioner and slathering myself from head to toe in the most luxuriously whipped body cream. Remarkably, I felt great and smelled amazing too. Across the room stood a beautiful ornate dresser and what looked like a hair dryer. But it wasn't any hairdryer. It was the latest and newest from Dyson. It had just been released and I was hoping Santa would pop one under the Christmas tree.. Sadly not. It felt incredibly light and when I flicked it on, it was super-fast and quiet. Ooh, I couldn't wait to use it. With the diffuser attached, my hair was dry in ten minutes which was amazing. Don't get me wrong. I wasn't blessed with fabulous thick curly hair, but curly nonetheless and at times, unmanageable. Sometimes you could say it was both a blessing and a curse and I had moments when I wished it was poker straight. One whiff of rain and it turned into a big frizz ball. But now it was behaving and resembled the hair of my dreams. As Mr Lee put it, spun gold.

I wiped clean every single lotion and potion I'd used and placed them back in the case and back where I found it. With a spring in my step, curls bouncing and feeling fabulous I headed back to my room. It didn't take long for doom to wash over me as my newly found happiness ebbed slowly away. What was I going to do now? Turning the handle, I smiled upon hearing Lan's gentle snores. She hadn't moved an inch apart from one foot poking out from under the covers. I sat down, careful not to wake her and pulled the covers over her, tucking her little foot back in. I looked about the room and sighed. It wasn't time for bed and after that wonderful shower, I was wide awake. Maybe I'd just take a little stroll around the building. I had a whole skyscraper to investigate. His jumper was still draped over the back of the chair, so I took off the nightie and put it on. Ummm delicious. I could still smell him on it. Thankfully it covered my arse and if I didn't raise my arms, would save the world from an apocalypse.

As my hand touched the handle, a tiny whisper called my name, "Rhy-lee." Sitting up rubbing her eyes she smiled shyly at me. I jumped on the bed and pulled her into my arms as she giggled.

"Well, who's a clever little girl?" I asked. She climbed onto my lap and said, "liàng nǚ" but I hadn't a clue what it meant. With a look of disbelief, she stretched one of my curls and let it bounce back. She was fascinated and giggled every time she did it. "As you're wide awake, let us go and find Mr Lee." I got up and held out my hand. She put her little fingers in mine but when we got to the door, shook her hand free.

Running to the wardrobe, she struggled to open the heavy doors but with great determination, managed. The size of her, she was just so adorable. With sadness, I wondered how she ended up on the streets and living what she knew as life! Removing a dressing gown from the hanger she put it on and then slipped her feet into tiny velvet slippers. So cute I wanted them myself but had visions of the ugly sisters forcing their chubby feet into Cinderella's glass shoe. This was all new to Lan and I was going to do my best for her when we left. Sure, it wasn't going to be anywhere as glamorous as this but she will be loved.

Approaching the door I could hear voices, definitely Gui's and a female. Maybe it was his mother? Trying to make out what they were saying and wondering if we should interrupt, Lan pushed open the door and skipped inside. Leaving me looking guilty as fuck and very obvious, I'd been earwigging. They just stared as I looked from one to the other. I smiled and walked in.

"Well, well, the children are awake," she said, rising from her chair, smoothing down her silk dress, looking at me with a look of disdain on her beautiful face. I bet she's a fucking lawyer or an ambassador for world peace or something. Ugh, I clenched my hands wishing I was still holding Lan's for support, were had the little rascal gone? I looked about the room and caught Gui looking at me in shock. He moved to the edge of his seat and leaned on his desk. He held my gaze for a minute as I awkwardly skulked to the centre of the room.

"Hello," he says, looking at me with longing. We stare at each other for an exceptionally long time. Like we are the only two people in the room and just grin. The woman edged closer looking me up and down and down again focusing on *his* jumper and my bare legs. She held out her perfectly manicured hand like a queen and as I shook it, was positive she squeezed it a little too hard. But what she said next annoyed the crap out of me. She's lucky I didn't slap her botoxed face. Still holding my hand she looked back at Gui and said, "She's far from the little scrubber you lead me to believe."

"That's enough Jingfei," he shouted. His chair scraped the floor as he stood. I pulled my hand free and wiped it on his jumper like I had been contaminated.

"I'm sorry, what did you just say?"

"Jingfei, I said that's enough. Do not have me repeat myself," he roared. He strode from behind his desk and stood next to her. Looking at them side by side they made a beautiful couple. She was slightly taller than me but not by much. Her skin was flawless and probably from skin whitening creams. Take a walk down China's beauty aisles in up-market department stores and you'd be surprised to find rows upon rows of skin whitening products. What I found bizarre is that most European serums and potions have self-tanning agents but they have skin whiteners and brightening chemicals. I didn't have a problem with ladies carrying umbrellas when it wasn't raining. Pale skin is on trend here and the word 'white' is jokingly used to describe the ideal Chinese woman. Now that I think about it, he did comment on my 'white' skin at the hospital. Back then I didn't think anything of it, but it was a compliment of sorts. They're also obsessed with fuller lips saying they bring good luck. Where I'm concerned, I don't think I'd agree with that one. Since bumping into Mr Lee, I've had nothing but bad luck! And both of us have full lips. I looked her straight in the eye. "Bad manners seem to be a common occurrence in this household. It's also a shame you don't have a beautiful heart to go with your beautiful face. But I suppose money can't get you everything," I said.

She casually put her arm around him, "I'm more than happy with what it's got me," she smiled. Gui shuffled awkwardly trying to move out of her grasp. But she only pushed herself tightly against him bridging the gap he made. If she only knew why I was here, that would wipe the smug look off her perfect face. Isn't she curious why I was staying in his home? I wanted to say it but what would I say? She lay her hand on his chest and then slowly slid it down his body with a superior look on her face. He watched me as I watched her hand stop just above his waistband. We both looked at each other. I'm not sure what I saw on his face, horror or tension. Maybe it was the thought of me pulling her hair out for insulting me! We Irish are known for our hot temper and fighting our corner. Why was he just standing there letting her do it? God dammit, what the fuck is the deal here? As if reading my mind, he pushed her hand away. His jaw tics as he glares at her.

"Stop acting like the cat who got the cream Jingfei, it's unflattering," he snaps. Oh for fuck's sake, she just pouted! Embarrassing.

"I'm just having a little fun Gui, what harm is it? So, what time will you pick me up? I'm so looking forward to having my wicked way with you tonight." She looked at me and winked.

Bitch!

"Well, I'd love to stay and chat Feng shui, but I've got things to do." I shrug.

"It's Jingfei," she gasped as Gui spluttered out laughing. "Who cares?"

She moved forward. "Like that?" She wiggled her bony finger at my obvious lack of attire. Thankfully, it was clear he hadn't told her anything. I looked at him first before I replied. He didn't look uncomfortable; in fact, he had a sneaky grin on his face. I don't think he cared what I was going to say. I know what I would have liked to say but couldn't because it sounded utterly ridiculous and unbelievable. He just stared. Like he wants me to say it. Maybe if I did, it might do him a favour. Get him out of something he needs an excuse to get out of? What am I even saying? This man is powerful and doesn't take shit off anyone. He's just humouring her, and I wondered why? I hadn't noticed until now he was wearing a three-piece suit. Navy which matched his eyes, making them stand out even more. God, he's so handsome. It takes the sound of a hard clapping noise to wake me from dreaming.

"Oh!" I shook my head making my long curls fall perfectly about my face. I flick them back over my shoulder and get up close to her face.

"There was no need for that, you almost burst my eardrum. I was going to give you a nasty look but I see you already have one!"

He sniggered again.

"Gui, are you going to allow her to speak to me like that?" He was back behind his desk now, both hands on the soft leather top, leaning forward as a lock of hair fell and caressed his check. Mmm. I loved his hair. His eyes flicked from me to her and back to me before he burst out laughing. I smiled back as his eyes drop down my body, not bothered if she was watching him do it, before locking eyes with me. That look gives me goosebumps.

"Well enough of this idle chit-chat, as I said, things to do."

Pronouncing her name perfectly, I turned to Jingfei and said, "I can't say it was a pleasure meeting you and I'm sure it's not the first time you've heard that?" I gave her a dazzling smile, winked at him and left. I purposely raised my hand to wave goodbye, my head held high and said, "Oh by the way, I hope your day is as pleasant as your personality!"

"Gui, she's not wearing any underwear," she gasped. I could still hear him laughing loudly making me giggle even more.

I fell back against the wall, humour replaced with anger. Who the hell did she think she was, scaldy bitch. Little Miss High-and-Mighty! Oh God, did I just make a fool of myself? All confidence drained from my body. Was I just a joke? But I saw how he looked at me. Oh for fuck's sake, what the hell would I know how he looked at me. Did I imagine that he gazed lustfully from the top of my head to the tip of my toes? Damned if I know?

9

I walked to the lift and pressed the button, the doors opening silently. Thankfully, a key or code wasn't required to gain access, which I thought strange, considering how security conscious he is. I stepped inside, closed my eyes and pushed a random button. I leaned against the cool glass and went over everything that just happened. Who was your woman? I was furious with myself for not finding out who or what she was to Gui. A few seconds later, the doors swished open. I peeped out, making sure all was clear before exiting. The corridor was long and dimly lit. It was probably what they call ambience lighting. The walls were adorned in an eclectic Oriental wallpaper, a delicate print in blush pink. It was perfect. Though it was long, I could only find one door which was halfway down. How strange. I was beginning to have second thoughts. Maybe this wasn't such a clever idea after all?

But of course, curiosity got the better of me. I walked toward the door with each step looking nervously over my shoulder. Not to be rude on this occasion, I gently tapped and waited for a response. Silence! Hoping the door was locked, I turned the handle and it sprung wide open with a clicking noise. How cool was that? Ideal for the orphanage. Trying to open a heavy door holding a baby and a shit load of nappies is no easy task. I dare say it cost a small fortune.

As I entered, the lights flickered on, frightening the crap out of me. I thought someone had turned them on behind me. But there was nobody there. Oh Jesus, it was his Playroom! I gulped loudly. Oh for fuck's sake, why am I surprised? It's funny but for a nanosecond, I wasn't frightened. Perhaps because I was aware of it after our conversation and oh yes, he's a Dom! So, this is where it's going to happen. I walked around the elegant room and studied every piece of furniture. I wasn't sure what they were called but thanks to my books, I had a fair idea of what fantasy they fulfilled. None of them freaked me out nor did they look like they could inflict pain. But that's the difference. It's not the paraphernalia, but the person who may cause pain or discomfort. My heart began to race. I don't know this man, this stranger and what he's capable of. Not long ago he thought it completely acceptable to chop off a child's arm. For fuck's sake, who am I kidding? Reality dawned. I clutched my chest, it felt tight. I couldn't breathe. What the hell have I got myself into?

I turned to run from the room and straight into a hard wall. Him. I screamed with panic and lashed out, pummelling his chest with heavy blows. He wrapped his arms tightly around me, gently whispering my name, his voice soothing as my beating hands stilled against him. His closeness brought on a strange feeling of calm and excitement. I rested my cheek against his chest for a moment, comforted by his sympathetic affection. I liked this side of him. "I can't do it," I cried. "I'm afraid. I was stupid to think I could go through with it. But being here, seeing this room has made my fantasies a reality and I'm not ready." I was full-on ugly crying now and knowing I was going to have a big puffy face didn't stop me.

He lifted me and I wrapped my legs around him like it was the most natural thing to do. The shock of his warm hands on my bare bum rendered me incapable of making another sound. He walked towards the bed. Of course, it had to be a four-poster! He sat down as I unhooked my legs and sat astride him. Oh my goodness. I could feel he was rock hard and it takes all my strength and will power not to grind against him. It felt so good. He gently runs his hand down my hair, holding it between his fingers. I can feel his breath on the top of my head. I don't move and I'm almost afraid to breathe. His scent and the bulge between my legs is giving me flutters. I get a vision of us naked and sweaty. Crap! I had never felt this way before. He kissed the top of my head. The air crackles between us. Can he feel it too?

"What scared you?"

"The pain," I gulped.

"I will never hurt you nor will you ever fear me. You will always have a choice. The bond between a Dom and his sub is special." He kisses the top of my head again. "There's so much shit and misunderstanding out there and you will find much of it in those silly books you read. Most of that stuff is impractical. I am not an abuser or a Sadist and certainly don't go about beating women up. We will discuss your limits and boundaries and that line will never be crossed unless you ask. You will know exactly what you're getting into before we begin."

"I don't like being told what to do and simply can't give up control. I am not a weak person."

"You're strong minded alright, I can't argue with that. So, know that every decision you make is what YOU want and are not being coerced into it."

"Will I have to sign a contract?"

"No. We have already touched on your fantasies and will discuss in greater detail, your likes, dislikes, kink and limits you may have."

"Oh, there will be quite a long list for that one!" My legs were beginning to cramp but I was reluctant to move for fear this moment would end. I mean, he was still rock hard, how I don't know because I'd hardly moved let alone taken a breath. Don't get me wrong, I fancy the hell out of him and would love nothing better for the both of us to end up in bed, satisfied beyond belief. But not here, in this room, where he's probably bedded numerous women?

"Are you scared of me Rhylee?"

"I don't think so?"

"It will never work if you are, no matter what I say."

"I feel more shy than afraid. I'm sorry but I have to change position, my legs have gone numb." I move onto my knees, my breasts brushing his face. A low growl escapes his mouth. I look down and see my hard nipples. He never even flinched, keeping his gaze on me at all times. I sat across his lap trying to stretch his jumper over my thighs.

"You know it would be much better if you removed it," he whispered.

I giggled nervously. "Ah no, it's grand. Not ready for that." I leaned my head against his chest so he wouldn't see me blush. He lifted my chin and we locked eyes.

"I love it when you try to hide your innocence, it's so appealing."

I gulped. This close I could see how perfect he was. "All you have to remember is to say STOP! Be very clear about what you want and what you like and dislike. You are the one in control and I will be guided by you and not by what I want. I am here to protect you. Do you understand?"

"Yes."

"We will honestly discuss all pros and cons before delving into this D/s relationship. If you come to this arrangement willingly, there will be no conflict of power whatsoever. Your desires will be my priority and in return, all I ask is for your compliance and obedience."

"Ah now, those words are for training puppies."

"You are not a sub, so yes, there will be some form of training."

"Suppose."

"How do you expect to learn? There will always be rules. Be it enjoyable rules. Rules and communication make it safe. The only way I can understand your desires and limits is through effective communication. You must be honest at all times when interacting. If you're not happy with something, say it."

"Makes sense I suppose."

"Don't keep quiet because I'm digging the scene. I am wholly focused on making your fantasies come true. Except for the crazy ones."

I giggled.

"I will base it on the information you give me. As the submissive, you have to accept that you are now mine, owned, surrendering all power. This is the whole point of being submissive. I will ask you the same question I asked you a few days ago. Are you willing to accept this?"

"Will I have to call you 'Master' or 'Sir'?

"No, you can call me what you want as long as it's respectful."

"I have no option but to accept this because of Lan, against my better judgement."

During our conversation, I never noticed his hand on my knee. His thumb gently swirling in a circular motion. I look up and he gives me the best come fuck me look as his hand slowly moves up my thigh. I'm starstruck. He lowers his head and kisses me. I try concentrate on the kiss, as his fingers edged closer. Jesus, I think I gulped into his mouth! His other hand was holding my hair in a gentle grip. It felt good. His tongue slid into my mouth reaching the back of my throat, while his fingers stroked between my legs on bare skin.

"Someone's been a very naughty girl. I should punish you for disobeying me. Perhaps a gentle spank to start with?"

"Gui," I breathe.

I didn't want him to stop what he was doing as his fingers circled my clitoris. Gentle pressure. Back and forth, up and down. He certainly didn't need a map as all 8,000 nerve endings were on fire. Okay, I don't think anyone has ever counted, but according to research, most women have approximately six to eight thousand nerve endings down there. The sensation washing over my entire body was like an out-of-mind experience and I didn't want it to stop. How have I missed this all of my life.

I opened my legs and as I did, he pushed a finger inside me. I gasped. I was so wet it squelched but I was too horny to be embarrassed. One finger was joined by two, then three which felt uncomfortable. They slid right in, taking me to the brink of an earth-shattering orgasm. Not caring what my orgasm face looked like, I gripped his waistcoat tightly, shuddering as I came. Oh God, it was never that quick before. It usually took me ages to find the right spot. I sat there content, enjoying the mind-blowing sensations rippling through my body. Neither of us said anything for a while as I fought hard to calm my heart slamming against my chest.

"Ummm. You're lovely when you come," he said gently. "That was quite a turn-on seeing you enjoying yourself, in such a state of ecstasy," he said as he sucked each finger clean. The fingers that were just inside me. I grimaced. "I had to taste you because I don't think you're quite ready to have me eat you out. Am I right?"

"Jesus yes," I squeaked. He gave a hearty chuckle. "I certainly don't have to ask if you had a good time. My wet fingers tell me all I need to know."

Still a little shy, I snuggled into his chest and listened to his strong heartbeat. He gently pressed my head against his chest drawing me closer.

"It was amazing, how did you do it? I mean, make me come so fast?"

"There's no formula for giving the perfect orgasm. I noticed you were more vocal when my fingers stimulated you up and down directly on your clitoris rather than side to side or circular strokes. It seems you have a preference.

Every female experiences orgasm in her unique way, it's not rocket science. You taste nice by the way."

"Oh," I managed to say, shifting awkwardly on his lap, feeling his thick erection beneath me. He kissed the top of my head before gently gripping my waist, lifting me and placing me on my feet like I was just a little doll. He stood and fixed himself as best he could but to be honest, there was no hiding what was going on down there.

"Now, let's get you cleaned up." He pushed me back gently and went into another room. I could hear water running and assumed he was running a bath. To my horror, he returned with a towel and facecloth. I leaned back resting on my elbows and asked what he was doing.

"Taking care of my sub like I said."

"I don't understand," I said, raising an inquisitive brow. "This is something you are going to have to get used to. Now is as good a time as any to begin your training." He kneeled in front of me and I pushed myself out of his reach. "Don't dare tell me you're going to wash me down there," I said, pointing a finger at my crotch and swivelling it in a circular motion.

"But yes, a Dom likes to take care of his sub."

"Omg, with a fucking facecloth, that's ridiculous. I can wash myself, thank you very much!"

"Rhylee, I don't like drawing references to your choice in literature, but on this occasion, I feel it's necessary. I'm sure there are references where the Dom takes care of his sub, after a scene. Aftercare?"

"Yes, but you more or less trashed everything that was in *those* books!"

"You're perfectly correct, I did and it was wrong of me to do so. Not all books are equal and one or two may get it right. So?"

I folded my arms and sulked. "Suppose so!"

"Good. Scoot to the end of the bed and spread your legs wide while I warm this up."

"Wait, what."

I was about to object when he stopped mid-step and in a stern voice, said 'NOW!'

I gave in and did what I was told but didn't pull up the jumper. Instead, I stretched it as much as possible, almost getting it past my knees. But as soon as I lay back, it sprung back up. 'Fuck it'! As he walked into the room, I covered my eyes with my hands trying to block out the embarrassment. I felt strong hands on my ankles as he pulled me to the edge and pushed them wide apart. I squinted my eyes shut under my hands and bit gently on my lip.

"Omg! It's so embarrassing. This had to be one of the most humiliating things I've ever done."

"You know, most subs find this an enjoyable experience." I ignored him and concentrated on what he was doing. He gently moved his hands up my legs and under my thighs, pulling me to the edge of the bed so that it was at eye level. I could feel his gentle breaths on my pussy. Oh God, it was making me horny. I peeked through my fingers and found him staring at it in awe. I hope it was awe and not revulsion because it's ugly or weird looking. It looked like a vagina the last time I looked, damn him, it's a lovely vagina!

I stopped overthinking if my bits looked weird. I'm my own worst enemy. He wanted to do it, otherwise, he wouldn't have his head stuck between my thighs, right? I needed to ditch *negative Nora* and take my mind off what he was doing and chill the fuck out! Try to enjoy the moment. Closing my eyes again, I felt the hot cloth on me and it felt so nice. Okay, that's not so bad. But then he stretched out the lips and wiped, in under and in between. The sensation was mind-blowing and it was beginning to feel too good. Omfg! I was getting aroused. This can't be happening. How can this make me horny? I clutched the sheets and held on tightly. The bed dipped slightly. I raised my head and watched him drop between my legs.

"Spread your legs more, I want to see how beautiful you are."

"O dear God," I whispered. Before going any further, he blew gently, almost taking me over the edge. It was too much. I wanted to take hold of his head and grind against his mouth. All these new sensations were so overwhelming. My legs were spread wide and I was obscenely open to him. It felt dirty but thrilling.

"Are you okay up there," he asked, glancing up at me.

I lifted my head and nodded.

"Um hmm," I moaned. I wanted to pinch my nipples. No, I wanted him to suck and bite them. He moved the cloth up and down over my clit, then side to side. Was he torturing me for being cheeky? He knew fine what he was doing. I was on fire. He placed a finger on each side and moved slowly up and down the inner folds. I started to pant heavily. He suddenly stopped. I wanted to scream, 'Oh sweet Jesus please don't stop, I'm about to come.' He revved things up to another level using both hands. One hand slowly circled without penetrating as the other traced circles over my clitoris giving me double sensations.

"You have a beautiful pussy."

I tried to control my breathing.

"What? Oh, thank you, I suppose!" My body started writhing, going into contortions. I pulled the jumper up so I could touch myself. My nipples are extremely responsive to touch, especially the closer I get to orgasm. They were hard and sensitive to the cool air, seriously enhancing my pleasure. I squeezed them gently between my thumb and forefinger, twisting them left to right, slowly increasing the intensity.

"Rhylee, remove the jumper so I can see your face." Without hesitation, I whipped it off and flung it over his head. He moved his hand over my tummy causing the muscles to clench. Taking my hand from my breast, he entwined our fingers. He blew gently on my clit just to get my attention. My eyes roll to the back of my head. With his tongue hard and flat, he licked from the bottom straight to the top like it was an ice cream cone. Fuck. It's too much and my knees try to close but he pushes them flat on the mattress.

"Don't move," he growled. My hands drop to the back of his head as I start to quiver. "I want you to come Rhylee."

I can't stop it. I arch my back, stretch my legs and curl my toes as I come! Now everything in me wants what's going to happen. He bites my clit and then sucks harder before licking up my juice.

"Holy God, what just happened?" I gasped.

"Two orgasms, that's what just happened," he grinned. Not taking his eyes off me for a second as he kissed my pussy then stood and fixed himself, for the second time. He ran a hand through his dishevelled hair, straightened his waistcoat and looked perfect. Not at all like a man who just had his face between my legs.

"Are you going to take care of me again?" He climbed onto the bed and lay beside me. In a split second, he was on top of me.

"Gui, I can't breathe," I giggled. He raised himself onto his elbows taking most of his weight off me as I let out a sigh of relief. I could feel how hard he was and just wanted to open my legs, desperate to feel his cock against my pussy. He kissed the top of my head.

"And how would you like me to take care of you?" I wanted to say, fuck me, so bad but couldn't.

"Tell me what's going on in that beautiful head of yours?" His face was so close I could see how luminous his blue eyes were and noticed the iris was rimmed with a small touch of amber, like fire. They were stunning.

"NO, you tell me what's going on in that beautiful head of yours first?"

"I believe you are doing what we call, 'Topping from the bottom!" He grabbed my hands and pushed them above my head.

"Ouch!" I could feel the stitches stretching under the strain but his hard cock digging into me took my mind off the discomfort. Especially when his waistcoat scratched my nipples. Here I am, naked and lying beneath this stunning man. Me!

"Yes, I believe I am, but didn't mean to. It was a nervous reaction which I hope you'll forget. Saying that, in the real world it would be an honest question."

"How is your arm?"

"Fine."

"Not hurting?"

"No, not in this position anyway. But if you removed yourself, God only knows how much pain it would cause and I'd probably scream the place down?"

"I see. Keep your arms where they are, if you don't, you WILL be punished!" He didn't look at all happy with what I thought was a hilarious reply. Yes, I had lied only because I didn't want him to stop. He raised his eyebrows in a YES, you heard me right kind of way. I was excited and eager to find out what he planned to do next. I liked what just happened. Maybe we could just have sex and leave all the nasty stuff behind? How about just cuddling? I love cuddling. I've never given a blow job and didn't fancy having his in my mouth. Only because of the sheer size of it. I suppose the inexperienced like me would find it very intimidating.

He climbed off me and I whined. Standing at the foot of the bed and not breaking eye contact, he slowly removed his clothes. Oh sweet Jesus. Was he doing a strip tease? Not sure. Didn't Evee say they were fun or was it fun for the guy she was stripping for? Damn, I wish I listened more to Evee's sexual adventures. Don't get me wrong, she's not a slut. She'd been with Josh for almost ten years and said sex every time was amazing. He's a big lad too and in the beginning, she said it wouldn't fit. But in time and lots of patience it all worked out. Sometimes he reached areas previously unexplored and said she wouldn't change his seven inches for anything smaller. It also helped that he was a considerate partner. After that nugget of information, I found it difficult to look at Josh without staring at his crotch.

I wanted a better view and went to raise myself onto my elbows.

"Remember what I said," he growled. With eyes locked on mine, he unbuttoned his waistcoat, then his shirt. I thanked God for the beautiful sight before me. He slowly slid down his zip and pulled his trousers down. No boxers! I licked my lips. His huge cock hung heavily between his legs. How could he even walk with that thing? I crossed my legs to stop the throbbing. How can someone be so fucking beautiful? He ran his fingers through his hair and the movement made his enormous cock bounce. I aimlessly nodded as I looked in awe at my first big dick. It was long and the girth was massive, pre-ejaculate seeping from the tip. But was it too much and more important, would it fit? He was very well-endowed and I know what Evee meant when she said, hung like a donkey! In Gui's case, a horse. But did penis size matter and was I about to find out? Jesus Christ, it's about eight-and-a-half inches!

10

He just stood there staring as I began to lose my nerve. I wanted to know what he was thinking. What! The! Fuck! was going on in his head? He walked back into the other room and I heard the shower go on.

He put his head around the door and said, "Remember what I said and it's not up for discussion." I nodded. He returned and once again I felt the hot cloth wipe me clean. He patted me gently with a towel and kissed me before leaving the room. I lay poker straight, like a statue and listened to him showering. WTF! Is he having a laugh? I lay there silently fuming. I can do this. It's not so bad. How long does it take to shower? How long did it take me? Oh fuck, it was way longer than an hour. My arm began to ache and it felt like only ten minutes had passed. My muscles weren't used to this position. If that wasn't bad enough, the wound was adding to the discomfort and I could feel the stitches stretching. I knew I had to endure it because of my big mouth. He asked out straight and I stupidly said I was fine. Put up or shut up! He's testing me. I can be still, quiet and obedient and up for whatever challenges he throws at me.

He emerged sometime later, I'd lost track of time. He was fully dressed wearing what I can only describe as the most beautiful suit I've ever seen, obviously tailor-made for the superclass. He probably spent more money on that single suit than I did on my car. Such is the nature of exclusivity and one of a kind. I wanted to ask him why the hell I was still lying naked and uncomfortable but instead said, "I love your suit, it's stunning."

He ran his fingers along the expensive fabric and fixed his cufflink. "Thank you." That's all he said.

"So, I see you're ready to go out on your date with what's-her-face. May I go back to my room now?" The realisation of what I just said pierced my heart. It upset me. Why did it hurt so much knowing he was going out with another woman? With her. He's nothing to me. I'm nothing to him? "I shouldn't have to remind you how important honesty is in this relationship. When it's not taken seriously and ignored, unfortunately, there will be consequences."

"Umm…..Pardon me, I wasn't aware this was a relationship but a convenience of sorts!" He ignored me and continued.

"For instance, I asked you a simple question earlier if your arm was hurting you. You blatantly said no, yet you winced when you raised it above your head."

"But…." He raised his hand.

"Let me finish. As I've said before, honesty is the groundwork for a trusting and safe relationship. The only way I can understand your limits is YOU being honest with me. To progress, you must be honest."

"Seriously, I don't know what you're talking about. Blame my muscles. They're not used to being in this position. And please stop mentioning relationships. We are not in a relationship. Let's be clear. I am here under duress." He let out an exasperated sigh or was it anger or frustration? "Whatever the excuse, you lied and you're still lying now! Why is it so hard for you to admit you made a mistake?" I didn't answer.

"Have you heard of mental bondage punishment?"

"Nope."

"It requires you to stay in the same place for a specified amount of time. Breaking from this position will warrant another punishment. Do you understand?"

"You want me to remain in this position for an hour or two because you feel I lied." Admittingly I'm my own worst enemy and as my mother once confirmed, 'a stubborn little bitch'. I pursed my lips together and just stared at him while he waited patiently for an answer which wouldn't be forthcoming. Grrrr! It brought back unpleasant memories of being a teenager. The constant standoffs with my parents. With an impatient sigh, he pushed his hands deep into his slim-fitting trousers showcasing his bulge. Even though I was laying down, my mouth dropped to my chest. If his beauty doesn't bring the room to a standstill, the prominent bulge in his trousers most certainly will. He caught me staring so I pretended to be looking at his waistcoat buttons. Phew, something else to lie about.

"Nice buttons," I mumbled.

He ran his index finger over them. "Eighteen-carat gold with diamonds. I know you love details."

"Wow, an engagement ring where I come from. Just in case the first four don't work out hahaha! So how much would one of those get-ups cost?"

I knew he was humouring me now.

"Get-ups....?

What's that?"

"Your clobber."

"Can't you just speak English?"

"Clobber is English. Your suit."

"100K stg, designed by the famous Stuart Hughes and made by the world-renowned tailor Richard Jewels."

"Holy crap. That's like a mortgage."

"One thing for sure which we both can agree on, you DO talk verbal diarrhoea when you're nervous!"

"Wait, what? I'm not nervous. Why would I be nervous? Should I be nervous? I get awful cramps when I'm nervous."

"I wouldn't be still standing here if you agreed you lied, I'd be sitting down to an exquisite meal, witty conversation and beauty to match." That stopped me in my tracks. "Worth knowing, I don't give second chances to others who have gone before you or after you. So, I will ask you again. Did you lie?"

I wasn't going to admit anything, call it pride or stupidity? "My muscles hurt as I've said already." He pressed his lips together and frowned.

In that voice he says, "As I've said already, keep your arms where they are, if you don't, you'll pay the consequences."

"Yep, got it, again!" I said, reverting my eyes up to the ceiling. I watched as his masculine frame and broad shoulders strode out the door with not even a backward glance. I stuck my tongue out.

"You're lucky, I could have made you kneel on a bed of uncooked rice which I've been told is quite painful," he said, walking down the hall. I was hoping he'd change his mind and stay. On another note, that man is oblivious to how hot he is. Evee would call him a panty dropper. I shouted, "Being a dick won't make it any bigger you know!" Wrong comeback, if he was any bigger, he'd split me in half. I lay there with just my thoughts for company. Why couldn't he just spank my arse and send me to bed without dinner? Punishment is meant to be exciting, isn't it? Word to myself, do not believe everything you read! Maybe he thought I just wasn't ready for REAL punishment? Yes, he's right! In one of the many erotic books I've read, one sub was punished by figging, literally making you hot. A finger-sized piece of ginger is peeled and shoved up your arse! The oils from the root have an immediate effect causing an intense burning sensation. No thanks! On the positive side, if the sub is allowed to reach orgasm it can be incredibly intensive.

My buttocks were beginning to go numb from lying in the same position for so long, but I wasn't going to move. He wouldn't know and if he asked, would I lie again? Damn him, I crossed my legs and felt the blood rushing easing the pins and needles. Anyway, to be precise, he said I wasn't to move my arms. I did a snow angel with my legs, obviously without the snow and not moving my arms. I'd been going to the gym back home and did several workout classes that could be done lying down. It would certainly pass the time and I'd get some kind of a workout. Toning and tightening my legs and stomach without even getting out of bed! Ha. Winner.

I started with twenty repetitions of the supine leg march. I couldn't put my hands by my sides. Followed by reverse crunches and finishing with straight leg lifts which was an hour class. It was wonderful doing it naked because the cool air felt so good, especially when I opened my legs. However, I couldn't block out the pain radiating from the wound spreading down my arm straight to my fingertips. It made me feel nauseous. I thought the pain was supposed to subside as it healed. Before long the sheer exhaustion of everything that happened with Gui took over and deep sleep beckoned. Or maybe I passed out?

I could hear voices, male voices ringing in my ears. Was I dreaming? They were speaking in hushed tones but I couldn't quite make out what they were saying. The strain on Gui's voice was unmistakably clear. I had to go to him. I forced my eyes open to find him standing over me and had to squint to clear the blur. The other man said, "She's awake." I blinked several times to focus and when I attempted to sit up, the pounding in both my head and arm felt like someone was sticking pins in me! In complete panic, he sat on the edge of the bed taking my hand gently in his.

"Thank you, doctor." The man smiled, turned and left the room.

"What's going on, why do I feel like shite? Actually, why do *you* look like shite?"

He looked like he'd seen a ghost and his hair was all over the place. I'd never seen him look so dishevelled.

"Shhh, you need to rest."

"Omg, I've been resting for fucking days!" I went to sit up on my elbows and cried out.

"Jesus, what the hell." I looked at my arm and saw it had been re-bandaged. "What's going on?"

"Your wound was infected and the stitches ruptured. The surgical incisions broke along the sutures." I looked at him like he was speaking another language. "The wound split open. Strained when I put your arms above your head, causing pressure for it to open. I'm so sorry Rhylee. The doctor said you would have been in severe pain and being in that position for so long didn't help. I was shocked seeing so much blood and honestly thought you'd been murdered!"

"Exactly how long was I in that position?"

"Five hours."

I don't know why but I began to sob. Was it because I knew he was out wining and dining or worse, having amazing sex with that woman? Or maybe because he left me all alone for five hours without even a thought because I meant nothing to him?

He caressed my cheek and his voice was so gentle, "Please don't, I can't bear to see you cry."

"I want to go home!" I cried. "Just let me go home."

"You can't, we have an understanding."

"Fuck the fucking understanding!! Understanding my hole, call it what it is, BLACKMAIL! I WILL GO HOME, you can't stop me!" I sobbed loudly and my voice broke into a scream, "You can't keep me prisoner!" Tears streamed down my face and I couldn't look at him any longer. I turned my back and pulled the covers up under my chin and cried quietly. The bed dipped and I felt his body stretch out and mould against mine. His hand gently caressed my hair and shoulders. My body shuddered with gentle sobs.

"There, there, hush my golden angel," he whispered. The doctor has given you a sedative which will help you sleep. Please don't cry. Can you forgive me?"

I sobbed and begged him to let me go until it felt like my heart was being brutally wrenched from my chest.

"Sshh, I've got you." He wrapped his arm around me pulling me tighter into him. Even through the covers, I could feel every shape of his muscular body. A calmness came over me and I wanted to stay like this forever. I felt his lips brush over my hair as he kissed the top of my head. I wished it was my mouth. He was so tender as I lay there listening to his breathing. I gave in and sighed, snuggling against him, feeling the beat of his heart... or was it my own?

"You haven't answered my question?" he asked. His voice was soothing and I could hardly keep my eyes open.

"There's nothing to forgive. We both know I lied because I'm a stubborn bitch."

"I would say, headstrong, obstinate, wilful, unbending, I could go on."

"If I told you the truth when you asked, we wouldn't be here now in the middle of this shit show!"

"We probably would, but under far nicer circumstances."

"God knows you gave me several opportunities, to be honest." I yawned. But at his question, I realised lying had its consequences, no matter how big or small. "Sometimes, it's better to keep your mouth shut and give the impression that you're stupid than open it and remove all doubt! I'm sorry," I whispered, before falling asleep.

Turning in bed sent searing pain up through my arm. But what a beautiful sight to behold. Gui stretched out beside me in a deep sleep, his arm resting protectively over me, a few strands of hair falling over his obnoxiously handsome face. I was in awe of this beautiful man sleeping innocently next to me. I wanted to lean in and kiss his plump lips but instead ran my fingers through his hair placing the strands neatly back in place. I wanted to see his whole face, so I carefully got up on one elbow giving me a perfect view. I studied every inch of his chiselled face like a greedy pirate studying a treasure map and wondered if his perfect eyebrows were professionally shaped? Was he aware we women would die for his super-long eyelashes? Life just wasn't fair.

I couldn't control my urge to run a finger over his plump lips. I stretched out my arm and noticed I was wearing real clothes. I was only interested in one thing, touching his mouth. I shook with nerves as my hand quivered above his face. Moving it gently over his bottom lip first, he opened his mouth and played at biting my finger. I screamed with fright. His soft lips turned into a contagious smile. "Good morning angel."

I made a face. "You almost frightened the crap out of me," I complained.

He chuckled mischievously. "Such a lovely way with words, young lady. How are you feeling, how's your arm?" he asked, playing with my curls, twisting them around his finger. "The truth."

"Hey! I'm not going to that shit show ever again. I've learned my lesson! It's very sore, that's why I woke up." He turned onto his side, propping himself up onto his elbow and looked at me. Oh fuck, bet I look like shite? His intense stare unnerved me. I flopped on my back and studied the domed ceiling.

"Hey, what's wrong Rhylee?"

"I'm sorry if I ruined your date?"

"My date?"

"Yeah, with Jingfei. She went out of her way to let me know you were having dinner and a little something something?"

"I had no intention of going out with her."

"But she said you were picking her up and you never objected."

"Jingfei likes to exaggerate and I learned that it's best to let her say whatever goes on in her head. I was working in my office. Well, that was the idea. Instead, I watched you for most of it on the security monitor until you fell asleep. And very entertaining it was too, in particular the gymnastics. That was a bonus. I came down to carry you back to bed when I found you in a pool of blood. The camera is positioned on the opposite side, so I didn't see the blood until I came into the room."

"But you said, 'witty conversation and beauty to match.'"

"Yes, I did. I was talking about you. I was taking YOU out to dinner."

"Me? You meant me when you said those wonderful things and not Jingfei?"

"Yes, you. I agree she is a looker, but her conversational skills are a lot to be desired. Non-existent to be precise.

She has nothing nice to say about anyone or anything and loves drama. Could you just imagine how an evening with her would go, especially after meeting you? It's all me, me, ME. She's even tried to trick me into thinking I was crazy for getting upset with her 'quirky' behaviour. We don't ever do dinner anymore unless it's for charity. At least then I have an excuse to mingle and escape her clutches. I shiver just thinking about it."

"But you dated her?"

"I did mention that didn't I? I tried my best to change her. I know that's wrong, but it was easy having her there at my beck and call. It's good publicity turning up with her on my arm for charity events. It kept the gossip columns busy and gained much-needed momentum for the charities. I found it convenient to send a car when her services were required."

"Oh God, you mean booty calls?!"

"I guess. The sex was good. I'll give her that at least. She was eager to please me and I took advantage. She assumed if it was mind-blowing, I'd forget about the lifestyle. She was like a power source of pure sexual energy. I couldn't believe how intense it was. Or how lucky I was, sex on demand. Call me arrogant, you wouldn't be wrong. When we were out, she always had my undivided attention. I never looked at another woman while we were together. I made her feel like she was the only woman in the room. But realised it wasn't real. I went along with it for a while until I got bored. Look, we are both adults and knew what we were doing. It was convenient for both of us. We're guilty of trying to change each other. If you feel you need to change someone, it's not meant to be."

"It seems you both benefited."

"I agree. We got what we wanted, needed. But enough about her."

I didn't know how to respond so quickly changed the subject.

"That's some chandelier, it's certainly a showstopper." I sat up and looked around. Where am I? Like, I know it's your house but it's not my room."

"You're in my bedroom. I wanted to take care of you myself."

Holy crap! His bedroom was huge and jaw dropping magnificent. Extravagant yet soothing. Floor-to-ceiling windows with panoramic views spanned from one end of the room to the other. "If this was my room, I'd never want to leave and would end up spending even more waking hours luxuriating in this sumptuous bed. I bet the thread count is like a gazillion?"

He looked amused and was happy to let me rabbit on. Both sides of the bed had sizable, mirrored dressers. Most of us have your common bedside lockers. Adding a hint of the dramatic were clusters of crystal orbs hanging over each one giving a touch of elegance. Evee would say, glitz and bling. I suppose it's an important part of any home, as most of our lives are spent sleeping. A sanctuary to take leave of our daily woes, intimacy and romance. The huge bed dominated the room, the ultimate in comfort and of course luxury.

"Is it handmade?" I asked, tapping the bed.

"Yes, it took 120 hours to craft this creation. Would you believe me if I told you the topper was made using a kilo of pure cashmere?"

"Yes, I would." It was fully upholstered and the dramatic curved winged headboard had traditional deep button detailing, upholstered in sumptuous grey velvet and trimmed with opulent crystal. A dream, bespoke bed made to impress and fit for a king, or queen. The white marble floor was timeless and associated with luxury, found in most high-end homes and interiors. It reminded me of a frozen lake. I found everything about it enchanting.

"It's such a beautiful room and amazingly, not one bit masculine."

"You seem surprised?"

"I am. I thought it would be quite industrial with exposed brick, iron or copper finishes and maybe polished concrete floors."

"So, what style would you say it is?"

"My style hahaha."

"Is that so?" he asked as he sat up beside me. I could see from the corner of my eye that he was naked above the waist. Oh, Jesus, I just couldn't handle it if he was completely naked so nimbly jumped out of bed and calmly walked to the window. I was grateful and relieved, feeling the swish of material flapping against my legs. I stopped in front of the mass of windows and studied the view.

"Rhylee, don't tell me you're frightened, shy??"

I turned my head and looked him straight in the eye. "Yes, I'm both!" He was behind me before I even had time to turn my head. He leaned in close and I could feel the swell of his cock against my back poking me gently. He wasn't one bit shameful either.

"What would you do if I gently pushed you up against the window, pulled down your pj's and slipped inside you?" I swiped around shocked. "I thought the 'understanding' would take place in the playroom? During the times you wanted to train me as your sub?"

He suddenly burst into laughter as his warm strong hands gripped my shoulders. I stood helplessly glaring up at him, annoyed he was laughing.

"What's so funny?" I asked.

"You can't slot lust and desire into a time schedule, I'm too much of a selfish fucker!"

"To answer your question, I wouldn't like it one bit. You make it sound dirty and grossly impersonal!"

"Ahh, you want romance? Unfortunately, you won't find that here. If you want the fairytale ending, you'll have to go to Disneyland. I hate to break it to you, but that Cinderella stuff doesn't exist, it's not real. I'm highly motivated by sexual desire, you could say I'm a sex-obsessed machine. You wouldn't be wrong to assume men are crazy for sex, while women just want romance. I have a high sex drive and pride myself on being in control at all times until I met you."

"But my arm!"

"I'm not interested in fucking your arm!"

"Oh my God, you've lost leave of your senses. You're acting like a caveman. I just can't believe how disgusting you are right now!"

"I have no problem dragging you around by the hair, some women like that."

"Ugh! You're just a fucking neanderthal who probably likes putting women in place. Isn't that the truth about submissives and submission?"

"Rhy, Rhylee!" I opened my eyes to find myself standing in front of the window. Startled, I turned my head towards Gui, a look of concern on his face. He threw back the covers and jumped out of bed, striding towards me in long measured steps. "What's wrong, are you okay, I lost you for a bit?"

I looked at him dazed and frozen to the spot. What on earth just happened? "Do you feel unwell? I'll get the doctor."

"No, no I'm fine, I think. I'm confused. Did you say you wanted to fuck me up against the window?"

"Christ no, I didn't. I thought you were just admiring the view so left you to your thoughts. But then you wouldn't answer when I asked if you'd like a bite to eat. You just zoned out."

"I can't explain it other than I was dreaming standing up. You were disgustingly vulgar and I'm surprised I'm not crying my eyes out in horror. It felt so real. It's all very confusing."

"Rhylee, tell me."

"No, it's silly."

"Still, I want to know what's upset you."

"You said you wanted to take me hard and to forget any romantic notions or silly fairytale endings I had in my head. How you lose control when I'm around you!"

He gulped. "Oh dear, that's brutal and not how I would conduct myself at all. On the contrary, I'm quite romantic, annoyingly so. Come here."

He held out his arms and without hesitation, I walked into his embrace. The warmth of his broad chest was like a magnet. I sighed and snuggled against him. "You're also a great cuddler." He laughed.

"Never been told that before." He held me tighter.

One thing I didn't dream, he was naked from the waist up. His skin was warm and soft and I could hear his heart beating gently. I peeled my face off his chest and looked up at him. Our eyes locked. He lowered his head as I tiptoed to meet his lips. He pressed them softly against mine as my heart thudded in my chest. It felt sweet and innocent. I tried to raise my arms around his neck but the pain stopped me. He pulled away gently and ran a hand through his hair. "You were right about one thing though and I'm not afraid to admit it. I do lose control. Just a little when you're around. It's never happened before. I pride myself on being a very controlled person, both in business and as a Dominant." For a moment, all I can do is stare at his beautiful face.

"You should have mentioned that and I wouldn't have sashayed around with no knickers on," I laughed.

"Fair to say you can blame that one on me. You will find the wardrobes full now."

"Oh wow? You shouldn't have."

"I didn't. You can thank my mother for anything nice that's happened so far."

I pulled away from him. "What do you mean?"

"Don't get me wrong, I wish it was me who had left the shit load of beauty products outside the bathroom door and a year's supply of kid's clothes for Lan."

"I do too."

"I didn't want to get involved emotionally and it caused numerous arguments with my mother. She said I was being cruel and heartless to both of you and that she didn't bring me up that way. At the time I was furious she got involved and wondered how on earth she managed to do everything from the confines of her bed, two floors down!! But the staff talk and everyone adores her and would do anything she asked even if it meant crossing me. When you walked in on us, I was stunned, you looked so beautiful and I had to fight like a demon to prevent an, umm, raging boner!"

I laughed out loud and punch him softly.

"It's not something I'd want to be exposed to Jingfei, life wouldn't be worth living! Now I try my best to keep her at a safe distance, but our families are in business together and she still uses that as an excuse."

"Do you need to be in business with them?"

"Both our fathers started it up and I keep an eye on it from time to time. Out of respect for my father, I treat her accordingly but if she had her way or had any encouragement from me, we'd be married."

"Crazy, sounds like some shitty tv show. Wouldn't it just be easier to put her straight? Like ripping off a Band-Aid? How is she going to feel when you do meet 'The One'? It wouldn't be nice or fair."

"She knows me too well. She knows that I'll never settle down with her or anyone else. She's more than happy to take any crumb that falls from my table."

"I'd say she's just holding out. She thinks if she waits long enough, you'll give in and marry her."

He smacked his hands together and roared out laughing, the noise making me jump.

"Seriously! Was that necessary? What did I say that's so damn funny?"

"Jingfei is as vanilla as you. Except she's repulsed with my lifestyle and has made it her mission to change me."

"Has she tried it? I mean, how do you know?"

"As I said, there's no denying she's a beautiful woman and sure why wouldn't you? We bumped into each other at an after-show party and ended up back here. She had a fair idea of my extracurricular activities so I introduced her to the playroom. I could see she was terrified and gave her every opportunity to leave. She insisted it was what she wanted so I took it real slow and was patient with her. She didn't visit for a long time afterwards and never mentioned it again. So as far as I'm concerned, marriage to Jingfei will never happen! Lust on the other hand is a different story. She fulfils the void. She gets the attention she craves and has accepted it. If she meets someone in the meantime, I for one would be delighted for her. It takes a man with bigger balls than me to take that on! Being a Dominant is part of my life. Marriage isn't."

"I still think it would be wise to remind her. She can stop wasting her life away hoping to convince you otherwise. You need to put her out of her misery. It's a train wreck waiting to happen and not one bit fair!"

"Fine. I take your point. I'll sort it out."

"So how did you know your mother left the toiletries?"

"I saw her Louis Vuitton travel case in the hallway and approached her about it. She said she was disgusted that I would treat you like that after you put your life on the line for her. Of course, she isn't aware of our arrangement and must never find out."

"So what did you tell her about Lan? I don't think I can take any more drama, it's just so surreal!"

"She thinks that I've given her a second chance and when you've recovered, you both will leave and go back to the orphanage!"

I turned my face away. Somehow, I didn't want to hear that word, leave. Leave him. It hurt and my heart was breaking. I should look at it as some fucked up adventure experience of a lifetime. He cupped my face, forcing it towards him until I had no option but to look him in the eye. He lowered his head until our foreheads touched.

"This is some fucked up shit you've gotten yourself into!"

"Funny, I was just thinking that." He smiled.

"Do you mind if I lay down for a bit, preferably my own room if that's okay?"

"Of course. Hey, are we good?" he asked. "Now that I've aired my dirty laundry?"

"Sorry, I'm just exhausted. That was a lot to take in and all the bed rest doesn't seem to be helping either. It's not like I get stabbed or made a sex slave every day."

"No, it's not. But you will heal and things will get easier."

"If you say so. But you're not the one in a compromising position. My whole life has been turned upside down. You can have this with any one of your subs."

"Yes, I can."

"Well then."

"They're not you. My life, a small part of it has been turned upside down too. I know that's probably hard to believe. I'm a very structured person. I know what I want and have never had any problem getting it. I didn't realise I was missing something until I met you. I'm just as shocked as you are, believe me."

I sat down, my mouth wide open. The sumptuous mattress beckoned me. I climbed under the covers and rested my weary body against the lavish headboard. I folded the covers and laced my fingers together.

"I'll apologise now in case I fall asleep. I don't want to because I'm sure it's not every day you explain or justify yourself to anyone?"

"You mean you like watching me squirm?"

"On the contrary, I won't deny I like seeing this side of you. It only confirms you're not a complete and utter prick, just impossible to read. And these little titbits into your psyche, although revealing to a certain extent, is somewhat refreshing."

"I'm happy and relieved to know that you don't think I'm an utter prick, or worse still, a serial killer."

"Hahahaha. No, not a serial killer."

"I know I'm not perfect and don't pretend to be. I make mistakes like everyone else but I believe you learn from them and move on. That's what makes you stronger and more adamant to be the best at everything you do. Sometimes perfection is a hindrance but you adapt. When you walked into my office wearing nothing but a slip of fabric, your curls piled high and the most luscious lips waiting to be ravaged, you were perfect! I knew I had to have you. Your innocence was overpowering and I was in awe of you. It didn't help either that you were so modest. It just made me want you all the more."

"Omg, I was a state and looked like shite! I was embarrassed you saw me like that."

"You're amazing just the way you are. Life is such that I rarely see natural beauty anymore because most women aren't happy for me to see them without all the paraphernalia. They spend a fortune on changing the colour of their skin, hair or the shape of their eyes. For what? To please someone or to fit in?"

"I don't agree with that. Most of us do it for ourselves. If it makes us feel better and gives us confidence, I'm all for it. To be honest, I would have preferred it if you hadn't seen me like that. It made me angry and very self-conscious. We all have our insecurities."

"But you see, for me it was a breath of fresh air."

"Not intentional I can assure you. Sorry, I didn't think I'd have the energy to pretend to like you today, but I'm proven otherwise!"

"I think there's a compliment in there somewhere. Rhylee, I don't go out of my way to upset people, not intentionally."

"You're just a magnet?"

"Harsh!"

11

I smiled up at him and wished things were different between us. I didn't want to be just his plaything. Oh, why couldn't we have met under different circumstances?

"You're gone again," he said.

I looked at him with a furrowed brow. "Gone where?"

"Daydreaming. I hope it was happier than the last one?"

"Just silly dreams."

"Tell me."

"Some things are best kept private."

"I see," he said with a sulky face.

I burst out laughing. "You're like a grumpy teenager, dimples and all."

"Are you hungry?"

"Can I ask you something?"

"After what I've told you, I'm an open book."

"Were you really going to take me out to dinner? Like out, out?"

He laced his fingers together and stretched his arms out like he was going to crack his knuckles. I had a feeling I wasn't going to like what he was about to say. "No."

"I knew it. It's because I'm a state and not in the same league as Jingfei or the women you date?"

"RHYLEE!" He said in a raised voice. "Listen to me. It's only because you wouldn't be mentally up to it. You wouldn't believe the pressure of being papped by egotistical arseholes trying to get an exclusive photo of 'Gui Lee's latest girlfriend. Most of them are just sleaze bags making up disgusting lies. It sells because everyone loves gossip. Not everybody is ready to see their photo splashed across every newspaper or magazine and their image picked to pieces. They're relentless and don't give a shit how impersonal they get. The headline on one of many would ask, 'Who is she, what has she got for Gui Lee to be interested? The front of another is emblazoned with the word's gold digger! Your hair is the wrong shade, your waist is too wide, you're too small, too tall. You get the gist. I would hate for you to have to go through that bullshit. Anyone else who's been out in my company has been born into it. Some crave it and perform certain things, good and bad to be constantly in the limelight. It's just that you're way too nice and a perfect target. I know you'll be a different person after you leave here. I guarantee you'll be the most confident version of yourself. Maybe then we'll give it a go."

"Jesus! You're right. I wouldn't have coped at all if they were mean. I have too many insecurities as it is."

"I think you're perfect. Though maybe not everything that comes out of that beautiful mouth of yours."

I wanted to stick out my tongue and say something to shock him like, 'If I wanted to hear from an arsehole, all I had to do was fart! He stood in front of me holding out his hand.

"Why are you smiling?"

"Just another one of those thoughts I mentioned which is best kept private."

"Come, if you're up to it, I want to show you something." He pulled back the covers and gently pulled my feet to the edge of the bed. "It's okay, you won't need slippers where we're going." He took my hand and helped me off the bed, leading me to the lift. "You okay," he asked.

I nodded. He pushed R. "What's R?"

"Rooftop. You haven't answered my question, Rhylee. You should know by now I'm not accustomed to repeating myself."

I looked at his twitching eyebrow and giggled. "I'm sorry, yes I'm fine."

"What's so funny?"

"Gosh, you're so intense. Do you need to know what every look or laugh means? It's not rocket science."

"With you, yes I do."

"Are you sure you want to know?"

"Yes!"

"Positive?"

"Just say it, Rhylee."

"So, I've noticed that when you're about to lose your patience, your eyebrow slightly twitches then raises right up. It's a great indicator of how annoyed you are."

"Nobody has ever pointed that out to me before. I'm surprised they haven't sprung right off my face because of you."

I looked at him and we both burst out laughing. "Omg, that's funny."

The doors swished open and my breath was taken away. I stood rooted to the spot. He placed his hand on my back and gently nudged me forward. I walked onto the softest green grass on a wraparound garden. It was spectacular and the thousands of fairy lights made it magical. It was stylish, intimate and utterly stunning. I clapped my hands in excitement which made him smile. I was sure it was one of the biggest roof gardens in the city. Beautifully furnished with sumptuous sofas and a ginormous whitewashed dining table adorned with candelabras, the dancing flicker of the flames adding to the romantic ambience. It had mostly grass with paved walkways and parquet grey decking, glass balustrades on all four sides with beautiful plants, flowers, trees and of course, the views. It took my breath away.

"Oh Gui, it's like something from a fairytale, a magical wonderland, a secret garden."

"I call it a moment of lavish fantasy to lift the spirits." He took my hand and led me through a trellised arch cascading with white flowers. There was a small intimate table set for two surrounded by giant urns overflowing with pink peonies and hanging above, a crystal cage chandelier, complete with glass birds and flowers within. The epitome of breathtaking grandeur. "This is where I was taking you. Seeing the look on your face right now, I know it beats any pretentious five-star restaurant and confirms I made the right choice."

"Oh yes, yes, yes. I love it. I can't take it all in."

He held out a chair and beckoned for me to sit. "Let's start again and pretend yesterday never happened, shall we?" I nodded and sat down in disbelief.

"Well, not all of it," I blushed. He raised an eyebrow.

Each place setting had a tiny menu placed on silver-rimmed plates. "I hope I made the right decisions with the menu?"

I read it from start to finish, my mouth watering in anticipation.

Red onion & smoked ricotta tart, fine bitter leaves w/honey truffle

Goat's cheese & mint ravioli, confit tomato, balsamic pearls

Salted caramel parfait, hazelnut crunch, milk chocolate ice cream

Selection of cheeses & fruit.

"Oh wow, sounds like a gastronomical delight. It's seriously making me hungry. Vegetarian, for you too? Or are you having a big juicy steak?"

"Nope, same as you, going to ditch meat while you're staying here."

Before I could answer, our meal was served in an elegant and sophisticated manner. The servers laid our food down with smiles on their faces and whispered, "Enjoy your meal."

I smiled back. "Thank you so much, it all looks amazing. Oh sweet Jesus, the truffle honey is to die for. I'd even eat a soggy sock if it was covered with that," I gushed.

"I'll be sure to let the chef know," he said smiling.

I can't help myself but if I'm enjoying my food I'm very vocal, with repeated oohhs and aahs right through the meal. My mother said it was one of the most embarrassing things to have to sit through. Each dish was prepared with great care and attention to detail. The presentation and the taste were both perfect. I never even noticed the dishes being cleared when the main was presented. "I'm so looking forward to the next one. I love ravioli but never had goat's cheese with mint. How are you enjoying your veggie meal so far? Are you savouring each delectable morsel as much as me?"

"There's nothing in the world at the moment which gives me a better thrill than watching you enjoying your food. Damn, it's almost turning me on."

"I'm sorry. I make ridiculous sounds when I'm loving my food."

"Do you make them while enjoying anything else? Or is it just food?"

I blushed. "Just food," I giggled. "No one or thing exists if I'm eating a mouth-watering meal with amazing flavours I've never experienced before." It had been difficult keeping quiet downstairs at the dining table, often almost forgetting where I was. I knew he was watching my every move and even surprised myself remembering the table etiquette my mother painstakingly taught me. Which proved I can do things if I try hard enough. At least now I can avoid my mother's disapproval at dinner.

"Tell me about your family, your parents. Life back home in Ireland."

"Oh God, now you've put me right off my food and we haven't got to the desert yet!"

He laughed then turned serious. "Surely they can't be that bad?"

"Not really. I suppose there's worse out there. Do I have to, it doesn't make for a riveting read."

"I'd like to know and I promise I won't judge," he said with a wink.

"I won't judge," says the man with a sex dungeon in his home."

"I prefer playroom or play space."

"Alright, only if you tell me yours, deal?"

"Deal."

"I'm an only child. I was brought up by my parents with a very strict father who wouldn't tolerate being answered back. Even if you were righting a wrong or standing up for yourself. To him, it was disrespectful. I sensed my mother didn't like me and felt we never bonded. I was taken to see a psychological therapist at the tender age of five because I was so strong-willed and frequently exhibited certain characteristics. My mother often mentioned that she couldn't handle my determination to do things on my terms and found it frustrating. She said I constantly had a sulky face from being stubborn and she was tired of always trying to convince me to wear something I didn't particularly like. I can see her point now to be fair. I remember the repeated arguments over what outfits she wanted me to wear going to school. I insisted that my socks were brilliant white without a mark on them. One day she broke down, inciting rage from my father who in turn dragged me to school to discover I wasn't wearing any knickers. That's when they made up their minds. They needed answers, so they made an appointment for me to speak to a professional. Her name was Dr Deer and she was a lovely lady but I don't remember what the outcome was. She asked me to draw a family picture and asked why my dad wasn't inside the house with mammy and me. I said it was because he was always out working. Another thing she asked was what colour my mam's eyes were. I remember I had to think about it."

"What about your dad?"

"He's a stickler for attention to detail. Even if I was only colouring, he'd be looking over my shoulder getting frustrated if I went outside the line. So now it's a curse because I go insane and overboard with attention to detail. I was the only child on the street who went to bed at seven and had to listen to them having fun until I fell asleep. When I got older my issues changed. I was extremely self-conscious and it didn't help that my mother forced me to wear the tightest tops. She'd make me wear my school uniform on a Sunday if I wanted to go to my grandmother's. It was so humiliating walking to the bus stop past the other kids in their Sunday best while I was wearing my uniform. Listening to the taunts and jeering. She swore it was because I looked like an angel in it. As I mentioned before, I wasn't allowed to give up meat until I was eighteen and absolutely no tattoos or piercings until I was married. I rebelled against the no-piercing and had my nose pierced when I was twenty. My dad was disgusted and didn't speak to me for at least three months. I went to secondary school and college without issue and became a Garda."

"What's that?"

"A police officer."

"Wait, you were a cop?"

"Yeah, but not a street cop. I worked behind a desk."

"Did you wear a uniform?"

"Are you going to go all pervy if I say yes?"

"Probably!" He smiled, leaning on his elbows, his interest piqued.

"Yes, all Gardaí wear uniforms whether they're at a desk or community policing. I'm actually still a Garda."

"But how. China. Here. You work in an orphanage. Are you undercover?"

"Hahahaha no. You'd be locked up by now if I was. I'm on a career break for three years. Younger members of the force can only apply. If successful, the three-year break works out at three annual payments. Officers can apply for a variety of reasons, including foreign travel or further education. However, applicants with particular skills or who work in high-demand areas couldn't. So, this is my first year and I was loving it until I bumped into you!"

"Ooh, that's harsh. I'm gobsmacked, amazed really and can't get my head around it."

"Why?"

"Well, the blatantly obvious reason for a start, is that you're teeny tiny."

"Luckily for me, the height restrictions were replaced with a physical competence test, otherwise I wouldn't have got in."

"But surely it's difficult reprimanding people taller than you?"

"My uncle is a high-ranking Garda Commissioner and at the request of my parents, I was posted in an office and not as a community officer which I had applied for."

"That must have caused some arguments?"

"I didn't speak to them for a while, which was difficult living in the same house. But fair play to them, they kept out of my way as much as possible. Plus, they knew my temper was simmering and didn't want to unleash the beast. I threatened to leave the force which only made them happy. I kept waiting for the go-ahead to go out as a community officer. Until someone mentioned that I wasn't on the list, never was. I couldn't get a straight answer from anyone. Nobody could tell me why I wasn't going out but only that I couldn't. I had to make an appointment to see my uncle and that's when he admitted everything. I was furious, telling him he wasn't being fair. He said he only did it because my parents were sick with worry. You see, from the start, they believed I was going to work in admin so accepted it. But when I told them I'd be on the streets. They fell apart. They begged him to keep their daughter, his niece safe and so he did. You'd swear the roads were a hive of criminal activity back home. From the time my application went in, my path was already mapped out without me having an inkling. I couldn't do anything. The rest you know."

"And boyfriends?"

I give an awkward smile. "Have been few and far between, nothing special."

"I find that very hard to believe."

"I'm just picky. Your turn."

Just as he was about to speak, dessert was served. I closed my eyes and savoured the saltiness of the caramel and then the explosion of flavour from the hazelnut crunch. Didn't some famous chef compare salted caramel as a class 'A' drug of the confectionary world? I opened my eyes and found him staring. "Ahem, what are you staring at and why haven't you touched yours?"

"I'm waiting to hear your dulcet tones and watch you suggestively lick your spoon."

"Sorry, it's not going to happen. I'm way too conscious in front of you to be a sensualist celebrator of food."

"Spoilsport."

"So, spill. I want every detail of your life, family and friends."

"Are you sure you can stay awake that long?"

"Oh yeah. I'm wide awake and buzzing on a sugar rush after that dessert. Please can you express my gratitude to everyone? It was simply delicious."

"Thank you, I will. I know everyone is eager to hear anything you have to say. You're somewhat of a celebrity around here."

"Shut your face! You're having a laugh."

"Think about it. You took on a professional gang of child criminals and saved my dear mother. Nobody has ever heard anyone raise their voice to me. Not even my mother after I punched a photographer in the face. You stepped right up to me and prevented something awful from happening to Lan. You've screamed at me on several occasions and the one I most enjoyed was," 'Being a dick won't make it any bigger. Everyone loved that too."

"Oh, dear! I didn't think anyone else was listening." I laugh out loud. I was about to ask him to continue when one of the staff whispered in his ear and handed him his mobile.

He glanced at it in his hand. "I have to take this, please excuse me for a moment. Get comfy, I'll join you shortly," he said, nodding towards the sofa.

"Is everything okay?"

"Of course, just something that needs my urgent attention. I'll get you something to drink?"

"No, thanks," I protested as he hurried away. I could hear how annoyed he was with whoever was on the other end. Damn, I should have made more of an effort when Evee was trying to teach me Chinese. That's it, I'm taking lessons. Funny that. Was he intentionally avoiding telling me about his family? Will I ever get to hear about his life? I walked over to the white linen sofa and sat down pulling one of the many throws over me. The overstuffed sofa felt as soft as a cloud and I knew if my head hit the cushion, I'd be gone. Yawning deeply, I fought hard to keep my tired eyes from slamming shut. The force was too strong….

12

I didn't sleep well. I tossed and turned, crying out every time I lay on my arm.

Still uncomfortable with the unorthodox circumstances of being here didn't help. And then there's Gui. There's no denying that I fancy the hole off him. I get butterflies every time he looks at me. But how can I have feelings for this man who, on one hand, worships his mother, and on the other, has maverick tendencies? His unconventional approach to life went against my better judgement. Even though I knew I should walk away, I found him impossible to resist. There's no surprise that I was attracted to the power and dominant nature. He wasn't the right choice for a functional, long-term relationship but had some nice traits too. My mother would say he was a wolf in sheep's clothing. I knew he wasn't a player or a cheat and hoped that one day, he could settle down. I wasn't the one trying to change him. That wouldn't be an option. He is what he is, and change can only come from within, on his terms, not mine. I have no issue with him being a Dom. I think it's sexy and wouldn't want to change his lifestyle for anything. He spelt it out loud and clear, there'd be no fairytale ending with him.

I just had a problem with how he treated people. Empathy. Yes, that's what he lacked. For once and for all, I was going to think of it as a learning experience and something I was going to enjoy. Hopefully?

I woke up in an empty bed. No Gui or Lan. I glanced around the room half expecting to find him sitting in the wingback chair watching me. I threw back the covers and sat up rubbing my tired eyes remembering last night. What a night. Everything about it was wonderful. Apart from me doing all the talking. Only for that bloody call I'm sure we'd have snuggled and talked all night until the early hours of the morning. I was wearing the same silk pyjamas and there was a matching nightgown at the end of the bed. I eyed the wardrobes. He did say he filled them. I wonder…

Sliding my feet into matching satin slippers which also magically appeared in front of the bed, I pulled open four doors but the two in the middle were still locked. How bizarre. I was more interested in what was in there than the rows and rows of beautiful designer clothes hanging up. I won't be a kept woman. If I accept these gifts, am I a whore? I shook my head. Of course not, I agreed to this arrangement after all. Did I though? I was blackmailed! Kind off. Yes, I could easily have turned a blind eye and behaved like a selfish uncaring bitch. Letting him take the law into his own hands. Probably wouldn't have been the first time either. Isn't that what he said? He could do what the hell he liked. However, I did choose to be a decent human. I'm not sure who I was trying to convince.

Tucked at the bottom was something brown, I got closer. It looked out of place with all the beautiful pastels and neutral colours. I carefully pulled it out. It was my scruffy weekend bag. How the hell? I sat on the bed and pulled the zip. There was a letter on top addressed to me in Evee's handwriting……I tore it open.

> *Oh my god hun. WTF! I can't believe it. You poor thing. Mr high and almighty phoned and explained what happened. Just like you to save the day. Of course, I demanded to see you myself but was told in no uncertain terms, NO! He made it quite clear, no callers. He didn't' need to be so rude about it. He asked, no, demanded that I pack some clothes and he'd have it collected. I would have thought Mr Gazillionaire could afford a couple of pairs of knickers! Seeing as he has a shit load of money. Yes, I Googled him. Had to make sure you weren't kidnapped by some raving lunatic cult leader. Have to admit, he's a bit of a ride. I certainly wouldn't mind being holed up with a handsome billionaire bachelor. Speaking of knickers. What the actual hell Rhy. I couldn't find anything decent. Felt like I was raiding my granny's drawer. Can't believe you're still wearing 'Bridget Jones' pants! I know you insist they're comfy and keep you warm, but really. You are a young attractive woman who wears granny knickers. It's just not right. I was actually morto folding them because they're so bloody ginormous! Wouldn't be surprised if that's why you were charged for excess baggage on the flight over. Hahahaha. I hope His Royal Rudeness doesn't clap*

eyes on them. Hmmm. I said if I didn't hear from you soon. I'm calling the police and I didn't care if he owned half of China. He had the gall to laugh when I said that. It just doesn't make sense. Why aren't you in hospital? I know you wouldn't want me to contact your parents. Should I? He said your phone was stolen and he'd replace it. Hopefully, I can speak to you then. Certainly, won't be banging his door down after the muscle experiment gone wrong called for your bag, bloody hell Rhylee, the size of him. Thought he'd escaped from the zoo!!!!! I will see you soon lovely x

Thank goodness the envelope didn't look like it had been tampered with. It's not something I'd want him reading. I'd never hear the end of it. My face went red as I imagined him going through my bag and pulling out my jumbo knickers. Oh, Jesus. What on earth could I have said? It's true, I loved them and that's all I wore. Ultra comfortable high-waisted granny pants, my shameful little secret. Only there's nothing remotely little about them. But of course, they weren't the ones you had to suck in your breath to get them over your tummy. Yes, I put my hand up and admit I'm a creature of comfort. I won't apologise. You will never find lace or frilly thongs or sexy lingerie in my arsenal. Maybe not quite the right choice of words? Eew, all that riding up the crack of your arse and finding the right moment to discreetly pick them out. But this now has created a major problem. My jumbo knickers are for my eyes only and not male consternation. I can't wear them here. I didn't even want them in the same room as me. I looked around and contemplated throwing them out the window or flushing down the toilet. I imagined the headlines, 'City comes to a standstill with multiple casualties as giant knickers falls from the sky.'

I rummaged around to see what else she packed. Bed socks. Love my bed socks too but wouldn't be strutting my stuff in them either. Some loungewear, ten pairs of granny pants, Jesus…and my toiletries bag. I emptied it and shoved my Bridget Jones's inside and wrestled with the damn zip. It was a tight squeeze and the zipper looked like it was about to give under the huge strain of trying to contain ten pairs of cock blockers. I felt relieved knowing they were out of sight. I hoped. I threw it in the hold-all and pushed it to the back of the wardrobe.

Now that the drama was diverted, I noticed another door. For fuck's sake, was I walking around with my eyes closed most of the time? Through the doors was a beautiful marble ensuite. Everything was white and marble with brass hardware. I splashed my face with cold water, brushed my teeth and dipped my fingers into a pot of something and moisturise my face. I ran my fingers through my curls and checked my face. Nothing I could do about that now. I walked to the living room.

When I entered, Gui was reading his newspaper and Lan was sitting on one of the sofa's combing her doll's hair. As soon as she saw me, she jumped up and embraced me like I was the returning prodigal child. He folded his newspaper and smiled at me. I lifted her up onto my hip and grimaced in pain.

"I wish you wouldn't do that." He spoke to her in an irritated tone to which she immediately tried to climb down.

I held her tightly and kissed her cheek. "Sshh sshh it's okay Lan." I sat down and held her tightly to my chest trying to stay calm. Screwing up my face, I look at him.

"Why do you have to speak to her in that tone? I wish you wouldn't. She's only a child. It upsets her and me." She looked up and I smiled and kissed her chubby cheek. She giggled so I did it again, again and again. Her giggles were contagious and we were all laughing in no time. I heaved a deep sigh and said, "Gui, good or bad. Only for Lan, I wouldn't be here." She climbed up on the sofa and patted the cushion, handing me her doll as I plopped down beside her. "She's beautiful. Is she your baby?" I asked. I looked at Gui. "Can you ask her please?"

His tone was a little gentler when he spoke to her. She giggled and shook her head. I hated that I didn't know what she was saying and that I had to rely on others to translate. But she's young and will probably speak English before I grasp a few Chinese words.

"She said don't be silly, it's a doll."

"Aw, that's sad. I suppose she's grown up a tomboy. It's hard to believe she never had any dolls and the valuable lessons they nurture." I held the doll and embraced her, pretending it was a baby. She shyly moved closer watching me cuddle and kiss her doll. She hesitated but then slowly took her from me. She kissed her forehead and coyly embraced it before putting her in the pram. She tucked a blanket around her and skipped over to Gui to show him. I remembered back to my own childhood and the roomful of toys I had. Baby dolls, Cindys, puzzles, balls and jigsaws. Suppose it made up for my mother's lack of maternal instincts? When I was old enough to stay over at

Evee's I was shocked to find her mother gently caressing her cheek and saying in a calm whisper, "Sweet dreams lovely, see you in the morning." The more I stayed over, the more differences I saw lacking. I don't ever remember being told "I love you," and hugs and kisses were few and far between, maybe non-existent. My toys helped me because I became the mother and what wasn't done for me, I did for them. My dolls sat down at the dinner table where they were encouraged to eat their veg so they'd grow up big and strong. I think that's when my mother started having a glass or two of wine with dinner. Sometimes the bottle? Only for Evee's family, I wouldn't have known about hugs or snuggles. I'd get embarrassed if her mam pulled me in for a hug when I was leaving to cross the road to go home. After a while it was me running to them to kiss them goodbye or greet them hello. Only for them, I would have probably grown up not wanting children of my own because of my difficult childhood.

I looked at Lan as she waited eagerly for Gui to interact. I don't think he had any idea how to play with kids. For a minute he just sat there looking from me to Lan with a bewildered look on his face. I smiled encouragingly at him. "Go on, you can do it. Make me proud."

"I don't want to. It's not something I do."

"I understand, but it's not about you now. It's about showing a child who hasn't witnessed how to love or be loved, give love. Don't be too self-conscious to let go or you'll look awkward. Playing with children doesn't come naturally to most adults so try not to worry about how you look. Didn't you play much as a child?"

"Yes, actually I had a wonderful childhood. As many toys as I could wish for and before you say it, tons of unbridled love too."

"Well, there you go then. You know what to do. You have the skills. You weren't one of the unfortunates who didn't get to play growing up. Play helps children's development."

"It's just that I feel embarrassed about it. Maybe because she's not mine."

"Lan won't know the difference and I'm certainly not going to laugh. Think back to when you were Lan's age if you can."

Lan pointed to the pram saying, "Yīng'ér. Yīng'ér zài kū."

"What did she say?"

"She said baby, baby is crying."

"Omg, that's amazing." He bent over and carefully lifted the doll and said, "Sshh." Then cradled it gently to his chest. My heart melted. I wanted to jump up and squeal, knowing how hard it was for this tough man to put his emotions out there.

Then he completely shocked me by speaking baby talk. Watching Lan's response was adorable. She was totally engaged. She rummaged in her doll's baby bag and pulled out a bottle and handed it to him. I thought he was going to object and say he'd had enough. Instead surprised me by sitting on the floor and giving the doll her bottle. He glanced at me and winked as I beamed with delight. He looked at the bottle and said something to her. "I told Lan her baby was a very good girl for finishing her bottle." He lifted the doll and placed her against him talking to Lan as he rubbed the doll's back. He handed her back and she continued to rub.

She walked over to me like she was holding a new baby. I kissed the doll's head and she put her back in the pram pushing it out the door and waving goodbye. I never saw her smile so much. "Thank you for that. The more you play with her, the easier it will get."

"I'm not quite there yet playing happy families."

"But that's not what that was. You were a play buddy, not her father."

"You know a lot about this kind of stuff."

"It's about making someone happy with your interaction. Take your subs. I'm sure they're happy and fulfilled during play because of you?"

"Different but I take your point."

"Not so sure you do. They would never assume you are a boyfriend. They know you are their Dom and wouldn't dare cross the line." I blinked back the tears and covered my eyes as I slumped back on the sofa. He was beside me in a second pulling my hands away from my face.

"Rhylee, what is it?"

"I'm the one feeling silly now. Just seeing you with Lan and knowing how hard it was for you to drop your guard. You were great with her, so sweet."

"It wasn't as easy as it looked. I felt intimidated and out of my comfort zone."

"I know and I'm sure one day you'll be a great daddy," I sniffled.

"Not on my bucket list and I'm not ready to join fatherhood."

"Never say never I always say."

"I'm enjoying life too much to be responsible for a baby human. The commitment isn't there. I'm anything but nurturing."

"Nurturing just doesn't happen overnight, such a quality develops from a tender age and you said you had a wonderful childhood. You had a positive support system around you as a child. I watched how you were with Lan, helpful, caring and patient. I think you showed more patience with her than you have with me."

"She's a child and doesn't know better. You're an adult who insists on testing my last nerve and my inability to stay in control."

"Exactly, she's a child who doesn't know any better so needs to be shown. To be nurtured."

"Look, I've been around my friends' kids and if you ask me, they're even more feral than Lan. Spoiled to the core and let do as they like. Wonderful children but would test your last nerve. The best thing about kids is handing them back when it's time to leave. I don't think there's a better feeling. Walking out and leaving the chaos behind. It's just not for me."

"Can I ask you something?"

"Um hmm."

"Are you afraid of commitment? Some men find it hard to commit to one woman."

"I don't think so. I haven't met *the one* I want to share the rest of my life with. If it happens, everything will take its natural course." His words kicked me hard in the gut. I knew he was feeling uncomfortable with how the conversation was going. He stretched out his long legs and laced his fingers behind his head. They say clothes maketh the man and while that doesn't usually include loungewear, he still had the oomph factor. He was dressed in cream sweats and a snug white v-neck tee shirt. His tight tee hugged every inch of his muscled body, stopping short above his waistband which hung low on his hips.

Few people could pull off wearing track bottoms let alone look as good in them as he did. He had it all, the complete package. I could see an inch of smooth golden skin where the hem of his tee shirt rolled up. I wanted to touch it so bad.

"What are you staring at?" he asked, glancing down at his body.

Staring far too long than I should have. I hesitated to look at him, dragging my eyes away. "Nothing, just thinking."

He brushed a strand of hair from my face and stroked my cheek. Oh, sweet baby Jesus that was hot. "I doubt it was nothing? What is it?" He asked. "And why do I get the feeling you're always keeping secrets from me?"

"Honestly, how could I possibly have secrets?"

He didn't answer. I waited…. "Hello, who's daydreaming now?"

Finally, he glanced at me, meeting my questioning gaze. "Don't know about you but I feel like I've done a session with a therapist!"

I rolled my eyes. "Yeah, nobody could accuse us of being verbally constipated."

He glanced at his watch. "I'm afraid I must leave you. I have a meeting at one and it's almost that now. Why don't you try on some of your new clothes? I'm sure you'd like to wear actual clothes for a change?"

My gaze left his face as I considered the idea. "Not really. To be honest I'd rather chill in pjs or joggers. Nothing quite like comfy dressing, feeling snuggly and relaxed. It's a lazy girl's paradise. Aren't you going to change for your meeting?"

"For the first time, I'm going casual."

"Ooh, look at you in your lazy man's paradise." We laughed in unison. "I suppose the empire is not going to run itself."

"Indeed. As much as we all loved *seeing you* at the last meeting," he winked, "I'm hoping to get some work done without any interruptions?" I remembered and blushed at the recollection of my childish behaviour. He took my hand and kissed it. "Believe me, it won't be facts and figures running through my mind. There are far nicer things I'd rather be doing over my desk." I nervously giggled and felt my cheeks turn redder than a stop light. "I'll never tire of the way you blush when I speak about intimacy, sweet. So before I lose my last scrap of control, I'll go."

I asked the question and blushed knowing the answer. "So, what would you be doing over your desk?"

"Fucking you!"

He stepped away, quickly striding out the door, eliciting a sexy laugh. I stared after him in an 'I need to jump your bones' kind of way. I squealed in shocked delight, kicking off my slippers and tucking my feet tightly under me. I wanted him so badly and have never felt so horny since the day I met him. But now, all I want to do is have sex with him. I don't want a fuck. I want him to make love to me. But I wasn't going to get that with Gui.

He made it crystal clear. No romance! Okay, right now, I'd take anything. Even an unemotional fuck would suffice!

As I sat there dreaming, a tray was placed over my lap. I tried to sit up to make it easier to balance but in perfect English was told to relax. "You need to get your strength up," she said.

I looked at her quizzically as she bowed slightly, smiled then hurried from the room. She was a tiny little thing, probably around my age and stunning. She wore a black top and flared trousers with ballet pumps. Wait! Was she one of Gui's little helpers in the shower that night? I still can't get my head around the bowing and nodding. I know it's a greeting and a gesture of respect. There are even bows for apologies and gratitude. Mind-boggling.

I was still trying to figure out all the customs and formalities. I've made quite a few faux pas at the orphanage already, but they didn't seem to mind. You're forgiven because you wouldn't be expected to remember all Chinese customs and there are quite a few. The higher the person is in status to you, the lower you bend your head. Looking back now, I should have known Gui was a force to be reckoned with when the doctor almost kissed the floor.

13

The tray was perfectly laid, with toast, fluffy scrambled eggs, juice and tea, accompanied by a flower in a tiny vase. Resting against it lay a note. 'The eggs are free range; the butter and tea were specially flown in from Ireland. The juice was freshly squeezed by my own loving hands.' Enjoy G. I chomped on the toast and couldn't help smiling to myself. What would it be like married to him? Living with him twenty-four-seven, sleeping beside him and waking next to him. Cuddles and extreme spooning. Sure, that's what spouses are for. Sign me up. I was giddy just thinking about it. All the sex too. I'd say we'd be at it like rabbits. Having him as my plus-one forever would be amazing.

He said he's very sexual and then there's the elephant in the room, he's a Dom. Hmmm. I'm not sure I'd make a good sub. I hate being bossed around and told what to do. Don't like the idea of having my identity taken away. Then there are the rules and the punishments and the controlling and surrendering. It's a different way of life. But then there's the other side. Feeling loved and adored, cared-for and safe. Maybe he's only kinky in the playroom?

It was something I was going to ask and hopefully get to finally hear the story of his life so far.

I must have been hungry because I ate everything. The eggs were delicious, soft and creamy. Mine always turned out like rubber and most times would probably bounce off the wall. I put the tray down beside me and stretched my legs. I pulled up my top and rubbed my full belly. It frustrated me that my stomach always looked so pudgy after eating. It looked like a 'mummy tummy' or 'baby belly.' I pushed my tummy out further and caressed the bulge. Evee would laugh saying, "It was my only talent being able to push it out to look nine months pregnant."

I tricked my mother once, almost giving her a heart attack. She said she couldn't understand why I would pretend such a thing and that it wasn't one bit funny, under the circumstances. As I stroked my tummy, I didn't realise I was being watched from the doorway. I looked up. The sight of him standing there, a look of sheer horror written all over his face. His stony features made me sick to my core. I quickly pulled down my top and sat upright. Not sure why but he made me feel guilty. For a moment I stared at the door, my heart racing. "What's up?"

He ran his fingers through his hair and remained quiet. I tapped the cushion beside me and giggled. "Fucking hell Rhylee!" he said.

He flopped down next to me staring wide-eyed at my tummy. "I wanted to give you this. It just arrived." He handed me a Kindle, still staring at my tummy.

"I didn't know what the fuck I walked into, watching you rub your stomach, smiling to yourself. My reaction was shit no. Run! I wasn't expecting to see that and it freaked me the fuck out. Then I was overcome with emotion imagining how you'd look pregnant, beautiful."

"I'm sorry you had to see that. I always look like a beached whale after stuffing my face. I get some relief by rubbing my tummy to ease the bloating. As you just witnessed, I also push it out to see how I'd look preggers. Sorry, not a good look I admit and judging by the look on your face, it's something nobody should have to see.

Changing the subject, thanks for this. I've always wanted one. I hope you won't be too late for your meeting?"

"To be honest, I'm not sure I can after seeing that?"

"Ah c'mon. Really? I'm sure you've seen worse?"

"I've seen many things but I wasn't prepared for that."

"Just forget about it."

"That won't be easy."

"I don't know why you're making such a big deal about it. Be thankful it's not real and you're not the baby daddy. God forbid!" I bounded to my feet and stomped out of the room. He didn't come after me and I was glad because I would have fucked the Kindle straight at him. I just don't understand how he can get right under my skin. How many times since I've met him have I got angry or stormed off? Too many. For God's sake, I didn't do it that often at home.

Knowing Lan would immediately sense something was up I took the lift to the rooftop to clear my head. What is it with that man? I walked the full square of the rooftop and discovered a hanging egg chair in the corner. It was covered in real flowers with big comfy cushions and a wool throw. It was such a romantic spot making me wonder who it was for. Certainly, didn't see him solving the world's problems swinging from side to side. Probably Jingfei? It wouldn't surprise me one little bit. She's made a little spot just for herself. I settled back and looked out through the glass balustrade wishing it was my special place. I turned on the Kindle and downloaded some books. Wow, the Wi-Fi was super-fast. I opened *The Wait* by an up-and-coming Irish author. It was about a young girl, vanilla in her lifestyle and interested in spicing things up just like me, who just happened to get involved with the utterly gorgeous Nathan Aldridge, business tycoon and Dom who captivates and seduces her. Ooh, what a coincidence, could have been written about me. I dived right in.

So engrossed I never noticed the sun set over the rooftops. There was a slight chill in the air, so I draped the throw around me, wrapped my arms around my knees and stared out into the oncoming darkness. The trouble with juicy books is that you lose track of time and can't put it down. It certainly was a beast of a book and I was surprised how much I got through. I rested my elbows on my knees and cupped my chin in my hands, staring out into the night. It was so peaceful up here.

For some reason, my mother popped into my mind. What on earth would she make of my situation? Revulsion, I'd imagine. Of course, she'd be all over Gui like a rash but would slap him about the head if she knew about our arrangement. Murder would be more in line if she found out. As much as we banged heads and argued, I was still her little girl. Of course, I loved her in my own way, but our relationship was strained at the best of times. We all know that sons are the mother's favourite. No matter what mischief they get up to or the trouble they may cause, they are easily forgiven. My poor dad. It wasn't easy for him to live in a house with two stubborn witches. Certainly not fun if we were both advocating the same argument differently. He would never take sides. Inevitably things ended with a 'let's agree to disagree,' situation with us both storming off to our bedrooms. Checking I was okay he'd pop in with a hot chocolate and a chat. I'm sure he did the same with mam but with something much stronger. Probably a gin!

I was snapped out of my thoughts as the chair furiously rocked from side to side. I screamed with fright thinking I was in the middle of a fucking earthquake. Gui's head appeared over the top. "Fuck's sake Rhylee." He came around and straightened the chair up. "She's over here," he fumed. A look of anger on his face. "Tell everyone they can stop searching," he shouted.

Filled with fright, I opened my eyes and lifted my head out from under the blanket. "What's happened," I asked in a trembling voice, my eyes fixed on his expression. I had never seen him in such a state. He looked frightened out of his wits. If he was scared, what the hell hope had I? I tried to shuffle out of the chair but his hand on my knee stopped me. "Will you tell me what's going on?" You're frightening the crap out of me now."

He kneeled and took both my hands. "Do you know the trouble you've caused?" His voice was hoarse and I found it incredibly sexy.

"But I haven't done anything. I've been here the whole-time reading. Whoever says otherwise is lying."

"Do you know how long you've been gone?"

"A few hours maybe?"

"Rhylee, you've been missing for four hours. I've had security search the building three times."

"I'm sorry, time flies when you're lost in a good book."

"For fuck's sake I'm serious Rhylee!"

"Don't you raise your voice at me, especially when I've done nothing wrong? I've been here and any of your multiple cameras would have shown you that."

"I don't have them running constantly on my private floors. Up here was checked twice but I can see they weren't so thorough, which is unsettling. They'll have some explaining to do when I get my hands on them! I honestly thought you ran away. Or worse, kidnapped! That somehow you bypassed cameras on the other floors. My security system is state-of-the-art and I've had little need to activate it everywhere, until now."

"Should that not have been a priority when your mother went missing?"

"My mother doesn't live here all the time, even though she has her floor. Don't change the subject."

I couldn't control the wave of emotions that came over me and I burst into tears. "This is just not fair. I can't take it anymore. My head is melted with everything that's happened to me in the past few weeks. Do you believe that I could leave this place? I mean it's like the damn White House with the amount of security you have. I think someone would have noticed the crazy blonde girl running and screaming out the door in a pair of pajama's!"

He gave me a longing look. "I was worried senseless," he said in a soft voice, hugging me tightly.

"I just assumed ... you ran away. You need to let people know where you're going."

I sniffed meekly and let him hug me even tighter. His scent and hard body pressed tightly against mine was making me giddy. He was worried about me, more than he'd let on. I smiled to myself. Gui wasn't the type of man who worried about anything. Delight filled me and I didn't want this moment between us to end. He rested his hands on my shoulders and gently pushed me back.

"There's an iPhone downstairs for you. There won't be any restrictions on it and you can call, text, email or do whatever you kids do these days."

"Oh, you shouldn't have. But thank you so much."

"I have to leave on business, for probably a week. Something urgent requires my attention. I want to be able to contact you at any time night, or day."

"I see," I said with a heavy heart. As much as we bumped heads, I didn't want him to leave. What the fuck was I going to do? At least I had Lan and now a Kindle and a phone. I looked forward to texting Evee. She'll be shocked to see that the tyrant is allowing me to communicate with the peasants.

"When are you going?"

"Tonight."

"So soon."

"Hey, what's this, you look sad. Dare I say it? You're going to miss me?"

"Me, no. Not one bit. Just your ability to drive me around the bend!"

"Aw, I'm sorry. Are you feeling neglected? I'll barely have time to eat or sleep let alone take the piss out of you. I'll try my best in between meetings to make time for that though, I promise." He winked then burst out laughing.

"Oh my God, you just can't help yourself, you little shit. You're such an annoying prick! You enjoyed that, didn't you?"

"I did," he said with laughter in his voice. "But seriously, you'll miss me all the same. Won't you?"

"Won't!" I sulked.

"At night I can sext you."

"Ah for God's sake, only horny teenagers do that."

"Were you one of those?"

"No, I wasn't and that's the truth."

"Sure, who knows, I might turn you on?"

"Doubt it."

"Famous last words. I'd put money on it."

"You think you'd get me excited with a text, hahaha."

"I'm so confident that I'll let you go home if you don't get yourself off afterwards. But you can't lie."

"It's a deal."

He held out his hand and we shook on it. "What do you get out of it?"

"I have everything I want, you. You're going to be my sub and that's what I would have chosen."

"Bet if I was your sub now, you'd have me over your knee?"

"I know I'd like to but you didn't do anything wrong."

"I was thinking about our arrangement. It won't begin until my arm is healed. Right. Which means I'll be here far longer than expected?"

"Yes, I suppose you are now. I never thought your arm would get infected, even though we did everything to help it heal. Having you in the playroom so quickly didn't help. But there again. It was a blessing in disguise. God only knows what could have happened if the infection hadn't been detected when it was. Are you disappointed?"

"Em, no, not really. No nicer place to recuperate. It's what comes afterwards that scares me. Do you use your hand when spanking?"

"Depends on the discipline."

"Can the sub choose?"

"Never. It's mostly between a hand, paddle, wooden spoon, cane or belt. Could even use a slipper if needed. To be honest, using your hand can be painful and is the least severe."

"For the sub?"

"Less severe as a punishment but hurts like hell if you're the spanker!"

"Aww, poor you."

"Also, there's less chance of bruising or welts and soreness is minimal. To be honest, you're a beginner so my hand would suffice."

"Oh, that's very thoughtful of you. Thanks!"

"Although I do like the sound of a paddle on a bare arse. That one would certainly put you off misbehaving."

"Do you own a cane?"

"Yes, I have several. Most of my submissives would agree that this is by far the severest of them all and luckily rarely used. And some would rather have the sting of the belt. Everyone is different."

"I think canes are barbaric! They all are."

"Don't make up your mind just yet. They all have their uses in different ways. Some subs crave a little pain with pleasure. Erotic spankings can be such a turn-on with a belt."

"And have you been whipped on your bare arse with a belt?"

"Of course not."

"Well then. I don't think you are in any position to say it's a turn-on!"

"During a scene, it's quite easy to tell if a sub is loving or hating something and I work off that. They get particularly vocal when it dips between their cheeks."

"Oh!" I gasped.

"Afterwards, I spend a lot of time with all my subs. Checking they're okay and asking how they thought the scene went. It's usually the ones being punished who get all bratty. Not realising that that's what got them punished in the first place."

"Can a sub choose his or her punishment?"

"No, but I know what's right for them and what their limits are." He took my hand and stood, pulling me up with him.

"Let's have dinner before I leave."

I looked up at him and was blinded by his beauty. "What's the matter? Why are you looking at me like that?"

I laughed. "It's nothing."

He bent down and threw me over his shoulder like a sack of potatoes. I squealed and kicked with giddy laughter.

"Gui, seriously, put me down."

He playfully slapped my behind. "That just won't do Miss Murphy."

"Honestly, you don't want to know."

"You wouldn't be slung over my shoulder if I didn't," he said, gently slapping and whistling like he hadn't a care in the world. "Each slap is only going to get harder. So just come out and say it."

He slapped me again before I got a word out, this time he wasn't so gentle. It was an open hand across my left cheek as hard as he could slap.

"Ouch! That fucking hurt," I shrieked, trying my hardest to kick out. But with one arm he effortlessly held my legs together and continued to swipe with the other. The next one brought a tear to my eye.

"Stop! It's no fun anymore. You're hurting me. Okay! You're a fucking ride. That's what I was thinking. Now put me down."

His hand stilled then rubbed my cheek gently in deep thought. "What the fuck is a ride?"

"Look it up. Prick!" I tried to lash out with my feet again. He stopped rubbing. And before he raised his hand again, I blurted it out. "It just means I'd fuck the life out of you! There! I said it. Now can you please just take me to my room without making eye contact?" I begged.

He slapped my arse and laughed that laugh again. I let out a sigh as he lowered me to the ground, rubbing my backside and looking anywhere but at him. "Go and set up your phone and I'll meet you for dinner in twenty minutes."

I turned to leave when he slapped my sore arse, "You little ride." He threw his head back and laughed out loud. Huffing, I just kept walking until I got to my room, closed the door and fell against it. I can't believe I told him that. How embarrassing! If my desperate please-fuck-me eyes didn't give him any inclination, he fucking knows now. It's going to be so easy for him. I flung myself on the bed and picked up the iPhone box. Something to take my mind off Gui for a while. I set it up and texted Evee.

14

Rhylee: Hey you, surprise…….
Evee: Omg. Did you steal his phone? Are you being held against your will?
Rhylee: Hahahahaha. No. Well not really.
Evee: What do you mean, not really?
Rhylee: Will explain in more detail when I see you. I'm fine, swear. But……..
Evee: But what? Tell me Rhylee. He hasn't laid a finger on you, has he?
Rhylee: Well, yes. Three to be exact, lol!
Evee: What does that mean? Only that you added lol I'd be calling the police. What??
Rhylee: He put them inside me.
Evee: Oh my fucking god!! Did you sleep with him?
Rhylee: Not yet. But I'm sure I will. I told him he was a ride….
Evee: Jesus, ye didn't?
Rhylee: I did.
Evee: Right to his face?
Rhylee: No, I was over his shoulder.
Evee: The fuck??

Rhylee: I wouldn't tell him what I was thinking when he asked. So, he flung me over his shoulder and spanked me.

Evee: OMFG! So fucking caveman. Are you okay?

Rhylee: Ah yeah. It was all in fun. I liked it. You know I like the idea of being spanked.

Evee: Yeah, but it's usually naked and over a knee. Over his shoulder doesn't sound as erotic. Were you naked?

Rhylee: Yeah, sounds shit and no, fully dressed.

Evee: Bummer hahahahaha. Sooooooo. What's the story? Have you kissed yet?

Rhylee: Yes.

Evee: Annnd!

Rhylee: It was brief and amazing. He has a beautiful mouth, soft juicy wet lips.

Evee: Hahaha, sounds like you're describing a fanny!

Rhylee: Seriously Evee!

Evee: What. Can't you take a joke? So, what else?

Rhylee: He's going away on business tonight.

Evee: Is that how you got his phone?

Rhylee: No, he gave it to me so he can contact me while he's away.

Evee: You mean a booty call?

Rhylee: How are you always right??

Evee: I'm more experienced in these matters.

Rhylee: Yeah, right little slapper.

Evee: Hahaha

Rhylee: Hahaha

Evee: Am I allowed to visit?

Rhylee: Not sure. I'll ask over dinner. Omg, I'll ask if you can sleep over. There's a rooftop and a pool. Hold on. I've got a text. He's waiting for me. I'll text you after dinner.

Evee: Can't wait. Missed you so much xx

Rhylee: Missed you too hun. Later alligator xx

I pulled open the massive doors to the wardrobe, wishing I hadn't left it until now to look through the mass of hanging clothes. I didn't want to keep him waiting, especially since he was leaving so soon. I didn't know how long we had so tried to find something quickly. What the hell was I supposed to wear anyway. Everything I looked at was too beautiful to put on just to wave goodbye. I reached in and pulled out my bag Evee had packed with my comfy clothes. Vest tops with matching shorts and knee socks, my movie outfits. Not sure what Gui will make of them? I brushed my teeth, put on some cherry lip balm and combed through my curls, turning them into beautiful golden waves.

When finished I headed for the dining room. I came to the door, hand above the handle and as my fingers were about to close around the doorknob I froze. The sound of a woman's laughter stopped me dead in my tracks. Oh, for fuck's sake, not her again! I looked down at what I was wearing knowing it would certainly give her something to bitch about. My hand rested on the handle as I contemplated changing into something elegant and sophisticated. No, fuck her. I pushed open the door and found them on the sofa, Jingfei lying down with her head on his lap. What the actual fuck! I wasn't mentally prepared for that! My insides knotted but I kept it together, walking with purpose to the furthest chair away from them. Neither of them made any attempt to move and I could feel him staring as I passed by. Prick! Before she could say anything, I jumped in first.

"Hi Jingfei, how are you? I thought I heard the shrill screech of cats fighting but it's just you."

She went to retaliate but Gui jumped up, making her head flop abruptly onto the cushion. I tried not to laugh but it was just so funny seeing her head bounce about. She sat up and fixed her hair, not taking her eyes off me. I waited patiently for her big comeback. She wasn't the type to let any woman have the last laugh, especially at her expense.

She walked elegantly to the dining table and turned dramatically to me. "Rhylee, I'd love it if you would join us for dinner before we leave for London." And boom, there it was, mic drop. The gloating bitch effortlessly knocked the wind right out of me. A smug look on her face as she draped her napkin over her lap. Gui's piercing gaze shot me a tender look as the hair rose on the back of my neck. His plans hadn't included her. Had she forced it on him? He held out my chair and I graciously took it. He hadn't done it for her and I tried hard not to gloat.

"Oh, Jingfei, turn that frown upside down as no amount of fillers will get rid of those lines."

"Gui, are you going to allow her to speak to me that way?"

He raised his hands. "I'm keeping out of it."

I smiled and she smiled as she fumbled with her hair. Dammit. I didn't want a bitching session. Nor did I want to see how far he'd let either of us go.

"I didn't know you were going away on business too?" I looked at her like butter wouldn't melt. She looked at Gui first before answering. Like she sought his permission to speak.

"Well, no, not business. I heard Gui was flying to London and I haven't been for ages. So, I thought, why not. And I can't wait to see your little cottage again in the countryside, it's so quaint."

He raised an eyebrow. I silently giggled. For once I wasn't the cause.

"I hardly think ten bedrooms and fourteen bathrooms are small! Jingfei it's bigger than your apartment."

She coughed and fanned her face with her hand. This woman is special all right. I inwardly roll my eyes. "I need to go shopping too. Harrods, especially the food emporium. Oh, and the chocolate hall which hadn't opened when I last visited. Would you believe it's taken four years to complete? Rhylee, do you like chocolate? Gui and I both have a sweet tooth. How about I bring you back a selection of treats." She asked.

"Yeah, thanks," I fake a smile. Dinner was served and we ate in awkward silence. When the table was cleared, she stood. "Gui, I'm going to freshen up. I'll see you in the foyer at nine."

He looked at his watch and nodded.

"Try not to wreck the place when we're gone darling," she said laughing sarcastically and without a second glance left the room. Smoke begins to steam from my ears. I wanted to shout 'Cunt' when she left. Gloom tugged at my heart. She had him all to herself.

"If it's any consolation, she won't be staying with me. I booked her into a hotel when she invited herself along for the ride. She'll be livid when she finds out. I'm not sure either why she mentioned the house, it was only a shell when she was there."

"Why do you need a house in the UK?"

"My second largest company is in London. I needed a base, so I bought a plot of land in the countryside and myself and Keane designed it."

"You know she's only showing me that she has more in common with you than me, that's all. I'm tired Gui with the mind games, sick and tired. I'm going to bed. Have a safe flight."

I turned to leave but he caught my hand. "Rhylee," he whispered.

"No, don't."

He turned me around to face him. I glanced up at him, my heart pounding. Once again, the world stood still as we stared into each other's eyes. Not even a blink between us. He gently brushed my hair to the side and started kissing my neck in a way that made my heart skip a beat. His hands roamed my body as I returned his insatiable kisses unable to control the surge of want running through me. This time, there was more than hot lust and need in his kisses. As we devour each other, my hands slide teasingly into his hair. He groans against my mouth when I tug. I feel his erection poke my tummy and smile. Shamelessly I place my hand flat against it and stroke it over his clothing. He reacted with moans of agreeable pleasure. "Fuck Rhylee." So, I pressed harder, then let go, losing my nerve. "Such a tease," he groaned into my mouth. "Such a sexy little thing aren't you?" he murmured. "Stunningly beautiful with a cute Irish accent that makes me hard every time I hear it." With both hands under my bottom, he lifted me against him and lowered me onto the dining table.

"I'm not like this," I pant.

"I know," he says, voice rough.

"It only makes me want you more." Neither of us could control our erratic breathing. He ran his hand up my legs and rested them on my thighs. "Nice outfit by the way. I was rendered speechless when you walked through the door. You have the perkiest tits I've ever seen."

"And you've seen loads," I giggled.

"Hey, that's a compliment. Sure, I've seen my fair share. But none compare to how yours feel or taste. Are you trying to coerce me?"

"You're between my legs with the hugest hard-on. Somehow, I don't think I need to?"

"That you certainly don't. You need to give a man a little more warning when you're going to enter a room dressed like that."

"Are you sure it wasn't the compromising position I found you in?"

"She acts like we're still kids. It used to turn me on back then."

He pushed up my top and licked my sensitive nipple, then the other. I let out a groan.

"You like that don't you?"

My voice was gruff when I answered "Yes." I tried to touch my other nipple when he took both my hands and gently placed them at my sides.

"Do not move them. How does it feel?"

"Your cock poking me?" I innocently replied.

"Cheeky. No, your arm. Is it hurting, don't lie."

"It's fine." He hooked his finger under my waistband and slowly inched my shorts down.

"Fuck! No underwear, you are naughty."

A scream came from behind us as the light came on over the dining table. I lifted my head and saw Jingfei with her hand to her mouth in the doorway. I was relieved my shorts weren't around my ankles and tried to pull my top down. He slapped my hands away.

"I gave you an order."

She cleared her throat and as cool as a cucumber said, "Gui, it's time for us to leave. You know the pilots don't like to be kept waiting."

"I'll meet you in the car."

"But."

He swung his head around. Oh God, this was so awkward. I tried desperately to close my legs.

"You know I don't like to repeat myself. Go! Car! Now!" He demanded.

I could see she was upset. She looked at me with disdain and if she could, would have called me a dirty little slut or something just as nasty to make a point.

"Now, where were we? We don't need these although I would have loved to pull them to the side and fuck you, next time."

I gasped. He removed my shorts and stood there looking at me. With the light shining directly above us I wanted to cover myself up. Then his warm breath sent my heart into a flurry. "Everything stopped when I saw you sitting so innocently on the hospital bed. Like a delicate flower, to be handled with care."

He kissed and sucked making me buck. Every nerve ending in my body is like a live wire. It felt so good. He flicked his finger over my clitoris making me catch my breath and lift my hips off the table. It made me forget where I was. "Your body is so responsive, there's no way you could ever disguise how horny you are. For me, the biggest turn-on is your reactions. Oh, the fun we're going to have in the playroom."

"It gives me butterflies just thinking about it," I pant. "It gives me butterflies too."

"Does it?"

"No," he laughed. "Men don't get butterflies."

"Oh, funny man."

He licked from the bottom right to the top. I gasp, turning my head to the side. "Rhylee, look at me." I do and feel his hard tongue darting in and out, circling the nub, dipping it back in, deeper, harder. I felt like I was going to combust into a ball of fire. His tongue masterfully fucked me as the tip of his nose rubbed against me. I don't think I've ever had anyone do that to me before. I felt like I was going to explode. He massaged it between his finger and thumb and with his other hand, slid two fingers inside me, withdrew and plunged in again.

"Omg, it feels so good," I pant.

"To answer your question, I just get a tingly feeling deep in my balls."

"How do you even know all this stuff?"

"Trial and error…. If you don't ask, you learn nothing." He abruptly stood and I was conscious of the cool air. He tore open his jeans letting his cock spring free. Oh, my fucking God it was overwhelming. He took hold of it and even his huge hand couldn't fully wrap around its girth.

"Jesus Christ, God help me," I gasped.

He slowly stroked his arousal. The sight of his huge cock was driving me crazy. With want or fear. "I'm going to fuck you and watch you come all over my cock."

My mouth drops open. This guy is sexy as fuck and standing right between my legs. Am I dreaming? He grips himself, slowly stroking up and down against my swollen pussy and I shiver. The more he stimulated me the more it throbbed and tingled.

"Stop, it's too sensitive," I groaned. Holy fuck, I need his dick inside me now. The sensations were driving me crazy. He leans over and kisses me passionately.

"You're so fucking beautiful." He smiles against my lips. He pushes my knees up to my chest and rudely exposes me even more. My eyes bulge wide open. I take a deep breath as he teases me, pushing the tip of his shaft in. His eyes close in pleasure as I feel it throb inside me. His face strained as he tries to keep it together. His jaw taut.

"Jesus, you're so fucking tight and that's just the tip.
You're going to kill me."

"Stop Gui, I can't," I stammer. "I don't want it to happen like this." My eyes hold his.

"Trust me."

"Please Gui, not here."

He hesitates. The tip of his cock pulsing inside of me.
A flash of nerves shoots through me as I wait.

"If it wasn't our first time," he says, "I'd take you here. But it's getting harder to restrain myself." He groans as he pulls out and I feel the heavy weight of it throbbing against my thigh. Nothing is as sexy as a man in control. My eyes well up and without hesitation, he's pulled me tightly against him. He wraps his arms around me and kisses the top of my head. Amazed at how he showed self-control, I wanted him even more. Sliding his palm around the nape of my neck he pulls me closer and whispers in my ear, "Sshh my angel, please don't cry. I'm so sorry. It's getting harder to control the urge." He exhales heavily. "The ever-growing ache to have you and touch you is unbearable. It's quite unlike anything I have ever experienced and the need to dominate you grows stronger with each day."

I sniff back a sob and squeezed him tighter. I smiled, feeling how hard he was against my tummy.

"You better put that away," I giggle. "This is all new for me too, Gui. I want this as much as you but not over a dining room table," I sigh.

He stared at me, eyes dark. "Yes, you're right. But when your balls are bursting, picking somewhere to fuck is not an option." He raises his brow and smiles.

He unhooks my hands from around his neck and picks up my shorts. Holding them out while I balanced myself on his shoulder, putting one leg in at a time. He pulled them up and ran his hands up my legs. "You know, even though you're a short arse, you have amazing legs."

I giggled. "A dear friend, who's no longer with us, would say, 'I've seen better legs dangling out of a nest.' He called me Sparrow. Or Murph the Smurf." I watched in awe as he attempted to put his massive cock back into his jeans.

With a deep intake of breath, he clenched his eyes shut and gasped out loud. "Jesus, that hurts like a bitch!"

"I'm sorry. But now you know how it feels." I giggled. "Is that your way of getting back at me, leaving me with blue balls?" he asks.

"Maybe." I winked. "Would you be angry if it was?"

He thought for a moment. "No. I can handle it. Bring it on short arse. I hate leaving you like this. But I must go. You could invite your friend over while I'm gone. You'd like that wouldn't you?"

"It would make me feel much better, thank you. As much as I love Lan, I can't talk about girly stuff."

"As long as you're not ripping the back off me, I don't mind. I know what girls are like when they get together. Turns into a bitch fest. Just promise me you won't leave the building."

"Do you think I'd get so much as my big toe out the front door without your goons dragging me back by the hair," I reply sarcastically.

"True but they will never lay a finger on you."

"I wish you didn't have to go."

"Me too, I'm rock hard… won't be a comfortable flight." I frowned.

"Is my little angel going to miss me?" I laugh out loud. "Yeah."

"Are you easily aroused?"

"Well, that's a bit random. Not normally, but…"

"But what?"

"You get me going quite easily and not just a small horn. But to the point where the veins are bursting from my cock."

"Omg," I gasped.

"Hey, there's no reason to feel embarrassed about a normal bodily function. I haven't had erections like this ever. But don't worry, I'll take care of it on the plane and think about fucking you all night long."

"Shut up, you dick. Who even talks like that?"

He laughs out loud as his hands drop to my arse squeezing each cheek gently.

"So, what would you be thinking?"

"You want to know?"

"Unless I'm going to be embarrassed?"

"Don't ask questions if you're not prepared for the answer, you know you want to hear in the first place. I'd bend you over the bed and pound you nice and hard, fill you with cum like the naughty little girl that you are. Show you who's boss."

I could feel my face going red and giggle a stupid nervous laugh.

"I knew you'd get embarrassed. Honestly though, are you okay?"

"Yes, you stopped when I asked. I know it was hard but you did. It could have ended horribly."

"I will never force myself on you as much as I'm losing the strength not to."

"Well, that doesn't fill me with much hope," I giggle. He took my hand.

"Don't worry, as much as you don't believe it. I am a gentleman. Will you walk me to the door? I don't want to say goodbye just yet."

"That door," I said pointing towards the door where Jingfei had screamed her lungs out ten minutes ago.

"No silly, the basement. You haven't been down there yet, have you?"

"No. Prisoners aren't allowed access to certain parts of the building."

He stopped in his tracks. "Do you feel like a prisoner?"

I smiled and proceeded to walk. He stood still, almost pulling my arm from its socket.

"Ouch. I did at the beginning, not so much now. I like being here. I like being in your company. Except when you annoy the crap out of me."

He smiled. I smiled.

"You know, the only part of the building you aren't allowed access to, and that's the front door. You are free to explore everywhere else should you wish."

"But now you're leaving." He pulls me along and smiles over his shoulder.

"Not for long."

"Doesn't make me feel any better knowing the wicked witch of the west is going too."

He scratched his head. "The wicked witch? Then burst out laughing when it dawned on him. "As in the Wizard of Oz."

"That's the one," I giggle.

"You'll need your dressing gown. It can be a little chilly when the doors first open. It's only the air-con for my cars."

"Wait, what. Hold on a minute. Are you saying you have a system just for controlling the humidity for your motors?" "Absolutely. Ventilation and temperature are important factors in any building typically for one-of-a-kind motors."

"That's just crazy!"

He smacked my arse gently, "Go get a jacket or something warm. I'll meet you back here."

We rode the lift in silence. The doors opened and the cold air hit me in the face. "Jesus Christ, you didn't lie about the chill. It's fucking baltic."

He placed his hand on my lower back, steering me from the elevator. I liked how it felt. The garage was huge and held about twenty cars as well as bedrooms, a service area and a glass-enclosed gym which could be accessed independently. It was only a garage. But the most stylish garage I had ever seen, keeping in tune with the modern aesthetics of the floors above.

"Omg. This is amazing. I'd be happy just living here." He pointed to another glass wall unit. "Over there, for instance, is my cigar room. One of my guilty pleasures. Storing them properly is the only way to ensure quality.

Unsurprisingly, proper humidity is of the utmost importance for an enjoyable cigar experience."

"I'll keep that in mind and I'll say it again, crazy."

A chauffeur walked up to him and bowed, handing him a leather folder. "When you're ready Sir. Traffic is fine and we're on schedule."

"Thank you, Chang. I'll be there in a minute."

My eyes followed Chang back to the car and watched him climb into a black Bentley. I found Jingfei, her face pressed right up against the glass staring at us. I waved. But not even an 'oh hi' girlfriend wave. He flicked briskly through the folder and then gave me his full attention.

"Again, I'm going to show you more of the restraint I'm slowly losing around you and refrain from kissing the face off you while she's staring at us like a mental patient."

"It's okay, I think she's seen enough. More than any woman in love should have to witness."

"Jesus, I'm never going to hear the end of it either." He frowned. "Fuck it." Without hesitation, he took my face in his hands and pulled me against him, kissing me once again. "Gui," I murmur. "It's unfair." He groans against my mouth and only because she's watching, I step away and tut. "You did that on purpose?"

"Of course, I did, she might get the message I'm not interested."

"Gui, you need to be direct. Some Dom you are." That makes him smile.

"It's difficult. Why don't you call Evee, and invite her over? The chefs and staff are on standby, and I'll text you later."

"Can I ask you something?"

"Anything."

"Will you have the cameras on? Will you be watching us?"

"There are no cameras in the private bedrooms. So, unless you eat, drink and party there, then no. Why, what are you planning, Miss?"

"I'm not planning anything. It's not my home so I wouldn't take advantage. I would just like to think that I can talk and walk freely."

"Unfortunately, all cameras can't be shut down, for insurance purposes. Rest assured, I won't eavesdrop or ogle. If Evee is joining you, let Daiyu know and she'll have her picked up."

"Daiyu?"

"Don't worry, she'll be around to look after you while I'm gone."

"Could I just go home until you come back? It would be much easier for me and less awkward. I'm still not familiar with your social etiquette and don't want to upset anyone."

He thought about it for a minute and exhaled. "I'd be happier if you remained here. The medical team are close by should anything happen. Meaning I wouldn't be constantly worrying about you. As for Daiyu, she takes everything in her stride and won't bat an eye. I would think after living with me all these years, she's well versed."

"Okay, I understand."

"Look, you'll have a wonderful time. There's also a cinema room. And the gym."

"As if. Can I show her the playroom?"

"It's a rather private part of my life. But I know you share everything. All doors are unlocked."

He looked at his watch.

"I'm sorry, but I must go." He wrapped his arms around me and then kissed the top of my head. "I'll text you."

"Can't you call?"

"I'll be in meetings from morning till night." He saw the look of disappointment on my face.

"I'll try my best to call at least once a day. Please don't take it personally if I don't."

He squeezed my hand and strode off towards the car. Oh my God, I began to cry. What the fuck? What the hell was wrong with me? I was making a holy show of myself. I stood there motionless, wiping the tears from my cheeks.

He looked out the window and frowned, as he spoke on his phone. Fucking hell. He couldn't even wait till he was out of sight. Always the businessman! The car pulled away slowly as I raised my hand and waved. Oh my God, lady muck had the fucking audacity to smirk while giving me the finger. Scanger! I strolled around the garage checking out his jaw-dropping car collection. A few I recognised. I like cars but having more than one or two is impractical. Sure why not if money or space wasn't an object.

15

Deflated, I stuffed my hands into my dressing gown pockets and turned to head back upstairs. What the actual fuck! Standing behind me was that woman again. "Forgive me, I didn't mean to scare you, I'm Daiyu. I'll be looking after you during Mr Lee's absence." She dipped her head and smiled like she was happy to look after me. She stretched out her arm for me to move forward and we rode the lift together. She stared at me but didn't speak. I could only imagine the secrets she knew. The doors opened and again, she opened her arm and pointed like the grim reaper. I exited and walked towards the living room. "Allow me, Miss Murphy."

"No, sure it's quite alright. You don't have to do that. I'm more than capable of opening a door."

"I have my orders Miss Murphy and this is my job. I do not want to disappoint Mr Lee."

With that, I moved aside and let her open the door. I walked inside and was greeted by an overzealous scream. I gripped my chest in fright.

"Holy shit Evee, what the fuck? You frightened the crap out of me."

Daiyu moved closer. "Mr Lee saw how distressed you were so arranged for Evee to be brought here immediately," she said. We ran into each other's arms squealing like we hadn't seen each other in months.

"Omg, I'm so happy to see you, Evee."

"Me too, missed you hun. What's the craic?"

"I'll organise tea for you both," Daiyu said. I looked at her and seeing the determined look on her face, thanked her. She left the room, closing the door gently behind her. Evee took my hand and led me over to the sofa like she had lived here all her life.

"For fuck's sake, how many sofas do you need in a room?" We both looked around then burst out laughing. "I can't believe you're here. I saw Gui on his phone and assumed he was in business mode before he even left the building. But he was making arrangements to get you here. Bless."

"He was speaking to me?"

"You?"

"Yeah, he called to say he had to go away on urgent business and you were upset. I was to be ready immediately because a driver was on the way to pick me up. He didn't want you alone too long. Bit bossy for my liking."

"I don't know what to say. I'm sorry. You could have had other plans?"

"Don't be silly. I would have dropped them for my bestie."

"Aww, thanks, babe."

"And obviously to have a nosey round. This place is fucking huge. So, where's he gone anyway?"

"How would I know? I'm not married to him."

"Not yet haha!"

"Are you fucking crazy? He's not interested in me that way?"

"There's plenty of time. You know the saying, a relationship is like a fart, if you have to force it, it's probably shit!"

"Omg Evee, you're such a disgusting smart aleck."

"True, if I wasn't so modest, I'd be perfect. So spill. I want to hear the good, the bad and the dirty."

As we got comfortable there was a tap tap on the door. We looked at each other. "Shit! Do I say something?" I asked. "Come in," Evee answered in a queen's voice. I nudged her in the ribs.

"Why are you speaking like the queen?" The door opened and Daiyu laid the small coffee table in hushed silence. She moved elegantly, placing down a beautiful tea set and cake stand. Then handed me the new iPhone. I noticed there was a message and opened it at once knowing it could only be from him.

Gui: Hope you're happy x.

Rhylee: Thank you so much. I'm more than happy. It was very kind of you.

Gui: It was the least I could do when I saw how upset you were. As much as I would have hoped, I'd be a fool to think I was the cause.

Rhylee: It was a combination of many things. Of course, I was upset that you were leaving and would have preferred to be at home if you weren't here with me. Also, I'm not sure how I'm supposed to act around Daiyu.

Gui: Forget she's there. She knows what to do, don't overthink.

Rhylee: She knocked on the door and I didn't know what to do. I felt silly.

Gui: If she knocks again, don't say anything. Don't worry, you're not being rude before you say anything. She's just announcing herself so she doesn't catch you in a compromising position. If, however, you were, just answer with 'just a minute.' That's all there is to it.

Rhylee: I would just prefer to do things myself and not have anyone fuss over me.

Gui: Daiyu takes her job very seriously and has served people in the highest positions. As I said, you will forget she's there.

Rhylee: But that's rude too.

Gui: Rhylee, she is not there to make friends with you and won't expect you to become her best buddy either. It's her job to look after all my guests and she doesn't treat anyone any differently. Presidents, subs and friends are all treated the same. The same can't be said for Jingfei. She's the only person to ever infuriate Daiyu and that woman has the patience of a saint.

Rhylee: Does she think I'm a sub?

Gui: You are my sub. But no, you are a very special guest.

Rhylee: Okay.

Gui: Have fun with your friend. It will be a different kind of fun when I get back x

Rhylee: Thanks for reminding me. Not! Anyway, it meant a lot x

"Miss Murphy, would you like me to pour?"

"Em, no thanks. If you don't mind?"

"Of course not, I'll leave you girls, to it. Oh, Mr Lee mentioned that you'd be staying on the fifteenth floor while Evee is here. Everything is ready."

I looked at Evee with a blank stare, then at Daiyu. She smiled. "It means you have all of the fifteenth floor at your disposal. Would you like to go now and get settled? It's no problem at all."

"I'm grand here Daiyu, thanks a million." She smiled, bowed and left the room.

"Omg, you have fucking maids and a whole floor to yourself. Can't wait to see it." I filled her in on everything, leaving nothing out.

"Fuck's sake Rhy, nobody would believe you. Apart from him wanting to take the law into his own hands. You're the fucking modern-day pretty woman."

"Seriously Evee, what's with your language? It's getting worse."

"It's because you haven't been around to give out to me for fuck's sake." She threw her head back laughing as I buried my face in my hands. It felt good to laugh after the events of the past week. We chatted for hours, laughing at each other's stories.

"It's just crazy and I honestly don't know why I'm laughing. Sometimes I think about what's about to happen and it frightens the crap out of me."

"Rhy, he will never hurt you. You know that. It seems he has a lot of practice in these matters. If anything, it's going to be an amazing experience for you. Think of all the mind-blowing orgasms."

"I can never forget what he was going to do to Lan. It doesn't make sense. It's like he was a different person."

"Look, he didn't. That's all that matters now. Stop changing the subject Rhy. What if he wants to do anal?"

"Oh Jesus. I will in me hole! No pun intended. You just had to go there. That's disgusting. I'm so on team, not for me."

"It's not something that's 'on the menu' all the time. So when it's available, guys want to put their cock in there." She said matter-of-factly.

"No, I just couldn't. I think it's vile. Have you and Josh?"

"Yeah, we gave it a lash once. We read everything available to ensure it was an enjoyable experience for both of us. But it's too much like hard work. We got as far as getting the tip in. Believe me, it hurts like hell because the tip is the widest part. And it's not at all like what you see in movies or porn sites. That's all-pure fantasy. Those girls probably did a lot of anal training?"

"What the hell does that mean? Aerobics for your bum?"

"Yeah. You gradually introduce larger toys to stretch it out. Starting small and working your way up. I'd say Gui uses butt plugs being kinky and all. So no, way too much prep having it in the booty hole."

I shivered. "Nah, it doesn't excite me one bit. Not sure how you'd even orgasm from it?

"So have you woken him up with a blowie yet?"

"What on earth is that?"

"Ah for fuck's sake Rhy, it's a blow job!"

"Well sorry, I've never heard it called that before. Bet you just picked it up too. Stop pretending you're all up with street slang. I've only been gone a week. Bet Josh told you that?"

"Hahaha, he did. And you've been away almost two weeks now!"

"Have I? Wow, I've completely lost track of time. And for your information, we haven't slept together. You know I'm not into giving bj's either."

"From your description of 'Donkey Kong' I'm sure you'll change your mind?"

"Nah, as much as it's big and gorgeous, I'm not interested in having it in my mouth."

"Famous last words, that's all I'll say. Does he know he has his work cut out with you, no anal and no blowies?"

"As far as I can remember I've told him so much?"

"I just can't believe you landed your very own Dom. That's one of your fantasies."

"Changing to another subject I'm not too keen on either hahaha. How on earth have I gotten away with not speaking to my parents for so long? Especially my mother?"

"I had to tell her you were on a course way up in the mountains. She didn't even question it."

"That's a first for her."

"We know how nosey she is."

"I don't think she means to be, it's just curiosity."

"Rhy, who are you kidding? The woman has a degree in being a nosey cunt."

"Evee, I know she's the worst, but she doesn't deserve to be called that!"

"Hang on a minute, are you missing the aul cow?"

"I think I am. So much has happened. But it's not like I can pick up the phone and chat with her about kinky stuff.

'Hey ma, I'm thinking of becoming a sex slave crawling around on all fours wearing a dog collar?"

"Could you imagine? The priest would be called for divine intervention and your poor dad would never hear the end of it. He'd have to move into his man cave to get some peace."

"Ugh... the thought of them even knowing what I'm up to makes me want to puke."

"When can I see Lan?"

"Tomorrow, she'll be sleeping now. We are trying to get her into a little routine."

"We, as in you and Gui?" I raised my eyebrows.

"Yeah. Why are you looking at me like that?"

"I'm not. It's just that you have your own ready-made little family thing going on."

"Ah, would you stop? If Gui heard you saying that he'd run for the hills. She was going to bed at all hours and waking up early. Sometimes after waking me, she'd run in and jump on Gui like he was her very own bouncy castle. It was hilariously cute. But he wasn't very keen on the early wake-up calls."

"I bet he secretly loved it?"

My phone pinged. "Speak of the devil."

Gui: 'Don't forget to carry your phone with you at all times and by the way your bandage is waterproof. No more plastic wrapper.'

"Look at you all smiles. What's he saying? Did he send a dick pic? Let me see."

"Eveeee O' Mahony! You knacker! Don't be so rude." I slapped her hand away.

"I want to see it when he does and he will. I guarantee you. They can't help themselves."

"He's not a horny teenager for fuck's sake. Does Josh?"

"He did when we started going out first. No point now, I see it all the time."

"Did you reciprocate?"

"We sexted and there may have been an odd photo. Sexting is one of the hottest ways to communicate with someone. A little sext here and there is a fun way to spice things up. I think Josh constantly sent eggplant emojis. He was always on the horn hahaha. I bet Gui will send pretty descriptive messages about what he'd like to be doing to you or do when he gets back. If he asked for some naughty pics, would you?"

"I don't think he's like that?"

"But… would you?"

"Ooh, I'm not sure. If I got into it and he had me all horny, then maybe? As long as I wasn't pressured into it."

"Josh once texted, 'I'm on my way home to slam my cock into you. It's so hard right now just thinking about all the things I'm going to do to you.' It accidentally went to mam!"

"Oh Jesus Evee. You never told me that. I'm so sorry but that's hilarious." I howl uncontrollably.

I couldn't stop the fits of hysterical laughter to the point tears ran down my face. "I'm sorry," I said, fanning my face with my hand. "Go on, finish what you were saying before I rudely interrupted you."

"He did," she said with a note of horror in her voice. "Poor Josh. I'd say he was mortified?"

"He didn't call to the house for at least six months. Don't think he fully recovered after it either. I was just thankful it wasn't a dick pic. It's a mistake that you only make once."

We burst into a fresh bout of laughter. "I can just see your ma's face. Omg Evee what on earth did you say to her?"

"I said absolutely nothing. She forwarded the incriminating evidence to me saying, 'Really?!!' I realised getting upset about it doesn't unsend the message or won't make any difference to the outcome. Come on, let's go see what's on the fifteenth floor," she said with a mischievous grin.

We jumped into the lift and stared at all the numbers. "Go on, do it," Evee coaxed.

I pushed the button and the doors closed smoothly. We held hands like two best friends waiting to go on stage in the school play. The doors slid open in hushed silence and in unison, we popped our heads out. We entered straight into what looked like an open-plan penthouse.

"Oh my fucking God, it's massive," said Evee.

"I bet that's not the first time you've said that," I guffawed. "Gurl, you are fun...nee! This is amazing. How is it even possible?"

I had to agree, it was stunning. The kitchen and living area were designed to be the heart of the home. The u-shaped kitchen was fitted with luxury state-of-the-art appliances. It had five bedrooms all queen with marble ensuites. There was an office and a library. We both went off in different directions.

"Rhylee, you have to see this," shouted Evee from somewhere. "Where are you?"

"I'll meet you back in the kitchen."

"You are not going to fucking believe this?" She took my hand and led me towards two huge black doors. She pushed them open revealing a huge swimming pool.

"Holy shit!"

"Rhy it's a fucking swimming pool!"

"He said there was a pool, but I wasn't expecting this." It had a glass curtain wall, barrel-vaulted ceilings, custom-made furniture and stunning views of the city. "There's also a cinema room." Hearing no reply, I turned to find Evee stripping down to her bra and knickers. "Omg, what are you doing?"

"Going for a swim."

"In your knickers!"

SPLASH...

"Oh Rhy, jump in, it's soooo warm."

I looked at the ceiling to see if there were any cameras. "I'll be back in a minute."

"What's wrong?"

"I've no underwear on!"

"Omg, you dirty bitch hahaha. Not even your Bridget's?"

"Oh yeah you cow, I want to talk to you about that," I said as I raced back to my room and rifled through the dresser. I hadn't looked before so wasn't sure what surprises if any they held. I opened and closed each of the drawers. Tee shirts, vests and every kind of top you could want. Oh no. What if there wasn't any underwear? There was no way I was putting on my big knickers. I crawled over to the other side of the wardrobe and with fingers crossed, asked God above for an intervention and prayed for a decent pair of pants. Hallelujah, every drawer was brimming with tasty delicacies of the most beautiful lingerie I had ever seen. I blessed myself and looked up to the sky above, thank you, God. I promise I'll be good from now on. I looked at most of the labels and hadn't a clue who any of them were. Okay, I heard of Agent Provocateur and Coco de Mer. But not Myla London, Eres, Carine Gilson to name but a few. All stunningly sexy. I picked a black underwired soft cup lace bra with matching briefs from Net a Porter. I stood back and looked in the mirror. Wow, I looked so chic and sophisticated. Hanging above the dresser were various robes matching every set of underwear. I slipped the gilded matching robe on completing the luxuriously indulgent ensemble. One more peek in the mirror then dashed back to the 15th floor. I had taken note of the security cameras before heading back. They all looked the same.

Before entering, I scanned the room again. Not a single camera in sight. I entered like a model strutting her stuff making the pool area my catwalk. With shoulders back and head held high, I walked at a steady pace keeping my strides long and smooth.

"Omfg Rhy, look at you. You look fucking amazing. Work it bitch."

I stopped halfway out of breath. "Jesus Evee, it's not as easy as it looks. It's really hard walking tall and sucking your tummy in at the same time." I opened the robe seductively letting it glide slowly down my body making kiss kiss faces at Evee.

"Fuck Rhylee, even I'd ride ye."

I climbed carefully into the pool, not wanting to get my hair wet and came up beside my best friend. I noticed she had been joined by a couple of inflatables.

"Where did they come from?"

"You were taking ages, I can see why now. So I had a little nosey through that door over there. That's where I found them, along with towels and dressing gowns. Your boobs look amazing in that bra by the way."

"Thanks."

"Did he buy them?"

"Seriously Evee, how could I afford them? They're designer. I don't think he did."

"Then who? Please tell me it wasn't what's-her-face?"

"Fuck. I certainly hope not. I'd rather go fucking naked or wear my Bridget's if she had anything to do with it."

"Ah ha, the luxury knicker fairy?"

"I think it might have been his mother?"

"Whaat, his ma? That's a bit weird?"

"I don't know who exactly. Remember the debacle about me showering and finding all those goodies? Well, he said it was his mother who arranged them and not him. Plus, there are wardrobes full of new clothes for me and Lan. I'd like to think he had something to do with it but very much doubt it. A few pairs of the knickers alone would cost me a week's wages."

"As long as there's no crotchless ones in there I wouldn't worry about it." There was a knock and again we looked at each other in surprise. "Oh holy fuck, we're in our bleeding underwear," I croaked. I grabbed one of the inflatable doughnuts and threw it over my head. The doors swung open and Daiyu appeared pushing a drinks trolley. I held the doughnut up covering my boobs. She paid us no attention and continued about her business like we weren't there. She had her back to us now and all we could hear was clink clink. She turned suddenly, holding a gold tray in her hands. She placed it down in front of us smiling. She walked to the door where Evee had a nosey and entered the room.

"Oh she's going to give out to us isn't she for going in there?" She came out carrying towels and robes and placed a set on each lounger before exiting the room.

"I don't think we're supposed to stop what we're doing each time she appears and follow her every move, Evee."

"I know. I'm sure they're all down there in the staff room laughing their heads off at us?"

I flung the doughnut off me and moved towards the tray at the edge of the pool. She had left a huge jug, cocktail glasses with umbrellas and straws, and several bowls of nuts, nibbles and chocolates.

"It's cocktail time," said Evee over my shoulder. I filled her's to the top and poured a little drop in my glass.

"Ahh Rhylee, you're taking the piss, it's only a cocktail."

"I'm tasting it first to see if I like it. You know what I'm like. If I taste alcohol, I won't drink it. Anyway, you know I'm a lightweight and get tipsy on one glass of anything!"

"I remember, you'd get drunk smelling a bottle of cheap perfume!" I swallowed the dribble and licked my lips.

"Omg…That's divine. I think it's one of those virgin cocktails?"

"Ah no are you serious, sure that's no fun."

I handed her the glass trying not to spill any. I watched her dip her tongue in first, then take a sip.

"Definitely alcohol in there Rhy."

"Wow, that's amazing, I couldn't taste any."

She held up her glass. "Cheers dahling, let's get shit-faced."

"Oh Evee, try one of these chocolate balls, they're so decadent. I think it's the best choccy I've ever tasted and you know I'm a connoisseur."

"Is it up there with sex?"

"Yeah, probably."

"Throw one over so."

She just managed to catch it, almost falling head-first. "Oh Jesus Rhylee, you're right there. Much better than sex."

"I was only joking. It's moist and rich and all the chocolate flavour you could dream of."

"They'd turn me into a chocoholic!"

I swam over to the inflatable leaf and pulled it behind me, waddling back to my drink. I climbed up and grabbed my glass before the ripples moved it out of reach.

"This is the life Evee," I said as she paddled by on a giant swan.

"Sure is and if you play your cards right, it could all be yours."

"Oh for fuck's sake Evee. I wish you would stop coming out with that ridiculous shite!"

The look on her face was priceless and suppressing the urge to laugh wasn't easy. She looked like she was going to burst into tears at any moment.

"Soz for shouting at you but you have to stop. Look at him and look at me. We are different people. He dates models and actresses for heaven's sake. I'm sure when he gets what he wants, I'll be on my way. Anyway, he told me in no uncertain terms to forget any romantic ending. His actual words were, 'Forget any romantic notions or silly fairytale endings I had in my head."

"Well, women deserve three things. A King, a ring and some great dingaling!"

I spit my drink out. "That's so true."

"Mam said that to me during our tenth-anniversary celebration. She had way too many alco-pops. I couldn't tell her I didn't have any."

"Not even great dingaling," I gasped.

"Not really. He's very vanilla and even that didn't move mountains."

"I thought he was great in the sack. You always made out he was."

"I didn't want to ruin the illusion."

"Why have you stayed with him then?"

"Not sure?"

Without thinking, I rubbed my arm. "Does it hurt?"

"Not really unless I lift something heavy and it pulls on the stitches. Omg, I thought it was bizarre he texted that my bandage was waterproof. I didn't consider that before jumping into the pool with all the excitement. Getting it wet would have caused another infection and I'd be here for fucking ever."

"Top up?"

"Oh yes please, it's delicious."

"Here you are," she said, slurring her words.

"Me thinks you're phiss-hed as a fart! We're one hundred percent scuttered!"

"Scuse me. I'm, I am nosh, not scuttered, bloody cheek."

"I think I may be a bit drunk myself. Let's get out before one of us drowns and doesn't know one of us has drowned. I certainly don't want to look like a drunk idiot to a bunch of strangers!"

"Oh can you imagine, our parents on the way to work seeing the headlines, the Irish had drunk the city dry and not even the pool was safe!"

I clutched the side of the pool tightly, feeling rather giddy.

"Raise your hands in the air like you just don't care," chimed Evee.

"Oh Jesus, don't start, or I'll pee my pants." I slid off the inflatable palm leaf and walked cross-legged up the marble steps. "C'mon Aretha Franklin, out before you capsize."

She did a very unattractive belly flop into the water, glass still in her hand, not a sacred drop spilt. What on earth was in that drink? I was just grateful there weren't any cameras to witness our drunkenness. She dived under the water, glass still in the air and swam the short distance before surfacing at the steps. She was always the better swimmer growing up. I held out a towel as we slowly walked to the loungers. I let my hair drop and wrapped the towel around her tightly. "How do they get the towels so fluffy?" I asked.

Both of us found that ridiculously funny.

"I bet even Mr Shady as fuck doesn't know either?" she laughed.

"Well, that's not very hosh-pitiful Evee."

"Well, then. Tell me what he does. Bet you don't know? He looks like he has more security than the President and we all know the Americans and portion control hahaha."

"Oh, a comedian too I see, not just a brilliant singer."

"Hey, you forgot to mention pretty face."

"That too." I blotted myself dry and pulled on the oversized robe.

"Stand up missus."

I jerked her towel free and draped the robe around her shoulders. Sit down before you fall over."

I sat down and popped my feet up on the lounger and relaxed. "Omfg," I screeched. Evee shot up like a rocket.

"Wha, what happened? I swear I wasn't sleeping!" I pointed to the drinks trolley between the two loungers.

"How the hell did that get there? When did that happen, look, the jug has been refilled! Did we pass out or something?"

"She's like Mary fucken Poppins Rhy!"

"Be a shame to let it go to waste, you want one?"

"Absofuckinglutely, that shit is lethal," she said winking. "I'd murder a bag of chips right now, extra salt and vinegar." I relaxed back against the lounger and took a sip of the toxic concoction. It truly was delicious.

"Oh yeah, a fish and chip, yum. Evee, didn't you Google Gui when you found out I was here?"

"I Googled Mr Lii instead of Mr Lee, about one billion differences. So, see if you two got married."

"Evee, shut your trap. What the hell did I say earlier?"

"I can't remember. Anyway, stop interrupting. You'd be Rhylee Lee. Sounds like a porn star. You'd have to get rid of what's her face first."

"You just can't help yourself, can you?"

"I know you're dying to say something but you can't because you've bitten my head off for the same thing!" I choked back something between a laugh and a sob.

"You're bloody annoying! But I love you to bits. Would you look at that. There are slippers down there now. Anytime I close my eyes, something else appears. I wish I could close them and wake up in the scratcher. I'm exhausted."

"You could never keep your eyes open Rhy after a few drinky-poos. You've done well girlfriend."

"I've done well and lasted longer than usual, we've gone through two pitchers, Evee! Two!" I held up two fingers.

"Why are you holding up four fingers, Rhylee?"

"That's it, your blotto."

"Who's Blotto?"

"I held up two fingers, you're seeing double ye mad cow."

I stood and slipped my feet into the plush slippers. As to be expected, luxurious comfort. Evee stretched her big toe trying hard to slide her feet in, but they kept pushing away out of her reach.

"I feel like the ugg-ly shiss-ter trying to force my foot into Cinderella's glass shlipper," she hiccupped.

I giggled watching her playing footsie with her slippers and knelt by her feet.

"Look you nincompoop, it still has the tissue inside." I placed both slippers on her feet and pushed down.

"Oh yeah, comfy alright. These bad boys are coming home with me courtesy of Mr Lee himself with the matching robe of course."

She said shuffling her feet from one foot to the other. "Evee O' Mahony you are not giving your name for a pair of furry slippers!"

"But they're not *just* slippers, they're Ugg slippers. Do you know how much these bad boys cost?"

"Yes, I bought you a pair for Christmas last year."

"Yes, you did and I don't wear them because they're too good. Now I'll have two pairs."

"I'm checking your bag before you leave and I better not find anything which doesn't belong to you."

"You're such a spoilsport Rhy!"

"I'm serious."

"But he won't miss them."

"I mean it! Before it turns into an argument, let's pick our rooms."

"Please, please, can I have the four-poster bed?"

"What, the one in the playroom?" She stopped in her tracks and grabbed my arm. "Just stop right there Rhylee Murphy. You didn't tell me he had a playroom. Like a dungeon?"

"Em, a five-star dungeon haha. No, it's not a dungeon. It's not even in the basement. It's like a Fifty Shades playroom a la Christian Grey, but bigger. And not painted like the red room of pain. I was going to show you tomorrow."

"Omg, is he going to take you there and strap you to the St Andrews Cross and flog you for being a naughty girl?"

"Evee, stop winding me up. I have no idea what he's going to do."

"So how long have you known about it?"

"From the very beginning." She narrowed her eyes. I held up my hands, "Look I'm telling you now."

"So has he introduced you to a few of his friends yet, butt plug, nipple clamps or Mr whip?"

"No, all we've done is kissed and…"

"Yeah, annd?"

"I told you already, he slipped his fingers in."

"That's it?? That's not very scandalous, at all. I did that behind the bike shed when you were sitting on the grass talking to the buttercups waiting for me."

"Omg, you little liar, you said you were having a sneaky smoke with one of the second years!"

"I was, the smoke came after he fingered me."

"How could you, in public and behind the school? What if you had been caught?"

"I'm quite sure you would have sent smoke signals or something?"

"Did you do anything else behind the bike shed?"

"Yep, everything imaginable."

"Where was I while you were up to no good?"

"Sitting on the grass talking to the flowers."

"Evee, when you said you were going for a quickie, did you mean sex?"

"Guilty as charged."

"It all makes perfect bloody sense now, the red face and hair all over the place. You even said it was very windy back there because there were no trees!"

"I couldn't very well say I just had sex up against the wall."

"Well yes, you could have, should have. Thought we were best friends back then?"

"Oh stop being a drama queen. I never said anything because I didn't want you to think I was a slut. If you knew what I was up to, you wouldn't want to be my friend or hang out with me. We all know how prim and proper you are. I could just imagine you on your knees with rosary beads praying for my wandering soul every time I went behind the bike shed."

"Jesus, I'm not that bad. Does poor Josh know how much of a little slapper you are?"

"Hey, that hurts! But yes, he does. He was the second year."

"Omfg, what else don't I know? Is Evee O' Mahony even your real name?"

"C'mon, drama Queen I'll show you, my room."

16

Indeed, there was a room with a white four-poster bed. The fastest way to make a statement is with a dramatic piece of furniture and that means a striking unadorned four-poster bed. As with all the other rooms, I was totally in love with this one too. Evee squealed and dived onto the beautifully made-up bed flopping on her stomach.

"Even the bed linen smells rich," she murmured before passing out.

I giggled and gently removed her slippers and robe and pulled the covers up over her. It wasn't long before her soft snores filled the room. I had five other rooms to choose but picked the one next door in case she needed me. Plus, I was too tired to check them all out again. My room was like something out of the Hamptons. Cool hues of blue and off-white, panelled walls with white wooden floors. I could just imagine the countryside and a view out onto the ocean or a beautiful beach.

As I walked around the room it stood out the most because I could see myself living here. I took off the robe and only then remembered I was just wearing underwear.

It was dry but I was worried Evee's might still be damp. Couldn't be sending her back to look after babies with a cold. She was out for the count and didn't budge when I pulled back the covers to feel her underwear. Just mumbled that she wasn't drunk. Bone dry too, making me wonder how long we were drinking cocktails. Before I climbed up onto the sumptuous bed, out of curiosity I pushed open the door attached to my room. Of course, it was an en-suite but in my house, it would have been the master bathroom. Nothing was on show so I opened the press under the sink and found toothbrushes and toothpaste still in packs. I was delighted because I'm sure the sugar levels were through the roof in what we just drank. Hated going to bed without brushing my teeth. Next to it was a leave-on mask, wow. I slathered it all over my face and climbed into bed. My phone pinged and who would have thought that little ping could excite me so much? I dragged myself across the vast expanse of the huge bed to the other side. I must be drunk because I didn't remember removing it from my pocket, hell, I didn't even know if it was in there in the first place. Please don't let me be hungover tomorrow. It had been a long, long time since I was drunk.

Gui: Hey.
Rhylee: Hey yourself.
Gui: How's things?
Rhylee: All good, how's things with you?
Gui: Just about to go to bed.
Rhylee: What a coincidence.
Gui: So, what did you do when I left?
Rhylee: Don't you know?
Gui: Should I?

Rhylee: Ah no. Just thought you'd know.
Gui: Do you want to tell me?
Rhylee: Had a lovely time. Went for a paddle. I can't believe you have all this. It's a home within a home. Thank you for letting Evee stay over. It's just amazing having her here.
Gui: Delighted you're happy. Anything else?
Rhylee: We had one or two cocktails and lots of chocolate then headed to bed. Where is it from, it's orgasmic.
Gui: I think it's a woman thing, chocolate. I know women who literally salivate just thinking about it.
Rhylee: How about you? Drinks?
Gui: I don't drink that much really, never through the week as I get hungover now these days.
Rhylee: When did you last get drunk?
Gui: It takes a lot to get me drunk. Last month, I ended up on the Vodka with the boys. I'm guessing longer for you.
Rhylee: The only time I got drunk was in my early twenties.
Gui: I was always drunk in my younger days. But as with anything and as you get older, the key is moderation.
Rhylee: Says the old guy lol.
Gui: So what are you wearing?
Rhylee: Going there, are we?
Gui: Just a simple question. I didn't ask to see your tits!
Rhylee: I don't know how to reply to that….
Gui: I'm only winding you up.
Rhylee: So, you don't want to see my boobs?

Gui: Only if you want to?
Rhylee: Omg!! Absolutely not!
Gui: Worth a try I guess.
Rhylee: How would you feel if I asked for a dick pic?
Gui: Wouldn't bother me tbh. But I know you're not like that.
Rhylee: What do you mean?
Gui: If I sent you a photo of my cock, you'd run a mile lol. Bet you're even blushing now…
Rhylee: Yes, to both.
Gui: Okay, let's change the subject. I'm getting horny just thinking about it.
Rhylee: Thinking about what exactly?
Gui: You.
Rhylee: Oh!
Gui: I'm sure you're aware of the effect you have on men.
Rhylee: Just you it seems.
Gui: I'll bid you goodnight before I regret what I may say.
Rhylee: Okay, nite nite.
Gui: Goodnight Rhylee.
Rhylee: When do you get back?
Gui: The end of the week if things go according to plan.
Rhylee: Can I ask what exactly it is you'll be doing?
Gui: I'm trying to close a multi-million-dollar deal on a media agency that helps startups and small businesses create and launch campaigns.
Rhylee: No big deal so!
Gui: No lol

Rhylee: I'm sure you could do it in your sleep.
Gui: I'm glad one of us has faith in me.
Rhylee: You'll smash it.
Gui: On that note, I'll bid you goodnight.
Rhylee: Nite nite.
Gui: So that's still a no for a pic of your tits?
Rhylee: Goodnight!
Gui: I'll leave this with you… how is it possible to be so sexually attracted to someone by just talking? Think about it.

Oh my God, he said he's sexually attracted to me. I clutched the phone to my chest. I sat up and plump the pillows behind me. Did he want to see my boobs? Surely not? Maybe he just likes winding me up? Is it something I could do? Posing for photos always made me uncomfortable so I couldn't imagine taking a selfie. Evee was always snapping away. She's so comfortable with her looks. Then again, she took a great photo and always looked amazing. The camera adored her. I always had to pull a silly face or stick out my tongue to feel natural. I got up on my knees and looked at myself in the huge mirror. The mask had completely sunk in, obviously needed it. She was right though, my boobs did look amazing in this underwear. On this only occasion, you could say they were my best asset. I held the phone far enough away to ensure they were in the photo. Facing the mirror, I kneeled up and kept my legs wide apart. I arched my back which made my legs look longer and thinner. Then leaning forward, pouting while touching my lips and looking directly into the lens I snapped a few selfies. Flicking through them, I looked half decent. Thankfully I hadn't gone for a swim so my hair was sexy in a loose ponytail. I tossed the phone onto the bedside locker and flopped down on the bed in exhaustion. It's a hard life being a lady of leisure. I was just about to slip into unconsciousness when my phone pinged. I smiled, stretching over to get it. Blinking my eyes to get rid of the blur, I opened his message.

Gui: FUCK! You're so fucking hot! I'm going to explode.

I rubbed my eyes and read the message again thinking I was reading it wrong. Have I missed something? Nope, that's what I read alright. My heart felt heavy.

Rhylee: Did you mean to send that to me?

I gazed at the flashing cursor waiting for his reply and drew a deep breath when it appeared.

Gui: Who else would I send it to?
Rhylee: I'm sorry, you've lost me.
Gui: The sexy photos you just sent me.

My shoulders slump as I read the message again. No, no, no. Omg, omg, omfg what the hell have I done?

Rhylee: But I didn't send any??
Gui: I'm sorry. I should have mentioned that your phone is synced to my iPad. Believe me, it wasn't intentional. The iPad was for you and I picked up the wrong one. I know you don't want to hear this but I'm glad I did.

Rhylee: I really can't talk about this now. I'm actually in shock. Can we talk tomorrow?
Gui: Of course. Please don't get upset about it. I'll say one thing and leave it, 'Beautiful.'

Two minutes later my phone pinged. I looked at the screen and read the notification. Gui Lee has sent you an image… I quickly opened the message.

Gui: You're to blame for this xx

The image was of Gui's thigh showing the length of his long hard erection, straining against the fabric of his joggers. Under different circumstances I would have found that sexy. My heart was racing and my breath came quickly as I placed the phone on the bedside table and curled up in a ball, too shocked to register what just happened. I had no doubt I'd toss and turn for the rest of the night.

Evee came running in and jumped on top of me like it was Christmas morning.

"Rise and shine sleeping beauty."

"Oh God. I'm not in the mood. What time is it? I've just fallen asleep. Please don't tell me it's time to get up?" The sheet is stuck to my cheek and my mouth is as dry as a Weetabix.

"Get up. It's 8.30 and a feast awaits us in the kitchen."

"Oh no. You didn't cook breakfast, did you? You can't cook!"

"Excuse me, I've learned loads having to fend for myself since you moved into his lordship's castle." She pulled the covers off me and grabbing my foot, dragged me off the bed. "Rhylee Murphy you're still in your underwear. Did you go to bed in wet clothes?"

I stumbled up and dragged my feet across the floor to the bathroom to brush my teeth. One eye open, the other closed. I put my hand to my pounding head and groan. I knew drinking Daiyu's concoction was a bad idea. I felt like shite. What the hell was in it? Then pushing my arms through a robe followed her into the kitchen. Indeed, it was a feast but I wasn't sure I had any appetite. She sat sipping her juice studying me. I glanced at her.

"Something's up, what is it? I know that face."

Embarrassed, I felt tears in my eyes and looked away.

Evee was beside me before I even took a second breath. "What is it, Rhylee? What could have possibly happened while we were sleeping?"

"Gui texted me."

"And?"

"And we chatted for a bit."

"And?"

"He jokingly asked to see my tits."

"Doubt he was joking. Chancing his arm, more like. So, you're on a guilt trip because you did? Look there's no reason to feel embarrassed about that. We've all done it and sure you're, almost, nearly married anyway."

"I didn't mean to send them. I didn't send them at all."

"Hun, what are you saying, you either did or didn't?"

"Not intentionally. My phone is synced to the iPad he got me but he took the wrong one. I was messing about taking selfies. Fuelled along with some Dutch courage and unaware they were popping up somewhere else. You know me Evee. I hate posing for selfies."

"So, what did he say? Was he repelled?"

"Well, no, of course he wasn't repelled. What the hell?"

"Duh!! I'm sure he went to bed with a smile on his face and a couple of pounds lighter." She winked. "More interestingly, did he reciprocate?"

"You're disgusting and no, he didn't return the favour and I know for sure he wouldn't have hesitated if I'd asked. And he said they were beautiful."

"So, what's the problem? Every girl's wish is to be told she's beautiful."

"He didn't say I was beautiful."

"Babe, it doesn't matter if he said you or the images were beautiful. It's the same thing."

"I don't want him to think I'm one of those girls."

"I'm one of those girls Rhylee and I'm not a slut. I know that's what you're thinking. Look, you didn't intentionally send them. So no need to bash yourself up about it. Forget about it."

"I know you're right. I think I'm just mortified more than anything else."

"Show me if you haven't deleted them already?" I pulled the phone out of my pocket and handed it to her.

"What's the password?"

"Doesn't have one. What's the point? I'm sure I'll have to give everything back when I leave?"

"And what's he going to do with all your shit? You look amazing by the way and you're hardly showing anything. The way you were reacting or should I say overreacting, I thought you had sent nudes! C'mon, the food is calling to me. Then you can show me the playroom afterwards. Need to build up my appetite for that. Then you can introduce me to Lan, the cherry on the cake."

I didn't share Evee's enthusiasm for our visit to the playroom. To be honest, I wasn't keen. I opened the door and the lights flickered on. We both popped our heads inside before entering. She whistled and said "Wow a cheesy sex dungeon it isn't. This is when you know you've truly made it financially. You have a special room for your hobbies."

We stepped inside but I stayed leaning against the door frame. "Come in for God's sake, it's not going to bite you. At least sit on the sofa."

"I'm grand, you go on and have a nosey."

She stopped and opened a drawer. "Omfg!"

"What is it, what did you find?"

"Come and see for yourself. You might as well acquaint yourself with these things before it happens."

I peered over her shoulder into the velvet-lined drawer. Butt fucking plugs in all shapes and sizes. Evee held one up to the light. "Wow, it's glass and shaped like a Christmas tree. It's very pretty."

"You wouldn't be saying that when it's being shoved up your arse!"

"That's true, but it won't be my arse, will it? I have a dresser where I keep arts and crafts. Mr Lee has one for keeping butt plugs."

I grabbed the offending object out of her hand and shoved it in the drawer slamming it shut. She wasn't one bit put out and opened the next one. "Ooh, nipple clamps. Hate these little bastards. They hurt like hell."

"When did you ever wear nipple clamps?"

"Josh and I have tried loads of things but not this kind of high-end bondage gear." She held up a pair to her breasts. "Bet these are real diamonds too?" She placed them back in the drawer and looked around. Without hesitation, she ran and dove onto the bed.

"Jesus Evee, be careful. Imagine if you broke it?"

"Hey, this bed has seen more action than the Playboy mansion. Bet he's had gang bangs and everything on it?"

"Please Evee. That's not something I want in my head when he takes me here." She patted the bed and I reluctantly joined her. We lay down and stared up at the ceiling.

"As rooms go Rhy, it's beautifully decorated. He certainly didn't spare the cash."

"So, Anastasia Steele, how many playrooms have you been in?" I giggled.

"None, but I can see he has very expensive taste. If you want a high-class playroom, be prepared to go bespoke. I'd say everything here is handmade and one thing I did find out, his net worth is estimated to be 2.5 billion or thereabouts! Let's try it out."

"No way, I'm not role-playing Evee."

"You're such a spoilsport."

"Okay, come on then."

"Take the robe off first."

I scooted off the bed and took off the dressing gown clutching my chest as I searched the room for cameras.

"What on earth are you doing Rhy?"

"Looking for cameras."

"Well, it's a bit late for that when he's already seen you naked and had his fingers in your hoo-ha!"

"Oh yeah, Jesus, I suppose you're right."

"So before we begin. What's your safe word?"

"Seriously Evee! Alright then. Hairy banana."

"No. I'm not accepting that."

"Big cock."

"Nope."

"Peony then."

"That's better."

I lay on the bed trying not to giggle. "Is it strange there's no bedding?"

"Who needs them? The mattress is leather, easy to wipe clean."

"Eew, that's gross!"

"Why would you want to cover up anyway? Rhy, this bed is not for sleeping in or cuddling after a session. The whole point of this room is exposure."

Taking my wrist she placed a leather fur-lined cuff around it and fastened the buckle. "Not a sign of cheap Velcro in sight," she whispered as she attached both to the restraining points on the headboard.

"How's your arm?"

"Grand so far."

"Whoops forgot to check they aren't too tight. Can't be cutting off your circulation now can we."

She kneeled up on the bed and shoved her finger into each cuff. "Perfect wiggle room there."

"Jesus, how do you know this stuff?"

"The books we've read. You've read enough of them Rhy to know. Don't you think it sounds mad calling a room pretty, when you know what shenanigans go on here, sex, floggings, more sex?"

"It's certainly something I won't forget in a long time. Not sure my life will ever be the same either?"

"Ooh, I forgot the most important thing." She slid off the leather mattress and opened another drawer.

"Better not be anything that hurts."

She waved a silk strip of fabric about her head. "It's a blindfold silly." Tying it gently over my eyes she sat beside me.

"Are you turned on by his power and domination, Rhylee?"

"I'm not sure about that yet. Maybe. He turns me on, big time. Don't you think he's hot as fuck?"

"Yeah, he's alright I suppose. But all this stuff. And you hate being bossed around. You turn into a cheeky bitch. If it doesn't turn you on, you shouldn't be doing it."

"Oh, this is supposed to be pleasurable for both parties. I won't know for sure until I'm his submissive. Books can only take you so far. This will take me there. He's not a sadist so he won't intentionally hurt me if that's what you're worried about?"

"He was going to chop Lan's fucking arm off a few weeks ago. You can't sweep that under the carpet!"

"I will never forget that, ever. But I've seen a different side to him now. I've no idea what the hell he was doing then, but that's not the man I know."

"Omg Rhy, listen to yourself. You can't say he's not the man you know, because you don't fucking know him. He could be a drug dealer. As I've said, he's shady as fuck. You know fuck all about him except for the size of his cock! You do realise he's blackmailing you?"

"I gave my word so I will have to see it through. As soon as the deed is done, I'm gone."

"That's going to be hard for you when you fancy the hole off him."

"It's impossible living with a guy you think is hot without developing feelings. I've had crushes before. I'll get over it?"

"So, you know the way you have these super sexual dreams. Has Gui taken centre stage yet?"

"Let's just say that in my dreams, Gui has spent a lot of time between my legs."

"He only wants to get his big cock wet Rhy!"

"Yeah, I get it. He only wants me for sex! And … What's the problem? You know I'm not into that crap, but what can I do?"

"Do you not want to have sex with him?" I thought for a minute.

"Of course I do, but I want meaningful sex."

"My lovely innocent Rhylee. We are going around in circles here. Do the deed and come home. Just don't tell me you're still waiting for your Prince Charming to come riding in to sweep you off your feet and live happily ever after. Life is not a fairytale hun. If you're looking for romance, move on. He told you so babe. It's not like he's going to hand you his balls on a silver platter!"

"It's not so much his balls I'm after, it's his heart."

"Well then, you're truly fucked. Right up the arse!

Promise me one thing and I'm not joking." I nod. "Please use a safe word."

"I promise. C'mon, let's get dressed and leave this to the professionals and go see Lan."

17

She looked up from her book as I slowly opened the door and her expression of curiosity changed to one of delight when she saw me standing there. She flung her book to the side and shot out of bed like a runner waiting at the starting line. She hugged and kissed the face off me like an excited puppy. It tugged on my heart so much.

"Rhylee, Rhylee I've missed you too much."

"Omg, where did you learn that? I can't believe it. It's only been a few days since I saw you last."

"I go to school now."

I turned to Evee. "I'm sorry I must be having blackouts or something. She knew no English when she came here."

Evee got down on the floor next to her and she went all shy hiding behind me. I took her hand and coaxed her around.

"Lan, this is my best friend, Evee. She's come to visit us for a few days." Evee held out her hand smiling and Lan shyly took it.

"Hello," she said, all coy. Evee spoke to her in Chinese and I was so envious she could.

"What did you say?"

"I asked if I could see her baby?"

Lan looked at me and I nodded. She ran to the cot and gently lifted her doll like it was a baby.

"Isn't that amazing? She's never had a doll in her life and we had to explain what it was and what to do."

"You've spent a lot of time with her and that rubs off on innocent children. They're quick learners and soak things up like a dry sponge."

"Yes, but I hardly spoke to her. I mean, I didn't teach her much English."

"Well, someone has and it shows how intelligent she is to pick it up so quickly."

"I'm embarrassed, she knows more English than I do Chinese."

"It's easier for children, don't worry about it. You don't have a teacher either."

I hugged Lan tightly, feeling like a proud parent. We played together for the rest of the day and then watched a family movie which fascinated her. She had us in giggles. Jumping up and patting her little hands on the screen then running behind it to see if they were hiding there. She was mesmerised because she thought they were real people. She sat between us and rested her head on my arm. I lifted it slowly to cuddle her. She took my hand and held it tightly before falling sound asleep. The days excitement was too much for her.

"Oh Evee, she's breaking my heart. Just look at the cuteness of her. How can people leave children so young to fend for themselves?"

"People don't care, hun, that's why we're working in an orphanage."

"As Gui's not here, she can stay in with me."

"Doesn't he allow that?"

"He said there was no point getting that attached. But sure, that went out the window the moment I met her. I think Gui has changed too but wouldn't admit to it. Best to keep on his side so he doesn't enforce his rules."

"I bet the only reason he didn't want you sharing your bed with her was so he could pop in whenever he wanted. I certainly wouldn't kick him out of bed for eating a packet of Tayto!"

"Evee, you have a boyfriend!"

"No harm in looking. I would never cheat on Josh."

"I asked you before and I'm curious to see if your answer is still the same?"

"Go on."

"Is Josh still your forever?"

"I guess. I do love him."

"Yeah, but are you in love?"

"I think so."

"You think? Marriage, you said never?"

"Was young and carefree then. Neither of us believed in walking up the aisle. You more than me. We've grown up. If he asked me, I'd probably say yes."

"Probably? That's not the answer I'd want to hear Evee."

"What about you? Your parents put you off marriage for life."

"Hahaha. I know. I'm not sure. If I met someone. The right person, then yes, I would. But you know me. I don't want to go out there to find him and he's not going to come knocking on my door."

"I have a good feeling about Gui."

"A good feeling or gut feeling?"

"Both."

"Come on Evee, I don't want to talk about this again!"

"Just hear me out."

"No! It's all crap!"

"That's rude! Just let me ask you this."

"Only if you promise you'll never mention it again. I want your hands and feet out in front. None of this crossing fingers and toes crap you do!"

"Seriously, I only did that when we were younger. I haven't crossed my fingers since I was a teen."

"You couldn't lie straight in the bed. So, think about it before I remind you."

"I don't need to. The last time I crossed my fingers was when my parents noticed the alcohol had been watered down and called us in for questioning. Mam made us promise that we never touched it so I crossed my fingers behind my back."

"Omg, so you did rob the alcohol and topped it up with water? You never told me that."

"Well, who did you think was doing it?"

"Honestly, I believed you when you said it wasn't you as did your parents."

"It wasn't actually for me. The girls from our class convinced me to fill a lemonade bottle. I poured a drop from each bottle of alcohol and they drank it before the school disco. I'd meet them at the top of the road and they'd be almost puking drinking it."

"Yuk, that must have been revolting?"

"I'd say so. Everything that was already opened in the drink's cabinet went into it. I even lashed in some holy water."

"Come to think of it, I remember them falling all over the dance floor and Father O'Shea phoning their parents to come and take them home. That they were a disgrace. I thought they were just being arseholes, knocking into everyone, but they were drunk, oh my God!"

"Yep, that's them. Sharron's mother made her jog all the way home while she drove behind. So then, how recently have I crossed my fingers?"

"When our parents took us out to dinner before we flew out. The waiter asked you how long you had been a vegetarian. I noticed you crossing your fingers when you said, "Since you were old enough to make that decision."

"Ah no, that's different. I never promised."

"It's the same! Hands and feet out front and promise." She reluctantly spread out her fingers and toes and promised.

"Right then. Let's sort this out now. If Gui asked you to marry him, would you?"

"But…"

"Yes or no Rhy."

"But you're not letting me explain."

"I just want a simple yes or no at this particular point in time."

"It's too hard."

"Lawd ham mercy child." That made me giggle. "It's a simple question!"

"Yes, okay. Yes, I would. Happy now. Let's leave it there. I'm going to bed. Are you coming?"

I lay awake hoping Gui would text, but nothing. My mind was racing wondering if he was out with her. I wasn't jealous. Just knowing how smug she'd be, breaking her neck to get in the door to tell me. He said he wasn't interested. But if someone flings themself enough times at you and is willing to do anything. That's a no-brainer. He's only human. It's not like he's having an affair or having secret liaisons behind my back. It's nothing to do with me although I'd be gutted if something happened. Only because he said he wasn't interested and that ship had sailed a long time ago. I don't think he'd shag anything that moved. But I didn't know him at all. I'm sure he has more self-control. Apparently, he was slowly losing that around me. The guy I fancy who keeps telling me what he wants to do to me is probably doing it to someone else right now. I'm his side chick. Or is she? I'm nothing! I need to get over myself. If I'm like this now, I can only imagine how I'd be if we were a couple! Bunny boiler alert ...... When this ends, I'm done and I'm taking Lan with me. Away from the 'mad hatters tea party' and unsubscribing from the shit show I've unwittingly signed up to!

18

Considering what went through my mind that night. I had a wonderful sleep and woke to find Lan wrapped around me snoring her little head off. We'd slept in my room because I was terrified Lan would discover the pool while we were sleeping. Now that's an idea. I'm sure Lan wouldn't have a clue what a pool was.

As soon as we had breakfast, I'd take her for a splash. I pressed the tip of her nose, "Boop."

She brushed my hand away giggling. It was amazing to see how easily she slotted into her new life. I didn't want to think about her future and had made up my mind that she was definitely going back to the orphanage with me. Unless Gui had a change of heart and adopted her? That's the life she deserved. Until then, she was going to live the life of Reilly! She sat up and rubbed her eyes, yawning.

"Good morning sleepy head," I whispered. She bent down and kissed my cheek.

I never knew what was on for breakfast. No matter, it was always a lovely surprise and delicious. Today it was pancakes which were one of my favourites. Evee came through the door carrying a bowl of sausages and bacon.

"Thought you might be here when I discovered the table was set for non-vegetarians."

"Hold on a second, you don't eat sausages or rashers anymore?" She stuffed a whole sausage in her mouth and groaned.

"Yeah, well about that. I didn't need to mention it before. And you're only finding out now because I'm here. Fell off the wagon as soon as you moved out."

"First of all, I didn't move out. Secondly, did you give up meat because you thought it would make me happy?"

"I was eating it all along, just not in front of you. Sorry. Anytime I said I was going to meet Josh to watch a movie, we were going for a McDonalds."

"I'm shocked. Not that you're eating meat, but that you had to hide it from me. I hate that you needed to do that."

"I just felt guilty, Rhy. You were so excited when I said I wouldn't eat meat again."

"Seriously, you're a big girl now and can make your own choices. It wouldn't bother me one bit."

She kissed my cheek then flopped beside Lan, kissing her too. She spiked a few pancakes with her fork. Piled them on her plate, topped with bacon and covered them with maple syrup. Lan's eyes boggled. She pulled on my sleeve and pointed to Evee's plate. "Would you like to try?" I asked. She nodded and sat back in her seat excitedly. Evee moved her plate in front of her, handing her a knife and fork smiling. She struggled to cut through the crispy bacon so I cut it for her. She opened wide and I spooned it into her mouth. She chewed for a minute then giggled, swung her legs and rubbed her tummy in a circular motion, "Yum yum, I like very much."

I cut the rest of her food into child-size pieces and she happily fed herself, crumbs and chunks flying all over the place... Oohing and ahhing after every mouthful.

"There's more on her than on her plate," laughed Evee.

"Ah, she's doing her best. It's not long since she was eating with her fingers."

We watched in silence as she casually spooned a bite into her mouth and methodically chewed and swallowed it. She stretched over and took a sausage and bit the top off. We stared at her intently waiting for a reaction. "Umm, I like very much."

After having our fill, we each lay on a sofa. "Oh God, I ate too much. I'm going to be the size of a whale leaving here," I said, rubbing my tummy.

Lan sat beside me and pointed at my tummy, "Baby?" I sat up embarrassed. "No, I ate too much honey."

"I'll say it again. Why on earth would you want a gazillion sofas," Evee asked.

"Funny, I asked that too the first day I got here. Don't think he was impressed either. I think it's safe to go swimming now, it's well over half an hour since we ate," I said to nobody in particular.

"Oh Rhy," she laughed. "You're such a dope. You don't have to wait thirty minutes after you've eaten. Swimming right after you've had something to eat isn't dangerous at all. Our mothers put that silly nonsense in our heads."

"Really? Omg. All these years I thought that was true. So it's only an old wife's tale?"

"Yep."

"I just can't take any more. Finding out you're not a vegetarian and that you can actually swim after eating. What next, I wonder?"

The three of us lazily strolled back to my room to search for swimwear. I handed Lan a tiny pink swimsuit and she looked quizzically at it on the hanger. Evee mimed someone swimming.

"Like she'd have a clue what that is."

I found the match and we all giggled when I came out and stood next to her. "Jesus Rhy, I never realised how sexy you are."

I took Lan's hand and walked to the elevator. We climbed in and I asked Lan to press number fifteen, which she did. "Ooh clever girl," I said. The lift began its ascent to the fifteenth floor of the building, our floor while Evee was here. Lan wasn't interested in her new surroundings at all until we opened the double doors to the pool. When we walked through, she panicked and held onto my leg.

"It's okay Lan," I said. "Don't be afraid. I wouldn't mind but she loves the bath."

Evee ran and jumped straight in causing the water to splash all over us. I giggled, hoping it hadn't frightened her altogether. Evee swam to the side of the pool and handed me a little child's doughnut ring. I sat down and immersed my legs in the water. Lan copied me. She kicked her feet up and giggled when Evee pretended to get all wet. I slid in and held out my arms to her. She hesitated for a second and then placed herself carefully in my arms wrapping her legs around me. I walked slowly around the pool and she panicked a little when the water rose to her shoulders. Evee swam passed which made her excited. I walked back to the side and pulled the two inflatables into the water, placing her in the smaller one. She immediately started flipping her feet and when she realised it made her move, there was no stopping her. I sat in mine and followed her around, just enjoying how happy she was. A child's laughter can help you forget anything. "Where's the swan one we had the last time?" I asked as Evee swam past on her back.

"I'll check the storage room." As she climbed the steps, a member of staff walked in carrying the inflatable swan followed by a second pushing a drinks trolley. We all stopped what we were doing and watched as they fussed over whatever was on the trolley. The swan was placed in the pool with a bow and a smile. Lan thanked her in Chinese followed by my feeble attempt. I was quite sure they giggled, politely. They arrived and left in complete silence.

"I don't mind saying this Rhy. But all this special treatment, room service and glorious food and alcohol. I just feel there's going to be an extortionate bill coming at the end of it."

"Hahahaha, that's funny, imagine." We had such a great time and it did feel like a five-star holiday break. Just seeing Lan's delighted face floating by, sipping her pink drink through a curly straw was priceless. Until now I had always wondered what a life surrounded by luxury was like. For a long moment, I wondered what it would be like to be married to Gui instead of his plaything. I looked down at my hands and gasped. "Jesus, I hope these wrinkles come out?"

We sat on the loungers as I dried off Lan when Daiyu came in. She held out her hand to Lan. "What are you doing?" I asked.

"I'll take her for her bath now."

"It's okay, I'll do it."

"I have my instructions to look after Lan while Miss O'Mahony is visiting."

"Thank you Daiyu, I will take care of her." For a moment we silently exchanged determined expressions. But I was adamant about holding my corner. She smiled, bent her head and left.

"Right little Lady of the house, aren't we Miss Murphy? I don't think the boss is going to be happy that his instructions were ignored."

"Oh dear, I hope she doesn't get into trouble. But I can never spend as much time as I'd like when Gui is here. He says it's for my own good. That way I won't get too attached. I keep reminding numbnuts that she's coming with me when I leave."

"Yeah, like what the actual fuck would he know?" She hissed. I nervously looked about the room again for hidden cameras, wondering if he just heard me calling him numbnuts. "What's the matter Rhy? You look like you've seen a ghost?"

"I'm just trying to convince myself that he hasn't heard me slagging him off," I whispered. It's some coincidence that the inflatable swan was brought in two minutes after we said it."

"Sure what can he do, spank you?"

I shot her a knowing look. "Probably."

"Do you think he'll punish you for stopping Daiyu from doing her job?"

"I don't know is the answer and stop reminding me." I ran a bath for Lan in Gui's giant tub, filling it with bubbles. She giggled hysterically, bursting them with her finger. I washed her hair and blow-dried it with the Dyson. We changed into pj's and watched a movie in the den with giant bowls of popcorn. This time it was a Disney cartoon. I glanced at my phone, but nothing. As I put it down it pinged. I was smiling before I even opened the message.

Disgusted it was only Evee. "Stop checking your damn phone every minute like a lovestruck teenager!"

I threw the phone on the cushion beside me and gave Evee a nasty look. She pretended not to notice but ended up fake choking on some popcorn to keep from laughing. Suppressing the urge to laugh myself wasn't easy, but I managed it perfectly. Movie over, we watched Lan play with her dolls. "Are you allowed to leave the building?"

"No."

"Do you want to? Aren't you bored?"

"Absolutely not. There's so much to do here and who would be bored living like royalty in a Skyscraper of all places."

"Just thought you'd like some fresh air?" I sat up. Light bulb moment. "Wait here."

"Rhy what's wrong."

"Nothing, just give me a minute." I ran from the room and Evee had to hold Lan back from chasing after me. Catching my breath, I handed her a hat, scarf and dressing gown and put Lan into hers.

"Eh, like it's ninety degrees in here Rhy. What's with the winter woolies?"

"Cover your eyes and trust me. You're going to be amazed." I took their hands and led them slowly from the room. The lift began its ascent to the rooftop. Once outside I pulled off Evee's scarf. "Tah Dah!"

She blinked a few times and gasped, "What the fuck, what the actual fuck Rhylee!" Lan held my hand tightly as I showed them every inch of the rooftop. I couldn't help smiling like it was mine.

We sat down on the beautiful white sofa and Lan snuggled into me. "I wonder what's going to appear this time?" Evee laughed.

"Nothing, because we're sober." We burst out laughing. We sat in silence, enjoying the peace and cool evening breeze. But his gorgeous face kept popping into my mind. I'm being tormented by thoughts of them together. I wish the fuck he'd get out of my head!

"How will you feel when you have to leave all this behind?"

"It doesn't belong to me so I'll be grand and plod on regardless."

"He doesn't belong to you either, but you'll miss him?" she said quietly.

"Yes, I will. I know so little about him and a part of me wants to run. Run and not look back. How could anyone have feelings for a man who didn't think twice about dismembering a child? Maybe it's not the first time? I could never be with someone like that. Of course, it's very easy to lust after him. Just look at him. Anyone with a pair of eyes can see he's a ride. He's like a God. Perfect in almost every way."

"Stop right there, you're thinking with your pussy!" I wince, it keeps coming back to the same thing. Some part of him is dead. What caused him to be shut off like this? Anyway, I need to stop thinking like I'd even have half a chance with him. Who the hell am I fooling, just me? Even Jingfei was stunning. And both are cut from the same cloth. Two beautiful people with neither an inkling of empathy nor compassion between them. But my head rules each time and thankfully will stop me from falling in love….

"None of this is your fault Rhy," Evee whispered, annoyed. Are you listening to me? Look at me," she demanded.

I turned my head slowly trying not to dislodge the tears welling behind my eyes. "Relax the cacks will you, I'm grand. There's nothing I can do but go along with it while I have Lan." Just then, Lan popped her head up and looked at me. "It's okay darling, go back to sleep." She raised her hand and gently wiped a falling tear from my cheek, then threw her arms around me. I held her tightly until she fell back asleep.

"You need to talk to Gui and find out when this ends."

"It hasn't even begun yet. He wants me fit and able before he even contemplates starting anything. I have something to tell you, which may upset you. But before I do, I want you to know that I've thought long and hard about it and I'd appreciate your support and understanding."

"What's going on?" She asks, full of suspicion.

"When I have Lan settled at the orphanage, I'm going home." She went to speak and I held up my hand and shushed her.. "Please just listen." She stood up and placed her hands on her hips. "I know it's just lust. But I am developing feelings for him too. I couldn't bear to stay here when I leave his house and him. Always wondering and looking over my shoulder. At least at home, I wouldn't be walking around Tesco's hoping I'd accidentally bump into him. Constantly wondering where he is and who he's with."

"Who he's shagging."

"Thanks, Evee! He'd just be a fantasy locked away forever in the deepest depths of my mind. Out of sight, out of mind. I know you understand where I'm coming from."

"Jesus Rhy, you can't fall in love with a man you're having doubts about."

"It's a sack of shit Evee. Just all fucked up!" Silence fell once again except for Lan's tiny snores.

"I'm exhausted and my brain is fried. I'm going to sleep in my room tonight. You're more than welcome to join us. There's plenty of room."

"Eh three in the bed etc, etc! I'll stay up here for a bit and do some pondering of my own."

I forced a smile. "Things are okay with you and Josh. Right?"

"Ah yeah, we're like pigs in shit."

"Ah hahaha. But seriously, you'd tell me if anything was wrong?"

"Of course, I can't hold my piss, as you know."

"Oh my goodness Evee, your language is getting worse."

"Okay Mother!" Kissing her cheek, I carefully scooched to the edge of the sofa trying not to wake Lan.

Riding the lift, I watched her tiny face and wished she was mine. I was told by my consultant that having stage five Endometriosis was associated with increased difficulty becoming pregnant or worse, infertility. Over the years I had several operations to remove scar tissue to alleviate the pain, each time, it was virtually impossible not to impact my fertility. Unfortunately, I was one of the unlucky ones. Something that will remain with me for the rest of my life. I lay Lan in the middle of the bed and went to brush my teeth.

My phone pinged. I jumped. My heart thumped. I looked in the mirror and ran my fingers through my hair. What the fuck was I doing, he couldn't see me, thank God. I collected the phone off the dresser and climbed carefully into bed not wanting to wake Lan. His name lit up on the screen and I smiled.

Gui: Hey.
Rhylee: Hey you.
Gui: How's things?
Rhylee: Grand. How's Jingfei?
Gui: Jingfei?? You want to talk about Jingfei?
Rhylee: Not really. Was just being polite.
Gui: Don't know how she is. She's out with some friends. Giving me a bit of a breather.
Rhylee: Oh, I see.
Gui: Have you missed me?
Rhylee: Are you being serious right now? Why would I miss you?
Gui: Because that's what people do and I miss you. Thought you'd feel the same.
Rhylee: Sure, why would you miss me?
Gui: I'm beginning to wonder…….
Rhylee: Oh.
Gui: I really do miss you. I miss watching you sleep.
Rhylee: Wait. What?

Gui: A guilty secret.
Rhylee: Are you serious?
Gui: I was checking on the patient. Mostly…
Rhylee: Mostly? That scares me even more….
Gui: Sometimes I'd sit there for hours just watching you sleep.
Rhylee: I don't know how I feel about that. Why?
Gui: Was drawn in.
Rhylee: Is that why there was a chair beside my bed?
Gui: Yep.
Rhylee: That's just creepy. You just sat there watching me drool?
Gui: Mostly.
Rhylee: What does mostly mean exactly? Do you realise how nuts that sounds?
Gui: Most nights I sat and fantasised. I had an overwhelming desire to put my hand between your legs to see if you were wet.
Rhylee: Fuck's sake, you didn't?
Gui: Absolutely not. But I masturbated so hard imagining my cock deep inside you. It was quite unlike anything I had ever experienced. Believe me, it has never happened before.
Rhylee: You mean the urge to fuck someone while they're unconscious?
Gui: No, masturbate. Never felt the need. I'm more than satisfied in that department. In fact, exquisitely satisfied.
Rhylee: Until now?
Gui: Yes.
Rhylee: Why now? What makes me so different?

Gui: Your innocence for a start.

Rhylee: How would you know anything about that? You didn't know anything about me then.

Gui: I knew the minute I saw you on the hospital bed.

Rhylee: Bullshit!

Gui: I know you haven't had much experience, sexually. I know you blush easily. I know you use bad language when you're nervous and I know you can be aroused even whilst sleeping.

Rhylee: Sure, it doesn't take a rocket scientist to know that. That's half of the female population.

Gui: Perhaps. But I don't think so. When you smile that smile my dick goes hard!

Rhylee: Omg!

Gui: That's why I didn't want Lan around. I was jealous she'd get all your attention. Or call it selfish.

Rhylee: Ah seriously. She's a baby. You'll be saying next you don't want to share me?

Gui: You're right, I don't want to share any part of you. You drive me to distraction and the ache to constantly touch you is unbearable.

Rhylee: I don't know what to say. I didn't realise and never would have known until now. You've hidden it very well.

Gui: Are you blushing?

Rhylee: Yes.

Gui: Rock hard right now.

Rhylee: Why?

Gui: My imagination runs riot where you're concerned. Even thinking about your mouth has me excited.

Rhylee: Easily excitable?

Gui: Just with you.
Rhylee: Can I ask you a question?
Gui: Of course.
Rhylee: When you said you knew I was aroused while sleeping, how? I know you said you didn't touch me. How else would you know?
Gui: The first night you were here. I hadn't anything suitable to dress you in for bed. I thought it would be okay because I wrapped you as tight as a bug. You probably got too warm and threw the covers off, revealing your breasts. I put the air-con on but it made your nipples rock hard. I swear, I almost lost my shit. All I could think about was sucking them. That was the only night I left you.
Rhylee: Omg …..
Gui: Sorry, I have to go. Jogging with a hard-on would be pretty painful. Chat soon.
Rhylee: Wait, how long will I be here for?

Gone…. Omg, what the actual fuck! Was he drunk? Surely that's the logical answer? He must have been because that was just bizarre! He said some things too before he left. But when we're together, he says nothing. But then again. We haven't been alone to have such conversations. As for what he just said about watching me sleep. Isn't that a little creepy? Omg, I hope I never farted. Oh, the embarrassment of it.

So, they weren't together. Well, not that particular time. With all the shit going around in my head, I didn't know whether to laugh or cry. I'm not usually the jealous type and it's only because I dislike the woman. The only reassuring thing is that he tried it already with her and it didn't work. No surprise there, she's a nasty cow! I wondered if she was feeling just as insecure as I was. "Yes." I sat up and fist-pumped the air immediately checking I hadn't disturbed Lan. She was exhausted and snoring delicately into the pillow. I rested against the headboard pulling the covers up under my chin and grinning like an eejit. He misses me. He said he missed me. Choosing to ignore all the freaky shit he'd said. Fucking hell …. he misses me! I slid under the covers with a huge smile plastered across my face and conked out.

It was annoying not knowing when he'd be back. Sitting up in bed I contemplated how I was going to react when I saw him.

Evee walked in carrying a breakfast tray. "Ooh look at the big smiley head on you, obviously on to your fella last night?" She settled the tray down carefully, handing me a cup of tea and a slice of toast. Lan sat quietly next to me munching on her cereal as she swiped through the pages of her book. "Sooo, what's the story? Any dick pics?"

"Sshh, don't talk like that around Lan, Jesus Evee!"

"I'm quite sure she doesn't know what a … 'dick' is," she whispered.

"Evee really!"

"Tell me for fuck's sake! Did you speak to him or not?"

"We texted."

"Annd."

"Okay, I know I shouldn't feel happy or smug."

"Go on."

"He said he misses me."

"So full of himself because he's texting, Bobby big bollocks!" I folded my hands over my chest and gave her a smug smile. She leaned back on her hands with a superior expression on her face.

"Told you," she said winking. "What else?"

"Em, he said he watched me while I was sleeping."

"What? When? How?" "Is he watching us now? She grabbed her dressing gown clutching it tightly to her chest as she scanned the room."

"Noo, it was during the first few days when I slept right through."

"I suppose there's nothing wrong with that. It's his house. Bit weird though. Is that it?"

"Yeah. Oh, I just happened to be naked."

"And there it is, the dirty bastard!" She whispered. "No fucking wonder he was in there watching you. Bet he had a wank too?"

"That's disgusting."

"Well, did he?"

"Yeah, he did!"

"I knew it! On you?"

"Nooo. Fuck's sake Evee, what do you get up to."

"How do you know?"

"Well, he said he didn't."

"You were unconscious for the first few days Rhy! Are you listening to me?"

"No, I'm not. You're talking crap." I stood up and paced the room, hands on hips.

"He's a sick bastard."

"Evee Stop, he got himself off and left. I believe him. End of. You've done nothing but give me an earache about him." As soon as the words were out, I was furious with myself for revealing something so personal even to my best friend. She looked at me accusingly and gave a small huff. For one horrible long moment, the room fell silent. I sat there watching her, knowing full well she was debating what to say.

"I'd fucking murder him if I knew he touched you without your consent or knowledge."

"I know you would and I love you for it. But please don't kill anyone. As gorgeous as you are, you'd look pretty shite in a prison-issued uniform!"

"Did he say when he and frosty knickers would be back?"

"Haha, frosty knickers, that's hilarious. No, he ended it suddenly saying something about it being painful having to jog with a hard-on!"

"Jesus, what the fuck were you talking about to give him a boner?"

"I swear, nothing. He says his imagination runs riot where I'm concerned. He's constantly in a state of arousal and usually able to control himself. Until now."

"Wow, you're causing the poor man some sexual tension. Bet he has big blue balls? Ah, he's sexually frustrated, you both are lol! Answer me this, does he make your vagina clap?"

"Honest to God Evee, where the hell do you get these from?"

"Well, does he?"

"Of course, he bloody does."

"If I'm still here when he gets back, I wonder if I'll feel the sexual tension between you?"

"I doubt it because I never did. It seems we've both tiptoed around our sexual attraction for each other."

"So, you never described his you know what," she whispered, turning her head to look at Lan.

"What's there to tell? It's big and lovely. You know I'm not particularly fond of them."

"Go on say it, the male appendage."

"But his is different."

"Did it look like a sausage roll? A bit of meat wrapped in puff pastry?"

"Eew Evee, no it didn't. It didn't have that extra bit of wrinkly skin."

"Ooh, then he's circumcised, wonder why?"

"That's exactly it. No wonder it looks so nice."

"Will it be as nice when he's fucking your mouth with it?"

"I won't do that and I'll tell him. What's so attractive about watching someone gag and drool all over your cock."

"That's the thing, they don't care what you look like or if you choke doing the deed as long as they come. Now, Josh is different. He knows not to shove it down my throat or place his hand on the back of my head. That's how he gets to have his cock sucked dry and balls like raisins."

"Oh Jesus Evee, that's hilarious. The things you come out with."

19

My phone pinged. I looked down and gulped. He's never texted during the day as much as I wanted him to. But he has now.

"So there's only one person that can be. What does he want?" I wasn't sure if I felt comfortable opening the message with Evee hanging over my shoulder.

"Em, a little bit of privacy, please. I pointed back to where she had been sitting before I got the message.

"Ahh, come on. We don't have secrets from each other."

"I know we don't, this is different."

"But."

"Evee, there's a limit to my patience and you're this close to crossing it. Back. Over. There. Now or I won't read it."

"You've been such a spoilsport since you moved into your palace!"

"Don't start me off. I'm not here by my own reconnaissance so stop trying to pop my last nerve!" I swiped the screen and read his text. Trying hard not to smile like a dick.

Gui

'Hey, I thought I might make it home tonight. Something has come up, unfortunately. Heading into another meeting now. Will try to message you later…

"So, what's the story?" she asked impatiently. I sighed and passed her the phone. "Can't believe he never mentioned it sooner," she said after reading the message. She lifted the phone and started to read again. As long as it's not his dick that's come up, you'll be grand."

"Honestly, you're such a dirty cow!" Lan sat on my lap pointing to the image in her book.

"I'm going for a swim, care to join me?" I looked up at her as she stood by the door.

"What's that look for?" She took my phone out of her back pocket and threw it on the bed beside me. As it landed it pinged.

"Evee, what have you done? You've guilt written all over your face."

"See you when I see you, hopefully not too soon." She squealed and ran. I opened the message.

Gui

'I don't know what to say. Only that it's taken me by surprise. I'm horny too xx

Omg, what the actual fuck! "Evee," I screamed. She must have messaged him while I was with Lan.

Evee

You need to hurry back and sort me out. I'm sooooo horny. I need your BIG Dick inside me x

I sat there in complete shock. WTF! My face turned red as I re-read it. What the hell am I going to say? I'm going to kill her with my bare hands. She's dead! I took Lan's hand. "Let's go find Aunty Evee," I said, trying to stay calm. I pushed open the huge doors and searched her out.

She stared at me from the middle of the pool. Our eyes locked. I looked at her hurt and angry at the same time.

"Get out of the pool now."

"No way. You'll murder me."

"How could you Evee? It's not even funny. I'm angry and pissed off."

"Are you angry with me because I said what you couldn't?"

"Evee, you had no right to do that. You don't even know him, we don't know him to joke about something like that. Now he looks like a fool."

"A horny fool actually," she giggled.

"STOP!" I shot her an angry look. She gazed at my disappointed face and realised she'd gone one step too far. "I think you should leave. This is another one of your messes I have to sort out!" I turned and paused at the door and faced her.

"What you did was cruel! I'm disappointed in you, Evee." I think she was startled by my tone more than anything else. I was fuming in the hallway when I pulled the door closed behind me.

Instead of going back to the room, I took the elevator and went up to the rooftop. Knowing Evee all my life, I knew she'd be pissed off with me for not thinking what she did was hilariously funny. And it may take an hour or two for her to come around. I had plenty of time to wait. He said he was going into a meeting but I couldn't leave it like this. I looked to the sky hoping he'd tell me what to say.

I sat there distraught for about thirty minutes before I gathered my thoughts, Daiyu appeared. "Miss Evee has left and she asked me to give you this. She handed me a folded piece of paper with Evee's scrawl on the front of it. I'll take Lan for her lessons now if that's okay with you?"

"Oh, okay. Yes, thank you." She smiled at me as she held out her hand to Lan. "I'll bring you some calming tea."

"Ah no, it's okay. I'm sure you have more important things to do."

"I would like to."

"That's very kind, thank you." She bowed and went to leave when Lan shook her hand free and ran back and hugged me. I held her tightly. She's such a clever loving child with great empathy. It's so important to be a good listener and show empathy even at such a young age. I kiss her and wave her off. I opened Evee's message.

'I'm sorry. I acted like a dick. Please forgive me x.'

I'll deal with her later. Right now, I had more pressing things on my mind. As I contemplated what to say, my phone rang and Gui's name lit up the screen. It was him. He's fucking ringing me. Fucketyfuck, what the actual fuck was I going to say? My heart was racing. If I didn't answer he'd know I was purposely ignoring him. Maybe he'd think I was in the shower or something. It continued to ring. Shit! Ring Ring.

Just stay calm.

"Hello."

"Hi there," he purred. Oh, sweet Jesus, he was acting all weird. I bit the inside of my cheek as I waited for him to talk.

"So… you're horny?" He said. I winced.

"Gui, before you say anything further, I didn't send that message. It was Evee. I'm so sorry." He stayed silent.

"Please say something," I whispered. I held my breath. "I see." He inhaled sharply. "I should have known. You're not at all the kind of woman who talks like that. But I have to be honest. It made me hard when I read it." I gulped and swallowed the lump in my throat. I could hear music and noise in the background.

"That's some meeting you're at. Where are you?"

"I'm at a bar. I couldn't sit there with my dick misbehaving. I had to make an excuse to leave and hide my boner with my briefcase." I stifled a giggle.

"I see. Do you wish I *had* said it?"

"Yes."

My heart was hammering in my chest and I smile. The noise faded in the background. He must have left or moved somewhere more private. "If it makes you feel any better, I am horny." I scrunch my eyes shut. I couldn't believe I just said that. "Are you there? Mork calling Mindy."

He chuckled, "Yes I'm here and I wish you were too." My tummy did little somersaults. I punched the air.

"Are you flirting with me?"

"How would you feel if I was?"

"I'd feel hot and fuzzy."

"I hope that's a good thing?"

"It's the best feeling in the world." I could imagine him smiling at the other end of the phone. "Haven't you experienced it?"

"I can't say that I have. I wish we had met under different circumstances."

"Why? I frowned.

"I think I would have been a different man had I met you sooner. Things have passed me by, and I have accepted the path I've chosen."

Again, my heart hammered in my chest because I knew what he was going to say next. I didn't want the words to pass his lips. I scrunched my eyes tightly and held my chest. I was tethering on the edge of the sofa. Daiyu appeared and placed a tray in front of me and I wished it was a bottle of vodka. All the tea in China was not going to calm me down!

"You know that I'm attracted to you? That all I think about is fucking you. I'm sorry if that sounds crude but it's the only way to describe it. I dreamt of nothing but those lips around my aching cock. Bending you over and fucking you. God, I've wanted you so much I've had to constantly disguise a raging hard-on. But I don't want you to confuse this with anything other than sex. I'm not after a relationship Rhylee," he continued. Again, those words cut me like a knife. "I know I've said it many times. We are not dating. I just want to fuck, no strings. It's been hard since I've met you, no pun intended. I struggle without sex. I'm a highly motivated sexual person. I have needs. They need to be met. Since meeting you, they haven't. I haven't fucked anyone since you arrived."

"I don't want a relationship either."

"But I know you want the romance and the ring?"

"I do. But not with you. I know there's no future with Gui Lee so I won't pursue it. I don't chase men, never have, never will."

"Then what do you want?" I bit my bottom lip.

"Just say it, Rhylee. Tell me what you want. Please."

"I want you to fuck me."

He inhaled sharply and the line went quiet. I just wanted to drop the phone like it was a hot potato. Oh God, I was so embarrassed. Did I just say that out loud?

"I like it when you talk like that," he eventually said.

"A good girl being naughty. The best of both worlds. I can feel myself getting hard. Where are you?"

"On the rooftop."

"I take it you're alone?"

"God yeah."

"What are you wearing?"

"Lounge wear."

"Touch yourself."

"Wait. What, now?"

"Put your fingers in that pretty pussy and tell me how it feels."

I gasped and looked around, my heart pounding. I'd never felt so aroused. I pushed my hand into my panties and touched my pussy. "I'm wet," I breathed heavily.

"Fuck. How wet?" I could hear how aroused he was.

"Soaking."

"Fuck."

"Is your cock hard?" He gulped. My face went scarlet.

"Rock fucking hard. I want you to slip two fingers into that swollen pussy. Nice and slow."

I bit my bottom lip as I lay down and spread my legs as wide as possible. "My greedy pussy just sucked my fingers right in." I could hear his breathing catching. "Are you holding that big cock of yours?"

"Yes."

"Please tell me you're not still at the bar?"

He let out a guttural laugh and the tone of his voice aroused me further.

"I'm back home." I could hear his breathing picking up. "I want you to add another finger and fuck that pretty cunt like a good little girl."

The third finger barely fit and I could feel it stretching me out. How the fuck will that big cock of his fit? I panted heavily and my heart beat erratically.

"Jesus Rhylee, you're not even here and you're killing me." I could imagine the muscles in his shoulders tense as his stomach contracted with each tug of his hand as he got harder and harder. I quickly pulled my top up over my boobs and rolled my eyes when the cold air hit them. Oh sweet Jesus, it felt so good. My fingers were back inside me and we were both breathing heavily now. I could hear our strokes getting harder and faster and my body was on fire as I felt myself edging closer. I could hear how aroused he was and wished he was inside me.

"Oh fuck Rhylee, I'm almost there."

I put the phone on speaker, grateful I was on the roof. Hearing his deep grunts is inexplicably one of the hottest sounds I've ever heard. Pumping myself hard I twisted my nipple which took me over the edge.

"Gui, I'm there, come with me," I panted.

His breathing was rushed and heavy now. He let out a deep moan. "Fuck yeah," which echoed out over the rooftops.

I had no words. I could hear his breathing slowly subsiding. When my body ceased convulsing from the orgasm, I was soaking. The muscles in my thighs were burning from the effort of spreading them so wide. I pulled my top down and slowly sat up trying to control my panting.

"Fuck Rhylee," he whispered sexily. "That was fucking hot."

"Yes, it was."

"Did you come?" I blushed and felt the warmth of it as it crawled up my neck to my cheeks.

"Yes, it was unbelievable."

"You are unbelievable. Are you okay?"

"I'm in shock if I'm honest."

"Why?"

"I've never done anything like that before."

"Get used to it. I'll have you removing your panties at the restaurant when I take you out."

"Oh no," I frowned. Are you crazy? I couldn't do that. I'm a good girl."

His husky laugh made my stomach flutter.

"Are you sure about that? Wait and see. I have to go."

"Until next time," I giggled.

"Until next time, goodbye Rhy."

Did he just call me Rhy? Nobody but Evee has ever called me that. That's strange. I scorned myself out loud, stop making a big deal out of nothing. I poured myself a tea and snuggled into the sofa. So what happens now? I've more or less said we can fuck with no strings attached. So playing by the rules doesn't count anymore. No emotional ties. He was going to fuck me anyway as his sub, but now he's not on the clock. He made no secret that he was just using me for sexual gratification. His terms. What have I done?

20

Has he ever been in love, I pondered. He said his path was set. What does that even mean? It's like he's accepted that he won't find that special person. He just hasn't met her yet. I'm sure he's met loads of gold diggers only interested in his money. Why do self-respecting women chase men just for money? I felt sorry for them too. What a horrible way to live. Is that why he doesn't want to fall in love? I sat there and grieved for him. Nobody should be alone. I didn't want him to regret his decision. I didn't know much about Gui or his company, only what Evee said. I Google Gui Lee with two 'E's and wait for it to load.

Gui Lee - CEO of Lee Corporation & Holdings

Estimated worth - One Hundred and Twenty billion dollars.

Media, Banking, Property, Steel - Iron

One hundred and twenty billion dollars. Are you fucking shitting me! Holy fuck. Wait, what. I frown as I read it again and blink. Hmm, so that's what they're after, I guess. I just want him and his big, beautiful cock. I smile and sip my tea. His dick is out of this world. Not that I've seen many. Then the memory of what I said pops into my head. Oh shit. I can't face him after telling him that I want him to fuck me.

Stupid, stupid woman!

Makes it worse when I'm ridiculously shy in his company to the point where I feel uncomfortable and breathless. Sure I'm self-conscious in social situations the odd time I do go out. I can't help it. Until I calm the fuck down and relax, I'm quite closed off. Some people perceive it as being standoffish or unfriendly. Being shy doesn't mean I hate meeting new people. Shyness is a crippling disease many don't understand. It can be stifling sometimes. Didn't he say that was one of the things he found attractive about me? Or was it my innocence? Isn't it true that guys are inclined towards shy girls because it's inbuilt in their psyche to protect and they love the feeling?

I finished my tea and took the tray downstairs. Still hadn't a clue where the kitchen was so brought it to the lounge. Daiyu appeared. "I'm sorry, I didn't know where the kitchen was to drop this back. Thank you, it did the job." She smiled.

"You're very welcome. It's my special brew. When you're ready, Mrs Lee would like to see you."

My eyes bugged in my head. Is he fucking married! "Did you say, Mrs Lee?"

"Yes." She noticed my confused expression and giggled. I blinked, too shocked to speak. "Mrs Lee, Gui's mother."

I put my hand to my chest and let out a sigh of relief. I looked down at what I was wearing and we both scrunched up our faces. After what I'd just been doing on the rooftop, I needed a shower.

"I'll just jump in the shower."

"No time, just put on a pretty dress. It will make you feel better." I nod.

"Don't you worry about anything? Mrs Lee is a wise woman and not scary like Mr Lee."

I walked back to the room in a daze. Bloody hell. I'm going to meet his mother. Does he know? I'm sure if he wanted this meeting to take place, he would have introduced us sooner. She's doing it behind his back. I text him.

Help!! Your mum wants to see me. Does she know anything? What do I say if she asks why I'm still here? This is just one big pile of crap! Like what do I say?

He called straight away. "Hi."

"Hello." I frown.

"Does she know anything?"

"Such as?"

"Our arrangement for a start."

"No. Of course not. Relax. I'll call her."

"N-no, don't you dare? As long as she knows nothing, I'll be fine."

"Don't tell her anything either."

"Oh my God. Right. So I can't tell her that her son wants to fuck me senseless then?" He laughs and I giggle too.

"You can tell her that from the very first moment I saw you, I wanted my cock deep in you."

"Oh, okay. She'll like that." I can tell he's smiling. "You big goofball."

"You know what I mean. Smart Cookie waited until I left too."

"I blush when I lie and you know I talk crap when I'm nervous. She'll know."

"Look, I know my mother. She's just being nosey. Honestly. Try not to worry. She's mad about you anyway."

"Don't you mind me talking to her?"

"Sure what can I do from here?"

"That's not what I asked Gui." He paused for a moment.

Choosing his words wisely.

"I'd prefer it if you didn't. Only because I know my mother will interfere and try to push us together."

"That's crazy. Why would she do that? I'm sure she wants her son to marry well. Marry a princess, pop star or actress?"

"No, you'd be wrong. She's met them all and hasn't time for any of them. She calls them money-grabbing whor… well you get my drift. She wants a wholesome girl, just like her."

"Wait. You've dated a princess?" I gasp.

"Two."

"Wow. If I didn't feel like crap before, I certainly do now! Okay, I could talk forever but your mother is waiting. Wish me luck."

"Just think before you talk."

"No shit Sherlock!"

"Hey, keep talking like that young lady and you'll end up over my knee and not be able to walk for a day or two."

"Blah, blah whatever."

He laughed, not a chuckle, but a deep, throaty belly laugh.

"Hmm, I'm glad I amuse you."

He laughed even harder. I shouted 'little shit' down the phone. "Goodbye, Gui," I said sharply and immediately hung up. My phone pinged.

Gui
You're hot when you're angry. Little pocket rocket ...

For the first time I was appreciative of the clothes Gui filled my wardrobe with. I ran my finger along the rails before stopping on a blush pink skater dress. It was one of my favourites. Does she know he bought all these clothes for me? I slipped on a pair of white pumps and ran my fingers through my curls and washed my hands. Oh shite, what does she want? Oh my fucking God, does she know I was a total hoe with her son on the rooftop? I looked in the mirror. Cute is how I looked.

I walked slowly back to the lounge and Daiyu turned the hoover off when I entered the room. "You look very pretty. Are you ready?"

"Do you know why she wants to see me?"

"I'm sure it's just to thank you and say hello?"

"Oh okay."

"You're such a little worrier, aren't you? I will give you stronger tea next time." We both giggled. She glanced at her watch as the elevator doors opened... "Four thirty." She tapped her watch. "I will come back for you at six o clock because Mrs Lee needs her rest." I nodded.

My tummy flipped as the elevator doors opened and we stepped straight into her living room, completely dominated by everything floral. You could say Laura Ashley had designed it. The room oozed elegance and opulence with French-style furniture and delicately placed ornaments made me feel instantly at ease. In hues of deep blues and white, it was bright and calming. Boasting an oversized white fireplace, it was the focal point of the whole room. But the pièce de résistance was the lighting. A French country-style chandelier with a weathered washed cream finish complimenting the floral-inspired bobeches and delicate crystal bead strands. It was stunning and unlike anything I'd ever seen. It was the perfect room for relaxing. When I eventually lifted my chin off the floor, I noticed Mrs Lee sitting in a wingback chair with her feet resting on a matching ottoman, watching me. "Oh, I'm so sorry. Your beautiful room took my breath away. You must think I'm so rude. Hello." I smile meekly.

"Not at all dear, Rhylee, isn't it?" I nod nervously.

"Yes, I'm Rhylee."

She smiles as she looks me up and down. "Hello." She gestures towards the sofa. "Please, sit."

"Mrs Lee, would you like anything before I go," Daiyu asks.

"I'm fine, Rhylee, would you like some tea, a water perhaps?"

"No thank you. Daiyu has spoiled me already with her wonderful brew."

"Brew," Mrs Lee inquired.

"Sorry, tea. We call it a brew back home." She smiles. She has this warm, motherly feeling about her. Black hair piled elegantly in a bun and wearing minimal make-up. She's stylish wearing a Chanel suit and pearl earrings. Very attractive in her early sixties I'd say. This woman hadn't one grey hair on her head and her face was hardly lined. What the actual fuck?

"How are you Mrs Lee after everything?" I put my hand out to shake hers and she took it gently and patted the back of it. Her hands were so tiny. "Nice to meet you under better circumstances. I'm sorry I haven't been to check on you sooner."

"Don't you worry my dear, we all know who is to blame for that," she sighs. "And please call me Genji."

"So how are you feeling? I'm hoping you're much better," I asked.

"I'm on the mend and have healed wonderfully. Thanks to Gui who had a doctor on call and insisted on having a nurse move in. I was ready to go back home to my apartment sooner but wanted to see you before I did. I thought I would do it now, with Gui being away."

I rolled my eyes and flopped back against the sofa. "Why doesn't he want us to meet?"

"He has his reasons I'm sure but enough about him, how are you?"

I blew out a defeated breath. "I'm good, confused." She chuckled. "Why confused, dear?"

"It's all still a bit of a shock, to be honest."

"I hope my son has been nothing but a gentleman towards you?"

"Of course, he has." Hoping I wouldn't blush. "But."

"But,"she asked. Her eyebrow raised slightly.

"I don't know how to put it. We seem to argue and shout quite a lot."

"Dear God." She puts her hand on her chest.

"Are you okay dear? I didn't bring up my son to raise his voice to any woman."

"Oh, I'm fine. Don't get me wrong, I can be quite a handful. But he is in a league of his own! Her eyes held mine and she smiled softly.

"At last."

"Sorry?"

"At last, someone who's not afraid to stand up to him. All his previous lady friends put up with his domineering nature. I'm sure it was for the money."

"They all left?"

She nodded. "Thankfully. Except for Jingfei." I rolled my eyes. "I take it you two have met?"

"Yes, we have. Lovely woman."

"Indeed," she smiled. "She's a hard pill to swallow, alright. Not to everyone's taste." She winked and I get the feeling that I'm going to like this tough lady. "One word of advice. Don't let her get under your skin. If she finds a weak spot she doesn't let go. Only for family history, I'd have given her a left hook myself." I giggled.

"So tell me Rhylee. She narrowed her eyes. "Do you find my son attractive?"

My eyes bug. "I'm not going to lie. Yes, he's a very handsome man."

"Hmm," she smiled. Seeing right through my bullshit. Christ, if she even knew how fucking aroused, I get just thinking about him.

"But he's not my type." I knew she was fishing so I tried to convince her I didn't want to ride his cock. How the fuck do I get myself into these situations? I got a vision of his face between my legs and smile, crossing them to relieve the pending tingle. It's fucking ridiculous how fucking perfect he is.

She reached over and tapped my hand and said with a knowing smile, "Of course he's not your type dear." I faked a laugh to cover my lies and look away, embarrassed she knew I was lying through my teeth. "There's nothing to be embarrassed about dear. I sense these things. Plus, the look on your face gave away your true feelings. I think you're the perfect match for my son."

"Are you mad?" I smirked.

"No dear, not yet." She smiled sarcastically. "And I know my son will eventually see this himself. Over the years he's had to build this wall to protect himself. Each year it gets higher and higher."

"That's sad," I whispered.

"It is but I know you're the one to bring it crashing down."

"Oh, you're wrong."

"Am I?"

"I'm not sure how you know this but myself and Gui are completely different people, wanting different things. He'll end up with a rich heiress, I'm sure?"

"Some of the women he's dated are after one thing, the very idea of marrying for money is repugnant to me. Someone once said to me, you cannot marry into a higher rung on the ladder. I don't believe this and neither does Gui. Whether they are rich or poor it has no bearing on whom he will love. What were the odds of you two meeting?"

"Why would a man like Gui want to marry an Irish hick like me? Anyway, as I said, I don't fancy him and he doesn't find me one bit attractive either."

"I know you aren't interested in his wealth. I know every woman who tried to snag him was and failed, thankfully. Women want to be with him because of his wealth and is unattached. They think they can turn the bachelor." I listened on, eager to learn anything about him. "Gui hasn't had a serious girlfriend in years. He's had nothing but flings. But now that you're here, I can see he's a different person. You bring out the best in him. He's been so secretive about you but the fact he brought you here shows he's opening up. He hasn't dated anyone since you arrived either. That's not like Gui at all. He's always had someone on the side. Most times he's just using them for sex." I blushed. "When he gets what he wants he dumps them."

Omg. I'm one of those women I wanted to scream out loud. "One piece of advice from an old woman. Keep your emotions close to your chest Rhylee. Let him find his way. He thinks he doesn't want or need a relationship and one sniff and he's gone. We don't want to scare him off, now do we. Let him fall for you. I have eyes everywhere and apparently, he can't take his off you. His heart is already melting my dear because of you. And I couldn't be happier."

"I'm not sure what your *eyes a*re telling you. But I can assure you that Gui has no interest in me. When I'm fully recovered, I'll be gone from here and will never see him again." I frowned.

"I hope you're wrong dear. But if this doesn't go the way I want it to, I hope we can stay friends if that's okay with you. We can meet for lunch, dinner or even shopping. What do you think dear?"

"Yes, I'd like that."

"I will never forget, nor will Gui, what you did for me. It takes a really special person to do what you did." Her phone rang. "Excuse me dear, I need to take this. It's Wwan, my hairdresser." I rose from the sofa to leave. "No, no please stay dear. It won't take long."

While she took the call, I looked at all the photographs. Most were of Gui growing up. My God, he's such a fucking ride. One was Gui shaking someone's hand and smiling directly into the camera.

Do you realise you're the most handsome man I've ever seen?

Then there were lots of him with a little blonde boy around the same age. I noticed one at the back and stretched over to pick it up. It was him and Jingfei and wow, how handsome they both were! I hate to admit it, but they looked amazing together. She's stunning. There was a small black and white photo that showed a young couple, perhaps in their twenties, standing outside a church holding a baby. I'm sure it was Mr and Mrs Lee and Gui. "Rhylee," Genji called. "Would you like to join me at the hairdressers tomorrow and then we can have lunch afterwards?"

"I'd love to but I'm not allowed to leave the building."

She put her finger up, "Yes Wwan, book me and Rhylee in for 1.30 tomorrow. See you then darling."

I walked back to the sofa with a frown. "I really can't go, Gui will lose his reason."

"My dear, while the cats away ... what can he do over in London? What's the point of living to a ripe old age if you can't enjoy yourself?"

"It's what he'll do to me when he gets back."

"Leave it to me dear."

Just like Nanny McPhee, Daiyu appeared. "I'll take you back now, Mrs Lee needs her rest."

"Seriously Daiyu, you don't have to follow Gui's instructions and 'molly coddle' me. I've had plenty of rest. Can you let John know I'll need the car tomorrow at one o'clock? Rhylee and I are having our hair done."

"I will indeed. Any particular one?"

"The Bentley will do, easier for me to get in and out of." Daiyu made a signal that my time was up. I kissed Genji on the cheek. "See you tomorrow so. That's if Gui's goons don't catch me first."

She laughed. "Those are my goons. Gui doesn't have any. He insists I have security 24/7."

"Well, they're not very good at securing anything after what happened to you, I scoffed."

"I'm afraid I was to blame. I pulled the wool over their eyes. I'm quite smart for an old one."

"Okay so, see you tomorrow."

As I was leaving, I noticed a block of wood standing against the door which looked exactly like the one they were going to use on Lan. What the fuck? My heart stopped. Oh my God, does she know? Is she just like him?

For fuck's sake I was so confused. I paused at the escalator and turned. I looked at her and smiled. She had the most angelic smile I'd ever seen. This was obviously where Gui got his good looks from. No, she hasn't a clue. She has no idea her son is a monster. A monster she's trying to hook me up with.

21

Back in my room I lay on the bed and sighed. What on earth just happened? She wanted me to date Gui!

It hit me like a shit tonne of bricks. My phone rang and Gui's name lit up the screen.

"Speak of the devil," I said upon answering. "Two calls on the same day Mr Lee, people will talk."

"Very funny pocket rocket, what did my mother have to say? I'm not in the mood for this fucking shit today."

"Be nice," I giggled. "You won't believe me."

"Go on."

"She wants us to date and if she had her way, we'd be married with 2.5 kids." I bit my bottom lip trying to stifle a laugh.

"You're not serious? Did she say that to you? She's fucking unbelievable!"

"Yes."

"I don't know what to say, I'm in shock, to be honest. What did you say?"

"I said, 'You were very handsome but not my type."

"Is that true?"

"Yes. No." He sighed. "I said you didn't find me attractive."

"Well, we both know that's not true."

"And you'd be happier marrying someone from the same background."

"Is that what you think of me?"

"Well, no, I said that to put her off. I honestly didn't know what else to say. There are no flies on her. You won't like the next bit."

He exhaled loudly, obviously annoyed. "Go on."

"She's taking me to lunch tomorrow."

"She's whaat!"

"I told her I couldn't but she wasn't having any of it."

"I see. Once she has her mind made up there's no changing it."

"So I can go?"

"Well yeah. Although I'm not happy about it. But I can't do anything from here."

"Haha, that's what she said."

"Just so you are aware. If people know who she is, be prepared for photographers waiting outside."

"Oh no, I can't."

"Her team will be there so it won't be too bad."

"Team," I asked nervously.

"Security. She's up to something alright."

"Yes, she's trying to marry you off."

"Yes, I see that. She knows better and that I'm not looking for a wife," he admits softly.

"Nor am I looking for a husband," I mutter.

"We both know that's a lie."

"Get lost. It isn't."

"She'll be hell bound on playing matchmaker. Where is she taking you?"

"I don't know. My head is fried. Honestly not sure it can take much more."

"There's more."

"Tell me," he mutters flatly.

"We're having our hair done first."

"Of course you are! With Wwan?"

"Yes, that's the one."

"She's fucking unreal."

"Stop, she's just being nice."

"She knows fine what she's doing. Just out of interest, would you marry me if I asked?"

"Huh, em, well I."

"Good grief woman, it's a simple yes or no."

"It would be a NO then."

"Why's that?"

"After what you were going to do to Lan. Makes me sick every time I think about it. And that's not something you want in your head."

"I see. I'll talk to you later after I've dealt with my mother. Goodbye."

"Bye then." I imagined he wasn't too impressed with what I just said.

I opened the doors to the wardrobe and looked at all the beautiful clothes. What will I wear tomorrow? I'm going to make sure I look amazing just in case there are photographers. I secretly hoped I'd get papped and the image gets back to Gui. I'll wash and blow dry my hair tomorrow so it's extra bouncy. Or will I straighten it? Yes, something different. Then I remembered Wwan. Maybe I'll see what he has in mind. I pulled out a vintage pink skater dress. Far more grown up than the one I was wearing. The fitted bodice was covered in a fine gold brocade overlay aiming to draw attention to the waist while the bottom was a box-pleated skirt. Stunning. I could either go for trainers or heels. I decided I didn't want to look particularly cutesy or girly, but more sophisticated. The thing with skater dresses is that they can help accentuate your legs whether you're short or tall. Thank God! I'll take all the help I can get.

I opted for heels. I found the perfect match. A pair of nude LV square toe block heel pumps and a matching bag. I found myself getting excited. Was it because I was going outside? There was a gentle tap on my door. "It's okay, come in," I called.

The door opened and Daiyu stepped into the room, a Dior carrier bag in her hand. "Mrs Lee thought these might come in handy for your outing tomorrow?" She smiled.

"Thank you, what is it?" I asked as I peered into the bag.

"I'd say it's some essentials," she said, winking. She left me alone and closed the door gently behind her. I sat down and emptied the bag onto the middle of the bed and giggled. It was Dior skincare and make-up. That woman is one in a million.

To take my mind off everything I went down to the lounge or as we now call it, the toy room. There was every toy a child could want. No idea where it all came from. I'd like to think it was Gui, but I know better. The improvement I cannot help seeing in Lan has given me hope in Gui for his patience. I know he frowns when he walks in here because there are toys everywhere. Until now, his home has only seen order not chaos. I told him it wasn't Lan's fault. Tell whoever is buying all these toys, to stop! She was sitting at the table with her book and looked up when I entered the room. She jumped right off the chair and into my arms, squealing "Rhylee, Rhylee."

This child just makes me feel warm and fuzzy and I know everyone who meets her feels the same way. She takes my hand and pulls me over to one of the sofas, pushing all the cuddly toys off and tapping the cushion for me to sit. Once she saw I was comfortably seated she climbed up onto my lap. She looked sadly at my bandaged arm and pointed.

"I'm sorry," she whispered and burst into tears. I hugged her tightly.

"Sshh now Lan, it's okay. I'm fine," I said, trying my best to comfort and reassure her. She buried her face in my shoulder and cried uncontrollably. "There, there," I whispered.

She peeked up at me, her normally perfect hair in knots and her eyes red from crying. "They said if I didn't get your bag we wouldn't eat and it would all be my fault."

"Sshh, nobody blames you. I'm glad it happened.

Otherwise, I'd never have met you." She sobbed again. "Go get your hairbrush and I'll fix your hair." She wiped her nose on the back of her hand and sniffed. "And get some tissues too, I giggled." I cupped her pudgy cheeks and kissed her nose. "You're just so cute I want to eat you all up."

She hugged me again and then slid down my legs. I looked about the room and gasped. Jesus, if Gui was here his last nerve would be popping. I kicked off my shoes and began putting all the toys back into the storage baskets. Lan rushed back in, brush in hand and stopped in her tracks. I could see the confused look on her face like we were taking her newfound toys away.

"Let's tidy up all the toys you're not playing with and put the babies to bed." Reassured, she was eager to help.

At twelve-thirty, I sat on my bed trying to control my nerves. Dressed to impress, my hair and make-up were impeccable. Soon I'd be out of this building. There was a tap on my door. I took a deep breath to calm my nerves and opened it expecting to see Daiyu. Instead, I found one of the goons. "Mrs Lee is waiting for you. If you'd like to follow me, please. May I just mention too, if anyone should attempt to talk to you or ask questions, please ignore them. I know this may not be in your nature to be rude, but it's a necessity when associating with the Lee family. Do I make myself clear?"

I nodded. My nerves were already shattered and although he was humble and spoke in a gentle tone, it did nothing to settle them. I was close to bursting into tears. Getting upset about it though wasn't going to change anything, so I took a deep breath, forced a smile and followed him.

The chauffeur held open the door which made me feel awkward. It was uncomfortable being treated like royalty when you're just as ordinary as them. I climbed inside and was delighted it was just the two of us. I looked about and saw a second car behind. "Security will follow," she said.

"I was expecting everyone to be squashed into one car after what happened to you. I thought Gui would have certainly insisted."

"As I said dear, while the cats away. Anyway, I only ever have one riding up here with me and a car behind. You look absolutely beautiful, Rhylee."

"Thank you," I breathed deeply and closed my eyes. "Is something on your mind dear?"

"To be honest, I'm not a very sociable person. It's not by choice. I'm just not great at meeting people. So, I'm a little overwhelmed and I'm not sure if I want to run or cry." She patted my hand. "I would never have thought that.

You seem like a person who is pretty sure of herself. But don't you fret about anything? I'll do all the talking," she said as she flicked open her newspaper.

'Wwans women,' …. What a contradiction for an openly flamboyant gay man, was a state-of-the-art, ultra-modern hair salon with a feminine touch of elegance. Offering a variety of services and amenities to suit every individual. It was out-of-this-world luxuriousness at its best. I'd say it was the crème de la crème of hair salons. There was even a fully equipped cocktail bar. Everything was all under one roof, perfect for day-long pampering. Should you be lucky enough to afford it? It was the complete opposite of the hairdressers I went to back home. Wwan himself was feminine and lively and in an odd way, handsome. Passing some of the most beautiful women I had ever seen, we were whisked to an elegant private room at the back and handed champagne once seated.

Ladies love to pamper themselves now and then and to be pampered. This was the perfect place for that.

He skipped in and air-kissed us both. "My darling Genji. I'm so delighted to see you up and about. You know I would have seen you at home?"

"I had to get out. I was beginning to get cabin fever. And anyway, it's not the same."

"Who is this little fairy princess," he asked, looking at me from head to toe. I could have sworn, he didn't look at me like a gay man. I wondered if he was faking it for show.

"Wwan, this is Rhylee."

He took my hand and looked deep into my eyes. "It is a pleasure to meet you, Miss Rhylee."

"Lovely to meet you too."

"Oh my, that accent. I love it. It's so sexy. Where is it from?" he asked, still holding my hand.

"Thank you, I'm from Ireland."

"Ah yes. The Emerald Isle. I could listen to you all day." He nodded his approval and turned to Genji and smiled. "Is she one of Gui's?"

I pulled my hand from his grasp. "Huh," I say, "that's a bit rude!"

"Really Wwan." Genji looked at him disapprovingly.

"Hey," he says, putting his hands on his hips.

"Oh, come on Gen," he laughs, turning around. "We all know you've no time for Gui's women. And certainly wouldn't take her here to your private haven. But this one is special, would you agree? Anyway, I'm only pulling her leg. So, my little fairy, what are we doing for you today?"

I crossed my arms, rolled my eyes and giggled. "I'm not sure. I'd like to try it straight but I'm afraid my curls will be ruined," I sigh. "I'm not sure it will even suit me. Oh, I'm not sure now. Maybe I'll just leave it."

"Absolutely not. It will be beautiful and I'll personally do it."

"You just need a little confidence," Genji says. I looked at them both as they waited for my decision.

"Okay, let's do it but I don't want anything cut off the length. Promise me you won't put a scissors near me."

"Would I be right in saying you're somewhat untrustworthy of anyone yielding a scissors? I won't cut your hair little Rhylee. It's fabulous as it is and will look like glass when I'm done."

I let out the breath I didn't realise I was holding. I clasp my hands together and smile. "Okay, I'm excited to see how it turns out."

"Genji, your usual set and blow dry?"

"Of course. I'm a creature of habit. We'll both have a luxury manicure too if the girls are free?"

"You know fine I keep a team on standby when you call. It's not my nails I'd be worrying about. How about those brows? They're all over the place?" I giggled watching the rapport they shared.

"Sure, why not. How's yours, Rhylee?"

I turned and looked in the mirror running my index finger over each one. I think they're okay. I've never had anything done to them before. Wwan, what do you think?" He leans in and tips my chin up. "Nothing major is needed here but a nice shape would change the look of your face. I'll get Sylvee to thread them."

"Oh gosh, are you sure? I've seen many disasters on Tik-Tok and found it so overwhelming."

"My dear, they haven't been to Wwans. Everyone's journey is different. When you leave here, not only will you have the best hair, but you will have the best brows of your life."

"I'm not sure what threading means if I'm honest."

"I only recommend this process to my clients. It's the best method for enhancing and defining natural brows because it's so precise."

"I see. Will it hurt and is it an actual thread?"

"Emm, it hurts just as much as tweezing or waxing but there's less tugging on your skin. Look, any form of hair removal that whips the hair out from the root is going to involve a little discomfort. You've hardly any strays so it won't be too bad. Unlike Chewbacca over there," he laughs hysterically, pointing at Genji. I almost choked laughing.

"Wwan. There's simply no need for that."

By the time Wwan convinced me it wasn't open heart surgery, Genji was already under one of those blow-dry machine things while someone was doing her nails.

"Oh, I'm so sorry. Are we going to be late for lunch?"

"Don't you worry, we have plenty of time? Relax and enjoy it, dear."

Wwan held me tightly against him as we said our goodbyes. "My little fairy, I hope to see you again. It was an absolute pleasure meeting you."

"Oh will you release the poor girl before you squeeze the life out of her," Genji said as she playfully hit him with her handbag. "Why don't you come to lunch with us?"

"Darling I'd love nothing better, but Mèng yáo is sunbathing on a desert island and you know when the cats away," he said. Giving her a little nudge with his shoulder. He kissed her affectionately on the cheek and helped her into the car.

"You know where we are if you change your mind darling."

"The usual place," he quipped.

"That's the one," she smiled. They waved goodbye like they were never going to see each other again.

"I don't understand. Isn't Wwan the owner?"

"Yes, he is, why?"

"Why did he say that when the cat's away?"

"He meant when he's away. He thinks the girls will get up to no good. I'm constantly telling him that he has the best and they wouldn't take advantage. They look up to him."

"Who's Mèng yáo?"

"That's the manager. She's one in a million."

"I thought Mèng yáo was Wwan's husband or boyfriend."

"Oh heavens above dear. Wwan is as straight as Gui. Yes, I know he's conspicuously dashing and leaning towards the feminine side. But it's all for show. The clients love him and his persona. They all think they can turn him straight. Little do they know he's a man with skills and knows how to please a woman."

I certainly wasn't expecting that to come out of her mouth. "I, oh, umm. He hides it well," I gasped. "Does it not bother you though, I mean the acting? I had a feeling he was straight the way he looked at me. But then I was completely convinced like everyone else."

"I know the man. We'll marry one day but until then, I'm sure he'll continue being embarrassingly flamboyant. We dated before I married and over the years since Gui's father passed, have slowly rekindled our relationship. He's a good man and would do anything for me. Besides, she winked, Wwan and I have a bet about you."

"And what's that?"

She tapped the side of her nose and smiled.

"I'm sorry you lost your husband but I'm happy you have someone."

"That's what I want for Gui, someone special. Not someone he uses for sex because he's afraid to commit."

"Oh, I'm not sure we should be talking about stuff like that. It's very personal."

"I have these conversations with him all the time. In one ear and out the other. Drives me insane because I know he knows I'm right."

"Did he say he's afraid to commit?"

"Yes. He's afraid of getting hurt."

"Oh!" I turned my head and looked out the window. That's so sad. That big hunk of masculinity is afraid of getting hurt. "I hate to pry, but did something happen for him to feel this way?"

22

"Ah, we've arrived. Let's talk about it inside." I giggled when I saw the name, *The Usual Place*, what a catchy name.

"Thankfully not a pap in sight so we can walk in like normal people through the front door. I daresay, we'll be going out the back afterwards. I bet you. Gentlemen, anyone want to place a bet?" she asked her security team.

"And what would that be Mrs Lee?"

"That we'll be leaving through the back door later because of the paparazzi." He looked down the street and into the restaurant.

Two minutes later he was shaking her hand. "Go on then, there's nobody in there and it's fairly quiet. This will be an easy twenty."

"Assuming you win your bet."

"As per usual, no using your mobile or all bets are off."

"Reid, that hurts."

"Yeah well, it's just a gentle reminder after being stung the last time," he quipped. "

"I don't know what you're suggesting. It certainly wasn't me who tipped them off."

She smiled at him and winked as she turned to walk into the restaurant. He rolled his eyes and winked back. He gave her an affectionate grin shaking his head, "You're such a chancer Genji." She formed the OK sign with her fingers and cackled through the front door.

There was something instantly refreshing about this place. Floor-to-ceiling windows lead your eye to the most amazing views. The handmade furniture and deep walnut parquet flooring completed the design. Ambient lighting from the wall-mounted fixtures and enormous chandeliers created a comfortable and welcoming environment, making the room feel warmer and more welcoming, perfect for winding down, especially after a hard day's work.

"Ah Mrs Lee, what a pleasure. We haven't seen you for a while."

"Hmm, I wonder why? I'll have my usual table, please. I didn't realise you were still working here."

"Yeah, it's a handy number in between the modelling," she said, looking eagerly behind us towards the door. She was gorgeous and I wondered why she wasn't walking a catwalk full-time instead of working here.

"Will Gui be joining you this evening?" she asked, looking over our shoulder.

"No, he's away on business."

"Oh, I see." Her face dropped as did her fake enthusiasm. Oh for goodness sake, get over yourself, woman. Stop making a show of yourself!

"Let me take you to your table."

"No need unless you've moved it. I haven't gone senile just yet."

"Oh okay, if, you're sure." Awkward!

"What a beautiful restaurant. Do you come here often?"

"All the time right up to my eh, umm accident," she frowned. "This was Gui's favourite too until he broke-up with Cici," she frowned, tipping her head towards the door.

I looked enviously at the young girl dressed in a little black number, her black hair cut neatly in a bob framing her stunning face and legs that went on forever. The thought of them wrapped around Gui made me jealous. Just then she was joined by a rather exceptionally handsome man who she immediately cosied up to. They knew each other because now and again she threw her head back in laughter while resting her hand on his shoulder. She whispered something in his ear and he looked straight over. Oh my God, he was fucking gorgeous and I couldn't stop my mouth hitting the floor. He gave me an engaging grin and winked. My heart skipped a beat. Then he waved and shouted to Genji. Of course, it would be my luck that they knew each other!

He grinned and waved like a lunatic like they were best friends. Genji was just as enthusiastic to see him and waved him over. I blushed and glanced around the table looking for something to take my mind off the blood rushing up my cheek. He practically sprinted towards us, and every woman stopped dead in his wake. His blonde hair is styled to just fucked perfection flopping from side to side as my eyes roam up and down his perfect physique. He was the epitome of wealth. Wearing a slate grey pinstripe suit, probably handmade, white shirt and grey tie.

"He's handsome isn't he," she whispered out of the side of her mouth. Genji could hardly contain her excitement as she stood holding out her arms. And exclaiming when he bounded into them, almost knocking her off balance. "Keane my darling I can't believe you're here. Why haven't you called?"

"I just flew in and wanted to surprise you so popped in for a quick bite. You look marvellous considering your ordeal. How are you, mom?"

MOM! What the fuck? I dart a glance at Genny, my eyes bugging.

"Oh, don't mind me, I'm fine but let me introduce you to Rhylee."

"Rhylee, this is Keane Lee Turner."

Oh, for fuck's sake, even his name is sexy. "He's my other son." Standing awkwardly, I held out my hand. Looking from one to the other. He took it gently and pulled me in for a hug which made me sigh. His aftershave was sensual and masculine and he was built like a stone wall. I resisted the urge not to let go. He gave me 'the look.' The thing where they tell you with their eyes, they want to fuck you. You know the look and it only works if the guy is hot. Holy God!

Feeling the rush of desire flood through me I cross my legs in the hope it will stop. I try to think of something off-putting. Mother. Yes, she'll do nicely. She could stop the devil in his tracks.

"Well, well well, so this is Rhylee. I've heard so many wonderful things about you. What you did for my mother went above and beyond. My brother and I are indebted to you."

I lowered my gaze and blushed even deeper, which elicited a provocative laugh. His voice was sexy as hell, like everything about him.

"Please say you'll join us." Oh my God, how am I going to cope if he says yes? I felt like I was in a dream so I closed my eyes and opened them again, nope, he was still here exuding hotness, staring at me with those come-to-bed eyes.

Don't make eye contact, look away. I screamed in my head.

"I can't think of anything better than having lunch with two beautiful women," he said, not breaking eye contact. I wring my hands in front of me. My nerves were shot. "I thought Gui would have been back by now?"

"The deal fell through so he had to renegotiate a new partnership, delaying his return. In the end, it turned out much better than he could have hoped for. Thankfully, the new contract seems to be a better deal for him and the company. As Gui's father always said, 'Change your mindset so that every missed opportunity is a learning opportunity.' It hasn't helped his frame of mind though that Jingfei is constantly wanting his attention."

"I heard she tagged along for the ride. Gui's got his hands full so," he said in a lowered voice and winked. How on earth am I going to be able to eat in front of this God? "As if reading my mind, he waved to the waiter who was silently waiting in the background.

"Good afternoon Mr Turner, ladies, what can I get you?"

"Hello Haoyu, can we have the menu please and some bottled water? Ladies, any preference, he asked, looking at Genji and I. Knowing how much sparkling makes me gassy, way too eagerly I shouted, still. He looked at me, raising an eyebrow.

"Sorry, didn't mean to shout, sparkling makes me burp." He threw his head back and gave an almighty laugh. The sound of it doing things to my insides. The waiter handed each of us a leather-bound menu and as Keane took one, I noticed the beginning of a tattoo. Oh my God. I drool. Does he have a tattoo sleeve? I'm imagining it covering his magnificent biceps. That's sexy as fuck. I blushed thinking of him in just a pair of boxer shorts and wondered if it carried on over his chest. I love tattoos on men.

"Anyone know what they want," Keane asked, glancing up from his menu.

"May I please have 'Ho Fan,' I've always wanted to try it. He smiled and said, "You can have anything you want. Mom, anything tickling your fancy?"

"Kung Pao Chicken with chestnuts for me please." The waiter returned with a notebook in hand and Keane ordered for everyone including a selection of Dim Sums, Scallion Pancakes and mini spring rolls.

"Have you tried 'Chou Dou Fu,'" he asked me.

"I have no idea what that is."

"It's stinky tofu," Genji laughed.

"Oh no, I haven't and don't want to either. Thank you."

"Ahh, you must try it though. It's especially lovely with sweet sauce," he pleaded.

"The name alone is enough to make me gag."

He shook his head and laughed. "It's not as bad as it sounds, trust me. You're a pescatarian, you'll like it." How did he know that?

"Fine," I mumbled, *you're not going to let this go.* He called the waiter and spoke to him in Chinese.

"So Keane, what have you been up to?" Genji inquired. "I have no idea what you've been doing because you don't bother calling me! Do you know how much that upsets me?"

"Mom, I called numerous times but was told you were asleep, resting or out of it on pain relief."

At his admission, Genji rolled her eyes. "I don't believe you."

He tutted, shaking his head and took out his phone from his inside pocket. "Are we doing this?" He dialled someone on loudspeaker and then placed it on the table. The phone rang twice.

Daiyu answered. "Hello, Mr Keane. Your mother is at Wwan's and then going to *The Usual Place.*

"Yes, I'm with her now. I just want you to clear up something. Did you give mom any of my messages?"

There was complete silence and I thought the line had gone dead. "I'm sorry, no I forgot. I wrote them all down and left them somewhere. I'm very sorry."

"It's fine Daiyu. Don't let it upset you. Take care," he said. Although he was talking on the phone, his eyes were locked on mine. He hung up and turned to Genji. "See, you know I don't lie."

"I'm sorry darling. I've just missed you," she said gently. He shrugged, sliding his jacket off his broad shoulders, then leaned over and kissed her cheek. Oh my God, I took my fill of his muscular arse and it was everything I imagined. Knowingly, he quickly turned his head catching me red-handed. Fuck it! A dirty smile escaped his lips and I blush. Oh, for fuck's sake. How embarrassing.

I couldn't put my finger on it but there was chemistry between us. I'd say women threw themselves at him and he had sex on tap. Like Gui, he was out of my league. His shirt was taut across his chest and he obviously trained hard to have that body. He was very similar to Gui. Both beautifully stunning alpha males who commanded attention. With confidence and magnetism, they'd have no trouble attracting women. You wouldn't stand a chance if they walked into a room.

Gui was taller and broader, with sallow skin and dark hair. Keane, although quite tall, was a few inches shorter and blonde, both had blue eyes. Oh my God, I wonder if he's a Dominant too. The naughty thoughts running through my mind of Gui and Keane, half-naked, were sinful. I concentrated on the waiter opening the bottled water and bite the inside of my mouth to stop myself from smiling. I'm sure it was written all over my face.

"Eh hmm, Rhylee." Snapping sadly out of the porn movie we were all starring in, I looked shyly at Keane. "I'm sorry, my mind was elsewhere for a minute."

"Anywhere exciting?" he asked, with a knowing look. "Not at all, just something I have to do," I blushed, which amused him greatly.

"So, you work at the orphanage. It takes a special kind of person to do that and I can see why you'd be very good at it."

"Ahh, it's not so difficult. It has its ups and downs, like everything really, that's life." Why did I find it difficult to look him in the eye?

"Don't you feel overwhelmed by it," he asked.

"Not at all. It makes me sad sometimes but there's mostly happy endings."

"Are you a 'They all lived happily ever after,' kind of girl?"

I sat back in my seat and studied his handsome face. I was not sure what to make of his question when Gui asked the same thing. "I'm not sure anymore, to be honest. People change, situations change."

He rubbed his chin as he pondered my reply. For fuck's sake, everything he did was sexy! Did Genji know what was happening here? Could she feel the chemistry? Don't get me wrong. I'm not saying anything could happen. Gui is the only man for me if only it was reciprocated. Yeah, he admitted certain things but not his emotions.

"Have you always looked after children?" He rested his chin on his palm, elbow on the table, his attention fixed on me. There it was again, that feeling like he was undressing me with his eyes. I inhale heavily as I try to control my breathing.

"I'm actually on a career break for three years."

"Oh really. And what is it you do?" He asked the question with genuine interest.

"I'm a police officer."

That certainly made him sit up straight. I smirk. "That surprises me. Isn't there a height restriction?"

"It was abolished and replaced with a physical competence test."

"I was wondering because you're tiny."

"The requirement for male officers was five nine and female officers five five. Before you ask, I'm five-two."

"Yeah, those two inches are very important. You know how men get confused when it comes to inches." He winks.

Genji had remained silent through our whole conversation and then piped up. "You're so tiny," she said, clutching her chest. "Your poor parents must worry when you leave the house to guard the streets? No wonder you were so brave in tackling that gang."

"That was the job I applied for but ended up behind a desk."

"The most important thing I want to know is, do you still wear a uniform?"

"Keane, stop teasing." He raised an eyebrow, crossing his arms over his chest. I smiled at his inquisitive gaze. "Do you have a uniform fetish, Mr Turner?" Oh God, I don't know why I called him Mr Turner. It sounded so sexual.

"Nobody can argue that they don't find men or women attractive in uniform, Miss Murphy. It's no secret that some men fall for uniforms of authority, like police uniforms or even business suits. I, however, am more attracted to nurses in uniform. It's a big turn-on but not a sexual desire and certainly not a kinky fetish. Although I have been known to dabble."

I didn't quite know what to say and the look on Genji's face was priceless. I wanted to delve further but was too embarrassed to ask. Even if I was brave enough, I couldn't ask those kinds of questions in front of Genji. "Interesting," I smiled sweetly, trying to hide my agitation.

"Rhylee have you ever been told you have a smile that warms the heart." I blushed and it brought a smile to his lips. I was relieved when the food arrived. Now all I had to worry about was managing to put the food in my mouth and not all over me. The conversation flowed freely around the table and I completely relaxed, feeling less awkward.

Keane was nothing but charming and humorous and I loved the banter between us. I was so mesmerised that I had to concentrate on what he was saying. Whether it was his calm manner, inquisitive ways, or infectious laugh, I couldn't help being even more attracted to him.

Just then the room lit up with a bright flash. "I just knew it wouldn't take long for them to crawl out from under their rocks," Genji said, pointing towards the window.

There were at least ten photographers pressed up against the window, shouting for us to come outside. A look of irritation crossed Keane's face. "More than likely they've been tipped off."

"Tipped off about what?"

"I've had many unpleasant encounters with paparazzi myself and found that they won't stop until they get a story whether it's real or not. Gossip sells."

"They assume you're Keane's girlfriend. Accompanying him for dinner with his mother," said Genji. "Who knows, but I'm guessing that's where they're going with it. The boys' personal lives, especially their relationships, are constantly under scrutiny. Photographers can hit the jackpot all too often, especially when girlfriends are in the picture. They can be, at most, ruthless and relentless. I wish they'd leave us the hell alone."

"Looks like I owe you twenty bucks, Genji," says Reid grimly. "This is how we're going to handle this. Both cars are positioned out the back and blocking anyone trying to gain access. Genji will go with me in the first car and Rhylee and Keane in the second. Usually, the first vehicle gets the brunt of followers while the second is mostly ignored." Keane rubbed his face and shook his head.

"They want Rhylee and won't be interested in the first car, no offence Mom."

"None taken dear, but you're right."

Keane looked over at Cici. "Don't you dare get her involved," Genji fumed. "It was probably her who called them in the first place."

"We have no other option. They'll be searching for two females and there's only so much the tinted windows block out."

"If you have to, but you know I can't stand her after what she's done to our family."

"Mom, it's our only option. Better the Devil you know." He strolled off towards Cici. Explained the predicament and walked back with her. "So mom and Cici will go with Reid in the first car. The other car will have security and myself and Rhylee will go in my car. They certainly won't be expecting a three-pronged attack.

"I thought I was going with you Keane," Cici scoffed.

I looked over at her whining face and wanted to smirk.

"Don't be ridiculous Cici," said Genji. The girl huffed and puffed and was only short of stamping her foot. How on earth did Gui date someone like her?

"No, you're going in the first car," Keane asserted. "I thought we could go for a drink, but …."

"Please, let's just get out of here before I say something I can't take back," Genji pleaded.

My eyes darted between Genji and Cici and hoped one of them wasn't thrown from the moving car. Keane glared at Cici, raising an impatient eyebrow.

"Okay then," she stammered. But you owe me dinner." Genji moved closer and stood facing Cici. "I would think after what you did, neither of my sons owe you jack shit." Mic drop.... "Keane, let's do this." She turned and kissed my cheek. "Rhylee, Keane I'll see you both tomorrow. All this drama has me exhausted."

"I'll drive around for a bit and shake them off and drop Rhylee home later. You know what, let's just go out the front door. Cici, thanks, your services are no longer required. That way both cars can go as planned." He looked about and called Reid over. "Can you ask Cheng to bring my car around to the front, please? Rhylee, are you okay with this?"

"I have nothing to be scared about, right?"

"Nah, they'll just bombard you with questions about your relationship."

"But I don't have one."

"I know and you know but they don't."

"You're good to go, Mr Turner," said Cheng.

Keane took command of the situation. "Okay folks let's get the show on the road. They won't know what to do with themselves when we all leave together." He walked beside me and put his hand on my back. Not sure if he was aware he was doing it, but it was sexy as fuck. Once through the doors, I was almost blinded by the camera flashes. Keane took my hand and whispered in my ear, "Let's pose for a few photos and they'll leave us alone. If we don't, they'll relentlessly chase us."

I stood on my tippy toes and whispered, "Why didn't we just leave through the back door then?"

"Because I wanted you all to myself," he winked. "Also, they're professionals and take photos extremely quickly when you comply so it won't take long." He wrapped his arm around my waist and pulled me tightly. As they clicked away, I could feel Keane's embrace pull me closer.

"What will they do with these photos?" I asked.

"Most turn them over to a celebrity photo agency, which in turn sells them off to the highest bidder. So be prepared to see your face in some magazine or other tomorrow."

One photographer asked if we were dating. Another asked us to kiss. They asked my name, who I was, where I worked and how long I was dating Keane. As the flashing lights and yells of questions continued, without warning, Keane bent his head and kissed me. And I didn't stop him. It was a soft kiss, not demanding but more inquisitive. The photographers went into a frenzy.

When he pulled his head back, I glanced up at him for a moment and said softly, "You shouldn't have done that." He narrowed his eyes, then concedes.

"I know, forgive me." He took my hand and pulled me gently toward the car. "Shut up and come for a drink with me."

I stop. "I can't," I sigh.

"You can't or won't," he scoffs.

"I don't drink."

"Murphy stop being fucking funny, you can have a Cola or a hot chocolate."

Focusing on his beautiful car, I was acutely aware that he was studying me. "As long as that's all it is?"

He opened the door to the silver Aston Martin, "Hop in." He bid the photographers a good night and heard him say, "You got what you wanted, let's call it a night."

One of them replied, "Have a good one Keane, you lucky bastard."

23

He clicked his seat belt and moved closer, leaning his elbow on the middle console to face me.

"Don't tell me you don't like me because I know you do. I'm sure you've felt it too?"

"Keane, if circumstances were different and I was…" I paused for a minute, trying to think of the right words to say. His eyebrows raised in a silent question.

"Go on."

I clear my throat. "If I wasn't in the predicament, I find myself in and had met you elsewhere absofuckinglutely in a heartbeat."

"Wait, what?" He went to say something then snapped his mouth shut. "You won't see me because you're in a, he air quoted 'predicament,' that's fucking ridiculous Rhylee."

"Don't you dare raise your voice at me? If you knew my predicament you would understand."

"And I won't understand unless you tell me! What are you hiding?" Staring out the window I paused to watch the photographers compare photos. Caught in the surreal sense of everything that's happened over the past month.

"This is all too weird, Keane. It's like someone is playing a joke on me," I said with a heavy sigh. Just then I heard the sound of a camera snapping. "You're right, they're relentless."

With a loud sigh, he started the engine. "Have you decided yet," he asked.

"I'll go for a hot chocolate with you," I yawned. "But I can't guarantee I won't nod off, I'm ready for bed."

He covered his heart with his hand. "Oh, I'm wounded. Haven't you learned I'm a riveting conversationalist," he said wiggling his eyebrows. I suppressed a giggle. "Go on, I know you're dying to laugh."

I took one look at him and his magical brows and couldn't help bursting out laughing. "You're such a knob, Keane Turner."

The half-hour ride was quiet and the silence comfortable, only becoming awkward when we reached the location. He slowed down and pointed a remote control as we neared luxe ornamental gates.

"Where are you taking me?"

"To my home."

My interest was piqued as we drove along a never-ending road. Intricate cobbles were perfectly boarded with a riot of colourful blooms and beautiful lighting. Unable to catch a glimpse of the house because of all the mature trees. Suddenly it appeared from behind them. It was stunning. "Oh, it's beautiful," I gasped. "I thought you'd live in a penthouse or bachelor pad."

"This is my baby. I have a pad in town too but prefer being here."

"Is it Art Deco?"
"Yes, it is."

The grand house was white and the driveway perfectly complemented the exterior. In this case, picking out the cool grey used for the window frames and front door giving it a stylish impression. "Is it original," I asked.

"Architecturally pretty much as it was intended back in 1936 apart from a complete interior overhaul and an added extension. What I'm mostly proud of is that it's not obvious where the house has been extended."

"Ooh, I can't wait to see inside."

Of course, the hallway was elegantly stylish and welcoming. It seemed every effort was made to make it just as inviting as the rest of the house. After all, it's the first part of the home you see when you enter. I suppose it's a reflection of your taste and personality. It had a monochromatic scheme, bold and beautiful, a classic which never dates. With black and white marble floors and large wall mirrors reflecting the light. The staircase was painted white with a black handrail and the runner was pink. Yes, pink! It was all just stunning.

"Oh my goodness, this is spectacular. I can only imagine what the rest of your home looks like," I gasped. "Thank you. Where would you like to go next, the bedrooms," he said with a twinkle in his eye.

"Behave, Mr Turner," I said, slapping his arm. "Or I'll tie you up." Why the fuck did I say that?

The kitchen was something you see in all the best home interior magazines. "This kitchen is to die for Keane. It's like you climbed into my head. I love it."

"It's my pride and joy because I designed it myself."

"It's not original surely?"

"It's all handmade. The original was falling apart, unfortunately. I salvaged the handles and doorknobs and had extra's made because it tripled in size. The 1930s kitchen tended to be functional rather than social areas, hence why they were so tiny."

"I particularly love the panelling. We have this at home too."

"That's a recent upgrade," he said, "which I think makes the kitchen." He leaned against the huge marble island and crossed his legs watching me.

"Can I ask you something?" I knew exactly what was coming and only had my big mouth to blame. So much for thinking I was off the hook. How on earth was I going to answer? After an awkward silence, I glanced up at him with a mischievous smile.

"Sure, ask away." I sat on one of the ten grey velvet stools placed around the oversized island. He pulled one out and sat next to me. Oh dear, too close. What was wrong with the other nine?

"When I asked if you'd like to see the bedroom, you told me to behave. Do you remember what you said?"

"I don't actually. When I'm nervous I come out with verbal diarrhoea and hardly remember anything." Oh, I just hate lying. I should have just said it out straight because he's just going to say it anyway.

"I see. I'll remind you then, shall I?"

I stretched and gasped, "Ouch." I looked at my arm and gently patted the scar. "I keep forgetting that it's there."

He gently ran the back of his hand up my arm, lingered on my scar then continued down again. It gave me goosebumps. I watched in silence and turned my head when we looked straight into each other's eyes. You could hear a pin drop with the ensuing silence.

I gulped. "Could I have some water please?"

After a moment passed, he said, "I hope you know that I would never do anything to upset you."

"I don't think we know each other long enough for you to do that. Annoy me, yes," I smiled.

His full lips curved into a smile as he handed me a cold bottle of Evian. "See I remembered, you don't do sparkling because it makes you burp. It affects me somewhat differently."

I burst out laughing and shook my head. "No, don't say it. I'll never be able to look at you the same way if you say it out loud."

He studied my face for a minute then let out an almighty belly laugh. "Oh no, it's not what you think, I'm allergic to sodium," he said in between laughs. "Some waters have added salt."

The realisation made me laugh and cringe at the same time. "I can't believe I thought it was something else. Let's move on shall we."

"Sure, let's go back to what I was trying to say. Why did you mention tying me up? It's not something one would say."

I opened the water and glugged half a bottle, then suddenly burped. "Oh my goodness excuse me," I giggled. "Must be my nerves."

"Better out than in I always say," he winked. I slid off the stool and walked to the window which was a combination of large windows giving the appearance of a glass wall. I'm sure it was stunning during the day, allowing in an abundance of natural light. My mother and Evee always knew when I was fibbing because I did something strange with my mouth. I'm not sure if he had this power too so avoided looking at him. He followed me to the window and stood right next to me. He was that close, I could feel the heat from his body.

"Are you in the lifestyle?" he asked. I remained silent. He put his finger under my chin, raising it to face him. "Well, are you?"

His touch brought goosebumps out all over my body.

I playfully swatted his hand away.

"No! Are you?"

"Yes, I am actually." My eyes bugged.

"You are? What are you?"

"Isn't it obvious?"

"Dominant?"

"Yes. Do you know much about it?"

"I've read a few books."

"Is that all?"

"Absolutely. So, you and Gui are Doms."

"He told you?"

"Yeah."

"He's never divulged that to anyone, except Jingfei but I think that was to scare her off. So why did he tell you?"

"He found one of my books," I said, looking at him from under my eyelashes. A soft laugh escaped his throat.

I bit the inside of my mouth to prevent it from giving me away. Oh my God, who would have thought? Two fucking hot Doms. Wait until Evee hears.

"With those puppy dog eyes, I'd swear you were trying to top from the bottom?"

"Hahaha, don't you have to be a sub to do that?" He smiled and it was then I noticed his cute dimples. He sat and leaned back, both arms stretched wide across the back of the sofa and crossed his legs. There were two sofas, that's how ginormous his kitchen was. He curled an inquisitive brow and patted the cushion next to him. I rubbed my face with a heavy sigh and sat on the opposite sofa. His intense gaze lingered as I fidgeted with the hem of my dress.

"Would you like to be?"

I laughed nervously, as he leaned forward on his knees. Fuck's sake, not again! This can't be happening. How can I be dishonest when I'm submitting to Gui?

"No, it's not something I'm interested in or would be good at. I did fancy myself as a sub but wouldn't be good at submitting every minute of every day."

"What if it was bedroom or playroom only? You could decide what works best for you, all relationships are different."

"I couldn't imagine myself, kneeling naked at the front door waiting for Sir or Master to return home. Or be happy for him to make decisions for me and abide by his rules. Sorry, but no thanks. I am not naturally submissive and it wouldn't come easy to me."

"It can be tailored to fit our needs, your needs."

"Why are you trying to convince me? I'm sure there's plenty who would love to submit to you?"

"There are, but I don't want to have a relationship with any of them."

"Are you saying you want one with me?"

"Yes. What can I say but I fancy you like crazy. And yes, it is crazy. I never believed in love at first sight until I saw you. You're everything I've been missing."

"Wow, I don't know what to say."

"Say you feel the same way?"

"I find you attractive beyond distraction and as I said, if things were different. But my heart belongs to someone else even though they don't want it," I said sadly.

Before I took my next breath, he was beside me, taking my hand in his, a flash of electric energy ran through me. I looked at our joined hands. "I can give you everything you want. I'd worship and love you. I'd give you the 'Happily ever after,' you want. Grow old with me, Rhylee Murphy."

I pulled my hand from his and burst out crying. He said the words I wanted to hear but it was just the wrong man saying them. "This is all too much. Can you please take me back?"

"I'm sorry. But I believe in nothing but truth and honesty. I don't bullshit about feelings."

"I know, I'm just a little overwhelmed. It's a lot to take in." I sighed deeply as his warm fingers touched my cheek. "Just know that my feelings won't change. I've never been more serious about anything in my life."

"It just seems so unnatural and fucked up. I don't know which it is. I'm just confused."

"About what? Falling for someone you've just met? True. But it is what it is. I can't stop my feelings. You just can't turn them off like a tap." I hugged him and kissed his temple.

"If nothing else, I'm sure we'll be the best of friends."

"I don't need any more friends. I'm at the stage in my life where I want to settle down, get married and have kids. The cherry on the cake is two kinky people taking pleasure from making each other happy and living a perfectly normal life. I have friends who are in the lifestyle, married and living the dream. If you're wondering, yes, they do exist and it does work."

"I suppose it's easier when it's only part-time, unlike the master and slave relationship. I certainly couldn't take it full-time."

"There are also those who only practise their roles during play scenes."

"That would be my cup of tea."

"Did you know, kinky sex and being in a Dom/sub relationship has many advantages to your health and wellbeing, whether it's mental or physical."

"Ooh look at you trying to convince me to sign the dotted line. But I'll take your word for it," I giggled.

A soft laugh escaped his throat. "You have the most wonderful laugh I have ever heard," he gushed.

"Bet you say that to all the girls," I jokingly said.

He gave me a hands-on-hips serious look. "I know all this is hard for you to take in. But believe me, I'm just as surprised as you to be honest. And I don't know if there's anything between you and Gui because he's acting all shady. Just know that I haven't dated in over a year. I have my subs, yes, at the club but I've never taken any of them here, to my home. I need a drink. Will you join me?"

"I don't drink. Only because I've never found one, I liked. I hate the taste of alcohol. But saying that, Daiyu gave me some deliciously lethal concoction and I couldn't taste any alcohol. We drank two jugs and at one stage I was hallucinating. I was very surprised neither of us vomited and if we had, it would have been nuclear orange."

"When you say we, was it you and Gui?"

"God no. My friend stayed for a few days when Gui left."

"I was wondering. Okay, get comfortable. Prepare to be amazed. I have just the thing. Take a seat and watch me work my magic." He strode like a man on a mission to the giant double-door fridge and retrieved a selection of items. Stacking all the ingredients in his arms, his attempt at juggling without dropping anything was hilarious until a lime escaped and rolled across the floor. I stifled a laugh and he gave me a sidelong glance.

"So, what's on the menu?"

"It doesn't have a name yet. It's my concoction so of course it's delicious. I won't make yours too strong. I'm not lying, they're so nice it's very easy to go overboard."

Looking at everything he placed on the island, I picked up an exquisite bottle. "What on earth is this?"

"Vodka," he smiled.

"No way. The bottle is beautiful. It's like a work of art."

"It's no ordinary vodka. It's a bulletproof glass bottle with a flask made out of the radiator guards from vintage Russo-Baltique automobiles."

"Wow, I don't even know what that means, but it sounds impressive. Seriously though, why on earth is it bulletproof?"

"Just so they can put the hefty price tag on it."

"Go on, how much did you pay for it?"

"Gui gave it to me for my birthday and at the time, it cost $1.3 million."

"You can't be serious? That's shocking!"

"The look on your face," he laughed. I rolled my eyes and smiled.

"Look I get it, if you can, why not? It's his money, he can do whatever he likes with it."

He carefully folded up his sleeves before starting. He grabbed two tall crystal glasses off the shelf and filled them halfway with large chunks of ice and a shot of the ridiculously expensive vodka. Peeling the rind off two limes, he rubbed them around the rims before chucking them into each glass, then he squeezed through his fingers making sure the pips didn't drop in. "That's the most important part, the lime juice. Make sure you get every last drop." He added about a quarter of pineapple juice, then filled to the top with ginger beer. He crumbled a sprig of mint and chucked that in too and stirred. "Honest opinion," he said, handing me a glass. I sniffed it first then took a little sip.

"I know I watched everything you did. But I can't taste the vodka, which is crazy."

"Would you like some more?"

"Eew no thanks. It's lovely as it is. I could certainly drink them all night."

"Drink up then, there's still a few hours left."

"Are you trying to get me drunk?"

"A gentleman never takes advantage of a lady."

"Sooo."

"Go on, spit it out." I gulped the delicious drink. "Honestly, I love this and will make it all the time.

Obviously without the million-dollar vodka. So, do you have a playroom too?"

"I do, would you like to see it?"

"Yes," I whispered.

"Your wish is my command," he said, wiggling his eyebrows. Drinks in hand we carefully took the stairs down to the basement.

"Do you have a dungeon, Mr Turner?"

"You tell me," he said, pushing open the door. Before I entered, I stopped and asked, "Why do you have this if you've never brought anyone home?"

"My home is everything upstairs. The basement has its own entrance. If I'm entertaining, they enter and exit through the basement. I have never been inclined to continue it upstairs to my bedroom."

"Are you always so honest?"

"Absolutely. A serious relationship can't exist on a bed of lies. They eventually catch you out. So, what's the point? I guess that's why I was so reluctant to get into a serious relationship."

I was surprised to see how sincere he was and hoped we could come back to it. A kinky playroom wasn't the place. I studied his face for a minute then walked into the dimly lit room which was soft and romantic. Hanging from the ceiling was a ginormous chandelier.

"Wow, that's some chunk of ice," I gasped.

"It's actually from your neck of the woods." I looked at him, raising an eyebrow.

"Ireland?"

"Yes, it's a bespoke Waterford crystal piece I had shipped over."

I elbowed him in the side. "You're messing."

"Ouch, you're a lot stronger than you look. I'm not kidding. I saw one in the seriously posh hotel we were staying in and told my designer to get me one. It took over three months to make." He flicked the switch and it lit up the room, thousands of crystal droplets shining like diamonds. Elegant was the best way to describe it. He was lounging against the door frame, staring into my soul.

"Did you design this room too?"

"No, I had someone come in."

It was a beautiful room decorated in several tones of white mixed with industrial accents and brick, like a posh wine cellar. "It's certainly not a dingy dungeon," I giggled, walking over to a large, padded cross secured to the brick wall, one of many showpieces displayed in the room. "Are your subs always naked when they are here?"

"Of course, they are." I blushed.

"Do you know you blush when you ask certain things?"

"Yes, it's a pain in the face!"

"Oh, I'm so sorry. I didn't realise it was a medical condition. Forgive me."

I burst out laughing. "Nooo, it's any Irish term we say."

"Thank God for that."

I walked to the huge bed and sat on the edge and sipped my drink. "Do you make them strip while you watch?"

"They have a routine. They strip and wait for me in the kneeling position." He pushed himself off the door frame and walked towards me. I took a deep breath and knocked back the last of my drink, wishing I had a second one to follow. Not sure why, but all of a sudden, I felt nervous and could feel the hairs at the back of my neck standing on end. He sat next to me.

"Are you okay?"

"Yeah yes, I'm fine."

He took my glass and placed it on the floor. "Your hands are freezing Rhylee." He raised them to his lips and gently kissed them. I lowered my gaze and blushed deeper. If he kisses me again, my head will explode for sure. Just then my phone pinged in my bag which I'd forgotten was still across my body. It was either Gui or Evee and for once I hoped it was the latter. I detached myself from his hold and took out the phone.

24

*H*is name lit up the screen. Usually, I couldn't stop the smile spreading across my face but on this occasion, I couldn't help feeling guilty. "Sorry, it's Gui. Do you mind if I answer? I don't want to be rude."

"Of course not. Tell the big lump to get home before I have to go back."

"Hey."

"Hi."

"I heard what happened at the restaurant. Are you okay?"

"I'm grand. I felt like a celebrity."

"You sure?"

"Absolutely. Keane was like James Bond."

"Sounds like him alright. It's late. Did I wake you?"

"No. Keane's just showing me his playroom."

"He's WHAT?" I had to hold the phone away from my ear.

"We're chatting in the playroom drinking vodka cocktails. You have to try one when you get back. They're delicious."

"You don't drink. Especially Vodka!"

"Only because I haven't found one that I like. But since meeting you, I've discovered two and I'll probably have a drinking problem when I leave?"

"Are you drunk?"

"God no. Sure we've just started."

"Rhylee, what do you mean you've just started? It's two o'clock in the morning!!"

"Wow, is it?"

"How long do you intend to stay there?"

"Well, I'm not sure. I don't know how lethal Keane's cocktails are and if he can drive. I could stay the night?"

"No, you're fucking not. I'm sending a car. Please put Keane on."

"Are you angry with me?"

"Of course not. It's impossible to be angry with you. But not so impossible with Keane."

"Alright then, goodnight!"

I grimaced as I handed the phone to Keane and took the opportunity to leave them to it and went back upstairs. He was angry even though he said he wasn't. Jesus, what the actual fuck was all that about? He acted like a jealous boyfriend! Was he angry I was with Keane? I walked out onto the covered patio and watched the rain fall. The sound of it falling to the ground was soothing, reminding me of home. I watched the drops splattering against the leaves and jumped when a bolt of lightning lit up the sky. Keane came up behind me and placed a blanket over my shoulders.

"Well, that was a noisy one."

"Oh no, the call with Gui?"

"No silly," he laughed, "The lightning."

"Oh right. Is everything okay? I mean with you and Gui. He seemed pissed off?"

"I think he was just a little shocked you weren't tucked up in your bed and shocked you were in my playroom. I'm sure all sorts went through his mind and I can only deduce that he has feelings for you."

I turned to face him. "It's complicated, Keane."

"So you've said. Neither you nor Gui are very good at explaining this complication. You both have your agenda and I'm sure it will be revealed sooner or later. I'm very close to him, practically brothers and this is the first time he's ever been secretive with me. So, if he wanted me to know, he'd tell me." I pulled the soft blanket tightly around me as the wind picked up.

"This is the first time I've seen rain since moving here," I said, trying to change the subject. The rain was over, but drops were still falling from the trees.

He remained silent. "I love the smell after a rain shower." Silence…. He was quiet for a long moment. Just then his phone buzzed. "Your car is here. You know I would have taken you back."

"Of course, I do." He walked me through the house in silence to the front door and placed his hand against it, preventing it from opening.

"Help me, help me understand," he whispered. I didn't turn because I knew why my heart was beating wildly in my chest.

"Keane, let's not do anything we'll regret."

He reached out and grasped my shoulders and turned me around. "Until Gui tells me otherwise, I'm not going to give up." Without warning he leaned in, cupped my face and gently kissed me. I didn't stop him. A flash of electric energy raced through me as our lips met. And then I felt how aroused he was. He kissed me again and groaned when our tongues clashed. He rested his forehead against mine with a sigh.

"Why the fuck are things so damn complicated?" He kissed my forehead and released me, stepping away as he spoke. "You're lucky I was raised well with old-fashioned morals. Otherwise, you couldn't stop me from fucking you hard right now."

I moved closer and reached up to kiss his cheek as he held me in a loose embrace. "It's going to be tough, Keane. For everyone" I opened the door and walked slowly to the car. Oh my God, how long has that poor man been standing there?

"Good morning, Ms Murphy. My name is Jun Hie, Mr Lee sent me to take you home."

"Hello Jun Hie, I hope you weren't waiting too long out here?"

"Not long, I just arrived." I jumped in the back and realised I still had the blanket wrapped around me. I put the window down and held it out to him smiling.

"Keep it."

"You can pick it up the next time you're around."

"See you tomorrow so," he said, winking. I blew him a kiss. I pondered the whole journey back if I should have. Isn't that just encouraging him? I miss Evee. We've always had each other's back and it's at times like this I need my best friend. I took out my phone to see if there were any messages from Gui. Of course, there wasn't. I lost interest in the changing landscapes and sat back in my seat and tried to relax. Why do things have to be so bloody complicated?

Slowing to a stop, just about to put my hand on the handle when Jun Hie jumped out like a stunt man opening the door of the Mercedes for me. "I'm sorry if I got you out of bed?"

"Not at all, Ms Murphy. My day can start at any time."

"Well goodnight, Jun Hie. I mean good morning. Haha. You know what I mean."

"I do. Sleep well, Ms Murphy."

My head pounded as I took the lift to my floor. Was it all my emotions or the Vodka? I gently cracked open Lan's door to check on her but her bed was empty. Lord knows where she sleeps half of the time. Thankfully I no longer worried if she wasn't where she was supposed to be. She's safe now. She will grow up being loved and know nothing but love. She brings out the best in everyone she meets and it comes so naturally to her. I smiled, knowing how much Gui is crazy about her despite his constant complaining. She won him over without trying. I hope.

I sat on the edge of the bed and stared at the floor. I sat there for a long, long time, feeling a bit dazed and confused after the events of the day. I just can't get my head around it, Gui and Keane. What a head-melter. One admitted to wanting to share his life with me after just meeting me and the other playing his cards close to his chest. It's like someone is playing a sick joke on me.

There was a gentle tap and Daiyu popped her head around the door. "I have tea for you if you'd like some?"

"Oh, really you shouldn't have." She pushed open the door with her foot and placed the tray in front of me on the bed. "I feel so bad. Has anyone got any sleep since I got here, Daiyu?"

"Don't you worry about that, this is our job. If we weren't happy, we wouldn't be here. Mr Gui looks after us all very well. I can't think of anywhere else I'd rather be."

"I know but…"

"Ssh now my dear and sip your tea. I think you need it after the mad day you've had."

"Oh, you heard?"

"I'm afraid it's nothing new. One whiff that any member of the Lee family, particularly when the boys are about and the place is swamped. Thankfully Mr Turner was there and able to get you out of that situation safely. If they don't get what they want it can get quite nasty. And sometimes, unfortunately, it's not anyone from the family who gets the backlash, but the person accompanying them. Printing unflattering photos and making up lies. Thankfully your step into the so-called limelight went well."

"What do you mean?"

She took out her phone, scrolled and handed it over. There were a few photos but the one where he was kissing me made my eyes bulge. And it wasn't a peck on the cheek either. It was a full-blown snog with the both of us moulded together!

"Oh my God," I said out loud. "That didn't take long. How is it even possible? It's a stiff drink I need right now, not calming tea."

"I'll get it."

"No, I'm only joking. Nothing can fix that."

"Can I speak freely Ms Murphy?"

"Yes of course."

"You are a beautiful young, free and single woman. You have done nothing wrong nor should you feel guilty. However, it may be enough to help him prioritise and re-evaluate his life. I've been with this family since Gui was in nappies and I have a fair idea what he needs right now." I began bawling and she was beside me in a second, hugging me tightly. I returned her hug but started bawling again in despair.

"You're tired, hop into bed and I'll check on you shortly."

"What's Gui going to say when he sees them?"

"But what can he say, you're single. If anything, it will set him straight."

"But they're practically brothers," I wailed, in an incoherent howl that would wake the dead.

"The last thing I wanted was rivalry between them."

"There's absolutely nothing wrong with a little rivalry between brothers," she said reassuringly. She went into the bathroom and returned with a box of tissues, plucked one out and handed it to me. "Do you know what you need right now?"

"A lobotomy?" I said through a bunged-up nose. "Nope, a cup of my special brew hot chocolate."

"If you think it will help," I giggled. When she reached the door, I called her. "Thank you for being so kind to me Daiyu. It means a lot."

"It's very easy being kind to someone who has a kind-hearted soul." With that, the wailing began again.

"I'll go get that hot chocolate." I blew my nose and rested my head on the pillow. I felt emotionally drained.

As my eyes closed, my phone pinged. With a heavy heart, I sat up and reached for it on the bedside locker. It came up as 'The other half.' Who on earth? Had to be Keane. I couldn't help giggling. He must have added it after speaking to Gui. Cheeky fucker. I was glad in fairness it was him. I wouldn't know what to say to Gui right now. Then again, maybe he doesn't give a shit and it's just me having a guilty conscience. I'd hate it if I hurt his feelings. But does he have any? Of course, he doesn't. That man is emotionally impenetrable.

Keane: Hello, how are you? Hope you don't mind that I took the liberty of adding me to your contacts.
Rhylee: I can't save you as my other half. But I'm glad you did. I'm okay, are you?
Keane: Could be better.
Rhylee: I know how you feel.
Keane: Where are you?
Rhylee: Why?
Keane: Curiosity. I designed that building and know every room. Take a pic.
Rhylee: It's just a normal-looking room with an ensuite. But okay.
Keane: Ah yes, that's one of the suites. Your bed is very inviting lol.
Rhylee: It's far from a suite. Unless you call a bedroom and bathroom a suite? Is it inviting?
Keane: The two doors between the wardrobes open into a large lounge. Maybe?
Rhylee: Aww you're taking it back now and they're locked.
Keane: How is that taking it back lol.

Rhylee: You said maybe…..
Keane: But maybe doesn't mean, no?
Rhylee: lol.
Keane: Tbh it would have already happened if you had given me any encouragement.
Rhylee: Em, I don't think we're talking about the same thing.
Keane: I'm lost.
Rhylee: We were talking about the bedroom.
Keane: Anyway, as I said, if you had fluttered those long eyelashes, we'd still be in the playroom, getting up to all sorts.
Rhylee: Dear God!
Keane: I'm just saying is all, it would have and stop putting images in my mind lol.
Rhylee: Lol I'm just saying. And anyway, I can't be to blame for your dirty mind.
Keane: Okay then, let's just say you're not helping.
Rhylee: I still don't get how it's my fault though, still down to your dirty mind regardless lol.
Keane: But you sowed the seed!!
Rhylee: I sent you a photo of a bedroom and you turned it around.
Keane: Is it just me???
Rhylee: Is it just you in what regard?
Keane: Having these thoughts…
Rhylee: Well, no.
Keane: Could be even more exciting lol.
Rhylee: Do you mean, more exciting if I was on my own?
Keane: No, I mean more exciting if I was actually there lol.
Rhylee: Ah haha.
Keane: What's so funny?

Rhylee: I thought you meant I'd have more fun if I was alone.
Keane: Ahh no.
Rhylee: So, do you think we'd go for some Dutch courage first?
Keane: Nah, I don't need it lol.
Rhylee: I would, lol.
Keane: Aww.
Rhylee: Would we at least go to dinner first …..
Keane: Not sure lol.
Rhylee: Why?
Keane: Depends on how horny I was tbh
Rhylee: Omg! You're shockingly honest, aren't you?
Keane: Sorry.
Rhylee: You don't need to apologise. It's refreshing.
Keane: So, do you think it could happen?
Rhylee: We both know the answer.
Keane: I meant it when I said I won't give up.
Rhylee: Daiyu showed me photos of us on the cover of a magazine. Have you seen them?
Keane: I have. I didn't mention it because I thought you didn't know.
Rhylee: I'm worried it might upset Gui when he sees it.
Keane: Nah. He's a big boy. And can handle it. I'd say if anything he'll be more pissed off than upset. He's very territorial. Try not to think about it although it's easy for me to say. And anyway, it won't have reached that part of the world yet.
Rhylee: What did he say to you?
Keane: He asked if I was out of my mind taking you to the playroom and plying you with drink.

Rhylee: What did you say?
Keane: I said stop acting like a jealous boyfriend!
Rhylee: Omg, you didn't?
Keane: Yes. It was funny actually. He started shouting down the phone so I hung up and blocked his number.
Rhylee: Omg you didn't? Did you? Lmao!
Keane: No, I didn't. Just wanted to give you a giggle.
Rhylee: Well, you certainly did that.
Keane: I'll love you and leave you. I'm hitting the gym in a few hours and my trainer is going to be pissed if I'm falling asleep on the job.
Rhylee: Omg, you're a machine.
Keane: I'm hoping that's a good thing.
Rhylee: It is.
Keane: I'll see you tomorrow for lunch with mom.
Rhylee: Great. Something else to piss him off!
Keane: He won't say a word because mom arranged it. Stop thinking too much about everything. Nite nite
Rhylee: I can't believe you say nite nite. I do too.
Keane: Nite nite x
Rhylee: You need to know I don't want anyone getting hurt.
Keane: I know that x

Tap, tap…..

"Come in Daiyu." She walked in smiling and holding another one of her special brews. "You will sleep like a tree after this but you must drink it all up."

"Do you mean sleep like a log?"

"Tree, log, same thing. Turn around and I'll unzip you. Can I get you anything else Ms Murphy?"

"Can you call me Rhylee?"

"That would be inappropriate."

"I see. I'm sure it would be okay when nobody is around?"

She thought for a minute then smiled. "Okay if it makes you happy Ms Murp… Rhylee." We both giggled.

"Do you have any children," I asked.

"Yes, I have three teenagers, two boys and a girl and all doing well in college."

"Oh wow, you don't look old enough to have one, let alone three teenagers. Must be all your special brews."

"Oh thank you," she giggled. "Please try your chocolate, it should be at the perfect temperature now." I took a sip. "Omg, that's delicious. There's something in it I can't quite make out?"

"It's rum and I used Jingfei's expensive chocolates." We looked at each other seriously for a moment then cracked up laughing. "Nothing soothes the soul quite like a hot chocolate made with some expensively fine contraband," she said through fits of laughter. "I can only imagine her face when she discovers there's none left."

"Won't you get into trouble? I can't imagine her not throwing a tantrum?"

"Oh, she does of course. Mr Lee heard her taking her frustration out on one of the older members of staff. He told her off in front of everyone and reminded her that she was not the lady of the house. And to never raise her voice or speak down to anyone in his household. Funnily enough, it was Mr Lee who was eating her precious chocolates, purposely leaving the wrappers about to piss her off. Anyhow, she's sure to bring back plenty just so she has an excuse to be here."

"But why does she keep it here? Seems bizarre?"

"An excuse to see Gui if you ask me. She said she can't have it in the house with her diabetic mother which is a load of doggy do do. I meet her mother most days in the park doing Tai Chi and she's fitter than me! She stashes it in the sideboard in the dining room."

"The dining room?" All I remember is the dining table Gui almost fucked me on. I feel my cheeks flush with embarrassment.

"Anyway, I'm pleased to see you laughing after the night you had." She slapped her thighs, got up and walked to the door. "I could spend the rest of the day laughing about Jingfei but have to get to the fish market before all the good stuff is gone. Drink up Rhylee and I'll see you later."

"Thanks again for all you have done for Lan and me, you're worth your weight in gold."

"You're very welcome. You are like a breath of fresh air," she smiled.

I jumped up and kissed her cheek. She smiled and closed the door gently behind her. I crawled onto the bed, curling my legs beneath me and sipped the exquisite drink. It shouldn't make me feel good, but Jingfei wasn't the most popular person to have around, yet I still felt jealous.

I drained the remaining chocolate and pulled my dress over my head. Took one last look at my phone then fell into the most wonderful sleep ever. Maybe the hot chocolate helped. Could it have been my dream about two extremely hot brothers? Even in sleep, they were irresistible.

25

Having had a magnificent sleep, I woke feeling rested and refreshed. I had something to look forward to today. I checked my phone and then went for a shower. I did all the usual pampering and as I slathered oil over my body, noticed how well my wound was healing which meant my time as a sub would begin sooner rather than later… something I wasn't looking forward to. I scrunch-dried my hair and dressed in jeans and a pink tee shirt.

I made my bed and couldn't help smiling at how beautiful it was when made up. It was like something out of an interior magazine. I still didn't know where the kitchen was but grabbed the empty mug regardless. Lan wasn't in her room and I had no idea what her schedule was these days. I went to the lounge and sat on my favourite comfy chair in front of the windows and retrieved my Kindle from down the side of the cushion. Daiyu walked in carrying a tray. She looked around making sure the room was empty before saying, "Good morning, Rhylee."

"Good morning to you too. Honestly, you don't have to do this every time. If you show me where the kitchen is, I can make my own meals."

"Oh no, Mr Lee would be very unhappy. You should know, he's seen the photos and is fuming." My heart sank as I sat up straight. "But don't you worry, his bark is worse than his bite?"

"I think I've lost my appetite," I whispered as I rubbed my tummy. I felt the anxiety swirling and gathering momentum in the pit of my stomach.

"You need to eat something. At least have a slice of toast. I can't force you to eat but Mr Lee gets regular updates on everything you eat and drink."

"Oh my God, are you serious?"

"He's only concerned for your well-being." If she only knew why Mr Lee was concerned about my well-being. "I promise you, he isn't as bad as you think he is," she said, handing me a slice of buttered toast.

"Do you know when he's coming back?"

"Any day now. I'd say he's now wrapping things up quickly after seeing those photos." I watched absently as she buttered a second piece of toast. I took another bite and said very slowly, "My life is not worth living. If he's packing up early on account of me, it can't be good." A feeling of anxiety washed over me. "Don't you worry unnecessarily? You have done nothing wrong Rhylee. It's not like you're even dating. Between you and me, I'd say he's jealous."

"Ah no, I tell you, you're wrong there."

"Am I?"

"Absolutely."

"Hmm. My heart tells me otherwise. I've noticed a change in that man since you got here."

"Really. Ah no. I'd say it's to do with having his mother around. The relationship between mothers and their sons are special. They're the light of their life, so to speak."

"We'll see if that's true when she goes home at the end of the week."

"She's leaving? My life is defo not worth living." I took a chunk of toast and then stopped in the realisation of what was about to happen. The reality of it all made me feel sick. I spit the toast into my napkin. "I'm sorry. That was so rude. But I don't feel well. I'm going to go back to bed. Please will you send my apologies to Mrs Lee? I don't think I'll feel any better by lunchtime," I cried.

Daiyu sat on the side of the armchair and felt my forehead. "You've gone as white as a ghost if that's even possible. Let me help you to your room and settle you in."

"It's okay. I'm sure you have a busy afternoon ahead."

"Don't you worry about that? I'll make you my special brew." I peered at her quizzically, making her giggle. "I have many special brews for different occasions," she said with a twinkle in her eye. I took off my jeans and climbed into bed. Daiyu sat next to me and watched as I drank her special brew. I handed the mug back to her, wiping my mouth on the back of my hand.

"I'm not sure how you do it, but that was just as nice as all the others. Exhausted by thoughts and emotions, I still managed to drift off. But images of the playroom and having sex with Gui flashed across my mind, so sleep was anything but peaceful. It seemed like I had barely closed my eyes before someone was tapping on my door.

I opened one eye and gasped looking up at the gorgeous man standing over me, Keane! He came into the room looking handsome in indigo jeans and a fitted tee shirt showing off every toned inch of his sculpted body. His jeans hugged his lower body revealing lean hips and long, muscular legs. I'm dead!

"Hi, I did knock, quite a few times," he said, his beautiful mouth pulling up into a smile. I blushed as I realised, I was returning his smile. I tried to remember what I was wearing before propping myself up on my elbows. My curly hair was wild and messy.

"Here, let me help you." He reached across, grabbed one of the spare pillows, fluffed it up and placed it gently behind me. Arousal ran through me as the warmth of his body brushed against mine. I shook the hair off my face and dropped back against them pulling the covers right up under my chin. He sat on the bed and not in the chair next to it. Oh God, too close for comfort. But I don't think I could have handled the sight of him in *his* chair.

"Daiyu said you were feeling poorly?"

"To be honest, I'm stressed over those stupid photos and now Gui is coming back early because of them. Are you sure he didn't say anything else?"

"Okay, promise me you won't freak out when I tell you?"

"Oh my God, tell me."

"Promise first."

"I promise."

"He said he was nervous and jealous because I was with you. Shocked you were drinking and the fact we were in the playroom of all places certainly didn't help. If anything happened to you, he'd kick the shit out of me!"

"That it?"

"Pretty much." He lifted one dark brow quizzically. "You okay?"

"Why would he be nervous or jealous," I frown, confused.

"It's a long story and now's not the time. Is your hair naturally curly?"

I screwed up my face. "What?" he asked.

"I don't want to talk about my hair. Don't change the subject. Tell me." He shot me a stern look, so I pouted, making him smile. Then he cut off the conversation with a hearty laugh making me giggle, diffusing the situation.

"Yes, it's all-natural." He raised an eyebrow. "My hair, naturally curly, I'm afraid." He pulled a wayward strand and let it spring back before placing it behind my ear. Oh sweet Jesus, that was so hot!

"I love it and prefer it that way." I lowered my gaze, blushing even deeper. "I love when you blush too." I covered my face with my hands. "Stop, you're making me worse."

"It's true. I do." I looked at him through my fingers. "Cut it out. Talking like that will get you into trouble, Mr Turner."

"Ooh it's hot when you call me Mr Turner," he smirked. "Stop it, I'm not even joking."

"Yeah, yeah." He pretended to zip a zipper across his lips. "Mom couldn't make it either. Wwan wasn't feeling well so she's gone out to his place to play nurse. So how about we have a bite to eat on the rooftop? It will be soo romantic."

I elbowed him in the ribs. "Hey, that hurt, I was only joking, or am I?"

"You're such a tease. I'm no proctologist, but I know an asshole when I see one!"

He clutched his heart and fell backwards onto the bed making a gurgling sound. "How could you? Your cruel words have pierced my heart. And I thought you liked me?" I rolled my eyes and crossed my arms over my chest. "Have you finished, you're such a drama queen," I giggled. "From now on, I'm going to call you Keano."

"Why Keano?"

"Just because I like it."

"Won't a certain billionaire get upset if you have a pet name for me?"

"Ah come on, it's not a pet name. It's a nickname we use in Ireland, after the football legend Roy Keane."

"Aw, that's not cute at all," he fumed.

"The last thing I want to do is tease him by flirting with his brother!

"Oh, if only you would," he said, wiggling his eyebrows.

"I'll have lunch, dinner or whatever; only if you behave." He leaned up on his elbows. "Just answer me one thing."

"Anything."

"Did you enjoy our kiss?" We stared into each other's eyes and I couldn't look away. My heart began pounding in my chest and I was afraid he might hear it too.

"Yes," I said tenderly. He smiled knowingly and sighed as if to say that this was the only answer he had expected to hear.

"So?"

"So what?" I ask.

"Did it arouse you?"

My mouth falls open in horror. "You said only one thing cheeky," I giggled. "It's just…." I stopped myself.

"Just what? Go on."

"Just that if only things were different," I reply slowly, wrapping a curl around my finger.

He opened his mouth to say something but just sighed. "You need to find yourself a girlfriend. I'm sure you only have to look at a woman and she drops her panties.

Well …. am I right?" He opened his mouth to defend himself, but nothing came out. He knew it was true. I could see he was in deep thought. He turned his head in defiance and I burst out laughing.

"You may be right, but they're not the women I want to date. Hoebags according to mom."

I giggle. "They weren't hoebags when you were sleeping with them!"

"No, they were pretty fucking satisfied though."

"Ooh, too much information."

"What can I say, I'm a very good fuck and could go all night."

"Jesus, you don't half love yourself."

"It didn't stop one or two thinking they could convince me they were the one. That's not me now. I got all that out of my system a long time ago. That's why I haven't dated for a couple of years."

Standing, he held out his hand. "Come, let's go eat. The aroma of freshly made seafood emanating from the kitchen is making me salivate. And I want to continue this conversation."

I took his hand and then remembered I was just wearing panties. "Just give me a minute, I need to put my jeans on." He grabbed them from the chair and handed them to me.

"Sure, I don't mind," he says with a mischievous grin on his face. I pointed towards the door.

"Out! Now."

"Calm down," he says. "I was only teasing."

"Out," I growled. He held his hands up in defence. "Jeez, can't a chap make a joke?" He shrugged. I roll my eyes.

"Jesus, you're so dramatic."

"Am not."

"Drama queen," I add.

His face falls. "I'll wait outside then." I throw my head back and laugh out loud. "But you do make me laugh if that's any consolation?"

"I'll take that," he gushed.

"I'll be right outside and promise not to peek through the keyhole." He closed the door and I immediately eyed the handle and giggled. There wasn't any keyhole.

He stood close to me as the doors closed and we took the elevator in silence. Afraid to look at him, I made a point of studying the changing numbers.

He glanced at his watch as the elevator doors opened... "Two-thirty, I have to leave at five-thirty."

It was such a relief walking out into the fresh air and feeling the heat of the afternoon sun on my face. Keane is right on my heels. "I love it up here, it's so beautiful." He looks straight at me, "So beautiful."

I broke our stare and glanced around. "So where are we eating? Mr Turner."

"I think you only call me Mr Turner when you're nervous?"

"Well Mr Turner, you're talking crap."

Daiyu approached us smiling. "Lunch is set up in the pod Mr Turner."

"Thank you, please tell me you made your famous fish pie," he asked enthusiastically.

She giggled. "Maybe? Find out before it gets cold."

"Come," he took my hand and walked quickly to the other side of the rooftop. "Daiyu's fish pie is one of the most homely, comforting and moreish dinners I've ever had," he said excitedly. "It's one of the things I miss when I'm away." He took me through some trees and we came out in front of a glass dome.

"Oh, my goodness where did that come from? How romantic," I gasped. "I didn't see this the last time I was up here."

"It's just finished so it was probably cordoned off then. These are our new dome structures for outdoor dining. Made of glass accommodating up to ten people seated at a round table. You can dine in any weather whilst taking in the spectacular views staying warm and cosy. Or you can sleep under the stars with our circular bed option which is so romantic when it's snowing."

"Tested that option yourself, have you?"

"Indeed, I have with the lovely Nola. She was certainly enthusiastic about spending the night under the stars. She even …"

I screwed up my face. "Eew! I don't want to know how enthusiastic Nola was, thanks very much. And I'm not staying here either listening to your sexual conquests. Ugh." I turned on my heel and walked into the dome as he roared laughing. God, his laugh was sexy as fuck, lucky Nola! Jealousy twists in the pit of my tummy.

The pod was decked out with greenery, twinkling fairy lights, candles and a chandelier. He followed me inside and the retractable double doors closed in silence.

"Wow, that's amazing."

He raised his hand, "remote controlled." He held out my chair as I sat.

"I have to say, this is amazing. Did you design these too?"

"Thank you. I did. The idea came about when a company approached me, urgently needing extra office space. There was no way to extend and when I saw the rooftop, the idea was born."

"I'd say it's wonderful to work in one of these, I'd love it myself."

"I have ten on my office building and had to assign them because of all the arguments about whose turn it was."

"Oh, I can imagine." He lifted the silver cloche to reveal a perfect fish pie. "I'd say Daiyu made this especially for me. She knows how much I love her fish pie."

"Yum, it smells delicious."

"Looks like she's done one of her 'special' winks, brews.

Pass me your plate. How hungry are you?" He asked. "I could eat a scabby horse," I giggled.

"Oh my God, sounds dreadful."

I took a forkful of fish pie, held it to my nose and sniffed, stuck out the tip of my tongue and tasted it before shoving it into my mouth. "Umm, delicious. I see what you mean."

"I'm sorry, I'm still getting over what you just did."

I looked at him, embarrassed as he mimicked me tasting my food. I burst out laughing.

"I'm comfortable in your company and I don't say that very often."

"Go ahead, don't let me stop you." He poured us each a glass of Daiyu's concoction, and I sniffed the golden liquid. Keane propped up on his elbows and stared. "What?"

I ask, smiling.

"You're just perfect even with your cute little habits." I raise my eyebrow. "I am perfect, except for my millions of tiny little flaws. It's far from cute and I try my hardest not to do it in company. But growing up in a home where your mother was a shit cook didn't help."

He thinks for a moment his gaze inquisitive, his eyebrows raised in a silent question. "Makes total sense then," he beamed. He held up his glass. "A toast to Rhylee's adorable quirks." We clinked glasses and giggled. "Nola by the way is my golden retriever puppy." He took out his phone and showed me his screen saver.

My mouth fell open. "Oh my goodness, she's adorable. Was she at your house when I was there?"

"No, she was with the vet. I rescued her from the animal shelter and wanted to make sure she wasn't poorly."

"I love that. I just hate puppy mills."

"I rescued her because I was rescued."

"Aww, that's so sweet. Will you bring her next time?"

"Is that an invitation?" He gave me a hopeful grin and winked.

I giggled and smiled at him. "Only if you bring Nola."

"Ouch! That's why I must leave at five-thirty. To collect her from the veterinary clinic."

"Oh no, is she okay?"

"She was having a full check-up and boosters for her passport."

"And there I was thinking you had a hot date."

"I'm having that now," he smiled.

"I'd love to go with you," I said hopefully.

"While the tabloids are still buzzing about the possibility of you being in a relationship with me or Gui, it's a no-no I'm afraid. As much as I'd love to take you, it's near impossible.

My phone vibrates and Gui's name lights up the screen. My heart pounds hard in my chest. I look at Keane feeling awkward, "It's a text from Gui, do you mind if I read it?"

"Of course not."

Gui: Hey, how are you?
Rhylee: I'm grand, tnx.
Gui: Sorry I haven't been on for a while, it's mad out here.
Rhylee: Yeah, your mum mentioned there was a problem.
Gui: There was, but a quick mind and perseverance pay off.
Rhylee: Thankfully.
Gui: Jingfei showed me a magazine with you and Keane in it.

Fuck face Jingfei ...

Rhylee: Yeah, it was crazy. Hard to believe it's reached that part of the world already.
Gui: It was online actually.

Bitch!

Rhylee: Oh really?
Gui: You looked stunning and your hair, well, it was like spun gold. Wish it had been me.
Rhylee: Wished what?
Gui: Kissed you.

Crap crap crap

Rhylee: It was only a peck.
Gui: It was on the lips Rhylee!
Rhylee: Was it, I don't remember.
Gui: I'll be home soon and our agreement still stands.
Rhylee: A deal is a deal.
Gui: Enjoy the pod, bye.
Rhylee: Bye-bye.

What a bizarre conversation….

26

I put the phone down and absentmindedly dragged my fingers through my hair. "Sorry about that," I said with a heavy heart.

"Hey, what's wrong?" He was beside me in a split second down on his hunkers.

"Is our billionaire Dom being a dick?"

I couldn't make eye contact because I'm trying my hardest not to burst into tears.

"Come here, it's obvious you're upset." He stood pulling me with him and hugged me tightly. He gave the best hugs ever. I closed my eyes and wished this wasn't so complicated. I had the principal role in my own shit show, and it was freaking me out. Gui needs to decide what the fuck he wants! He hooked his finger under my chin and raised it. "What's the dickhead done now?"

We stared at each other, and the air crackled between us. He slid his hand to the nape of my neck and pulled me closer. "I can't help myself when I'm around you. I've been in a state of arousal since we met." His sexy smile captivated me. I went to say something but he dips his head and kissed me softly. My heart pounded when he slid his tongue into my mouth. I closed my eyes. His next kiss was demanding, teasing me and driving me insane. I lost control as my fingers ran gently through his hair and I forgot where I was.

"I want you and want to watch you come."

I jerked out of his arms and stepped back panting for breath. "Is that…?" I looked down at his erection and blushed. He looked at me questioningly. He reached for me again, but I stepped further away.

"I'm sorry Keane, I can't. It doesn't feel right." Panting heavily, he drags his hand down his face. "Why?" He shook his head. "This is fucking killing me, Rhylee."

I burst into tears. "This whole situation is fucking with my head too. It's like some seedy exposé you read about in a shitty newspaper."

He looked wounded and hurt. "Do you mean this," he said, gesturing at the air between us.

"Nooo. God no. Not us."

He put his hands on his hips. "I swear to God Rhylee, I'm fucking losing it here. You still won't tell me, will you?"

"I can't."

"What the fuck is going on?" He snapped. Tears rolled down my cheeks. He pulled me close, cupped my face and kissed my nose.

"I'm sorry. Forgive me. Please don't cry, Rhy." I inhaled deeply. He has such a calming effect on me and for those few minutes, all is well in the world.

"I need to know though and this may seem stupid. But you're not in any danger? I mean…"

"Sshh, I'm not. It's nothing like that. Please don't worry."

I frowned. His eyes narrow. "Is that the truth?" I reach up and kiss his cheek.

"I promise. I'm not in any physical danger. And no, I don't need a bodyguard before you offer your services," I giggled. He chuckles too. He pulls me closer into his body and hugs the life out of me.

"Jesus, I can't breathe," I spluttered.

"I'm sorry, I just don't want to let you go." He shrugged. "Come on. Let's drink ourselves blotto on Daiyu's special brew."

He kissed my temple and wiped the tears from my cheek with his thumb. "Well, that's gonna be hard. I'm afraid. Gui left orders that nobody was to serve you anything with alcohol."

"You're fucking joking?"

He took my hand in his and squeezed it gently. I sighed.

"Let's finish our fish pie or Daiyu will never speak to me again." I stared at him. He was so fucking hot. A million visions of him bending me over the table and sliding down my jeans flashed across my mind.

"What are you thinking," he asked. I blushed. "Nothing."

"Was it naughty?"

"Guilty," I giggled.

He smiles. "I'm sure we're both thinking the same thing?" He sighed.

"Really, what's that?" I asked him.

He points to his boner. "Need you ask? Surely that's a huge hint?" He smiled innocently.

"It is," I replied softly.

His eyes linger affectionately on my face.

"Stop it! Don't start, or you'll have me bawling again."

He raises his hands in defence. "You can blame my dickhead brother for that."

"I've lost my appetite, Keane. Can we just sit and chat?"

"Whatever you want Rhy. Let's go snuggle on the sofa in front of the fire pit. I'd like to know more about you if that's okay?"

Sitting comfortably in front of the fire pit, we both looked out over the skyline. "It's unbelievable to think we are on one of the tallest buildings in the world."

"I know," he said. "So …" He smiled. "Tell me about yourself."

"Not much to tell. You know all there is to know."

"Ah, but there were certain questions I couldn't ask in front of my mother."

I bit my lip to hide my smile. "Like?"

"Who was your last boyfriend or fling?"

"Ooh straight to the point. I've never had a boyfriend - or a fling."

His eyes bug out in shock. "None?" He coughed. "You're winding me up?"

"I'm deadly serious."

"What, never?" He thought for a moment. "Are you gay?"

"You ask that after playing tonsil hockey with me?"

"This is true. But I could have turned you straight."

"You're so funny."

"Can that happen?"

"God only knows."

"Ahh, you're Catholic, aren't you?" He said like he just solved a case.

"It's not because I'm religious for fuck's sake!" He burst out laughing and I do too.

"You're such a dick Keano."

"I just don't get it. How is that even possible? You're beautiful, kind and smart. Everything about you is sexy, smoking hot, full lips, huge blue eyes ... and your voice. If I hadn't seen you first, I would have fallen for your voice. When I first heard you speak, it almost stopped me in my tracks." I smile to myself.

"Don't exaggerate."

Every girl wants to hear that

"Wow, I don't know what to say. I'm sure you have men constantly trying to get into your knickers." Absent-mindedly he tapped his temple. He smiled and glanced at me. "Got it. You were a nun?"

"Bingo."

He looked at me in shock. "Really?"

"Don't be silly!"

"Oh."

"I suppose I just haven't met the 'one'... He rubbed his hand down his face in thought and then back up. Everything he did was sexy.

"Until now," he suggests. I laughed out loud.

I wish.

He lifted his arm and I snuggled tightly against him. I tucked my legs under my bum and rested my head on his chest like it was the most natural thing in the world. For now, I was content as I listened to his heart beating. I smiled up at his sexy face and he pulled me closer, kissing the top of my head.

"We should totally fuck right now."

I elbowed him in the chest. "Seriously…. Don't ruin it."

He smiled down at me. "I'm sorry, I just can't help myself." All of a sudden, he sat ramrod straight and faced me. "Hang on a minute. Are you saying you're a vir-gin?" His full lips curved into a smile. I nod my head.

"Uh-huh."

His eyes widened, "Oh my God!" We stare at each other. "I'm shocked," he said.

I blinked. "What?"

"Well, that's a first. I've never met a virgin before."

"You have now. Truthfully, I've hardly had any experience with men at all."

"I can certainly help you with that," he said, wiggling his eyebrows. I rolled my eyes. He sat there in silence watching me.

"I suppose it's not something you hear very often."

"Fuck no."

I could see him eyeing his crotch and shifting uneasily. I bite my lip and giggle. "I'm sorry, but how can someone so perfectly beautiful still be single? It's a fucking sin."

"Oh my goodness, will you stop?"

"Surely you've been attracted to someone?"

"No. Not really." I sigh.

The only man I want is untouchable …

"Are you waiting until you're married? Because I'll marry you right fucking now," he said in a deadpan manner. "Have a couple of kids and happily grow old together."

You're not him.

I studied his serious face. I couldn't help myself and burst out laughing. "You're such a comedian. It will happen when it happens. I'll wait for my knight in shining armour, I'm sure he's out there somewhere?" I smiled hopefully.

"But thank you for your kind offer," I giggled. "Come on, let's change the subject," I murmured.

He exhales heavily. "Can't believe you're knocking me back." He frowned.

"I know. Shocker huh?"

He gave me a beautiful smile and I knew he wasn't that bothered. Maybe his ego is just a little? I had a gut feeling that we'd be great friends forever.

"So tell me about your relationship with Gui and Genny. Why do you call him your brother?"

"My brother from another mother," he joked. "I was four when Genny took me in and raised me as her own. We lived next door and our parents were best friends since university. They all attended university in the USA, as did myself and Gui. We were sleeping as the house went up in flames. My father forgot to put the guard in front of the fire."

I gasped and squeezed his hand in mine. "Oh my God Keane. I know what you're going to say. It's okay, you don't have to."

He shrugged. "The alarm was raised quickly and firefighters rushed to put it out but it was already out of control. You couldn't see in front of you the smoke was so thick with strong winds fanning the flames. Firefighters tackling the blaze had to pump water from the swimming pool to fight the flames because the house was so large. Mason, Gui's dad, climbed up onto the garage when he was told not to enter the house because it wasn't stable. But there was no stopping him knowing the three of us were still inside. My room was on the garage side, and he carried me to safety without even a scratch. I was still sleeping."

He fell silent again. I squeezed his hand. "He went back in and that's when the house collapsed killing him and my parents." He stared down at me, obviously shocked by his memories. "There wasn't any doubt in Genny's mind that she was going to adopt me. We moved within a week because it was just too painful. She treated me as a son and Gui just grew up thinking I was his brother. We were so young and didn't know any better. On our sixteenth birthday, Genny told us. It made no difference to either of us. We loved each other regardless. And never once thought it strange that our looks were so different. Me blonde and him jet black, the resemblance is uncanny don't you think hahaha? Thanks to our close upbringing, we know exactly what the other one is about to say, like twins you might say. We've made loads of hilarious memories together, especially in uni. Girlfriends were unfortunately put through their paces, to make sure they were up to standard. And if they weren't. Adios. We have an unbreakable bond. We can always rely on each other to show how proud we are of each other's achievements. He's the first person I call for advice and vice versa. We will forever have each other's back and family always comes first."

"Oh Keane, that's devastating. I'm sorry for you all but what a wonderful outcome," I sniffed. "And you've kept your surname."

"I have. Most of my companies are LT Holdings, Lee Turner or KLT Architects & Developers. I wanted to carry on my father's name."

"Wow, that's amazing. So, your parents aren't Chinese?"

"Jesus, you'd do alright working for the FBI," he laughed. "My parents were both American, as was Gui's dad. They were incredibly wealthy, and my inheritance was put into a trust fund with Genny as trustee. It was a variety of assets, money, property, stocks and bonds and dad's business which Mason was a partner. Genny continued to run it until I was old enough to take over. I bought her out after five years which earned her a profit of over a billion dollars."

"Holy crap!"

"So that's my life in a nutshell, warts and all."

"Are you okay? I whispered.

"I'm fine. I've just never opened up about it to anyone before. Ooh, you're a right little FBI agent."

I stretched up and kissed his cheek. "What was that for, not that I'm complaining."

"Just because…eh obviously you two talk a lot. But do you talk about private stuff? Like girlfriends and such?"

His sexy eyes held mine. "We don't go into details about sex if that's what you're hinting at? It's so strange, he hasn't said anything about you. It's the first time he hasn't confided in me. Maybe he wants you all to himself and I can't blame him. It's bizarre because mom is not sure exactly what is going on either. Perhaps now you'd like to shed some light on the matter?"

"I think he felt obliged to look after me after what happened. That's it."

Liar liar liar.

"Sounds about right, he's a softy underneath it all." I let out a sigh of relief knowing I dodged a bullet.

"I'd love you to meet Lan and my best friend Evee."

"I'd like that too. Evee, that's an unusual name."

"It's traditionally an Irish female name meaning peace."

"What's she like?"

"Who, Lan or Evee?" I giggled innocently knowing full well he meant Evee. "We've been best friends since childhood. And she's like a sister to me."

"Oh, wow really."

"She's my bff and her parents treat me like I'm one of their kids. God help anyone who slags me off because they will feel the wrath of Evee. She has made it her job to protect me."

"I'll remember that one," he said, nodding his head slowly up and down.

"I know she will always have my back. She's wild and carefree and doesn't give a shit what anyone thinks of her. The total opposite to me."

"Is she hot and does she have a boyfriend? That's all I want to know!"

"Oh my God, nobody's safe around you."

"Hard facts, Rhylee, that's all I want," he said, smacking his hands together.

"She's stunning and has been with Josh since she was thirteen. They're mad about each other and at times make me want to puke. Ah no, I'm happy for them. Wouldn't be surprised if he proposes on her birthday. It's long overdue."

He looked at his watch. "Fuck, I have to go." His phone rang and he dug it out of his pocket. "Hey Dan., sorry, I lost track of the time. I'll be there shortly. How is she? Great, that's a relief. Yeah, see you then." He clapped his hands together. "Nola is a happy healthy little puppy."

"Aww, that's good news indeed. I won't walk you out if that's okay. I need to do something." I stood and held out my arms.

We hugged each other tightly. He kissed the top of my head and left. I sat down and phoned Evee. Having put it off for so long.

"Well hello stranger," she answered.
"Hi"
"How's things?"
"Grand."
"Just grand?"
"Yeah. I'm sorry I haven't called sooner."
"It's okay. I knew you would when the time was right. I've missed you."
"Missed you too."
"Don't start me off," she sniffed.
"Would you and Josh like to come over tomorrow and meet Gui's brother?"
"His brother?? I thought he was an only child?"
"So did I. His name is Keane and he's ridiculously hot. Wait until you see him."
"Maybe another time. Not up for meeting people right now."
"Why? What's up?"
"Just not feeling sociable?"

"Ah come on. I'm not in a mood anymore!"
"Would you?"
"Ye-ah."
"Fuck off!"
"What can I say, he's a ride."

We both burst out laughing. And just like that. The air was cleared between us.

I smiled to myself looking forward to seeing my pal. Fuck, should I have run it past Gui? Here's me treating his home like it's my own. Shit! I'll text him. Ten minutes later he replied. Fine….. From his reply, I'm guessing he wasn't in a good mood. I suppose he has a lot on his plate right now... multi-billion-dollar deals, his mother and who knows what else? Maybe I figured somewhere in there too? Shit! Probably why he's in a mood.

Pushing that thought to the back of my mind, I focused on Evee's impending visit. I was so eager to see her and could hardly wait for the next day. I was annoyed with myself for carrying it on for so long. In my mother's words, you're just a stubborn little bitch!

27

Lan and I were playing in the lounge when Daiyu appeared. She tapped on the door. "Rhylee, Evee is in the lobby, will I show her up?"

I stopped in alarm at her question. As if I was the lady of the house. "I'm sorry Daiyu. I should have said she was calling. Do you mind showing her in? Or I can if you like?

"No no, it's fine. Mr Lee mentioned you were having guests over. We need to know these things for security reasons."

"I'm sorry, of course." She smiled and left. I felt like an idiot!

Evee ran into my arms and swung me around like I weighed no more than a rag doll. Lan was jumping up and down with excitement. She lifted Lan and hugged her too.

"Where's Josh," I asked, looking over her shoulder.

She approached me as she removed her jacket, a sad smile on her face. "He won't be coming. He's at home."

"Oh, is he ill?" She put Lan down and took my hand, leading me to the sofa.

"He's home, home," she said, blinking away her tears.

"Home … as in Ireland," I gasped.

"Yes."

"Are his parents, okay?"

"We broke up." She said it with such sad finality like she had lost him forever.

I didn't say anything for a few minutes because I was shocked to my core. "When?"

"Last week."

"Oh my God Evee, why didn't you call me?"

"You had your own thing going on here."

I shook my head. "You are more important to me than anything. I can't believe you had to go through it on your own." My eyes welled up and I wrapped my arms around her. She began to cry, her sobs muffled as she leaned against my chest. Both of us were now softly bawling. Poor Lan stared, standing very still clutching her doll tightly.

"I feel so alone."

I held her even tighter. "What happened?" She started to say something but just bit her lip and began to cry again. "It's okay, take your time."

She pulled away and wiped her eyes on the back of her hand. Lan ran off and returned with a wad of tissue paper. "You're not supposed to wipe your nose on the back of your hand," she said innocently.

We both looked at her and laughed out loud. She kissed Evee's cheek and then went back to playing with her dolls.

"He said he was bored."

My eyes bugged. "What the actual fuck!"

"I have only ever seen him cry twice in all the years we were together. When his granny passed and when he told me he wanted to break up. I thought he had been acting strange and pushed him on it. He just said he was busy at work. After a dinner meeting, he came home blotto and blurted it out. There weren't any clear signs that we stopped working, because we always communicated, and sex was amazing."

"I don't know what to say. I'm gobsmacked. Bored with what exactly, YOU," I said, anger burning through me. I waited patiently for her to answer, filled with both anger and pain for my best friend. How could he after all these years?

"Mam and dad just arrived and are staying for a few weeks."

"Explains your horse-riding outfit."

"Yeah, you know mother, she thinks riding her horses solves everything. I'm meeting them at the stables after. Why don't you come too? They're dying to see you. Or are you still locked up?"

"Yeah. Except for that time when his mother took me out to lunch. Omg, wait until you see the photos. We were hounded by paparazzi and that's when he kissed me," I whispered.

"Who, Gui?"

"No, Keane."

"Jesus Rhylee. You have two men in heat and to top it all off, they're brothers. You've gone from a famine to a feast."

I scrolled through the images on my phone and handed it to her. She clicked on the headline of one of the images:

Is Love in the Air? As Keane Lee Turner and Rhylee Murphy are snapped leaving a private dinner with Genji Lee.

Keane Turner living up to his playboy rep leaving 'The H' with supermodel stunner Asha Carlton

"Rhylee, omg you look like a model. That's the only time I've ever seen your hair straight. It's stunning. And your dress. But who's Asha," she asked, pointing to the photo I'd missed.

"Hmm, don't know."

"Fucking hell though. He's fit as fuck," she gasped. We both drooled over one of the photos of Keane getting into his car.

"Wait until you meet him. He's the complete package, brawn and brains."

As she scrolled through the rest of the images, I couldn't get my head around it. How could this happen? They were supposed to stay together forever.

"Evee, I just don't know what to say. It doesn't make sense. Like he's the one who followed you over here. You never asked him to leave his family or his job. You even said that you'd try long distance."

She handed me back my phone. "I know. Maybe when he gets his head around it, he might be able to help me make sense of it all."

"He's a little fucker!"

"I know you're only looking out for me but don't say anything you may regret. It might be just a blip?"

"Have you talked since he went home?"

"Well, no, not yet. And it's been so hard not to call him."

"Are you okay meeting Keane? I mean you don't have to if it's going to upset you?"

"No, I'm fine, honestly. Don't worry. I won't fling myself down on the floor and have a mental breakdown."

"You sure," I giggled. She gave me a reassuring hug.

"I'm a hundred percent sure."

There was a hard knock on the door which frightened the crap out of us. Standing there in all his gorgeousness was Keane hiding behind masses of beautiful flowers and gift bags. Evee's mouth dropped open and she pinched me. He walked toward us and handed me a bouquet. "For you, beautiful." I smiled shyly. "You must be Evee, these are for you. And may I say, you are as beautiful as Rhy said you were?" She looked up at him like he was an apparition and blushed. She actually blushed. Oh! I've never seen her go red.

Lan hung back looking shy and nervous. This man had us all in a fluster. He removed his jacket, casually throwing it over the back of the sofa. His muscles flexed against his tight shirt. "Oh, my fucking God," she whispers. Both of us were transfixed by his every move. He got down on his knees and handed Lan a huge pink glitter bag. "And this is for the prettiest little girl in the house."

Evee and I looked at each other and awed. The look on her face filled me with emotion. I wasn't around when she got any of the other stuff. I swallow the lump in my throat. But dammit, it's so hot watching how he is with her. He's a natural. Unlike Gui. Feeling two pairs of eyes on him he looks over at me and raises his eyebrow in question. "What?"

"Nothing." I gushed. Evee is leaning on her elbows, starry-eyed, short of falling flat on her face. Or should I say, head over heels? Hmmm…interesting. Lan looks to me for assurance.

"It's okay sweetie. Keane got that, especially for you." She stood on tippy toes trying to peek into the bag.

"Would you like me to show you?" He asked. She looked at me and I nodded.

"What's in there?" She asked with a shy smile. He lifted the bag close to his face and whispered into it. "What's that? You want to meet Lan?"

"Who's in there," she said. She pointed to the bag not taking her eyes off it as she walked towards me. She leaned on my lap.

"Rhylee, who's in there?"

"I'm not sure but I think whoever it is wants to meet you. Go and see honey." She kissed me and then ran back to Keane. He moved the bag in between them. She waited a few seconds until curiosity got the better of her. Peering in, she gasped, looked at me and smiled. She kneeled closer and carefully took out the most beautiful life-sized doll I had ever seen. We all gushed.

"I don't believe it. That's incredible," I said. She placed the doll beside her and looked at me in shock, her mouth wide open. She stood there for a moment like she was looking in a mirror. The doll was the spitting image of her. I looked at Keane.

"How?"

"I can't take the credit for this. Gui sent me a photo of Lan."

"I don't understand. Why did he do that?"

"He knew I was coming over so asked me to go to 'Mini me.' It's a famous store which specialises in twin dolls."

"He asked you to do that, for Lan?"

"Told you, he's a softie." My heart melted. I wanted to phone him straight away to thank him. But remembered I was on his naughty list. He pushed the other bag towards her. "This one is from me," he smiled sweetly. Her screams of delight were infectious as she took out several outfits for her doll. My heart couldn't take much more.

"What's her name," I asked.

She put her finger to her lip and thought for a moment. Then asked her dolly. "She says her name is Rhylee." I put my hand to my heart and melted into a puddle. I nodded enthusiastically as she held up each outfit.

Evee whispered, "I'm bursting for a wee, where's the bathroom?"

"Last door on the right. And don't be nicking anything either." I winked.

Bending close to my ear she whispered, "There's only one place to hide anything and that's up my arse. You gonna look there?" As she left the room, she wiggled her perfect arse in her obscenely tight-fitting jodhpurs and giggled.

Keane was beside me in a heartbeat. "Fucking hell Rhylee. You never said she was that fucking hot. And Christ, that ass. I've died and gone to heaven."

"I did … I said she was stunning. Oh, and don't mention her boyfriend, they've just broken up."

He blessed himself and said, "My prayers have been answered."

I elbowed him in the chest and realised he was deadly serious. "Oh my God, you're such a player, Keane Turner. Yesterday you wanted me to have your babies. Disgusting!"

I laughed. "In fairness now, at the time I was genuinely serious."

"After what you've just said. Not gonna happen."

"My dear beautiful Rhylee. We both know your heart lies elsewhere and very close to home. Who am I to interfere with true love?" He tapped the side of his nose and joined Lan on the floor. I looked at him gobsmacked, my mouth wide open. I scratched my head. What the fuck has happened since yesterday. I clench my jaw in frustration.

"Oh my God, that bathroom is to die for," said Evee as she sat on the floor right next to Keane.

"I designed it," Keane beamed.

Her eyes widen. "You did," she exclaimed. I roll my eyes. Here we go. "Yeah, I designed the whole building."

"Wow really. Is that what you do?" She said tucking her hair behind her ear. Things like that don't impress Evee. She comes from old money. So, if he's trying to get into her knickers that way, he hasn't a hope. I have to admit, they look good together. Evee with her fiery red hair, fair skin and freckles and Keane, blonde, dimples and sallow. Their babies would be beautiful.

"What are you smiling about?" Evee asked. "Tell you later," I winked.

"Hey, there's no secrets around here, Miss Murphy. Or is there?" He asked, tapping the side of his nose again. We all looked from one to the other.

"Hey, are you two, okay?" Evee asked. I hate when mom and dad fight."

We looked from one to the other and burst out laughing.

Daiyu appeared. "Lunch is served in the dining room."

Keane stood and held out his hand to Evee. "Great, I'm famished," he said.

I giggled. "Who even talks like that?"

He whispered in my ear. "Someone trying to impress a fiery goddess." I tut. As to be expected. The table was beautifully set. I sat opposite Keane and Evee. I'd give anything to know what's on his mind.

He leaned forward. "Are you okay Rhy?" He asked. "I'm just wondering why all of a sudden, you're being an arsehole," I smirked.

He put his hand on his chest. "Ouch, that hurt!"

"What's going on here?" Evee asked. Did I miss something when I went to the loo?"

He shook his napkin all the time keeping his eyes locked on mine and dropped it across his lap. "Is there something going on Rhylee," he asked. I dropped my gaze and bite my bottom lip, suddenly not feeling hungry. I picked at my salad and listened to Keane and Evee chatting away like they've known each other for ages. Evee was always so confident and could talk to anyone. Nothing fazed her. I suppose I was more shocked at how quickly Keane turned his attention to her. This made me wonder if he'd do the same to her too. I know he's going to pursue her. I felt sick knowing how vulnerable she is right now. I clenched my fists under the table. He can go fuck himself if he thinks she's just going to fall so easily into his bed. Sick bastard. I was gutted because he fooled me too. I thought he was everything you could want a boyfriend to be. But not for me. Evee's phone rang. "Sorry, just a minute. Hi Dad. Yes, I'll be down now." She glanced over at me. "No Dad, she can't make it today. I will. See you in a minute. I have to go. Dads parked illegally." She hugged everyone and left.

I was half expecting Keane to follow her out like a little puppy. I was relieved he didn't. Taking Lan's hand I said, "You know where the door is, let yourself out."

He remained silent as I walked by. "Rhy, can I be completely honest?"

I stopped in my tracks and turned to face him. "I think you've shown your true colours, Keane. And it makes me very sad indeed. I feel heartbroken if I'm being honest."

He followed silently behind me. I didn't care that I dared to tell him to leave knowing it was more his home than mine. I plonked on the sofa and sighed. Keane sat next to me.

"I thought you were leaving. There's no reason for you to be here now."

Lan tapped my leg. "Can I get Rhylee's clothes?"

"Of course you can, you don't have to ask darling."

"It's not what you think."

"Isn't it?"

"I'm sorry for acting like a dick. I thought if I pretended that I knew what was going on, you'd end up telling me. Then I tried to make you jealous hoping you'd reveal something. Childish I know and I deeply regret acting like a total shit. Can you forgive me?"

"Wait, are you saying that shit show you put on was to fuck with my mind?"

He took my hand in his and kissed the back of it. I snatched it away. "Rhylee, I swear, that's all it was. The feelings I said I have for you are real. I was just trying to call your bluff."

"Well, it wasn't very nice. But it has made one thing clear in my mind. We will only ever be friends. Good friends."

He pulled me in for a hug. "I'm so sorry Rhy. I'd never hurt you. Please say you forgive me."

"I forgive you, you little shit. Don't ever do anything like that again."

"I promise. I won't," he pouted. "Rhylee."

"Yes, Keane."

"Can we have make-up sex?"

"Jesus! Grow up."

"Worth a try. I do think Evee is fucking hot though."

"That's okay because she is. I'll just say one thing. Please give her time."

He squeezed me harder. "One last kiss, hey?" I pulled away.

"About that."

"Go on."

"I should never have reciprocated. It was unfair of me to give you the wrong idea."

"When I want something Rhylee, I don't stop until it's mine. On this occasion, it became a challenge. I'm man enough to admit defeat. Probably my first and hopefully my last. Can I ask you something?"

"Anything."

"Would we have worked?"

"I said it before. In an ideal world and if circumstances were different. More than likely, I'd be pregnant now."

"Fuck Rhy, don't say that."

"It's the truth. I fancied you from the moment I saw you talking to Cici. You're everything I'd want but there is someone else. He just doesn't feel the same way."

"Dickhead!"

"But I realise now it wouldn't have worked between us."

"Why?"

"I think it was more lust than love if I'm being completely honest."

He pondered for a moment. "Who's to say?"

He stayed until I was too tired to talk anymore. Daiyu had taken Lan and her twin off to bed hours ago.

"I'm going to stay the night," he yawned. "I'm too exhausted to drive home."

"Do I need to lock my door?"

"You're safe," he said, wiggling his eyebrows. I kissed him goodnight. Too tired to shower, I just about managed to throw on my pyjamas and fall head-first into bed. What a fucking day?

28

My phone rang and Evee's name lit up the screen. "Shit, what time is it? I feel like I'd just closed my eyes." My eyeballs were burning in my head.

"What time did you go to bed?" she asked.

"Late. Keane didn't go home."

"Oh," she cooed. "Did he have a sleepover?"

"No, he did not Evee! He stayed in one of the gazillion bedrooms!"

"I looked him up."

"You Googled him."

"Of course, I did. He left an impression. But I'm not sure. There are hundreds of images of him. Everyone is with a different woman and they're all stunners. He's quite the player. Did you know?"

"I suppose he was just enjoying life. Getting it all out of his system."

"And has he?" she asked.

"He said he wants to settle down and have kids."

"Settle down when?"

"He's ready now."

"Do you believe him?"

"Yes."

"Hmm."

"What's that for?"

"Just thinking."

"You like him, don't you?"

"I do. I know it's crazy and it's much too soon after Josh and then he has the hots for you."

"Sshh, calm down Evee. Take a breath before you pass out. Believe me. Nothing is going on between us. Look, even if there was no Gui, nothing would have happened. It was all just banter and sexual tension."

"If you think there could be something. You have to at least try."

"But you said you 'would' and you never said that about Josh."

"Eew! I've known Josh as long as you and he's like my brother. Keane is a full-grown man, and I wouldn't be normal if I said I wouldn't, he's a ride. But that's it."

"Are you sure?"

"Evee, I swear to God I'm not interested."

"It's true, I'd like to get to know him."

I knew she was smiling when she said it. "Well then, just take it in your stride. You want to make sure Josh is out of your system. You've known him forever."

"Did I ever tell you when Josh and I had unprotected sex?"

"Doesn't ring a bell."

"The next day, he made me go and get the morning-after pill. He even made the appointment and asked his mother to take me because he couldn't look at me without feeling guilty. If I had been, I was okay with being pregnant. You know me. But he went berserk saying we were too young to be tied down raising a child. I asked when was it convenient for him to have one. Do you know what he said?"

"I don't think I want to know."

"He said never!"

"What the fuck Evee. Why did you stay with him? Everyone knows you want a shit load of kids."

"I think I stayed because I liked the security."

"If you'd told me this at the time, I would have kicked him in the balls."

"After being around Keane for those few hours, I could see the difference between them. I feel bad saying this. Josh is a boy who should have come with 'How to become a man' instructions. Keane is all man."

"There you go. You were childhood sweethearts."

"Anyway, enough dreaming. He's probably not even interested?"

"He thinks you're hot."

"Get lost! Omg really?"

"How do you know? Did he say that Rhy?"

I burst out laughing. "His actual words were, 'Fiery goddess.'

"Fuck off, no way. Omg," she gasped.

I smiled to myself. I had a good feeling about this and I was going to be fairy godmother.

"What time did you say it was?"

"It's just gone nine."

"Why on earth are you up so early?"

"I went riding with mam at seven-thirty. She's trying to keep my mind off Josh. I tried telling her that I was fine. And I am. It's like a weight has been lifted off my shoulders."

"I was thinking about it too. I think you felt you had to stay together because you knew nothing else. But wait and see. Let Keane make the first move. In the meantime, you need to get on with your life. Whether it's with Josh or someone else. Do you want to come over for breakfast?"

"I've had breakfast. We all can't be ladies of leisure, you know."

"Come over and watch me eat breakfast then," I giggled.

"Are you sure? Won't Gui be pissed off when he hears about it?"

"To be honest, I don't care." I did care. But I'd deal with it when he got here. Until then, I just wanted to see my friend.

I was still in bed when she tapped on my door.

"Why aren't you up lazy bones?" I exaggerated trying to sit up.

"Oh let me help you," she said, rushing to my aid. "Are you okay Rhy?"

"I don't feel the best, to be honest."

"Is it your Endometriosis?"

"I just feel sick, a little dizzy."

"Oh, should I get Daiyu?"

"Ahh, she has enough to do. Could you get me a glass of hot water with a slice of lemon please?"

"Of course. Where's the kitchen," she asked.

"I have no idea. But if you go to the living room, Daiyu will appear."

We both giggled. "Is she still doing that?"

"Yeah, thank God. Because I still don't know where anything is in this place."

"By the way. You look gorgeous." She stopped at the door and turned. "The green dress is stunning with your hair."

She looked down at what she was wearing. "Aw, thanks. It's one of mams. I raided her wardrobe when she got here. I think she purposely buys things for me and pretends they're hers."

"Nothing wrong with that," I said.

"I'll be back in a minute." I wasn't lying. She did look gorgeous. She was always a stunner. And she never acted like she knew. She's much taller than me with shining red hair down her back. Pale skin with a scattering of freckles, green eyes and huge lips. We have the typical Irish complexion coveted by many. We Irish are truly the fairest of them all. Saying that Gui is fairly pale. That's right, wasn't his dad American? I'm sure Keane mentioned that his parents and Gui's da were from America.

Lan came bounding through the door and jumped on top of me. "Whoa there Lan," said Evee, "Rhylee is not feeling too good."

She sat on my lap and slapped her tiny hand against my forehead. "Are you sick?"

"A tiny bit," I smiled.

"Will I get the doctor," she asked.

"Not this time honey." I kissed her cheek. Keane appeared in the doorway holding a tray.

"Mr Turner, a very good morning to you."

He frowned. "Rhy, stop calling me that." Then I remembered. It turns him on. Shit.

"For the patient," he says.

He wore a pair of jeans, tight in all the right places and a pink T-shirt. Only he could pull off wearing that colour. Evee had that look again and mouthed, "Holy fucking shit," and I giggle. Yep, he was hot. Lan shifted off me as he placed the tray gently over my lap and kissed my cheek. "The flower was my idea. What's wrong with you anyway Rhy? Did my mansplaining make you ill?"

I exhaled heavily. "I think I might just have a bug?"

"Gui knows."

My eyes bugged. "Why? Seriously, does he need to be told everything?"

"He's kind of a germaphobe so he needs to know. If I was ill, he'd call me and say, "Don't you come over here you germy prick!"

"Sshh, language," I giggled. I put my hand over my mouth to stifle a laugh.

"I know I shouldn't laugh at your expense, but that's so funny. Sounds just like him."

"Anything to make you feel better princess."

He sat next to me and poured hot water into my cup. "How many," he asked with tongs in hand.

"One slice please, thank you."

"Do you feel up to having a slice of toast?" he asked softly.

"It's fine. I can manage, don't worry. So, what are you doing today?"

He shrugged. "Not sure. I'm at a lost end. I had plans with Gui but that's up in the air now."

I thought for a minute. "I have an idea. Why don't you take Evee and Lan to the park?"

Evee pins me with a stare. "After what happened with the paps, I don't think so. Lan could end up getting hurt. And if Gui knew I put you in that situation again, well you get the idea."

"That's a shame. It looks like such a lovely day out there." Looking out the window, he rubbed his chin in concentration. "Hmm. Just wait here. I'll be right back."

As soon as he was out of earshot, Evee joined me on the bed.

"What the hell are you doing, Cilla Black?"

"I don't know what you're talking about," I smirk.

"I'm not ready to go out alone with him just yet."

"You won't be alone. Lan will be there too. Nothing much can happen with a toddler in tow."

"I know but it would be awkward."

"Evee, we don't know what he's even planning. Might be just a picnic on the roof," I say as I bite into my toast.

"It doesn't matter what or where it is. I'm not capable of adulting right now," she frowned. She was panicking now and speaking way too fast.

"Would you calm down for God's sake, you'll be grand."

To my utter surprise, she stopped freaking out. "You have to come too," she pleaded.

"I'd love nothing better than to get out of here. But I'm not well hun."

She took my hand in hers and looked at me with a sad expression. "You still haven't told me what's up with you."

"I'm not sure. Kinda feels like the flu?" I blew on the hot liquid and took a sip.

"Oh, that's so nice. Would you like some?"

At this point, she was now pacing the room. "No, I'm grand, thanks. But I just remembered, I have to help mam clean out the stables."

"Evee O' Mahony, stop telling fibs. Your mother wouldn't shovel horse shit if her life depended on it!"

"Well, she has to this time. The staff are all out sick."

"Omg, you're such a little liar. How can you stand there and tell me bare-faced lies?"

"It's true. Ask her."

I held out my hand. "What?"

"Give me your phone. I'll ask her myself."

Her eyes widened in terror. "I left it at the stables. Where would I fit a phone anyway? I have no pockets," she said, twirling.

"Lan sweetheart, can you ask Daiyu for Evee's coat please."

She climbed off the bed and when she got to the door, Evee screamed out. "Alright for God's sake, I'm telling lies."

"Sure, I know that. I feel bad that you did."

"But you wouldn't bloody shut up about it no matter what I said. What do you expect?"

"Don't go then. You explain to Lan why you've ruined her day out knowing she's been locked up here as long as me. Go on, tell her."

She gritted her teeth as she looked at Lan's sad little face staring up at her.

"You're such an evil bitch Rhylee Murphy."

"Sure, I know that too, you lying cow."

She narrowed her eyes at me and laughs. I laugh too. "Well, ladies. Do I have a surprise for you or what?"

I dusted the crumbs from my hands and smiled. "What is it," I asked as Evee sat next to me.

"We are going on a helicopter ride," he gushed with excitement. Evee and I looked at each other. He smiles and looks between us.

"So, what do you think?"

Evee points with her finger up to the sky. "You mean up there?"

"That's not the response I was hoping for."

"How?" she asked, rubbing her temple. "Have you hired one for the day?"

"Nope, I'm taking Gui's. It's on the helipad on the other side of the building. I designed that too," he said winking.

"Wow," I said. "This place is full of surprises."

"So Keane, just to clarify a minor detail," Evee said, exhaling heavily. "When you said, 'I'm taking Gui's helicopter. Are you taking Gui's pilot too?"

She squeezed my arm waiting for him to answer. "I'm the pilot," he beamed.

She put her hand over her mouth.

"I have a PPL, Private Pilot's Licence." His eyes flicker between the two of us, obviously disappointed she wasn't impressed. Probably used to women fawning all over him hearing that. "Please don't tell me you're afraid of flying?"

"I wasn't until now. Those things have an engine the size of a hair dryer." I burst out laughing.

"Well, you haven't heard this one, it's a beast with a jet engine and sounds like a fighter jet."

"You seem to know your stuff and it all sounds so interesting," I said.

"Ahh, you could say I'm an aviation nut. So is Gui."

"What? A nut," I giggled. "Evee, you'll be grand. Stop fussing. It's a chance in a lifetime." She smiled sweetly at Keane as she pinched me. My eyes widened. "Ouch," I roared.

"If that's the case, you have to come too," she said.

"Aw, I'd love to. But I'm going to lie down and try to go back to sleep. Try to shake this bug. Hopefully, by the time you get back, I'll be feeling myself again." I bite the inside of my cheek to stop myself from laughing. Keane on the other hand was beginning to look frustrated.

"Evee, I'd love nothing better than to take you for a ride."

"Oh Jesus," I sniggered.

"Fuck! You know what I mean."

She giggled at his faux pas which helped lighten the situation.

"You'll both love it and Daiyu has even prepared an amazing picnic hamper for us."

She bit her lip and nodded. "Okay, let's do this. Do we need to take a jacket?"

"Just come as you are." His eyes bugged and I sniggered again. He was certainly coming out with double entendres which could only mean one thing, he was just as nervous as her.

"Lan needs a coat, just in case," I said. "Come on, sweetie, get your hat and coat, maybe a pair of gloves too."

She came back into the room all wrapped up within an inch of her life. I climbed out of bed and hugged her, kissed Evee and Keane and practically pushed them out the door. Evee turned.

"But…"

"Buh-bye now," I said, pushing her out the door and closing it quickly.

Get the fuck out

"Make sure to take lots of photos," I shouted. I jumped on the bed giggling and rubbed my hands together. I couldn't have hoped for a better plan.

Knock knock…

Oh, for fuck's sake. Don't tell me she's changed her mind. Mrs Lee popped her head in.

"It's only me, can I come in dear?"

"Hello, Genny. Yes, of course." I said relieved. "Thank God it's you."

"Why, who were you expecting?"

"I thought Evee had changed her mind especially after Keane made arrangements. I know I put her on the spot. But a bit of encouragement never hurt anyone. Do her the world of good. I hope… Saying that, if she had done that to me, I wouldn't speak to her in like forever."

She smiled softly and kissed my cheek.

"How are you and how's Wwan? I hope he's feeling much better?"

She sat on the chair facing me. His chair. My eyes widened. The chair he wanked in watching me sleep. Oh, dear.

"Wwan is fine, thank you. Has man-flu. God help us. But Daiyu said you weren't too good yourself? So, I thought I'd pop in and see how you are."

She clasped her hands, index fingers pointing together and tapped her lips. Looking at me, all judge-like. Waiting for me to speak nothing but the truth. I hesitated. Was she on to me?

"Thank you, that's very kind. But no need to be concerned. I'm feeling much better now, maybe a little tired," I said, faking a yawn.

She smiled warmly. "Hmm," she said. I innocently smiled back.

"Still, I think I should call the doctor to be sure. Gui would be furious if I didn't. Your health and well-being are very important to him." We stared it out.

"May I speak freely?"

"But of course. You can say anything to me."

"Are you trying to put Keane and your friend Evee together?" I didn't answer.

"You see, I know he likes you very much and it might be a great mistake."

Does she know?

"I like him too but it wouldn't work between us."
"Your heart is elsewhere? Yes, I believe it is?"

She knows?

I thought for a minute.

Was there any point repeating myself, that we couldn't come from more different worlds blah blah blah...

"I don't plan on getting close to anyone because my time here isn't permanent. I have to get back to my family and my job."

"I see," she said. "I know my sons well and share a very close bond with both as you know. I can sense when something is off. At this particular moment, it's way off the Richter scale. Over the years, Gui," she looked for a reaction, "has never changed who he is or how he behaves. He is a man's man with a heart of gold but doesn't wear it so well. He built this huge wall around his heart to protect himself and through the years it became impenetrable. But since you came along, all that changed." She smiled. "For the short time you've been together he's relaxed more and is slowly letting his guard down. This is a huge step for him. He's learning to smile more and his sense of humour is shining through. He's a very funny man you know but not many people know that. Maybe being around you for a while has made him realise life is much better with you in it." She leaned back in the chair and crossed her legs. She wasn't leaving until she learned what she wanted to hear.

"Wow, I'm not sure what to say. But I don't think me being here has anything to do with the changes you've seen in him. Maybe having you here has softened him a little?"

"But I'm here every other day dear. He built me the most beautiful apartment and I get to see at least one of my sons whenever I like."

"Then maybe he's just mellowing with age like a fine wine," I giggled.

"He likes you, no doubt about that," she says all matter of fact.

I blinked. "Nooo?"

"He's crazy about you."

"That's not true."

"Yes, it is true."

"How do you know? Did he tell you that?"

"He didn't have to."

"Well then, how do you know?"

"I'm his mother. It's my job to know. Anyway, it's so obvious to everyone. Even Keane had a fair idea. But you know that already. Okay, I'm breaking a confidence here. He said he has feelings for you because he gets excited when your name flashes up on his phone."

I frowned. Yeah, I bet he does alright. After the underwear photos? Dirt-bird.

My face fell. "I don't think that would convince me, Genny. Unfortunately, we come from different worlds and both want very different things."

She settled back in the chair. "When Gui's father met the love of his life, me, a Chinese woman, it didn't go down well with his parents and the shit hit the fan. Pardon my French. All hell broke loose. They were hard people, especially his father, who tolerated the relationship only because I was at Harvard."

"You went to Harvard. As in the infamous university?"

"We all did. I loved it and that's why I sent the boys there. His poor weak mother was never allowed to voice her opinion. He had to fight his family to marry me. They threatened him with everything. From dis-inheritance to severing all connections with him completely. But that didn't deter him. He didn't care about the family name or money. I was the love of his life and he wanted me in it even if it meant losing them. Thankfully his mother had a heart after all and knew that she could never disown her only son. We weren't permitted to marry straight away. His father would only give his blessing if we lived together for at least five years and finished university. Once qualified, Mason would sit next to his father running his multi-million-dollar empire." She giggled, "That went out the window when I got pregnant with Gui. Mason was awarded first-class honours. His father couldn't have been prouder. Being pregnant I just about managed my degree."

"What did you study?"

"Law."

"Holy crap!" I gasped.

"We had some tough battles along the way but we got there. So, you see my dear. My son doesn't judge people by class. He judges them for the type of person they are. To him, there are only two types of people in the world, good or bad." She grinned looking very proud indeed. "I brought my sons up well."

I finish my toast in a daze. "Okay, then maybe I was wrong on that point."

"I can see something is playing on your mind dear, please tell me what it is."

Your son thinks he's God?

"I can't. I don't want to say it."

"I can't help you dear if you don't tell me." I got up and paced the room.

"Rhylee, you're frightening me now."

I plopped on the bed and faced her chewing my lip. Wondering if there was a better way of saying that her son was a criminal who took the law into his own hands. I took a deep breath.

"Take your time dear. I honestly can't imagine my son having done anything to distress you this much?"

I twisted my hands together. "Please know that this is very difficult for me to say and for you to hear. Soon after I arrived here, they found some of the gang members responsible for what happened to us. The others were locked up somewhere, but Lan was being held as a prisoner by Gui and his thugs. They were about to chop her arm off right there in front of me." I watched her eyes bug but she remained calm, I continued. "I pleaded with him to give the child a chance in life. So, you see, nobody in their right mind would live with a monster like that!"

She looked serious for a moment then fell about laughing. "Oh, my goodness Rhylee, you had me for a minute. What an awful joke to play."

I kneeled at her feet and took her hand in mine. "I'm sorry Genny, I'm telling you the truth." I crossed my heart. "I swear to God. Someone from security held her arm down on a huge wooden block as a silver sword lay beside it. Gui said scum like them needed to be taught a lesson and that was how he dealt with their kind. I'm so sorry Genny."

"That's absolutely ridiculous. Gui is a law-abiding man and would never step one foot out of line. Some of his close friends hold high positions in law not to mention he wouldn't harm a hair on your head. For God's sake, he wouldn't even kill a fly."

"Genny, I know this must be a huge shock for you but I was there. I didn't imagine it. The room was full of security, the chopping block, the sword and the self-righteous look on Gui's face."

"By any chance was it the 'Horse chopping sword,' she asked.

"Yes, yes that's it. I'm sure that's what he said it was called. From the Song Dynasty or something." I got up and started pacing again, my head a clusterfuck of emotion.

"I don't know what's going on but that sword is priceless and wouldn't cut butter. It's always locked away in a glass display cabinet."

"I'm only saying what he told me. What about the block then? I saw it in your apartment."

She thought for a moment. "I do have a wooden block."

"Omg!" I gasped.

"Several on each floor."

My hand shot up to my mouth as I stared at her in disbelief, too shocked to speak.

"Rhylee, it's not what you think. Those are steps for Coco and Bean, my Chihuahua's who are too small to jump onto the sofa or my bed. Gui had them made for me from an oak tree they felled from his property in London. They're all over the place."

I sank to the floor, too dumbfounded to register what she was saying.

"Rhylee, my dear, I don't know what else to say. What you've said is just bizarre. Gui loves children. Have you not seen him with Lan?"

"Yes, I have. He's awkward and uncomfortable." She pointed to the bed.

"Please pass me my bag dear."

I crawled over to the bed, my head in turmoil and grabbed her bag. She took out her phone and scrolled, then handed it to me. "Take a look and then tell me he's awkward or uncomfortable around her." There were hundreds of photos of Gui and Lan together. In each one, he had the biggest smile on his face and he looked like he was genuinely having great fun. The cutest one was of them both asleep with Lan half lying across his chest. He had built a wall of cushions just in case she rolled off. In another, he sat patiently with toy rollers in his hair as she painted his face in the most unattractive makeup. I giggled out loud. Another had him reading to her and one sitting at the dining table colouring. I handed her phone back, confused. Where the hell was I when they were playing happy families? I felt left out. It made me sad. What the actual fuck is happening?

"Who do you think bought her a wardrobe of clothes?"

"You?"

"It was Gui."

"He said it was you, that it wasn't in him to be that way inclined."

"I didn't. He also hired not just one, but several teachers to teach each subject. That's why she's so good at speaking English. He's also put the other boys in a correctional school where they'll learn skills and have employment in one of his companies at the end of it. They were all given the choice. Only one of them wanted to go back to his former life. You can't win them all as much as he tried."

"What the actual fuck. Pardon my French. So, you're saying everything is a lie?"

"Absolutely. I don't know about you, but it looks to me like he did it all to make you stay?"

"He tricked me. Well, that's just fucked up! Don't you think it's fucked up?"

"Knowing my son, he meant no harm and had his reasons. Tell me. If he had asked you to stay and recover under his roof, what would you have said?"

I thought for a moment.

"I would have said, fuck off you dirty bastard." Her eyebrows hit her hairline.

"Oh, well yes. That's the answer any normal person would have given. You made an impression on him. He played on your weakness, children and your good heart. So, he concocted the whole charade while you were sleeping.

It's not the only thing he did while I was sleeping.... Dirty bastard!

"Likely, he couldn't let you go so soon."

"Most people just ask you out on a date."

"I don't think that was enough for him. So really, he's just embellished a few lies."

"Omg Genny, stop making excuses for him. What he did was wrong. And weird. He's a fucking nut case," I squealed.

"Now now dear. I'm going to leave you alone to think about it. No matter how fucked up it looks," she smiled innocently. "You'll come to the right conclusion as to why he fabricated the whole thing. He had no intention of causing harm or offence." She clapped her hands together. "I think it's nothing short of brilliant," she brimmed with happiness. "I agree, on this occasion, my son hasn't taken the normal route. It just proves you mean much more to him than he's led you to believe."

I threw my head back and laughed. It was the funniest thing I ever heard. "No! It just proves he's sick in the head!" Her mouth fell open. "Rhylee Murphy! I'm sure you don't mean that. This is quite unlike him. He's never done anything like this for anyone."

"Should that make me feel special? How many times do I need to say this? What he's done is not normal. He needs help!"

"We both know that's a lie."

I dropped my chin on my chest. "We do?"

"Well dear, as I said. I'll leave you and love you. I'm hoping you'll understand why he did it?" She smiles.

We stared at each other in brief silence. "Oh, my fucking God," I say out loud.

I stare at her, my mind a train wreck. We sat in awkward silence for a while, and then she took my hand in hers and gently squeezed it.

"Oh, come here dear. I think it's adorable."

She pulled me into her arms and hugged me tightly. "I'm sorry, I know I shouldn't be excited. Try to see it for what it is. In my eyes, I didn't think any woman was good enough for him. Until I met Rhylee Murphy from Ireland." She squeezed my shoulders and then left.

29

I stared at the door long after she was gone. I screw up my face. I mean what the actual fuck! That was completely unexpected. Surely, she can't be right. I shook my head in disbelief, nah, surely not. He made it all up to keep me here. What a shit! I climbed into his chair and imagined how he watched me. If it is a lie, I don't have to stay any longer. Oh fuck! My heart dropped to the pit of my stomach. What do I do now? One thing I was certain of, I needed a stiff drink.

One of Daiyu's specials wasn't going to cut it this time. I'm damned if I do and damned if I don't. What an absolute mess. Feeling downtrodden I shuffled into the bathroom and turned the shower on. I stood there motionless, letting the steaming water run over my head, wishing my problems would drain away too. The shower did nothing in helping me come to a decision. I wasn't sure if it was anxiety or adrenaline running through me, but I needed to do something to relieve it. The gym. I needed to clear my head. The treadmill would suffice. I pulled out my weekend bag and rummaged through my stuff. I pulled out my sexy butt lift leggings which were a

Tik Tok sensation worldwide. I wasn't bothered how my arse looked because they were comfy and I loved them. I popped on a tee shirt and looked in the wardrobe for some trainers. I tied my hair up in a high ponytail and headed to the basement.

I exited the lift and looked about. I followed the glass wall around the gym and two doors automatically swished open. I eyed the machines not knowing what half of them were for because they were probably high-tech and top of the range. They looked different to the ones in the Garda gym. I was only interested in the treadmill. I set the incline to zero, to begin with, no point killing myself. I wasn't at work now. A nice brisk walk to start with followed by a gentle run. I turned it on and hooked it up to my tee shirt. I warmed up for ten minutes at an easy to moderate walking pace. It felt good. I was going to enjoy this. I increased it until I was slightly out of breath for the duration of my workout. I noticed a music button so hit play. Taylor Swift poured out through the surround sound. Wow, does he listen to Taylor while working out? It was easy listening so left it playing. It wasn't long before I started running and I couldn't believe how much I was enjoying it.

After forty minutes I started to cool down. I switched it off and stepped down and almost jumped backwards with fright.

"Jesus Keane. You almost gave me a fucking heart attack? How long have you been standing there?"

"Me? Give *you* a heart attack? Fuck's sake Rhylee, have you seen your fucking arse in those leggings? It's like two bowling balls in a fishing net. Lethal. My poor dick doesn't know whether it's coming or going between you and Evee strutting your stuff around the place. It's hard being a man around here these days. No pun intended." We both stared at each other and burst out laughing.

"I'm not messing Rhylee. I'm going to end up with blue balls."

"Omg, you and your brother need to go to confession. I'd bet you'd get at least ten Hail Marys!"

"I don't even know what that means, it sounds painful though," he laughs.

"It means you need to see a priest because neither of you have any filter and the language that comes out of your mouth is atrocious. A pair of sexual deviants is all I'm saying!"

"That's a bit drastic. We can't help it if we're hot-blooded males, now, can we?"

"Thinking before you speak would help."

"I have to fess up to something. I couldn't help it."

"What have you done?"

"I sent a video of you running to Gui."

"No, you didn't."

"Oh, I did."

"Why?"

"Because you're hot as fuck and I wanted him to see what he's missing."

"For the love of God, stop including me in shit! Did he reply?"

"Of course, he did."

"And?"

"Read it for yourself." He handed me his phone and then straddled an exercise bike with ease.

I read the message out loud…

Pick your fucking mouth up off the floor, keep your dick in your pants, I can smell your erection from here and get the fuck out of my house.

"Charming," I giggled. "Sure, no wonder he's pissed off, your caption is, please sit on my face! Seriously Keane, what age are you?"

"It's so fucking obvious he's into you."

"Don't be silly. He's pissed off because you're winding him up."

"No, it's not that. He'd usually say, "Go for it.""

"I don't understand?"

"Do you want to know?" He wiggles his eyebrows. "God, is it that bad?"

"We have the same circle of friends. Sometimes those friends may introduce us to other friends of the female persuasion. Sometimes the inevitable can happen and we could end up dating or sleeping with the same woman. So, if we're interested, we usually send a photo. It's only because it happened before. The lovely lady sold her story and more or less said who was better in bed and who had the biggest dick."

I look at him in disbelief. "Omg! What a bitch!"

"If he wasn't interested in you, he'd give me the thumbs up." He removes his jacket and throws it over the electric bike beside him and starts to pedal. I can see every muscle ripple as he moves and I reluctantly tear my eyes off him.

"So, who has," I laughed.

"Has what?"

"The biggest dick."

He went to say something but I stuck my fingers in my ears and giggled. "No no no, I don't want to know. I was only joking. However, I would like to know why they're called blue balls."

He climbed off the bike and began unbuttoning his jeans. A cheeky smile on his face. "Let me show you why." I ran screaming from the room, his laughter booming through the building.

I stopped at the lift and waited for him. "Keane Turner, you're such a dirty fucker." He kisses my cheek.

"I know."

"So how did the trip go and what have you done with my best friend? Have you locked her away in your Ivory tower?"

"I wish. She's amazing. Josh, that's-his-name, isn't it? Yeah, he rang when we were in the sky. Didn't seem happy when she mentioned she was in a helicopter with me."

"Oh no. How was she?"

"She seemed okay and didn't let it ruin the day. She told him she'd call him afterwards and then call you later with all the gossip. Hmm. Aren't you supposed to be sick?"

"Omg, I completely forgot about that. I had a little sleep, then showered and felt like I could run a marathon afterwards, so came down here."

He couldn't help raising his eyebrows at the obvious lie. "You are a dreadful liar, Miss Murphy."

I bit my lip to stifle my smile. "Are you staying a while?"

"Only if you change into something less distracting."

"Anything for you."

"Really?"

"Behave," I giggled and linked my arm through his. "Where's Lan?"

"She's having swimming lessons."

"Aww, that's brilliant. So what floor are you taking me to?"

"Depends on what you want to do. But I have to insist you take those fucking leggings off immediately. I can't concentrate on anything. If your man finds out I'm still here he'll kick the shit out of me."

"Who's your man?"

"Your fella."

I elbowed him in the chest. "As if. Where will I meet you?"

He thought for a minute. "The fortieth floor."

"Seriously, how many floors does this building have?"

"Sixty and the penthouse."

"Jesus. Does Gui own the whole building?"

"Yeah. It's divided between his businesses and homes."

"I suppose it makes sense."

"I'll drop you off on the way," he laughs. The doors open and I hop out. I turn to wave and catch him staring at my arse like he's memorising every inch.

I put my hands on my hips. "Really Keane. Are you saving that for later?"

He laughed out loud. "I know. Shocking, aren't I."

He smirked. I rolled my eyes. "Go on, get a move on. See you in a few." I wondered what was on the sixtieth floor. This place was like a maze.

Once again, I pulled out my ever-trusting weekend bag. I'm sure I'd seen my old tracksuit. Knowing now how excitable Keane gets, I wasn't risking anything. Yep, there it was. It looked like something you'd find in a bargain basement. I didn't care, it was comfy and hid a multitude. I sniffed it to be sure it was actually clean. As it wouldn't surprise me if Evee had taken it out of the laundry basket. Heading out the door, I ran back and threw on a dressing gown just to be safe. There was no way he'd get excited with what I was wearing now. I pressed the button and waited in anticipation. What on earth could it be? He had his own house so it couldn't be an apartment. Must be his office. But didn't he say businesses were on the lower floors? Argh, I'm all confused. Too many floors to remember. The excitement was getting the better of me.

I finally reached the fortieth floor and held my breath as the doors opened. Keane was standing there to greet me. His eyes widened.

"May I take one of your layers of clothing? Perhaps your dressing gown to start with m'lady."

I giggled and a husky laugh escaped his throat making my tummy flutter. "Do you know what Keane Turner? You always make me laugh, regardless of how I'm feeling and I love that."

"I aim to please, m'lady."

"So what exactly is this?"

"It's an apartment."

"No shit Sherlock, who's apartment?"

"Well, mine of course."

"But you have a house."

"That's in the country and I have several homes. Just like mom and Gui."

"It's funny when you say, mom. Omg, most people are happy with one home," I gasped. "So how do you stop undesirables sneaking up to these floors?"

"Ah ha," he says, tapping his nose. There are two escalators. One of them has fingerprint recognition."

"Of course, it has."

30

It was like a loft conversion. Dark wooden floors, exposed ductwork mixed with pristine white walls and plenty of steelwork giving it a hip industrial edge. It had a floor-to-ceiling fireplace in black steel with two built-in bookshelves on either side in dark oak veneer matching the oak wooden floors. The large doorless opening connecting the living room and dining room created a wonderful flow connecting the two spaces. It had a wall of windows like all the other apartments looking out over the cityscape and allowed for lots of natural light. A huge island as big as the one in his home took centre stage and boasted a smooth concrete waterfall top. The white marble distressed finish splashback complimented the presses and continued the charcoal and white colour palette featured throughout.

"Holy crap". I gasped. "That island is humongous. It's literally the size of Ireland, it's gorgeous".

"I'm glad you like it."

"It's fab and I could happily live here. It's very masculine but with a feminine touch."

"That's exactly the look I was going for. Best of both worlds. Let me show you the rest of the apartment."

The master bedroom was mostly white with large windows offering views of the surrounding city. The large steel frame headboard continued the industrial theme, while a giant heart made of white twigs hung on the wall above the bed, rendering it less sterile looking. It was gorgeous.

"I love the heart, it's very organic and romantic. I'd even hang one on the red brick wall in the lounge. I think the contrast would be amazing. And add LED lights behind it."

"I never thought of that. I love that idea." He dug his phone out of his pocket and made a call. "Hey Yichén. I'm at the Turner Lee apartment. Can you organise one of the hearts to go up on the red brick wall and showcase it with LEDs from behind. Thanks, appreciate it."

I snapped my fingers. "Wow, just like that. I don't understand why you all need a separate apartment when you don't actually live here. Couldn't you just come and stay with your mother? It's not like she doesn't have the room."

"I did in the beginning, but I swear to God, she had me driven around the bend. She never stops talking. She'd still be talking even if I was on the phone or emailing. We have to keep a close eye on business news, markets and stocks. One time I had turned on three channels to watch the headlines and for the whole day, never got to hear any news because she wouldn't stop talking. If she's not talking, she's hoovering. The only time she's quiet is when she's watching her murder mystery programmes."

"Oh stop. That's so funny."

"So that's why we ended up having one each. Both mom and I have a floor while Gui has several. Also, she wasn't very nice to our dates at breakfast. One look and she'd take an immediate dislike to them, which was most times. Poor girls, they never stood a chance. It was mortifying to be honest."

"Sounds like you both had a lot of dates."

He plopped down on the sofa and patted the cushion. "Come sit down. Are you sure you wouldn't be more comfortable without the dressing gown?"

"It is hot in here," I say, fanning my face with my hand. I remove the robe and his eyes bulge when he sees the baggy tracksuit.

"Jesus Rhylee, you would have been cooked alive in all that gear."

"Actually, could I have a drink of water please?"

"Is this you making a point," he asked, handing me a bottle of water.

"About what?"

"Wearing ten layers of clothes hoping I'd find you less attractive."

"I didn't know what I was walking into so wrapped up, just in case." I lied.

"I think you're trying to look as unsexy as possible because I behave like a horny adolescent around you. I apologise if that's the case?"

I patted his hand and smiled. "How did it go with Evee?"

"I'm not sure if I'm honest. She seemed very quiet and that was even before Josh rang."

"Quiet is good. If she was bored and really didn't want to be there, she would have talked incessantly. She's the same when we go to the cinema. If it wasn't her choice, she'd talk all the way through it. Just like Genny," I giggle. He breathed a sigh of relief.

"Phew," he said, smiling.

"Why don't you ask her out to dinner?"

"I was thinking about it but thought it might be a little insensitive. You know, with it being so soon after her breakup."

"It's only a bite to eat. It's not like you're trying to get into her knickers." I looked sideways at him, raising an eyebrow.

His mouth drops open in mock horror. "Here, don't look at me like that. I know I'm bad, but I'm not that bad. I'll at least give her a few days to get over him," he teased. I shook my head and punched his arm playfully.

"You're so full of shit Keane Turner."

"But seriously, she's so calming to be around and is so intelligent too. The complete opposite to my usual dates."

"Do you date bimbos?"

He hunched his shoulders and smiled. "She studied law for five years. Woke one morning and said it wasn't for her. Her parents were devastated. Only because she was so good at it. But they stood by her decision and encouraged her to do whatever made her happy. Afterwards, she felt really guilty because they had been so understanding. So, she did her finals, passed with honours and now has it to fall back on in the future. She calls it her settling down plan."

He raised an eyebrow. "Her what?"

"For now, she plans on doing whatever she wants. At the moment, Law isn't on her list. When her bucket list is empty, she'll settle down with the man of her dreams, set up a little law firm and live happily ever after."

"Wow. She has it all panned out. You can really see how she carries herself having been brought up in a loving home."

"Absolutely, her parents are the best. Wait a minute, you said usual dates? Do you want to date her?"

"I'd really like to but …"

My phone rang and Evee's name lit up the screen. "Speak of the devil. Won't be a minute." He squeezed my hand and left the room to give me a bit of privacy. He really didn't have to leave but I appreciated it, nevertheless.

"Hiya, are you okay?"

"I'm grand. We're definitely finished now."

"I wish I could come over."

"Don't worry about it, I'll be grand," she sniffed.

"Can you come here and stay for a while?"

Keane popped his head around the door. "I can pick her up if she wants and she can stay the night."

"Did you hear that Evee, Keane said he can collect you? Yes, absolutely. We can have a proper chat. I have loads to tell you. Yes. I can't say it now. Okay. Love you too."

Keane dived on the sofa all excited. "Well, is she coming over? Have I to pick her up?"

"For fuck's sake will you calm down? Yes, she's going to come over but she can't stay, unfortunately. Her parents are taking her out to dinner."

"Maybe I could take them all out?" He eagerly asked. "I think it would be awkward for everyone because of the situation and she's very emotional just now. They've definitely finished for good. She wouldn't be able to talk freely with you there. You understand, don't you?"

"Of course, I do." He looked really sad.

"But sure, see how it goes. Evee surprises me all the time."

"So, what have you got to tell her?"

"It's private, nosey hole!"

"Ah don't do that to me. I won't say anything."

"It's girl stuff, so mind your own business."

"Should I pick her up at her home or her parents?"

"If you really don't mind, she's at home."

"Of course, I don't. What time?"

"Now if that's okay." Before I could finish, he was off running out the door. "Let yourself out when you're done. Or stay if you wish." He left the sentence hanging and winked at me. He was gone in a flash. I headed back to the lounge. Jesus, who the hell has to clean all these floors? I wondered.

I had my back to the door looking out the window when Daiyu appeared holding a stack of towels. "Hi Rhylee, how are you?"

"I'm good, thanks. How are you?"

"Same story, different day," she laughed.

"Can I ask you something?"

"Sure."

"Are you the housekeeper for the whole building?" She dropped the bundle of towels on the sofa and tightened her ponytail.

"God no. I'm not Superwoman." She exclaimed. "Just five floors. Gui's cleaning company looks after the rest. I oversee the upkeep of Gui's floors, Mr Turner's, Mrs Lee's and mine."

"Yours?"

"I know. Sounds unbelievable. I have the floor just under Mrs Lee's. Gui, gifted a floor to me and my family. It was so generous of him to do such a life changing thing. I will forever be in his debt. Not only that, but he also put my boys through medical school and my eldest daughter has just received her law degree. I couldn't in a million years have afforded to put them all through university, even though I'm generously paid. He's so thoughtful, there's nothing he wouldn't do for us. I've been with this family since I was a teenager when Gui's father, put me into one of his properties back then. When he passed, Mrs Lee asked me to move in with her. I stayed for almost twenty years and now I'm here."

"Still can't believe you have three teenagers!"

"You're too kind," she beamed. "Would you like anything to eat while you wait? I believe Mr Turner is collecting Evee."

"Ah no, I'm grand, thanks. Do you know if Lan is still swimming? I don't want to go in because it will only distract her. She's just finishing up now, these are for her. She has English lessons now." She gathered the towels and left me to my thoughts.

I was so happy to hear how well the Lee family have cared for her. Imagine having a private apartment which took up a whole floor and no financial worries. If he was in front of me now, I'd hug him. And what about all the stuff he's doing for Lan? He's like two different people.

"A penny for them," I heard a familiar voice say. I turned and rushed into her outstretched arms.

"How are you holding up?"

"Do you know what? It's all such a shock to my system."

"Where's Keane by the way?"

"He's gone for a swim. Said he needed to cool down. Too much temptation in one place. Whatever that means." We both stared at each other, obviously thinking the same thing. Keane half-naked in just a pair of swimming trunks. I shook the thought right out of my head. It really shouldn't be in there.

Taking her hand, I led her towards the sofa. "Of course, it is hun. You were childhood sweethearts."

"No, I mean, I'm shocked with myself for staying with him."

"What, I don't understand."

"At the beginning, the both of us were totally head over heels in love, as you are. Young love and all that crap. But over time, if it's not meant to be, it fizzles and becomes a routine. I felt it creeping in but just ignored the signals. I regret that we've both wasted so much time sticking it out."

"This is all a shock to me. You never said anything."

"I think that's why I was spending more time at the orphanage. I didn't want to go home and continue with our monotonous routine. I just wish one of us would have had the balls to say something sooner."

"I don't know what to say, Evee. I think I'm more shocked than you. Is he coming back to get his things?"

"He took what he wanted and said to keep or donate the rest."

"Over, just like that. Bleedin sap! He had shit hair anyway".

"That's funny. He did love his hair. Don't get me wrong, I will miss him to bits. He's a good person and I will always love him as a friend. It's sad that it has come to this but I'll get over it. It's taken me too long to realise we weren't right for each other. We stayed together way longer than either of us deserved. At least we're young and have our lives ahead of us."

I stare gobsmacked. I take her hand. "You know what they say, the quickest way to get over it is to get under it," I said, wiggling my eyebrows."

She rolled her eyes and tutted. "No Rhylee, we said that. It was us, me and you. We made it up when Ava's fella dumped her."

"Oh yeah. I remember. And then we called her a slut when she slept with Isaac."

"That's only because we were jealous because he was a ride. He had just moved into the neighbourhood, from England I think and we loved his accent. He would do anything for a quick blowie, bless him."

"Omg yeah. He got her pregnant, didn't he? Wow, we were so young then."

"Do you know they're still together? Three kids later. She texts me the odd time."

"Ahh that's good, I'm happy for her."

"Okay. Spill. What have you got to tell me?"

She rubbed her hands together. "I don't know where to start."

"It's always good to start at the beginning, babe. Just take a deep breath and begin." She squeezed my hand encouragingly.

"Okay, I told you about the sword, Lan and becoming a sub."

She nodded. "Yes, go on." Evee stayed silent as I filled her in.

"Well, his mam called in to see how I was after you all left for the helicopter ride. We got chatting and she was gushing about Gui and hinting at us getting together. I just couldn't let her go through the rest of her life thinking her son was a saint."

"Omg, what did you do?"

"I told her the truth."

She gulped loudly. "Everything?"

"Well yeah. Except for the sex part."

"Oh, thank God! Fuck. What did she say?"

"She laughed."

"Huh?"

"She thought I was joking. She actually believed I was playing a sick joke on her."

"She's his mother, of course, she'd think that."

"She said that sword thingy is a priceless artefact and was very surprised it was out of its display cabinet."

"Shut the fuck up!"

"I'm serious."

"The blocks of wood are steps for her Chihuahua's, Coffee and Bean."

"Omg, their names are so cute."

I snapped my fingers. "Evee, focus. Wait until you hear the next bit."

"Could do with a bucket of popcorn. This is some fucked up shit, go on."

"He's put the rest of the gang in school and employment in one of his companies when they graduate." She gasped. "Genny said it was obvious that he concocted such a bizarre story to keep me here."

"That's fucking unbelievable Rhy."

"She asked me out straight, if he had asked you to stay, what would you have said?"

"You would have said NO because you're a good girl."

"Yes, I would have said no for sure. Or, even though you're hot as fuck, I'm not going home with you because you could be a serial killer. Ahh sure g'wan, give me a shout tomorrow instead."

Evee burst out laughing. "Oh, my God. What should I do?"

For five minutes, I pace the room. "I can't forget the way he is with Lan. On one hand, he's a psychopath and on the other, he's the man you want to introduce to your parents and make babies with."

"I can't believe he did all that to make you stay. You've got to give it to him. He's one smart cookie."

"That's if it's even true? When I fainted, he caught me, thank goodness. I never thought about it until now. Why was he even there?"

"I think he went after you to ask you to stay. As much as he's not the settling down kinda guy, or can't get his shit together, he wanted you. I'd say that was probably a huge step for him. He's never chased anyone in his life. I'm sure he has them dropping their knickers with just a glance."

"Omg I'm sorry but I have to scratch. It's driving me crazy." I rudely shoved my hand into my knickers and gave my crotch a good scratch.

"Eew, what the fuck are you doing, Rhylee?"

"The hair is growing back after I shaved last week and it's so fucking itchy. It's driving me crazy. I knew I shouldn't have shaved. I never shave. Hate the prickly little feckers growing back."

"Oh God, yeah, I hate that too. The bloody itch is unbearable. Just don't do it absentmindedly in front of anyone. They'll think you have crabs."

"Oh, Jesus yeah. I'll be back in a second. Just going to wash my hands." Five minutes later I entered the room sniffing my hands. "Have you used that hand wash yet, it's beautiful."

"Yeah, I grabbed one the last time I was here."

"Please tell me you're joking."

"Omg, you believed me."

"Well, you tell so many lies, what do you expect?

So where was I? Oh yeah, why me? It doesn't make sense. Even if it was love at first sight, I'd have a better understanding. What he wants from me he can do with any woman."

"The difference sweet Rhylee is that they're not you."

"But why am I so different? Did I mention he's dated, Princesses and models?"

"Fuck off. You're obviously unlike anyone he's dated. Something clicked when he met you at the hospital. There's no doubt he fancies you and I'm sure your personality had something to do with it too?"

"Omg, I think I was rude and I certainly didn't sweep him off his feet."

"That could be it. You didn't take any of his bullshit. I'm sure he's surrounded by head-nodders all the time."

"What's a head-nodder?"

"They're called 'yes' people. Maybe your being mean to him was a breath of fresh air?"

"Hey, I wasn't mean." I thought for a moment. "Blunt and sarcastic maybe."

"Just because he's not expressing his undying love for you right now, doesn't mean he won't."

"He told me there'd be no 'Happy ever after,' and he doesn't want a long-term girlfriend or wife. Some men aren't forthcoming with their thoughts and feelings, he was. I want the fairytale and he's not the one to make that come true."

"Okay, so he doesn't have a magic wand but wants to fuck you senseless until you can't walk. Nothing wrong with that? Just enjoy it and leave."

"But I like him too much and have feelings of the romantic variety which I can't separate."

"Rhylee, you either want to shag him or you don't?"

"Oh, I do but…"

I was about to deny it, but she put a finger to my lips. "There's no but. He's not the monster we thought he was. I think he's unorthodox and wonderful, the lengths he's gone to." She shook her finger at me. "So, you can either shut up and put up and enjoy the experience or leave and never see him again."

"God," I whisper. "I can't believe I'm even considering staying." The urge to just say yes thrummed through my body.

"What are you thinking," she asked.

"I've always been a good girl, good daughter, good everything. Now I'm going against everything I stand for. I want to stay but I'm scared. And then I'm scared of leaving."

"Omg, you've fallen for him," she gasped in disbelief.

"Yes, I have for my sins. But this is no ordinary crush Evee, it's way worse. I'm fucked."

"You will be, in more ways than one," she laughs. "It's fifty shades of shit!"

"Whether I go ahead with it or not. I've decided I'm going back to Dublin when I leave here. Selfish, but I have no desire to see him with anyone else and the thought of it is killing me."

"No Rhy, you can't go home. Don't decide just yet. Things can change, people change. I won't let you go!" I couldn't hold the tears any longer and completely lost it. She stretched over and pulled me into her arms.

"Baby has it bad."

"I'm like a blubbering idiot and don't know why. He said a few nice things to me and my mind is muddled. I just can't stop thinking about him and I want to feel his touch again. No other man has ever made me feel like this. I'm heartbroken at the prospect of never seeing him again. He's a man who goes after what he wants and he doesn't want me. It's just a convenient arrangement for him." I sniffed.

"At least Keane kept your mind off him for a bit?"

I looked up at her but only saw concern on her face. "I wouldn't have gone there. My heart wasn't in it. He said everything a girl dreams of hearing and he would do anything for you. It was an utterly delightful experience. He's wonderful and adorable and whoever gets him will be so lucky. I'll always treasure and value his friendship."

"But he's mad about you Rhy."

"No, he's not. I think he was a little confused. We both lost ourselves for a moment."

"But will the friendship survive when it all comes out?"

"He knows my heart lies elsewhere but doesn't know for sure where. He has his suspicions though." There was a slight look of relief on her face. I smiled to myself knowingly. It only confirmed that she does like him. "Fucking hell," I mutter. I think we both have a problem."

"Can I ask you something?" I nod.

"Of course."

"Did you see his cock?"

I jump up off the sofa coughing and spluttering. She gives me a cheeky grin. I clear my throat. "Fuck's sake Evee. No, I haven't seen his bloody cock."

Right on cue, Keane walked through the door. I cover my mouth with my hand. "Keane ..." His jaw drops to the floor.

"Well, this is awkward." He gave a sheepish grin. "Would you ladies like me to leave you to it?"

"No, please stay. Forget what you just heard," I pleaded as my brain tries to focus.

Nobody spoke and you could hear a pin drop.

"Oh no, is it that time already?" Evee squeaked. My eyes narrow at her. "The kids will be wondering where I am?"

"Keane moved closer, a look of confusion on his face. "The kids?" He repeated. His gaze flicked between the two of us. His crisp white shirt was unbuttoned at the top revealing smooth skin. His hair was still wet from his swim and combed to perfection. I'm sure Evee wouldn't mind running her fingers through it. She blushed when she spoke.

"My parents. They're waiting at the restaurant for me."

He laughed awkwardly. Thought you had a couple of kids you never mentioned."

"No," she giggled, "but would it make a difference?"

"Absolutely not. Can I drive you there?"

"Ah no. Sure it's not far. Peeking Road."

"Honestly, I'd like to."

She looked down at her hands. "Okay, thank you."

"My pleasure. Rhylee, you don't mind if I drive Evee to the restaurant, do you?"

"Jesus no, why would I mind."

"Why don't you come?" she said.

"I'm not that hungry and you know what your mam is like. Won't stop until I have to be rolled out of there. Anyway, I can't leave the building."

The words were out before I could take them back. "What do you mean you can't leave here? Who says,"

he asks, quirking an eyebrow. Evee grabs his shoulders and turns him towards the door.

"I'm sorry Keane. I have to go now. My parents will be up the wall. They know how anally punctual I am."

"Okay, I'll just get my keys." He left the room giving me a quizzical look. I put my hand to my chest.

"Fuck's sake, that was close. Why don't you invite him to join you?"

"I was thinking about it but you know what mam and dad are like."

"So? Your mam will be all over him and your dad will see he's nothing but a gentleman."

"When my heart starts beating normally again, I will."

"But don't drink anything. Do you hear me?"

"I may have some liquid courage."

"Evee, no. This is different."

"I'll be on my best behaviour mother, I promise."

He tapped the door with his knuckle. "Is it safe to come in? No cocks or dicks flying about?" I'm mortified and a blush rises to my cheeks. I grab Evee's hand screaming nervously with laughter. "Jesus Keane." We all burst out laughing. Evee hugs me tightly and I know she's shitting herself. She whispers in my ear that she'll text me later. Keane gives me a little cuddle and leans in closer.

"We'll finish our conversation tomorrow." The smell of his aftershave, citrusy and masculine hits me. I push him away. "There's nothing you need to know Keano." He runs a hand over his jaw. "Just be careful driving. Those tiny streets are dangerous. Fragile cargo on board."

He bowed. "I get it. Your wish is my command."

31

When they left, I grabbed my Kindle and sat in front of the floor-to-ceiling windows and tried to sort the mess going around in my head. Evee was right, fifty shades of shite. Fifty shades fucked is probably more fitting. I listed the negatives and positives of the arrangement, which is now null and void. But I still wanted to see it through. I wanted Gui to fuck me and not stop. My body tenses as I remember how it felt when he kissed me, touched me and put his fingers inside me. A blush crept up my neck and I crossed my legs to stop the tingling. A man like him is not interested in someone like me long-term. The women he dates are nothing like me. But I didn't want sleepless nights wondering what if. I don't need to justify my decision to anyone. I know the score so no need to feel rejected when it comes to an end. I took a deep breath and exhaled. He told me exactly what he was going to do to me. Yes, I want it. Confident for the first time that I have made the right decision. It wasn't just sex. He had given me the kind of orgasms I've always wanted but never had. Three times he made me come. My heart pounded as I imagined how it would feel, him coming inside me.

I'll never have anyone like him touch me. A man like him, powerful, handsome, smart and sexy. I'd do it just for that. We both get what we want from it I suppose. I could hardly contain myself and smiled with the thrill of what was to come. I want him! My phone pinged. It didn't excite me anymore because it was never him.

Evee: Well, you're going to be so proud. Keane is sitting at the table with the kids and he has the pants charmed off them. He's handling it like a pro. Not that he's even trying. Mam all of a sudden doesn't feel well and we both know what she's up to. If I was any way paranoid, I'd think you were up to it too. My nerves are a little frazzled but in a good way. Butterflies and all that shit. No matter what, I'm not going home with him… I know what you're saying right now. How dare you lol! Chat tomorrow x

Rhylee: Remember what the nuns preached to us when we were going on a night out? Keep your hands together and pray, keep your legs together and lay…. Just saying x

Evee: What are you saying, cheeky bitch hahaha x

I tucked my Kindle down the side of the cushion. Reading now was a lost cause. There's no way I'd be able to concentrate. How do I confront Gui about this newfound information? He could laugh in my face. What will he say? He can either say it's true or a load of bollocks. Why would a man like him need to lie to convince a woman like me to stay with him? Omg, that's exactly what he'll say. Duh! I can only imagine how many women want to sleep with him. One glance from him and they'd come. I take a few minutes to ponder, trying not to jump to any conclusions.

What a shit situation to be in. Maybe I won't broach the subject at all and just continue with the arrangement. Oh God, what shall I say?

Tap..tap and the door opened. "Oh hiya, what's up Daiyu?"

"I hope I'm not disturbing you?"

"Of course, you're not."

"Lan is going to bed soon and she wants to say goodnight."

"Oh right. I'll read her a bedtime story."

"She'll love that." She turned to leave just as I was about to scratch down below.

"Oh, Daiyu, wait." I jumped up and ran over to her. I looked about and whispered in her ear. "I'm embarrassed to ask."

"No, no go ahead. Ask away, please."

"Is there any chance I could get a quick wax? I know there's a salon downstairs. It's just so itchy after shaving," I say pointing at my crotch as I cross and uncross my legs to stop the itch. She bursts out laughing.

"I'll take you down now if you like."

"Omg, that would be amazing. Don't you have to make an appointment?"

"Never. Mr Lee's guests come first, always."

"So, I'm not the first to avail of this service," I said. She hesitated before answering.

"The salon is open to all his guests, both male and female. Both Mr Lee and Mr Turner avail of the services themselves."

That's not what I wanted to hear and maybe she was just protecting me?

The salon was of course state of the art. Very similar to Wwans. Maybe it was one of his? Anyway, in less than an hour, I had my private parts, legs and underarms waxed and a mini pedicure. It wasn't as painful as other times, probably the efficient therapist. I could have stayed longer but I wanted to read to Lan.

The results were well worth the discomfort because I felt amazing. No more itchy and scratchy.

Lan was now in her own room. Whoever decorated it certainly designed it for a little princess. It was beautiful. I sat up on the bed next to her and read two stories before she nodded off. Without waking her, I managed to prise her little fingers from mine, kissed her goodnight and crept out.

After checking my phone again, I took a shower and decided to sleep naked. This was something I did at home after having a wax because everything felt softer and velvet-like, more luxurious. A great wave of calm rolled over me as I hugged the covers and fell swiftly asleep.

Was I dreaming because it seemed that I had barely closed my eyes when I felt something tickle my lips. Then I heard him. His voice. It was as clear as day. Husky and sexy as fuck. My eyes shoot open and there he is, smiling, leaning up on his elbows stretched out beside me. I close my eyes tightly and open them again. I wasn't dreaming. "Hello," he said smiling, in a low gravelly voice. My heart flipped in my chest at the sound of it.

"Hi," I whispered as I stared at the God in front of me. A deep sexy smile crossed his face as he slowly licked his bottom lip. Jesus. I'm done. My heart quickened and my palms grew sweaty. It was a pinch-me moment. "Am I

dreaming? Please be real," I said out loud. "Did I just say that out loud?" I groaned.

He laughed. I love that sound, it does things to my insides. I've missed it.

The room was dimly lit with light coming from the adjoining room. It was the first time I'd seen the doors open. I rubbed my eyes and smiled. "You're back."

"I am. Sorry it's taken so long but I had to be sure the deal was airtight. I didn't want to have to leave you again."

"Oh."

He moved closer and cupped my head in his hands and kissed me deeply. His tongue was soft and eager. "Fuck, you smell so good," he sighed, biting my neck gently. I wanted more. I put my hands around his neck to pull him closer. His tongue hungrily explored my mouth as I ran desperate fingers through his hair. He wore dark jeans and a snug, white t-shirt that emphasised his muscled chest and strong arms. "I think I'm a little overdressed for the occasion," he hummed.

I prop myself up on my elbows and watched him strip. He knelt and pulled his t-shirt over his head throwing it to the floor and wasted no time removing his jeans. I watched in awe as his massive hard cock sprung free. Hmm! No boxers. My hungry eyes worked their way up from his perfect cock to his perfect face. All impressive in their own right. How can someone so beautifully perfect exist? He's huge, far bigger than I remembered. I watched as he slowly strokes himself, the muscles in his arm flexing and I release the breath I'd been holding.

In one swoop he pulled the covers completely off me and I shivered. His jaw dropped open and he looked at me like he'd never seen a naked woman before. "Fuck, you're naked." I felt a blush rising up my chest, my neck and then my cheeks, my eyes never leaving his. Eager eyes travel over my body. I silently thanked God for my wax appointment and promised to visit him soon. He looked at me like I'm the only woman he wanted. I wish. It's the same look I'd seen the last time we were together. "Fucking gorgeous," he muttered. Our eyes locked. "I've been so fucking hard because of you."

"I want you," I gasped and blush when I hear myself say those words.

Recognition flashed in his eyes and he smiled, showcasing his dimples. I bite my lip and his eyes traced the movement making him growl. "As much as I want to taste you, the need to fuck you is greater. I can't wait to be inside you."

"Then what are you waiting for?"

I looked down at his heavy cock hanging between his legs. "That's gotta hurt."

He raised a brow. "You wouldn't believe it."

I watch as he knelt between my legs and pushed them apart with his knee. I looked at his beautiful face and then his cock. That's gonna kill me. "You're so hot when you blush Rhylee Murphy," he said, slowly stroking his arousal. "Do you know how long I've waited for this moment? Too damn long."

He cupped my breast and moved closer. My breath caught as his tongue circled my nipple. Omg, it was unbearable. I arched my back and shudder as goosebumps popped up across my skin. He lifted his head, just enough to speak. "You have the perfect handful." The other hand slid down my body between my legs. He pushed his middle finger into me, followed by a second, then circled my clit with his thumb.

"Holy crap," I groaned. He inhaled deeply acknowledging how wet I was.

"Rhylee, fucking hell you're soaking wet. Just for me." The more he stimulated me, the more it throbbed and tingled. I lifted my hips but he had me pinned tightly to the bed.

"Oh God," I moaned loudly.

"No, it's still Gui."

I giggled. Then soft lips moved against mine and down my neck. Smooth hands gripped my hips. His eyes fixed on mine as he pushed into me slowly, a breath escaping through his clenched teeth. Then curses as he enters me. His voice was hoarse. "Fuck, Rhylee. So damn tight."

I gripped the sheets and breathed through the overwhelming sensation. Christ, I knew he was big, but nothing prepared me for this. It took my breath away as his thick cock stretched me out. I closed my eyes and focused on stopping the tears from falling down my cheeks. It was too much. I'm going to fucking die. How would my mother cope with the embarrassment? *I'm sorry Mrs Murphy, your daughter died from a massive cock!* She'd never be able to face Father Michael again with the shame of it all.

"Look at me," he said, staring down at me. "Do you know how good you feel?" He pulls out just to the tip then slowly buries himself to the hilt with a groan. I try not to scream so clench my teeth. "Fuck, you're so tight," he groaned. He did it a few times like he was warming me up. Each time it hurt less and I started to enjoy the dulling pain. He looked down in concentration where we joined, inch by inch disappearing inside me. "So good," he groaned. His hands tightened on my hips and I was sure they'd leave bruises. He leaned over and kissed me, gently biting my lip. "Just so you know, I won't last long. You feel so good. I'm losing it here."

"I'm just there too," I panted. When he was in me, thrusting away, there was nothing else in the world quite like it. I caught my breath as he circled my clit with his thumb. "Oh, sweet Jesus. That feels so good," I groaned. He pushes me over the edge, sending pulses of pleasure through me. My legs straighten and my toes curl as I cried out his name and come on his cock.

His body responded with a surge of desire and his thrusts sped up. I locked my legs around him and pulled him deeper. "Fucking hell Rhy, are you trying to kill me." He began to move faster…, faster as his cock went deeper inside me. There was nothing gentle about it. "Oh my God, oh my God, don't stop," I panted. My fingernails scraped up his back as he pounded into me. A groan escaped him as he takes one final push and released into me with heavy shooting pulses. I could feel his hot cum hitting my insides. He dropped exhausted on top of me, his heavy deep breathing once erratic now slowing to a calm. "Fucking hell," he gasps against my neck. He made a move to climb off me but I asked him to stay, loving how his cock felt still throbbing inside me. He lifted his head and rested his forehead against mine. His fingers skimmed my breast as he placed an arm on each side of me. "You know," he said, looking down at me with his just-fucked hair, "that's exactly how I imagined it would be, perfect. How was it for you?"

"Incredible," I whispered.

"You sure?"

"Absolutely." My heart was still pounding. He put a strong arm around me and rolled onto his back, taking me with him. I giggled. Resting my head on his chest, I heard his heart beating as fast as mine and hated when I felt him slipping out of me. He kissed the top of my head then lazily trailed a finger slowly over my tummy, resting his fingers over my breast. My nipples were hard and the touch of his hand made me horny. Seriously! Absent-mindedly he ran a fingernail over one and I jerk.

"Omg."

"Fuck, they are sensitive, aren't they," he said.

"Yes," I exhale, trying to keep it together. "Can I ask you something?"

"Of course." I nervously bite my lip.

"Will you be honest?"

"Wow, I'm intrigued now, go on."

"You hardly contacted me while you were away. I thought you changed your mind and that you felt it was all a mistake." He let out a long sigh.

"These past few days have been crazy. It was touch and go for a while. Just because I didn't contact you as much as I would have liked, doesn't mean I wasn't thinking about you. To be honest, I thought about you more than I'm willing to admit." I smile.

"I asked before, but you didn't answer. What age are you?"

"I didn't answer because I felt I was too old for you. I'm thirty-seven and you're only twenty-seven. If I remember correctly."

"That's not that old."

"Is that all you wanted to know?

"No, that's not really what I wanted to ask you. Was it all just a facade to keep me here?" I asked the question lightly like it hasn't been on my mind every minute of the day, all day, every day.

He sucked in a deep breath and slowly released it. He stopped massaging my breast and moved his hand down letting it rest on my hip.

"Yes," he said. No point lying now. You obviously know. Knew you were smart too."

My hands slid up his chest and I rested my chin on top. Tucking a strand of hair behind my ear, he stared into my eyes. "Go on," I encouraged him.

"When I saw you alone at the hospital, so beautiful and innocent, I couldn't let you just walk away." I rolled my eyes at him and smiled. "What, I'm serious. I'm surprised you never noticed the bulge. That's never happened to me, ever."

"Annd?"

"I followed you to ask you out but you fainted. In the back of the car with you in my arms, it came to me. It turned out much better than what was in my head. Your sensitive caring nature and empathy clinched it."

"But you still could have just asked me out, you know. That's how it usually works."

"To be honest. I thought if I could get away with it, why not. I decided I didn't want to waste time on dates and all that bullshit. I wanted you no matter what."

"Thank you," I said.

"For what? For being a dick?"

"No," I laughed.

"For being honest."

"Let's just say, you were on my 'To-do list' the moment I saw you."

"Erm, to-do list?" He traced my jawline from my temple to my lips. I resist the urge to bite his finger.

"To-do list?" I repeated.

"Yeah, to-do….."

– you on the bed

– you on the floor

– you in the car

– you on the table

– you in the shower

– you everywhere

I burst out laughing. "Omg, you are crazy. Do you know that?"

"Crazy, funny or crazy, call the psychiatric hospital?"

"A little bit of both. At least you can tick one of them off now."

He smiled. "So, what happens now that you know it was a big fat lie?" he asked. "If you need some time to think about it, I can at least give you that," he said.

"Perhaps a minute or two, maybe even five." I hit his chest giggling. "You're funny, do you know that? And tell more lies than Pinocchio."

A smile lurked on his lips. "I'll admit I'm not perfect."

"Nobody is Gui."

"You are," he whispered.

"I know we don't want the same thing. It's only sex for you and nothing else. You made it clear from the start. It was hard for me to accept. But I want to stay and enjoy whatever happens."

He reached out and caught a curl and we both watched as it slid through his long fingers. "Interesting," he remarks. "You might regret what you wish for," he warned, raising an eyebrow.

"Who knows? At least I have a safe word."

He dazzled me with one of his million-dollar smiles. "But seriously, after everything you've uncovered, I'm glad you're still here and not running for the hills."

I got butterflies hearing him say that. "I thought about it." His full lips curve into a smile and he kissed me hard. I kissed him back. The hand resting on my waist gripped me tightly and he pulled me on top of the length of his body. I pushed myself against his hard chest and straddled him. His hands ran up my back and back down to my arse, squeezing it gently. His gaze moved up to my breasts and he commanded me to lean back as he sucked a nipple into his mouth. My eyes rolled and I shuddered.

"I fucking love your tits," he growled.

I had once thought it crude and dirty how he spoke to me. But I realised now, it's how real men speak when aroused and turned on. How could I forget, it was one of my fantasies? I was only familiar with quick fumbles and disappointment from the men my age I dated. Few and far between because they did nothing to turn me on, thinking at one stage I might be gay.

I could feel him getting hard beneath me. "Seriously," I gasped. "You've just come. How is it possible? I thought older men took longer to get it back up," I giggled.

"I can't help it if I want to fuck you all the time. Wait…. Older men! Fuck Rhylee I'm nearly forty not sixty," he laughed.

Giggling against his mouth, I kissed him gently, slowly grinding over his cock. With the added sensation of my hard nipples brushing against his chest, it started a tingling tsunami down below. If I keep doing this, I'm going to come. I can't help it, I want him inside me again.

He smiled wickedly. "Are you taking control," he murmured. "I love how you feel on top of me."

I kissed him deeply. He gripped my curls, gently tugging my head back. He raised his head and sucked from one nipple to the other. It's when he gently bit down that I completely lost it. "Oh, holy fuck," I groaned. I shrieked when he flipped me over so I'm pinned beneath him. I could feel his huge cock between my legs. Our mouths were like magnets. He groaned as our lips touched and I opened my mouth and sucked his eager tongue, before gently biting it.

He growled. "Sorry," I panted.

"More," he grumbled. There's such want in his kiss. I kissed him back with the same ferocity making my lips ache. "You're such a great kisser," he breathed out heavily against my mouth.

He climbed off me and stood at the end of the bed. I lay there exposed. I could feel the cool air on my swollen pussy. I rose onto my elbows, half dazed.

"What's wro.."

Before I could finish, smooth hands glide down my legs and gently pulled me to the edge of the bed. He slid his hands under my thighs, lifted my bum and lined his cock up against me. I ran my fingers over his muscled chest and he groaned.

I gritted my teeth. "Are you okay Rhylee?" I bit my lip and nodded. I spread my thighs wider hoping for easy access. He looked down where our bodies met and with a low growl, plunged into me.

I let out a cry. "Jesus Rhy, are you okay? Do you want me to stop?"

"No, it's okay. You're just so big."

He pulled out giving me a moment to recover then eased into me, slowly at first and when he was sure my body accepted him completely, he fucked me relentlessly. "Oh. My. Fucking. God. I'm going to come," I said through clenched teeth.

He closed his eyes. "Fuck, you're so tight," he grunted. He pushed deeper until his body went rigid and he pumped into me. I arched beneath him and moaned loudly, our bodies shattering in a haze of pleasure. He eased out of me and lay next to me as our legs hung off the edge of the bed. He turned and stared. "That was fucking amazing."

"Mind-blowing," I said, as my legs fell flat like heavy weights.

"Sorry, it was just a quickie," he panted.

"A quickie. I don't think I can take much more."

He took my hand and entwined our fingers. "I can't get enough of you, Rhylee Murphy," he panted.

"Then don't," I swallowed hard. He kissed my cheek and stood up.

"Please don't go."

"I'm just getting some tissues unless you'd like a facecloth?"

I blushed. "Tissue will do fine, thanks."

Gui emerged from the bathroom with a look of concern across his face. "I think you've just got your period."

I bounded to my feet and look at the bedding. "Oh no, your expensive sheets will be ruined. Don't worry if I run it under hot water, it should come out."

He came behind me and wrapped his arms around my waist. "Don't worry about it. They're just sheets and period sex doesn't freak me out either."

I took the tissues from his hand and placed them on the bed before sitting down. I couldn't look at him. "I don't have my period."

He got down on his hunkers and took my hands in his. "I don't understand Rhylee."

"My period isn't due until next week if my dates are correct."

"Wait, let me get this straight," he said, running a hand down his face. "Are you telling me you're still a virgin?" I nodded. He stood abruptly and exhales heavily. "You're a virgin," he says again. "Like how the fuck can that be true? Why wouldn't you tell me something like that?" His jaw clenched. "Rhylee, I …" He turned to me, running a hand through his hair. Damn, he's even sexy when he's angry.

"It's not something you bring up in a conversation to be fair. I don't know why you're angry with me." I could feel tears streaming down my face and my lips began to tremble. That's all I needed, an ugly crying face. I yanked a tissue from under my arse and blow my nose. He lifts me gently onto his lap. I leaned my head back and looked up at him, as he wiped the tears from my cheeks. His face suddenly softened.

"Angel, I'm far from angry. Shocked more than anything." Hearing him call me angel opened the floodgates again. I clung to him, unable to stop sobbing. He held me tighter and I could feel his heart beating as fast as mine. "Sshh it's okay. You're such a sensitive soul, aren't you? Please don't cry. It's just not something I've ever experienced. I mean you're twenty-seven and hot as fuck. How is it possible? I just don't know what to think. Fuck Rhylee. I took your virginity." He shook his head again. I blow out a frustrated breath.

"I suppose you could say I'm too picky. I didn't sleep around and I certainly wasn't into one-night stands. It wasn't a race to lose it and I wasn't in a hurry either. That's why I've waited so long. I didn't like anyone enough to give it to them willingly until I met you." He opens his mouth to say something and then closes it. I reach for his hand. "You didn't take my virginity, Gui, I wanted you to be the one. It sounds corny but it's true. If I hadn't met you, I'd probably be a sixty-year-old virgin. I wanted a memorable experience and I was one hundred percent sure I wanted to share it with you." I watch him.

"Damn it, you're special Rhylee."

"I'm not."

"Yes, you are," he repeated. You deserve more."

I reach up and grip his face, a hand on either side. "I chose you."

He shook his head in disbelief. "Thank you. I'm humbled and honoured. Christ, if I'd known I would have been gentler. You must be in bits, I know I was rough. I'm sorry for that. Christ, your first time and I was almost barbaric."

My hand slides up his smooth chest. "I swear, that thing needs its own driver's licence. I doubt I'll be able to walk for a few days."

"That's so funny and I'm trying hard not to laugh. No regrets?"

I kissed him hard on the lips. "No regrets. It's something special I'll always cherish."

He pulls away and stares at me. His eyes hold mine. "I know it's not the same. It's my first time with YOU and that's special to me. Something I'll remember forever." I move my arms around his neck and pull him closer. "Thank you. I love that."

"Also, the more we do it, the quicker you'll get used to my ginormous cock, meaning it can only get easier. That's if I haven't put you off sex forever?"

I burst out laughing. "Are you kidding? I'm going to do my own To-do list. But I may have developed 'Dicknophobia."

He burst out laughing. God, I love that sound, it makes me all tingly. I've missed it. "Jesus Christ Rhylee, you're such a breath of fresh air." He kisses me gently, his tongue lapping against mine as he places me on the bed like a delicate flower.

"I'll be back in a minute. Don't go anywhere."

"I won't be going anywhere unless there's a wheelchair in there," I say out loud.

"Comedian too," he laughed. He returned moments later with a bottle of water and two tablets. "Get them into you, it should ease the pain, hopefully."

"Are you running a bath?" I asked.

"Yes, you can relax while I change the bed. I don't think you'd be able to stand in the shower." He moved toward me and I moved out of reach.

"Gui, I'm not that bad, I can walk by myself."

Ignoring my protests, I'm lifted against his hard body and carried to a bath full of luxurious bubbles. "Oh, that smells gorgeous." He grabbed a hair grip and gathered it into a high pony.

"It's not perfect but it will do for now. You relax there and I'll be back soon."

"Thank you."

He tucked a stray curl behind my ear and kissed me softly. "Back soon." Shamefully I eyed up his perfectly toned arse as he left the room. "Stop looking at my arse!"

I giggled. "I can't help myself." I lay back and try to calm the random thoughts racing through my head. Did I feel any different after losing my virginity? Was it emotional? I crossed my legs and yelped. Fuck, that hurt. "Rhylee," I heard Gui's voice and looked up. "I lost you for a minute there."

"Oh, sorry, I was miles away."

"In a good place this time I hope?" I nodded. He climbed in behind me and once I settled comfortably between his thighs, I relaxed entirely. His hands came up around my waist and he pulled me even closer, kissing the top of my head.

"This feels nice," I murmured.

"Good," he said quietly. I leaned back against his chest and looked up at him. "Are you okay Gui?"

"Can't complain, no one listens when I do anyway haha!" He touched my exposed neck with his lips. "All you've been through and you're checking if I'm okay. You really are an angel."

I slid my hand under the water and we threaded our fingers together. His free hand roamed down to my inner thigh and tapped gently. My breath quivers. He puts his lip to my ear and whispers. "Nothing strenuous for a while young lady."

"My mam always said, if you fall off your bike, you climb right back on and ride it for dear life. That's exactly what I'm going to do."

His lip curled into a smile. "I thought you never listened to what your mother says."

"I'm making an exception this time."

"Scandalous, young lady!" His fingers trailed up my thigh, to my tummy and cupped my breast, a thumb skimmed my nipple. Heat pooled between my legs and I felt him getting harder. "As much as I want to have you again, you need to recover. But don't worry, there's plenty more to come."

For about an hour we stayed there in comfortable silence as he gently bathed me with a huge natural sponge. He kissed the top of my head and pushed a button which empties the bath. "For God's sake, you and your gadgets. Can't you just pull a plug like normal people?"

He laughed. "I don't do plugs, they ruin the aesthetics."

"Of course, they do," I giggled.

His eyes narrowed. "Are you mocking me, Miss Murphy?" He climbed out and wrapped a fluffy towel around his waist then wrapped me up.

"How do you get the towels so fluffy?"

"That, you'll have to ask Daiyu. She holds all the secrets." He patted me dry from head to toe, being extra gentle with my inner thighs. I winced. "I'm sorry, should I call the doctor?"

The look of concern on his face tugged at my heart. "Are you mad? I don't need anyone else poking around down there."

He shot me an exasperated look. I held my hands up, "I'm kidding, but thanks, no need to call a doctor."

He lifted me onto the counter and gently dried my legs, down to my toes. "You have the cutest feet I've ever seen. So small and dainty. Just like you. When did you do your nails?"

"I had an emergency appointment with the salon downstairs." He raised an eyebrow.

"Whatever do you mean?"

"I'm too embarrassed to say."

"Seriously, after everything we've done and are going to do, you're still embarrassed?"

"Some things are best left unsaid," I yawned.

"I'll leave it there so. Come on, sleepy head, let's get you to bed." He held out his hand and leads me to the bedroom. "Oh, you have remade the bed. You must be used to the turnaround every week. Women in and out, quicker than a Tesco's conveyor belt." I giggled.

His eyes widened. "Cheeky monkey. I am single, you know. You'll be surprised to hear I've never had a woman stay with me in this bed."

"You've never had a woman here?"

"No. Only you."

"Yeah right. Ahh, you take them up to the bachelor pad where all the magic happens."

"Yes, I do. Not sure about the magic though. I try my best. Anyway, it's what they expect. Or the playroom.

Depending on the person. Believe it or not, this is my favourite room to sleep. It's unlike any of the other rooms. I find it calming. So, you are the first and only woman to sleep here."

My face lit up. "Wow, another first for me," I winked. We climbed into bed and lay facing each other. He ran his thumb over my lip and then kissed me. "I'm afraid to close my eyes," I whispered. He pulled one of my curls and let it spring back.

"Why's that?"

"It's silly."

"Tell me."

"In case I wake up and you're not here. That the wonderful night I've had with you was all a dream."

"Aww bless. You are a hopeless romantic, aren't you? Come here." He pulled me closer and I turn in his arms. We fit together like a jigsaw puzzle. He planted a kiss on the top of my head.

"At the hospital, I imagined you sniffing me."

"That's because I did. Smell is the strongest sense tied to memory. I didn't think I'd see you again."

"What was your first impression of me?"

"Apart from being sexy as hell. I found you funny and intriguing. A great sense of humour is always sexy."

"You think humour is a turn-on."

"Not necessarily, just yours. Some women try too hard, and it usually ends the night sooner than they would have liked. Must be the Irish sense of humour."

"Thank the fucking Lord we're good at something."

"But the sight of you made me hard as rock. Speaking of which." A smooth hand glides up to play with my breast and he gently tugged a nipple. I shifted my bum into him and gasped.

"Fuck," he hissed as I pushed myself against his cock.

I took his hand and held it against my heart. "Are you trying to kill me, Mr Lee?"

"I actually can't help it. You have the best tits. The perfect package. It's true what they say, good things do come in small packages. And you're beautiful." His mouth slides down to my neck and he kisses me. I rolled my eyes and tutted.

"Did you just tut me?"

"Yeah, it's just the things you say."

"Rhylee, there's no side twist to me telling you you're beautiful. It's just what I think. Genuinely... You are beautiful."

"Thank you." It wasn't long before the tiredness took over and we fell asleep spooning with his arms tightly around me.

32

I woke feeling refreshed after having had the best sleep ever, grinning like the cat who got the cream. What a night. I stretched and felt a heavy weight across my tummy. I looked down to find Gui's arm and I smiled. I turned slowly to stop him from waking and just stared at the beauty sharing my pillow. My inner thighs can one hundred percent confirm what happened alright. That I've been well and truly fucked by Mr Gui Lee noted business tycoon extraordinaire.

I ran my finger over his full lips and he stirred slightly. His face is just inches from mine. I couldn't help myself and moved in closer and lightly kissed them. He smiled against my mouth.

"Good morning, beautiful," he said in that husky tone.

"Good morning yeh ride." We both burst out laughing.

"Were you watching me sleeping?"

"No, I was just wondering how that God-awful foghorn sound could come from someone so angelic."

His eyes widened in disbelief, and I giggled.

"I do not snore Rhylee Murphy. How dare you. Did you sleep well?"

"Like a log."

"I want you, but it's too soon I know."

"To be honest, I'm afraid to look down there."

"Would you like me to check if it's all still there?" I giggled and punched him softly. "You can't be trusted, Mr Lee."

"I'm sorry, I can't help myself when you're around. I'm truly fucked." The smile on his face is everything and I get butterflies. I've never met anyone like him. Just listening to him makes me want to be naughty. He's such a ride.

Bless me Father, for I have sinned…. Will sin… Again and again…

Just then there's a loud crashing sound. "Omg," I shrieked. "What the hell was that?" As if it was nothing to worry about, Gui casually turned on his side and started playing with my hair. "Gui, I'm serious. What on earth was that noise? Aren't you one bit concerned?"

"More than likely, they're preparing for the celebration tonight."

"Oh. What kind of celebration?"

"Just my birthday."

I sat up straight like I had just been electrocuted. "Wait, what. Hold on a minute. Your birthday."

"Yes, my mother insists on celebrating both our birthdays every year. It's a huge family tradition. I know huh, strange at this stage in my life. But she loves organising everything, including the guest list. I'd never dream of stopping her although sometimes I've had words with her over the invites. Common denominator…all the single ladies. Saying that she's amended it three times since you got here." He looked up at me. "Hey, why so sad?"

"I can't even get you a gift and sure what could I get you anyway. You have everything you could want."

He pulled me on top of him and I rested my head against his. "I have everything I want, right here in my arms."

I turned my head because I didn't believe him. "Look at me," he whispered. Large hands cupped my face and he kissed me like he meant it. "I mean it, Rhy. Do you believe me?"

"Suppose."

"Good." His hands drifted slowly down my back and cupped my arse, squeezing it gently. "Come, let me make you breakfast."

"You, cook?"

"Don't look so surprised. I'll have you know I'm a great cook."

"Shall I get a fire extinguisher, just in case?"

"Any more of your cheek and I'll spank you."

"You go first, and I'll follow you up shortly."

"Why can't we go together," he eyed me suspiciously. "It's just, well, I don't want to give anyone the wrong idea. I'm sure your mother is already here. You don't want to give her wedding notions now, do you?"

"Shit. You're right. She certainly doesn't need any more encouragement." His eyes grew wide. The look of relief on his face floored me.

"I'm going to find Lan when I'm dressed. Are we invited to the party?" I said in a huff.

He climbed out of bed and retrieved his clothes from the floor and I noticed he was semi-hard. "Of course, you are, why wouldn't you be."

"I hardly think Genny would want me there with all the single ladies."

"Aren't you a single lady too?"

"Gui, I'm serious, you know what I mean.

I'm quite sure her list is for rich eligible females suitable to marry the apple of her eye."

"Rhylee, you're on the list. She had close to fifty eligible ladies invited and when you came along. She cut it by half."

"That's why I shouldn't be there."

"It's not a match-making party Rhy," he said softly. "You're blowing it all out of proportion. Eligible men have been invited too, he chuckled. You are one of her favourite people. Probably the only one outside of the family."

"Do you want me there?"

"Why on earth would you ask that?" I rolled my eyes.

"And don't be doing that eye roll thing either like I've asked you something ridiculous."

My face sagged. "What if someone catches your eye? But you feel me giving you the evils."

"There'll only be one person catching my eye tonight and that's you. Come on, I'm hungry, stop this nonsense and join me."

"It's still early and I'm knackered, I wonder why. I'm going to stay in bed for another hour. I'll find you later."

"Okay. Oh, by the way, I ordered some evening gowns and they'll be here around twelve. If you like, Evee can choose one too."

"But you've got me so many things already. Suppose it's easy when you have your own personal shopper. Do you?"

"Yes, I do. But everything so far including the dresses were chosen by me. It's the first time I've ever personally shopped for someone and it was quite enjoyable imagining how they'd look on you. You're taking me out of my comfort zone Miss Murphy."

"Is that a good thing?"

"I'm not sure."

As soon as he left the room, I called Evee. "Hey, where are you?"

"Well good morning to you too Miss Murphy."

"For fuck's sake, why is everyone calling me by my surname?"

"Has someone gotten out of the wrong side of the bed?"

"Evee, why are you talking like that? Omg, you haven't."

"NO, I have not. Seriously, stop making out I'm a slapper Rhylee."

"I'm sorry. Spit it out, Evee, I say, waiting. Where are you?"

"I'm in Keane's."

"Omg, you little tramp."

"Calm down ma, we didn't sleep together. Although it was very tempting. But I was a good girl."

"Whatever, are you here or in his house?"

"I'm here, why? What's wrong? Are you okay?" Each word started to rise in a higher pitch.

"Calm down, I'm fine. Has Keane mentioned that Gui's having a birthday party tonight?"

"He mentioned something alright but I think I had too much Dutch courage to remember. Is he turning forty-eight?" She giggled.

"Cheeky bitch, thirty-eight!"

"Still a cradle snatcher."

"I knew you'd get drunk."

"I was sober until I came back here and he started making all these fab cocktails."

"Hmm, sounds familiar. Where is he?"

"Not sure what room he's in. He left me at the bedroom door, kissed me goodnight and closed it in my face. Like what the hell."

"I'm sure it was a little more romantic than that. Was he as pissed as you?"

"I would think so. He said I was wifey material. What's up anyway, my head is pounding. Do not say I told you so either! All I know is that I'm going to enjoy whatever it is. Just like you."

I cleared my throat. "Shall I book a flight home for you too?"

She sighed heavily. "Yeah, suppose."

"Evee, I was only joking. Just because I'm doomed, doesn't mean you are too. I know for sure he likes you. That's something, isn't it? Hey, answer me."

"Suppose."

"Anyway, why the hell are we still talking on the phone? I'll be there in a minute. If he is beside you, now is a good time for him to go for a swim."

"Jesus, he's not here Rhylee!" She snorted.

I let myself in and found her fully dressed in bed. She looked at me with two huge panda eyes. "Omg Evee, your mascara is all over the pillowcases."

"It will wash out, don't worry about it."

"And you look like a panda." Well that got her up like a bolt of lightning and straight over to the mirror.

"Jesus, I can't let Keane see me like this, state of me."

"Here, I brought you some wipes."

"Omg, you're the best."

"Just tidy up under your eyes."

"Anyway, what's up?"

"You're not going to believe it. Gui has arranged for evening gowns to be sent over for us."

She jumped onto the bed with such ferocity, I almost bounced right off. "No fucking way? That means I'm invited too."

"I'm sure Keane asked you last night but you just have brain fog."

"Maybe. I can't wait to see the dresses. Hope the personal shopper has good taste?"

"HE has great taste," I winked.

"I'm raging I can't even get him a birthday present. What do you get the guy who has everything?"

"You, naked and wrapped in a bow."

"He's already had me, twice."

"Rhylee Murphy, no way. OMG! Are you okay? Come here to me. My baby's not a virgin anymore woo woo."

"It was everything I imagined it would be, but better. I'm so sore down there though. Were you the same?"

"Don't remember. It hurt a little but I don't think I was as sore afterwards. I think I was more in pain after horse riding to be honest. Then again, you said Gui's dick is a mofo. When he pulls his boxers down and that mofo bounces out like it's on hydraulics."

I burst out laughing. "That's very precise actually." I giggled.

"Where on earth did you hear that?"

"I think it's from some rap song?"

"I'm wondering if they'll do our hair and makeup too. I'll find out."

"Feck's sake, I'm hungry. Any sign of breakfast."

"Get up and find out Princess Evee. Seriously. What are you like? Gui wanted to make me some, but I got a little upset and said I was going back to bed for an hour."

"What happened?"

"Ahh, he acted so relieved when I said we shouldn't be going for breakfast together so early in front of his mother. Giving her wedding ideas. I swear to God Evee. You should have seen the look of relief on his face! Like I just saved him from something horrendous."

"Don't take it personally hun. The word marriage leaves a nasty taste for a bachelor like Gui and I'm sure the thought of marriage to anyone would frighten the bejesus out of him. For now, he's just set in his ways."

"Jesus, I can hardly keep my eyes open. You go and have a bite to eat. I'm going back to bed. When the dresses arrive, I'll text you. I'm sure you don't mind hanging around with Keane?"

"Will I bring something back?"

"No, I just want to sleep, thanks though."

I crawled into bed and sleep didn't come easy. All I could think about was that I didn't want to go to the party. I hate things like that. Plus, it was going to be attended by some of the most beautiful women. How would I cope seeing them all over him and hanging on to his every word? All trying to impress or become the next Mrs Lee? I knew it was going to happen, sometime. I just didn't want to have to see it.

Three hours later there was a tap on the door and Gui popped his head in. "I hope I didn't wake you. I was here earlier but you were snoring your head off so I let you be."

"I was not snoring my head off you cheeky sod."

"Now, would I lie to you?" He laughed.

"No, Pinocchio you wouldn't." He pushed the door open with his foot carrying a tray full of deliciousness, sourdough toast and poached eggs.

"Thought you might be peckish?"

"Ooh that looks amazing, thank you. The eggs look so perfect."

"See, you didn't believe I could cook."

"Still don't. I am impressed, Mr Lee. Good looks, multiple orgasms and you're not bad in the kitchen either. I've hit the jackpot."

"I try my best. By the way, the dresses are here. I've had them put in my apartment above. By all means, choose the one you like. But I think you'll look stunning in the gold one. Hey, they are all amazing, I picked them."

"So who's going to your party? Any Queens or Princesses? Bet there are loads of models."

"You have nothing to worry about. Rhylee you're going to make yourself sick. Normal nice people, I promise. Well, Jingfei will be there, so maybe not haha. It's at seven-thirty on the roof. Private drinks before in the lounge for a select few. I'll try to stay by your side most of the time. But will have to mingle too. You'll have mom, Keane and Evee. So, stop worrying."

"Would it be okay if myself and Evee went down to the salon for hair and makeup?"

"All taken care of. Mom has organised everything. Wwan and his ladies will be here at four. She said to come up for some bubbly before then."

"Four!! Omg. Surely it doesn't take that long to get ready?"

"Afraid so. Mom makes a party of it."

"Thank you. It all sounds amazing."

"Angel don't look so frightened. Once you're in makeup, you'll completely relax."

"I'd relax even more if I didn't have to go."

"Ah don't say that. You'll feel different when you're in the middle of it."

"Em what do I say if I'm asked who I am?"

"You can say you're a family friend if you like?"

"I like," I smiled.

"It's just that if you said you were a friend of mine, the vultures would circle."

"It's okay, a family friend is fine. After all, it's true. I'm friends with you, Keano and Genny. Oh, and Daiyu."

"Keano?"

"Oh, it's just what I call Keane. An Irish nickname."

"I see." His face sagged. I leaned in and kissed his mouth.

"It's just a nickname," I said softly. Sure, I call you a ride."

He placed the tray down on the floor and dived on top of me. "You're lucky your…. What do you call it? Oh yes.

You're lucky your hoo-ha is indisposed or you'd be riding my cock right now ye little ride."

I burst out laughing. Oh, my goodness, he's just the cutest.

"What's so funny? Isn't that how the Irish say it?"

"Yeah, you're not Irish, but it's just hilarious when you say it." He chuckled.

"I love when you smile and giggle. Makes my day."

I rolled my eyes. "I'm not just for Christmas you know," I giggled. "A Rhylee can be for life too."

He rolled off me and I immediately regretted what I'd said. "I was joking. I don't know why I said that. I know you don't want a 'wifey for lifey', you've told me often enough."

"I just don't want you getting hurt. I'd rather have this short time with you than nothing at all. I hate banging on about it. It's hard for me to change who I am. I've dated women who in the beginning were happy to accept the situation. I mean, why not. They loved the fame, limelight and gifts. Who wouldn't? They became complacent and thought they'd be the ones who could change my ways. Looking for more than what I was willing to give them. Some moved on selflessly, others sold stories or lied. On rare occasions, I'd be the one who ended up getting hurt."

"I'm not them. I understand you've built this great big wall around your feelings. I feel sad, knowing you won't allow yourself to find happiness. Everyone deserves someone to love and be loved. I hope when you realise this, it won't be too late."

He smiled but there was sadness behind his eyes. "Do you know what Rhylee Murphy, you are the only one to see right through me?" He kissed the top of my head and I grabbed his hand.

"I would never want to change anything about you anyway."

He squeezed my hand. "I have to do a few hours in the office. So feel free to organise your day however you want. I'll come to get you at six-thirty. Is that enough time to get the war paint on?"

"Oi, you cheeky fucker! I'll see you then." I flopped down on the bed and pulled the covers over my head. "Grrrr!" My heart was pounding fast in my chest and I needed to calm the fuck down. There was no way I was going to the party with a nervous rash crawling up my neck. I heard the door open. "Rhylee, it's me, Daiyu. I have something for you." I pushed the covers under my chin and smiled. She was standing there with a glass of something the colour of a radioactive cesspool. "Please tell me that's not for me."

"Gui asked me to whip up a natural remedy for you. He says your nerves are gone because of the party. This is a family recipe and one hundred percent guaranteed. Before you say it, there are no side effects and it won't give you diarrhoea."

"Omg, I'm worried even more now because you said that."

"See you're worrying unnecessarily. All the more reason to drink it. Come on now, it's not that bad. My kids drank it all the time during their exams. I even blended some apples to make it taste better, especially for you."

I reluctantly climbed out of bed, the whole time keeping my eyes on the vomit-green concoction.

"Mr Lee has never fussed over anyone like this. He likes you. It's a good sign."

"It seems everyone and their mother thinks that except Gui."

"Give it time. You'll see. We have an old Chinese proverb that says, relationships are decreed by fate. It suggests that you and your partner were meant to overcome all odds to meet and be together. If fate brings a couple together, it means that there is a reason for the union to occur, reasons that only higher powers or the universe may know. I agree with that. You and Mrs Lee were both somewhere you shouldn't have been. Fate brought you together and brought you to him."

I smiled and took the glass. I sniffed the contents, blessed myself and knocked it back. "That looked worse than it tasted, thanks so much. Fingers crossed it works."

"Trust me, it will."

The rest of the day flew by. Genny and Wwan had us all in hysterics. Or maybe it was the bubbly. Yes, I had a few. Sure why not. And I swear to God, seeing Wwan outside the salon, he's one hundred percent straight. Evee and I picked our dresses and Gui was right. The gold one, although extremely sexy and provocative, looked stunning. If I hadn't drank the green gunk, I doubt I'd have the courage to wear it. It was a sequin slip dress, which clung to my body like liquid gold. It had a plunging V-neck and spaghetti straps with a full thigh slit and sweeping train. The back was daringly low, barely covering the top of my arse. Thank God it had a clever built-in bra. I stood in front of the floor-to-ceiling mirror and didn't recognise the person looking back at me. My hair was scraped back into a high pony and straightened. My makeup was so beautiful that I kept sticking out my tongue to make sure it was really me.

"Well, all I can say is that we both scrub up well for two hicks from Ireland," Evee gushed.

"Eh, I would hope so after almost three bloody hours in hair and makeup."

"Here," she says, pushing her phone into my hand. "Snap away. We're never going to look like this ever again. Gui is going to fucking shoot his load when he sees you." I turn to her and start spluttering, champagne spitting everywhere. "Oh my God, Evee." I giggled. "I'm almost after choking."

"So what do we do now, just wait?"

"Gui said he'll come to get us. Drinks will be in the lounge for a select few before the party starts."

"Select few. Hmm. That means the chosen ones. Can't wait to see who the special ones are. Apart from us of course."

"Oh. My. Fucking. God." We both turned to find Keane dressed in a navy tuxedo, a smile beaming across his face.

"You both look amazing. Seriously hot."

He kissed our cheeks and held out his hand to Evee. "May I accompany you upstairs for drinks?"

She looked at me for direction. "You two go ahead. I'll wait for Gui."

She squeezed my hand. "See you up there Rhy."

"You won't be waiting much longer," Keane says. "They were just finishing his hair when I left."

Evee burst out laughing. "What the hell is he having done to his hair? I'm scarlet for him."

Looking guilty like he just revealed a big secret. He quickly added that he was only having it blow-dried. Evee burst out laughing again which was beginning to infuriate me. "Take her upstairs before I slap her."

"Rhylee, come on. What straight man has his hair blow-dried?"

"Jesus, what's the big deal anyway," I fumed.

Keane politely coughed. "Actually, I've had mine done too."

"Oh." Evee gasped. It was my turn to laugh.

I hadn't sat down since I put the dress on. I suppose now is as good a time as any to make sure I don't burst out of it like the Incredible Hulk. I sat down carefully and held my breath. Nope, nothing straining under the pressure. Thank God because I wasn't wearing any undies. No matter what I tried on, you could see the top of them peeking out. The only problem was the thigh-high slit. Sitting down you could see my whole leg and then some. I'd have to hold it some way without making it obvious I wasn't wearing underwear. I stretched out my leg to admire the shoes which were specially matched to the dress. The dry oil I'd sprayed on my legs shimmered gently making them look half decent.

Someone wolf whistled and I looked up to find a fine thing, Gui leaning against the door frame, looking hot as fuck and sophisticated in a dark suit. I blushed. We stared at each other.

"Fuck Rhylee. Stand up, let me see you." His voice is deep and sends shivers through me. His full lips curved into a smile as I stepped shyly forward to meet him. "Fuck, you smell delicious too," he says nuzzling into my neck, biting it gently. I cross my legs trying to calm the tingling. "Turn around. I want to see your arse." He trailed a finger down my bare back then down between the cheeks of my bum, making me gasp.

"Very naughty Miss Murphy. No underwear. How do you expect me to keep it together knowing you're naked under there? I'm well and truly fucked." He boldly moved his finger over my hole and I took a deep breath. It felt good, and I moaned. Oh no, I just moaned out loud.

"You like that, don't you?" He whispered in my ear. He pressed harder. There was no hiding the strangled groan which came from my mouth. I wanted more and shamefully started pushing against his finger. He removed it straight away and turned me around.

"Jesus, I want to fuck you right now. You're to blame for this. I look down and his cock is tenting painfully against his trousers.

"That's gotta hurt," I giggled. I could kiss it better."

"Are you trying to fucking kill me altogether," he groaned.

"What can I say? You do have the hugest dick I have ever seen."

A smile broke across his plump lips. "Can't be hard. Certainly, the biggest one you've ever seen, I bet."

I giggled and put my arms around his neck. "You'd be right." He moved his gaze down to my mouth. "As much as I want hot red lipstick smudged over my cock right now, I won't ruin the masterpiece. You look more stunning if that's even possible."

"Ahh, it's amazing what a shit load of makeup can do."

"Do I detect an air of confidence about you Miss Murphy?"

"That you do. That Chinese medicine Daiyu knocked up did the job. Thanks for looking out for me."

He cupped my face with two hands and kissed my nose. "When you walk through the door, I want you to shine. Pay no heed to Jingfei either. I'm sure she'll try to knock your confidence because you look fucking stunning. Ready?"

"Ready as I'll ever be."

He held out his arm and I linked him. We took the lift in silence. By the way he looked at me, I knew if he could he'd rip the dress right off me and fuck me senseless.

I pointed at his crotch. "How's it going on down there?" He lifted his jacket. "Almost gone. I thought about Jingfei licking it and it worked a treat."

"Oh my God, Gui." I sighed. "That's mean."

"God you are a proper softy, aren't you," he says and kissed my forehead.

33

*H*eads turned when we enter the room and I wished we could have walked in holding hands.

As he said, there weren't many people there. About fifteen and I knew a handful of them already. Jingfei shot me daggers and I refused to make eye contact. I could see she was wearing a red silk dress and her hair was down around her face in curls. As much as she irritated me, the woman looked stunning. She certainly wasn't hit with the ugly stick.

Wwan and Genny were on the sofa and I'm sure she sounded like she was pissed as a fart. "Christ. The night will be a night to remember if my mother has one more drink. I asked Wwan to keep an eye on her."

"What do you mean?"

"She starts on anyone she can't stand. And there's a few of them here tonight. I've never seen her this tipsy so early."

"I think she started in hair and makeup. We were there for a long time and the champagne was flowing freely. Surely it can't be that bad?"

"We'll see." We joined Evee and Keane and I couldn't help noticing how Keane looked at her. It was so obvious he was into her. He was star-struck and I don't think she has a clue. I crossed my fingers. She looked beautiful tonight. The dress she wore was the one I had originally picked first. Only because it was pink. It looked stunning against her auburn hair. She looked like a Princess. If anyone didn't know Gui or Keane, they'd think we were two beautiful couples.

"So old chap, how does it feel almost hitting forty," Keane asked.

Gui burst out into laughter. "You'll know next month, *old chap*."

Evee tugged on Keane's sleeve. "It's your birthday next month?"

"It is. I hope you're into older men," he said, wiggling his eyebrows.

"But why didn't you just have a joint party," I ask.

"And what's the fun in that?"

"So, you'll be doing all this again next month?"

"Yes, and the month after for mom."

My eyes widened. "Bloody hell. Someone likes to party," Evee giggled. "I'll have you know, some of our best deals have been brokered at one or two of these parties," Keane said.

"Ahh, is that what you call working the room?"

"Yes, and Gui knows how to shake hands and kiss babies."

"And ladies I bet," smirked Evee. I gave her the evils.

What the hell was wrong with her lately?

"Speaking of which, I see someone I need to say hello to." He squeezed my hand and walked away. I watched him walk casually over to a woman with long black hair and just as tall as him.

Keane followed my line of vision and whispered, "She has nothing on you."

"Ah sure it's not my business who Gui talks to." Nevertheless, I still couldn't help watching them together. He had kissed her cheek and she had kept her hand on his arm. It was obvious they'd been close at some stage, clearly comfortable in each other's company. Now and again, he would say something and she'd giggle demurely. She still wanted him. It was so obvious.

Evee lowered her head and whispered in my ear, "I bet she wants to strip him naked and ride him until she passes out."

"Yeah, and every other woman here tonight I'd say." Just then, he turned his head and his eyes sought out mine. The way he looked at me gave me goosebumps all over. I smiled and he smiled back before returning his attention to the raven-haired beauty.

"Seems to be a lot of flanter going on over there," said Evee, nodding towards Gui and the mystery friend.

"What's that," Keane asked.

"Flirtatious banter."

"Ah no, they're just good friends who dated a long time ago. She runs one of his companies. He's on good terms with a few of his exes. Not many men can say that."

"Can you?" Evee asked.

He took a sip of champagne before answering. "No, I can't. If it doesn't work out, I don't see any point."

I would have loved to get him something he'd remember me by. He wasn't a materialistic man even though he had the top of the range in everything. He didn't flaunt his wealth either. I'm disturbed out of my daydreaming by Evee snapping her fingers like she's Beyonce.

"Hello. Come back to us."

"Fuck's sake Evee, I almost slapped the face off Jingfei for doing just that! Grab your phone and follow me."

"But the party," she cried.

"It will still be here when we get back. Keane, will you excuse us for a few minutes."

"Yeah, sure." He looked between the two of us. "Is everything okay?"

"Everything is grand. I just need Evee's help with something. We'll be back in a jiffy."

"Right then, I suppose I should mingle."

I grabbed her hand and pulled her towards the elevator. "Fuck's sake where's the bloody fire Rhylee?"

"I'll explain when we get there," I said, shoving her into the lift. The doors opened and we stood in the corridor.

"Where are we?" I opened the door and pushed her inside. "What the fuck are we doing here? Omg, we're not having a gang bang or anything like that, are we?"

"Jesus Evee, you've got some imagination."

"Says the pot!"

"Okay, sit down and listen. I want you to make a video of me."

"Doing what exactly. Riding the spanking bench?"

"I'm going to strip naked and pose in a submissive position."

Her eyes widened. "Why?"

"Something special for Gui's birthday. And don't go off on one saying I'm a little slapper. You did it all the time."

"Yes, I did. But I was in a long-term relationship. Of course, I'm not going to judge you. But are you sure this is what you want to do? I'm just saying because I know how shy you are and I don't think I've ever seen you in the nip. Except when we were kids."

"Yes, I'm sure. It's something he'll never forget."

"So have I to video you undressing too?"

"No, it's not a striptease. I'll undress and pose. Not sure which position yet. I suppose whichever is more comfortable. Then wait for him to come get me."

"Okay, I'll take the video and send it when I go back to the party. I want to see the look on his face. No wait, do you know what you should do?"

"Go on."

"Stick a butt plug in."

"Absolutely not. Are you fucking crazy? I don't want to give him any ideas. Anyway, the size of him would split me in half."

"Hmm. Nipple clamps?"

"Nope."

"Ball gag?"

"Fuck off Evee."

"Just trying to help," she giggled. "Go on then, get your kit off and show us your tits."

"You're disgraceful. Does your mother know you use that kind of language?"

"Says the one making a porno." We both burst out into laughter. I slid the straps off my shoulders and let the slinky fabric pool on the floor.

"Jesus, it's baltic in here." I shivered. I carefully placed the designer gown over the spanking bench.

"Bloody hell Rhylee you're not wearing any knickers," she gasped.

"I couldn't. You saw how low the back of the dress is."

"Omg, look at your boobs."

My hands shot up to cup them. "Oh no, what's wrong," I said in a panic. "Are they horrible and saggy?"

"Are you mad? They're the firmest tits I've ever seen, you lucky bitch."

"Phew, thank God. Should I leave the heels on?"

"Try with and without. See what's comfy." I left them off because the heels were poking into my arse. I kneeled on the small rug just inside the door where I assumed that's where his subs waited.

"Oh Jesus, I feel sick," I groaned.

"Look, isn't this another one of your fantasies?"

"No. Never wanted to be a sub."

"Well sure you're here now. Might as well give it a lash." The room was cool and my nipples were hard. I placed my palms on my thighs and straightened my back. "Oh, would you mind moving that big leather chair a few feet in front of me?"

"Oh yeah, that's so sexy. He'll probably sit there and wank staring at you. Wouldn't be the first time."

"Shut up Evee, stop acting the maggot! Okay, shoot before I go stiff and can't get up. Wish me luck."

"You look amazing, Rhylee. Stare straight ahead and don't look or talk to me when I'm videoing. I'll start back here then circle, paying particular attention to every part of you. Breathe naturally and don't be holding in your tummy. Not that you need to."

"Jesus, I know, I know," I say, nervously.

"Are you ready?"

I clenched my teeth and nodded. "Okay." I swallow. "Go ahead. Oh, don't forget to say Happy Birthday on it." The video was only about five minutes long but it felt like hours.

Evee hugged me and dashed. Stopping suddenly at the door.

"Oh Jesus," she giggles, "What floor do I press?" I waited patiently and I hoped Daiyu's snot green concoction was still working its magic and I didn't have an ugly rash up my neck.

The door swung open and my heart almost stopped with the fright. Nevertheless, I kept my eyes straight ahead. "Jesus fucking Christ," he gasps. From the corner of my eye, I could see him removing his jacket and placing it over my dress. He walked to the strategically placed armchair and sat down.

"Fuck Rhylee, I'm in shock. I'm so proud of you. I know how much of a perfectionist you are and this is no exception. With time it will get easier and who knows, you might just fall in love with being bossed about?" He laughed.

I tried hard to suppress a smile and hold the position, glad I was doing a decent job at being a sub. *His* submissive, for one night only. He leaned forward, putting his hands in the prayer position on his knees. His glossy hair fell over his face and I fought the urge to push it back.

"Look at me," he growled. I remained still and turned my head to face him. He smiled. Damn, how can a man have lips so enviously luscious?

"Fuck me," he drawled. I made a move to stand, hoping I wouldn't fall over like a baby giraffe. "Crawl," he said in that voice. "Keep your eyes on me." I did as he said and crawled toward him, feeling my arse and boobs swaying from side to side.

I got to him and opened his legs wide. Never taking my eyes off him, I opened his belt and slowly pulled down his zip. Teasingly, I slid my hand inside his trousers and set the beast free. He drew in a deep breath as I ran my thumb over the head of his rock-hard pulsing cock. It was wet with pre-cum and I licked it like an ice cream while massaging his tight balls. Hearing him groan sends bolts of pleasure through my body, turning me on even more.

"Stop, Rhylee I'm about to come."

Ignoring his protests, I sucked his cock into my mouth. He let out a groan and pulled me up. "Stop! I want to come inside you, not in your mouth." He desperately slammed his lips against mine, sucking the groans right out of my mouth.

"Fuck, you taste so good." I felt a pulse of desire between my legs and kissed him harder. His smooth hands drifted slowly down my body and cupped my arse moving me on top of his cock. He bent his head and sucked a nipple. Then moved to the other one alternating between sucking and gently biting. I groan out loud.

He knew my nipples were my weak spot. He stood up like I weighed nothing and carried me to the bed. He lay me down gently and in haste ripped off his shirt and trousers. His thumb brushed over me and then he smothered my moans with a kiss. Taking my ankles, he gently pulled me to the edge of the bed and raised my legs flat against his chest. I felt muscles I never knew I had ache with the strain.

"I just want to bury my cock deep in you." He grabbed my arse and pulled me closer. Gripping himself he slid his cock up and down. "So wet."

I bit my lip and watched as he pushed into me. He watched me as he filled me, inch after inch. I gasped, arching my back, feeling him go balls deep in one push, skin on skin. We both groaned out loud. "Fuck, I'll never get used to this," he gasped.

I closed my eyes as he pounded into me. He released a frustrated growl. "Rhylee, look at me. Do not close your eyes." His eyes look almost black.

"Sorry," I whispered through clenched teeth, feeling the onslaught of an orgasm. His expression immediately softens. "Oh God, you feel so good inside me," I mumble. He pulls out slowly to the tip and inhales heavily. "Fuck, I can't. Hold it." He rammed into me and I feel my breasts bounce with each hard thrust. A deep frown creases his brow as he comes inside of me.

"Oh, my God." I whimpered. "That was fucking amazing."

He pulls out of me and gently placed my legs down, then braced his hands on either side of my head. "You okay angel?"

"I'm okay." He collapsed on the bed beside me. "It gets even better each time." My breasts rise and fall as I tried to reign in my erratic breathing.

"I love your tits and how they move. Especially when I'm fucking you. Everything is fake these days. Fake is the new norm."

"Did you know, men lose fifty percent of their thinking ability when they see nipples."

"Yep, I well believe it." I turned on my side to face him and winced. He scrambled to sit up in a panic. "Christ, was I too hard?"

I shook my head. "I'm grand, honestly. I'm sure it will ease with time. Anyway, it's a nice pain."

He kissed the tip of my nose. "You look beautifully fucked."

I turned away embarrassed."

"Hey, you need to learn to accept compliments." I huffed a laugh.

"It just makes me feel awkward and I know it's silly."

"Of course, it's not silly. You're just not used to receiving them. And that's just because you don't put yourself out there. YOU would be different if you lived a little."

"Thanks," is all I could muster.

"Saying that, selfishly I don't want you to."

"What do you mean?" He ran his hand over his face and sighed.

"Tell me, what is it?"

"I can't. I feel like a dick."

My stomach was in knots as I spoke. "O-kay." His jaw clenches. I sat up and looked at him. "You have me worried now."

"Fuck it. I watched you laughing and giggling with Keane and I've never been a jealous man. But it hit me right in the fucking gut."

I tried to remember and couldn't place when they were both in the same room together. Apart from now at the party. But I barely spoke to Keane. "It shouldn't bother you."

"It does because you don't laugh like that with me or look at me the way you look at him."

I thought for a minute. "Hmmm. Did you watch us while you were away?"

"I couldn't help myself."

"But surely you know we're only friends."

"I know that he fell for you hard and I can't blame him for that. It's understandable. I'm jealous of everyone who is with you. And I'm a dick for not doing something about it. That's how fucked up I am."

"I agree. That's some fucked up shit right there." I giggled. I took his hand and kissed his palm. "That's the type of shit every girl wants to hear. The first part anyway. You're not a dick, you're just afraid. Come on, people will be wondering where we are."

"Is that all you have to say?"

"No point in saying anything else. Except get dressed." He cupped my face and kissed me passionately. "Let me just get some hot cloths."

"On this occasion, I don't mind. But I'll do it myself."

"Well, I honestly don't mind if you do me," he chuckles. "You're mad, we'd never leave this room if I did. Don't forget your face. Ronald McDonald isn't a good look for either of us!"

"I'd say the only person wondering where we are is Jingfei."

"Exactly. The very person I don't want boring a hole in my head for the rest of the night."

We cleaned up and headed back to the party which by then had moved to the rooftop.

"I couldn't have wished for a better birthday present. You are the perfect sub and I can't wait to do it again. Thank you."

"Aww, you're very welcome." He tipped my head back and kissed my lips as his hands gently squeezed my arse when the doors opened. We both pull apart but not before I see Jingfei looking at us in shock and disbelief. Fuck!

"What do we do now? Do we go our separate ways or both walk over to Evee?"

"You're overthinking again, angel."

"Maybe," I say. I followed his lead and we join Evee, Keane and his mum.

"Here's the birthday boy. I was wondering where you two disappeared to. Everything ok," she smiled, looking from me to Gui. He grinned, fixing his tie. He kissed her cheek.

"We're good." She looked at me and winked. I smiled innocently. I looked at Evee and she gave me a thumbs up. I gave her a wink. I looked at Keane and I'm not sure what I saw. Acknowledgement, maybe.

"Angel, er.. I mean Rhylee, would you like a drink?" We all turned to Gui and his faux pas and laughed.

"I need a stiff one because I can feel Jingfei's eyes scalding me." We all burst into laughter. "Surprise me, nothing too strong though."

"Water it is so." He shot me a smile that would make me drop my knickers if I was wearing any. I rolled my eyes dramatically. Evee leaned forward and whispered in my ear, "So, angel, how did it go?" I checked Keane wasn't listening.

I replied, "Amazing. He absolutely loved it."

"I'd say so from the look on his face when he opened it. Probably got a hard-on right there!"

"Oh my goodness," I said in shock. She squeezed my hand tightly and I could see her trying not to squeal. "I'm just going to see what's keeping Gui. I saw Jingfei follow him and he may need rescuing?" Said Keane.

"I'd say so, that one is away with the fairies and needs to cop on to herself," said Evee.

"Keane dear, I'll bid you goodnight now. Tell Gui I'll see him tomorrow. I can hardly keep my eyes open. Not sure what they were putting in those drinks. I'm way too woozy."

"Mom, I'm surprised you're still standing considering you started at lunch."

"Don't be so cheeky you." She hugged him and blew me and Evee a kiss. A few minutes passed and Keane returned with our drinks.

"Jingfei and Gui are back there deep in conversation. "About what," Evee askes.

"The fuck if I know. Maybe one of us should probably rescue him in about ten minutes."

"That would be you," I giggle.

"No way, she tried to keep me there too. It needs to be someone she dislikes." They both turn to me.

"You cheeky fuckers. She doesn't know me at all and has no reason to dislike me."

"She thinks you're stealing her man," says Keane. "Well, that's just nonsense. She didn't have him in the first place," I fume.

"Angel, you go rescue your man while we go for a dance."

"No Evee. Come with me," I cried.

"Pull up those big girl knickers and be off with ye. Ooh, you're not wearing any, oops."

"Sorry, what did you just say?" Keane asked. "Nothing," we squeal together. She grabbed his hand and dragged him towards the DJ.

Fuck. Do I really need to do this? If she had her way, she'd keep him there all night. As I approached, Gui leaned in and hugged her. It wasn't a normal hug either. We women know these things. She stood back and her face was beaming. When she spotted me, she wrapped her arms around his neck and pulled him closer. I didn't know whether to turn and leave or just stand there like a spare. She whispered something and he turned.

"I'll be back in a minute. Rhylee, I'm just getting Jingfei an orange juice. No fighting you two."

"Don't say anything yet," she whispered enough for me to hear.

"No, no I won't, although it's the best news ever. I'm thrilled." He hugged her again and left us alone.

Fuck's sake. I just knew she was bursting to tell me and was enjoying dragging it out. "I'm not sure what exactly you think is going on between you and Gui. But I should tell you before you end up looking foolish."

"Nothing is going on. But say what you have to say."

"You have the nerve to stand there lying when it's so obvious you were fucking him." I crossed my arms in defence. "If you have nothing nice to say, you can just fuck right off Jingfei."

"Aww, you eventually learned how to pronounce my name. Well done."

"Goodbye JINGFEI!"

"Aren't you curious to know what has put a smile on his face and made him so utterly happy?"

"Is it you fucking back to the planet you came from?" Her eyes bugged right out and I had to bite the inside of my cheek to stop me from laughing.

"I am surprised that Gui would find you entertaining because he doesn't like vulgarity." I turned to leave.

"Before you storm off like an adolescent, you should know that I'm pregnant."

"And why would I need to know that?"

"Only because Gui is the father."

"You and Gui?" I choke out. She nodded. My heart felt like someone was squeezing it tightly. So that's why he was over the moon. "When I realised what you two had been up to, I decided to tell him. If it makes you feel any better, it wasn't planned. These things happen in the throes of passion when you throw caution to the wind. Needless to say, we're both over the moon and he or she will get nothing but unconditional love. You saw it for yourself. Of course, he was shocked at first, but you saw his face."

The breath I'd been holding escapes my lungs in a gargle. "Wait. What. I don't understand."

She made a pathetic attempt at a laugh. "Come now Rhylee, you do know how babies are made." He told me I was the only person he didn't use a condom with. I looked at her smug face trying to hold it together as my heart shattered into a thousand tiny pieces. If I didn't leave right then, I was going to start wailing like a banshee. I didn't let the tears fall. I refused. Not in front of her. The smug wagon. So that's why he was going to get her juice. Of course, it is. No alcohol for the woman carrying his baby. It should have been me.

"How long?" I asked. "When?"

"We started getting closer a couple of months ago. But then you came along. It didn't matter though, I was already pregnant." She rubbed her tummy for emphasis.

I stiffened. It takes every ounce of willpower not to make a spectacle of myself. "I didn't tell anyone until my first check-up. That's the real reason I went to London."

I drew in another deep breath. "I went to the same hospital where the royal children were born. And that's where we'll have our baby. Gui has prioritised the renovations of the London house so we can all live there. Probably for the first six months or so."

I couldn't help it. Even though I bit my lips together the shaking wouldn't stop, and I fought to contain my composure. I needed to leave before I made a show of myself. Even worse. Slap a pregnant woman. A moment ago, he was fucking me hard. I'm going to be sick. Whatever we had is over. We can never recover from this, ever.

"We'll know on the next scan whether it's a boy or a girl. Which would you prefer? To know or be surprised on the day. At least Gui can come with me now for the rest of the hospital appointments. I'm sorry, I didn't mean to bore you with all the details. It must be a shock for you?"

"I'll survive."

"What will you do now?" I looked her straight in the eye. "I'm going to leave."

"Yes, I think that's the right thing to do. Go back to Ireland. No point hanging around here anymore."

I turned and left.

34

My fist slammed against the button for my floor and I burst into tears. I knew I'd have to leave here someday, but not like this. Only for I saw it and heard it myself, I wouldn't have believed it. So, this is what it feels like to have a broken heart. I want to go home now and for once, I want my mother's arms around me. I removed the dress and hung it in the wardrobe. I pulled out my weekend bag and packed what was mine. I sent Evee a text.

Back at the apartment. Don't tell anyone. Especially Gui. Will explain it all tomorrow. Enjoy the night xx

Sitting at the kitchen table looking at flights home through bleary eyes I heard keys in the front door.

"Rhylee …. Rhylee, where are you?"

"I'm in the kitchen." Evee came bounding into the kitchen and stopped in her tracks when she saw my face.

"Oh no, what's happened."

She pulled out the chair next to me and took my hands in hers. "What are you doing here? I only texted you fifteen minutes ago."

"Obviously I wasn't going to stay there knowing something shit must have happened for you to be here. I wasn't leaving you alone. So, what's wrong? You look like you've been crying to get into the Guinness Book of records." Tears trickled down my face.

"She's pregnant."

"Who's pregnant?"

"Jingfei," I sobbed.

"So?"

"She's having *his* baby." I was now wailing like a banshee.

"Please don't tell me it's Gui's."

I blew my nose into my sleeve and nodded.

"The cheating scumbag. Doing a line. Wait until I get my hands on him. I'll cut his fucking mickey off! What did he say?"

"He didn't tell me. He just found out before me. That's what they were talking about when Keane went over to rescue him."

She abruptly stood up. "What are you doing?"

"I need a drink. Do you want one? Drinking to oblivion will help you forget."

"Yeah, go on then."

She opened the fridge and moved things about. "We only have Vodka I'm afraid."

"That'll do."

"You hate Vodka."

"They all taste like shit to me anyway. I'll have a Vodka and Coke."

She filled pint glasses, classy, with ice and added Vodka and Coke. "C'mon, this is a sofa situation."

Once we were sitting comfortably. I filled her in. A second pint later, we were feral.

"So, the only way to get over a breakup or a betrayal is to…."

"Oh, fuck right off Evee, don't start that shite." We fell over laughing.

"Do you realise Rhy, we're the only people not to take our own advice," she hiccupped. My phone vibrated. We both stared at it like it was a bomb about to go off.

"Fuck! Who is it," I asked.

"I can't fucking see from here. I haven't bloody got extra vision eyes."

"Hahaha, you mean x-ray vision."

"Hahaha, that's what I said." I stretched over and fell off the sofa. Pushing the hair out of my eyes, I sobered up quickly. "Fuck, it's Gui."

"Answer it. He's only going to keep phoning before he breaks the door down."

"What will I say?"

"Oh God, I don't know."

"What if he's pissed off? I left the building."

"Fuck him, he stuck his dick in another woman and got her up the duff!"

"You're not going back, so make it good."

"Did you say anything to Keane?"

"Em, oh yeah, I said you got a call from home."

"Deadly. You're fucking amazing. Evee O'Mahoney, don't you dare scream down the phone that he's a two-faced backstabbing whore." She folded her arms over her chest and plonked back down on the sofa in a huff. "I mean it."

I took a deep breath and answered. "Hello."

"Rhylee, is everything okay? Keane said your mother phoned because your dad is in hospital. Is he okay? Why didn't you come and get me?" I looked at Evee giving her the evils.

"You were preoccupied and yes, my dad is in hospital." I blessed myself. "But he's doing fine." I blessed myself again. "I'm booked on the next flight home tomorrow. Ah no, thank you, no need to fly me home in your plane. Honestly. If it's okay. It would be better if you didn't. I'm really tired and have to leave early. I will. Yes, I'll be back as soon as he's home from the hospital. Of course, I'll miss you too." My eyes welled up and tears trickled down my cheeks. Evee sat down beside me and put her arm around me. "Yes, goodbye Gui." I hung up and flung the phone across the room then broke down sobbing.

Evee pulled me into her arms and I sobbed uncontrollably against her chest. "Sshh darling, you'll be okay. He's a fucking gobshite!"

"He acted like nothing was up. Of course, he was very concerned about my dad. Thanks, Evee."

"Sorry, I forgot I said that."

"You know I hate lying about serious stuff like that." We both blessed ourselves looking up to the ceiling and apologised for fibbing.

"He wanted to accompany me and said he'd fly out a specialist doctor from here if it would help."

"Huh, like we don't have specialists in the back of beyond Ireland. The nerve."

"He's only trying to help. Look, thank fuck it's not true. Why would he leave Jingfei? That doesn't make sense."

"Probably because she's not due for at least another seven months. The dirt bird wants his cake too! You couldn't make this shit up. Have you booked your flight?"

"Yeah," I sniffed. "You wouldn't expect me to stay, would you?"

"God no, absolutely not. I'm just thankful you weren't in a proper relationship."

"Me too."

"I know it's not what you want to hear, but in time you'll forget him."

"I can't blame him for anything. We weren't a couple. So I'm not going to be hard on myself. It's just going to be hard cutting him off."

"It is what it is. He certainly didn't know this was going to happen. Or that he'd meet you. Don't cut him off altogether. I know you love him."

"Please don't tell Keane why I left. I'm not sure when they're going to tell people."

"I won't. Don't want him thinking I'm a lying backstabbing whore."

"Absolutely. I can't believe I'm going home."

"Neither can I. I'm all alone now."

"No, you're not. You have Keano."

"Do I? He mightn't want anything to do with me now that you won't be around."

"Evee, that's not true. He told me he likes you and I've seen how he looks at you. Don't you dare think like that," I yawn. "I have to go to bed."

"Do you want me to bunk in with you?"

"Absofuckingletely … NOT. We'd spend the night talking and giggling and crying. Anyway, I'm sure I'll have no problem sleeping after all that alcohol."

"Shout out if you need me."

The ten-hour flight home went by in a blur. I wouldn't let Evee come to the airport because I can't handle goodbyes. Dad was picking me up and I had no idea what I was going to tell him why I wasn't going back. Not like I can say, the man I love got another woman pregnant. I need to think up something, otherwise, I'll just bawl it all out. He was waiting in arrivals holding up a huge sign, 'The best girl in Ireland.' Oh, Jesus, it brought a lump to my throat.

I was ready to cave and tell him about the shit show I left behind. Leaving my suitcase in the middle of the floor I ran into his open arms blubbering. "Hey, what's all this about? You'll be back in no time and we get to have you for at least seven months."

I looked up at him, making sure I was hugging the right dad. "Of course, you're broken-hearted but it will all be worth it in the end." I pulled back and looked up at him again, confused.

"Evee called us last night to tell us what happened.
Imagine being a billionaire."

"Wait, what."

"She explained everything so we wouldn't keep bringing it up and upsetting you."

"Bringing what up Dad."

"About that billionaire guy."

I almost choked. "She told you about Gui?"

"Yeah, that's what I said, the rich guy."

"Do you mean G.U.Y?"

"Yes, what other guy is there?"

"You wouldn't believe me if I told you."

"Told me what?"

"Nothing Dad. Anyway, what about him?"

"She said he donated a couple of million to have the orphanage completely renovated. That the children went to several orphanages with the staff until the work was completed. I'm so happy you didn't go to one of the other orphanages like Evee did. We know how much you love those kids."

My eyes were as wide as saucers. And just like that, it was done. Love you, Evee.

Mam was delighted to see me and even shed a tear or two. She looked the same except she wasn't dying her hair blonde anymore. Her slate-grey bob suited her.

"You look gorgeous Mam and your hair is fab. You should have let it go grey sooner."

"Do you think so?"

"Definitely."

"So dear, would you like to go out for dinner to celebrate or get a takeaway?" she asked.

I looked from one to the other. "Celebrate what?"

"Why you coming home of course."

"Ahh no. That's okay Mam."

"A takeaway it is so," dad grins.

"Is vegetable Szechuan still your favourite?"

"Yes, Dad."

"But without the water chestnuts, mushrooms, bamboo shoots, mangetout and broccoli?"

"Patrick, it would be just as easy to ask for a vegetable Szechuan with just onions, peppers and bean sprouts."

"I don't know. Who ever heard of a vegetarian who doesn't like most vegetables," he sighed.

"I'm a pescetarian, Dad."

"Oh, is that what they call people who don't eat veg."

"Patrick, she's only in the door, stop winding her up or she'll leave us again. Are you sure you want Chinese food? I thought you'd be sick of it by now?"

"Our Chinese takeaways are not the same as over there. They changed the dishes here to suit our palate. I'm going to my room for a little sleep. Is that okay?"

"You go and rest and I'll call you a half-hour before the food arrives."

"Thanks, Mam, I'm exhausted." As I made my way up the stairs my phone pinged.

"Rhylee dear, I put fresh pjs in the hot press, save you going through your case."

"Thank you, that's very thoughtful." Growing up, mam would always warm up my pyjamas in the hot press. Or if I was working late. It's the little things. I removed my makeup and changed into my lovely warm new pjs. Thanks, mam. I climbed under my duvet and opened my phone. Gui's name lit up the screen. Usually, I'd get excited seeing it but it didn't feel the same now.

Hey, hope you got home safely and your father is okay. Let me know if you need anything. Lan hasn't stopped crying since I told her you've gone home for a while. She thought this was your home....

I was sad that I didn't get to see Lan before I left. I just wanted to get out of there as quickly as possible. From what Gui said, she probably wouldn't have let me go. I'll phone her in a few days. I don't know if her situation will change. Now there's a baby on the way, I can't see Jingfei treating her like her own. It's something else for me to worry about. I texted Evee and thanked her for getting me out of a hot mess and that I'd call her in a few days when I settled back in. What the fuck was I going to do now? I can hardly sit around with my parents all day. I fell asleep almost immediately.

Surprisingly, I had a wonderful sleep considering what had happened. Mam called from the bottom of the stairs that the food was on the way. I stretched, then turned over and looked at my phone. There was a message from Keane.

> ***I can't believe you never said goodbye. I know you're coming back at some stage. But I'm missing you already.***

I shut the phone off and went downstairs. I sat at the kitchen table leaning on my elbows. As mam walked by, she stopped in her tracks. "Oh, my goodness Rhylee. What on earth happened to your arm." She put the napkins down and moved closer to get a better look.

"Patrick," she called out. Look at Rhylee's arm." Oh for fuck's sake. How the hell was I going to explain that? Dad put his glasses on to take a better look. Not that he needed to, the scar was huge.

"Jesus Christ Rhylee. What happened? Is it sore?" he said as he went to poke it. Thankfully I was saved from any further interrogation by the doorbell. I grabbed my sweatshirt from the cloakroom and put it on. Out of sight, out of mind. Hopefully. I'd have to think of something to tell them. Or should I just embellish the truth? No,

I'll tell the truth if they ask. Too much lying going on. Dinner with the parents was surprisingly nice. We had loads to catch up on and mam filled me in on all the local gossip. Afterwards, we watched a movie, all three of us without any bickering! It was fair to say they were being very good adults, for a change. While mam made a cup of tea and dad read the newspaper, I thought about Gui and I felt a pang in my heart. The changes he was going to have to make. Would they move in together? I know it's not the life he wanted and I wondered if he felt trapped. As for his lifestyle, what's going to happen there? Surely, he can't just end it. It's just not fair. I feel like shit. Fuck, I feel like I've broken up with my boyfriend. The fact I'm never going to see him again is killing me. To make it worse, my bestie is not here to help me get through it. I didn't even get to do a 'scene' or any kinky shit. It's not like he cheated on me. We weren't anything. But it still hurts. It's going to be hard not to look at magazines or stalk him on social media to see what he's doing. It's gonna hurt seeing him have a life without me. Evee won't offer up any information either knowing it would only upset me. I suppose it's best if I just rip the plaster off and be done with it. At least I'm not at the 'Bridget Jones' stage, cocooning in a blanket, drinking anything that has alcohol in it and binge-watching Netflix. No, I won't sit around ruminating about him. It's his loss, he just doesn't know it yet. Looks like I'm back to having my own separate life again. God help me! I will survive.

Eh, sure I will, I suppose. Oh my God. How do people cope with real break-ups? At least I won't get the 'you'll find someone better soon.'

"You okay darling? Asked dad. "You're in a world of your own."

"I'm fine, honestly." Mam walked in carrying a tray. "Nothing, a nice cup of tea and a bit of apple tart won't fix."

"Aw, you made my favourite."

"She was baking all night." My emotions got the better of me and I started bawling. Mam put her tea down and pulled me into her arms, making me sob harder. I know it's difficult for her to be maternal, which she's always struggled with. Maternal instinct is a myth in our house, and I was always reminded that not all women have it.

"Let it all out, darling. Those children made an impact on you, huh? It's not going to be forever. You'll be back in no time." Dad handed me a box of tissues and kissed the top of my head. I felt so guilty letting them think I was missing the children. Of course I did, but not as much as I missed him.

The days flowed by into weeks and I had several texts from Gui. He mentioned nothing whatsoever about the baby or becoming a father and I'd be lying if I said I wasn't interested. Evee couldn't tell me anything either even though she's been out with Keane many times, the subject was never brought up. The suspense was killing me not knowing.

I made an appointment to see Susie, my doctor because the Endometriosis pain was unbearable. I decided on the way there that I wanted to go back on the pill. It was the only thing to give me some relief. It was either that or a hysterectomy and I wasn't ready for that. I loved my doctor having been with her since I was a baby. She was like an older sister. She welcomed me with open arms and before my appointment, we had a chat and a cuppa. I filled her in on my time in China, obviously not everything and tried not to get emotional. What the hell was going on? My hormones were all over the place.

"So, before I fill out your prescription, have you been sexually active?" My eyes bugged.

"Yes, about three weeks ago, why?"

"We just have to be sure you're not pregnant."

"But you know I can't be."

"I know. It's just a precaution and peace of mind." She handed me a pregnancy test. "Here, do two and I'll get your prescription ready. I went through the process and carried them out on tissue paper.

"So, what are you going to do while you're back home? Surely you must be bored out of your tree."

"You know me, Susie. I hardly go outside the door. Since I've come back, mam is different with me. You know how it was for me growing up, constantly arguing. I don't feel awkward around her anymore. So, I'm okay hanging around the house. Never thought I'd say that."

"It's true, absence makes the heart grow fonder."

"But I was hardly ever at home, spending most days in Evee's."

"Yes, but you always came home. That's the difference." She came around beside me and looked down at the tests. She moved closer and picked one up. She put her glasses on and then turned the main light on. "Rhylee, you're only pregnant!"

"Stop messing. Jesus, my heart."

"I'm not messing, look. It says your pregnant." I jumped up and sprinted towards her.

"It has to be faulty."

She handed me both tests. "That's why we do two different brands." One had a little line and the other did actually say, pregnant. "Oh my God Rhylee. Wait, do another few." She opened her drawer and handed me the box. Do them all." She took my hand and squeezed it. We sat there in silence waiting for the ten tests to confirm I was one hundred percent pregnant.

"Oh my fucking God Susie. How is this possible?"

"I'm not sure. But we knew there was a small chance you could."

"But I'd just come off the pill after all those years thinking it would still be in my system. And then, of course, the Endometriosis. The reason I was on it in the first place." I burst into tears. And then Susie was in tears beside me. "I just can't believe it. I'm going to have a baby."

"Just to be sure, we're both crying like banshees with happiness? Right?"

"Oh Susie, absolutely. I'm just in shock. You know how much I've wanted a baby. You know I was broken-hearted after being diagnosed with Endometriosis." Then I was smiling and laughing like a demented lunatic. I blink at her. "Fucking hell," I say, leaning against the wall. "I'm going to be a mother after all."

She hugged me tightly. "Is there a father on the scene?"

"He's in China. I don't think he'll be in the picture.

I'm going to do it alone," I say faintly.

"Will you tell him?"

"No, there's no point."

"Either way Rhylee, it's the best news ever."

I nodded, clutching all twelve positive tests in my hands, smiling. "Would it be weird if I kept these?"

Her eyebrows shot right up, and then she laughed. "Eh, in your case, no. How do you think the folks will take it?"

"I don't know. They'll be just as shocked as I am. I'll wait for the right moment. Get it out of the way."

She plonked back down behind her desk and scrunched up the prescription. "You won't be needing this so," she laughs.

"So, what symptoms do I have to look forward to?"

"Sore boobs, fatigue, nausea with or without vomiting and increased urination."

"Lovely."

"I was a temperamental bitch. All I can say is Jack is a saint for putting up with my mood swings."

"You got a good one there. He's one of a kind."

"Yes," she says, satisfaction in her voice.

35

I walked home in a daze hugging myself. I was going to be one of those women I envied cradling their bumps, pushing a pram or taking the kids to the playground. I had a huge smile across my face and didn't care if I looked like a crazy woman. What do I say to my parents when they don't even know the baby's father exists? I wasn't scared to tell them. Actually, I had to tell someone before I burst with excitement. So, I ran like Forrest Gump all the way home.

I swung open the kitchen door, out of breath with hair stuck to my purple face. Mam was leaning against the island, drinking tea and talking to dad. "Mary, mother of God, what's wrong?" she asked panic-stricken, looking over my shoulder to see if someone was chasing me.

"Mam, Dad, I'm pregnant." Mam turned white as her cup smashed to the floor.

"Ah Mam, your favourite china." Dad turned, pausing with the cup of coffee halfway to his lips.

"Is this one of your jokes?"

"Oh Rhylee, you know I don't like that sort of joke," she said, sweeping up the pieces.

"Mam please sit down." She did as I asked, looking from me to dad. "I've just come from Susie's. That's where I was this morning. I've done loads of tests and they were all positive." Mam clutched her chest "But how? Your Endometriosis," she said.

"Guess I was lucky."

"Can we ask who the father is?"

I took a deep breath. "Dad, you know that billionaire Evee told you about. Well, it's him. He doesn't know and I'm not going to tell him. We fell out so I'd rather he wasn't in the picture."

"The guy who donated to the orphanage?"

"Yes, his name is Gui Lee."

"But why wouldn't you tell him? Is that why you came home?"

Mam was out of her chair and pulling me up into her arms. "Oh Patrick, what does it matter? It's none of our business. Rhylee is going to have a baby. Isn't it the best news? We're going to be grandparents. Oh, I've always wanted to say that. When are you due?"

"I think in about seven months. Susie is organising the hospital appointments. Mam, will you come with me?"

"Really, omg I'd love to darling. Dad can drive us there and we'll have lunch afterwards."

"Dad, are you okay with all this?" He stood beside me and placed his hands on my shoulders.

"He doesn't want the fairytale ending?"

"Afraid not Dad."

"Well then, I'm happy if you're happy and I'm happy you're here. My little girl is going to be a mother. It's a miracle."

The three of us hugged as mam and I sobbed uncontrollably. My phone pinged. I dug into my bag and pulled it out. Gui's name lit up the screen.

"I'm going to lie down for a bit. I feel tired after all that running."

"You're tired darling because you're pregnant." We both smiled like lunatics. I dragged my feet up the stairs and undressed. The trousers which once fitted perfectly were now digging into my diaphragm. When did that happen? Studying my tummy in the mirror I just looked a little bloated. Maybe it was a symptom? I was still in my first trimester. I snuggled in my comfy chair and Googled bloating in pregnancy. Yep, bloating as it happens is a common symptom. I didn't care as long as it didn't make me fart. I read his message.

> ***Hey. How's your father? I'll be flying to London on Friday because I've had to alter the plans for the cottage. I'll pop over Saturday to see you. Miss your cheeky smile.***

Oh my God, he hasn't even mentioned he's going to be a dad. He's altering the plans because of the baby. The bloody nerve of him thinking he can just drop in. I don't think so. I bet Jingfei doesn't know he wants to visit me either. Grrrr! I'm so annoyed! I got up and paced the room, deciding what to say.

> ***Hi, dad is good, thank you. I'm sorry.
> But I won't be here this weekend.***

As soon as he read my reply, he phoned. I wasn't ready to speak to him yet and didn't care if he knew I was avoiding him. I switched off my phone and went for a nap. Naps were a regular part of my routine, often napping on the couch most afternoons. I could even nap standing up if necessary. I had zero energy, so dad insisted on driving me everywhere. Sleeping became my new best friend during the first trimester. But finding a comfortable position with sore boobs and painful nipples was a feat. Then when I'd eventually doze off, I'd be up having my tenth pee. Again, I didn't care what this pregnancy was going to throw at me. As long as I had a healthy and happy baby. Gui continued calling and texting…

Rhylee, I know you're ignoring me and I don't know why? I can only assume this is goodbye. I hope to God I'm wrong because I'd miss you like crazy. I never thought I'd feel this way and thinking I may never see you again has made me question every choice I've ever made. You showed me a different way of life. And I like it. I can't stop thinking about my birthday present either. It was the best and most unexpected. The kinky things we could have discovered together. I miss you x

There was a gentle tap on my door. "It's only me darling, your mother." That always made me laugh. She sat on the edge of my bed and handed me a large gift bag. "Just a few things I thought you'd like." I sat up and peered into the bag.

"For me?"

"You can return anything you don't like. It's been quite a while since I went shopping for you."

"Ah Mam, you shouldn't have." I opened each item which was wrapped in tissue paper. I held up the first item of clothing. It was a massive, rather unsexy bra.

"It's a sports bra and was highly recommended by the sales assistant. I did Google most things, just to be sure they weren't bullshitting me." I burst out laughing. I've never heard my mam use that kind of language. She got me a few sports bras and matching knickers. A beautiful calming candle and various things for the bath including body oil.

"That oil is to stop the stretch marks. Didn't have anything like it in my day."

"Ooh, I'm going to try one of these bad boys now. My boobs are killing me." I walked out of the en-suite with a huge grin. "Oh Mam, the relief is unreal. Thanks so much." Needless to say, sports bras became my other best friend, wearing them night and day. I gave her a huge hug and she wouldn't let me go for more than a few minutes. "I want you to know that I couldn't be happier darling.

Your dad and I are here for you. You and the baby will want for nothing."

"Oh Mam, don't. I'll be bawling again."

Gui phoned several times and I ignored them all. I had visions of him landing his plane in the middle of the road right outside our house and quickly decided I shouldn't any longer. I phoned Evee and resisted the urge to tell her my exciting news. No surprise, she and Keane were now dating and I couldn't be happier for them. I wouldn't expect Keane to keep such a secret from his brother anyway. Closer to the time I'll tell her and hope she'll understand why I didn't tell her straight away.

The weeks and months flew by and my life became busier than I ever would have thought. The best part though, I now had a bump. A bump big enough to cradle.

Just like Jingfei, I wanted the sex of my baby to be a surprise. I hoped she was doing well because believe me when I say, I had some melters myself. My due date was fast approaching, and my baby bag was already by the front door and we kept one in the back of the car, just in case.

Knowing I was well-prepared helped reduce my anxiety, a smidgen. Mam and her knitting club knitted enough to dress my baby right up till they were a teenager!

The time had come to phone Evee. She answered on the second ring. "Hey babe, how are you?"

"I'm grand. How are you?"

"Put it this way, my social battery is drained."

"That's what I like to hear. Where are you?"

"Just about to put a wash on, why?"

"Are you alone?"

"Yeah, what's going on?"

"You might want to sit down for this."

"Is it a sofa situation?"

"Absolutely."

"Please tell me you've won the lotto?"

"Sort of."

I could hear her smiling. "Hang on, I'm getting a drink."

"You'll need one to be fair," I laughed.

"Okay, go. I'm sitting comfortably and have a drink in hand."

I took a deep breath and exhaled heavily. "I'm pregnant." Silence. "Are you there?"

"Sorry, I thought you said you were preggers!"

"I did."

"Fuck right off you little liar!"

"I swear to God, I'm not lying. I'm so sorry I didn't tell you sooner. It's just that I knew how close you and Keane are getting and I didn't want Gui to find out." She shrieked loudly, almost bursting my eardrum and I held the phone away from my ear.

"Bloody hell," I giggled.

"OMFG! Rhylee. You better not be joking. Are you fucking shitting me right now?"

I was in fits of laughter and then I was crying. My emotions were completely fucked up from one minute to the next.

"Oh my God, you're going to be a mammy," she said, elated.

"I didn't think I'd get pregnant on the first go," I admitted.

"Are you okay?" she asked, concerned.

"I'm getting through it. The symptoms are shite, especially nausea. Most of my favourite foods make me gag. You know what I'm like for mashed potatoes with loads of real butter. Well, the sight or smell of them now turns my stomach."

"Fuck, you're pregnant before me," she said giddily. "You are going to be the best mam ever. Speaking of mothers, how did frosty knickers take it?"

"She couldn't be happier. We've been getting on amazingly since I came home and even better since she's going to be a grandmother. I wish you were here too."

"Don't you worry, I'll be over as soon as I book a flight. My best friend is having a baby. I wouldn't miss that for the world."

"Can I ask you not to tell Keane? As much as I'm pissed off with Gui, knowing he has a second baby on the way would I'm sure be a great shock. Especially for someone who didn't want a family to begin with."

"If you're sure that's what you want, then I won't say a thing. I promise and I don't have anything crossed. I swear. Still no mention of him and Jingfei having one. It's like a big secret and as much as it's killing me, I don't want to be the one to bring it up first. I'm waiting for Keane to announce it."

"That's just bizarre. Evee."

"I know, mad."

"Sorry, I have to go."

"What already. But we haven't been speaking for long."

"My water just broke," I said calmly.

"OH. MY. FUCKING. GOD!" She screeched. I calmly walked downstairs. Mam and dad were playing Monopoly. They both looked up.

"It's time."

Dad looked at his watch. "Time for what luv?"

I pointed to my bump. "Baby wants out. In two seconds flat I was strapped in the back of the car with mam holding my hand and showing me how to breathe.

"How are you feeling darling?"

"My back is in bits, to be honest and I need to go to the loo."

"That's the baby's head pressing against it."

The day had finally arrived and I was about to bring my baby into the world. A world without a father. Confirming I am indeed a dumb blonde, I stupidly thought that once I was settled, the baby would pop out shortly afterwards. Fuck was I wrong. The doctor monitored me and said

I should go for long walks around the hospital because I wasn't ready yet, telling me it could be hours or days and they may induce me after thirty-six hours to prevent infection.

Holy fucking hell, the contractions started and walking was the last thing on my mind. I wanted drugs! Real fucking drugs! "Ow, ow, ow!" I cried. Mam began timing the contractions because they were getting stronger and closer. The day turned into night and still no sign of my baby wanting to leave the comforts they had grown accustomed to. I was grateful to have a private room because I looked like shit. Hair stuck to my sweaty face, bloated and a shade close to Barney the purple bloody dinosaur. I lay back and wondered if hallucinating was a symptom because I could have sworn, I saw Lan.

The door opened slightly, then closed and I could just about hear whispering. The door opened again and mam and dad were speaking to someone in a hushed tone. When she came back in, her face was pale. "What's wrong Mam? You look like you've seen a ghost." I tried making a joke of it but she wasn't taking the bait. She sat on the edge of the bed and held my hand. The door opened again and Evee bounded in and almost jumped on top of me with excitement.

"Evee, be careful for God's sake," mam screamed.

"Oh my God Evee, you're here. I can't believe it."

"Oh wow, look at the size of your tummy and your boobs are only massive. Are you sure you're not expecting twins," she giggled.

"You must have got a flight right away," I sobbed. I noticed she looked guiltily at mam and then back at me.

Weird! She sat down and held my other hand. "Okay, you two, what the fuck is going on. Ow! I don't need drama right now. Ow! Evee, in case you haven't noticed, I'm about to shoot your godchild out of my vagina!"

"Rhylee Murphy," said mam, shocked by my language. "Whaat! I'm going to be a godmother, I'm going to cry."

"Well, I'm reconsidering, spit it out!"

She cleared her throat. "Rhy, I want you to do something you're sometimes incapable of doing and that's listening without interrupting."

"Bloody cheek," I said, fuming, snatching my hands away to cradle my bump.

"In front of your unborn child, do you promise not to interrupt me or have a fanny fit?"

"I promise, just get on with it for fuck's sake." Mam raised her eyes to heaven. The doctor came in, poked about down there, nodded at her and left. Why did he nod at her? I'm the one having the baby. Charming!

"I'll sit over there just in case," says Evee. "Even though you promised, I just don't trust you."

"Cheeky bitch!"

"Rhylee, your language is atrocious," sighed mam. "For two young ladies, your language is most unbecoming. You'd think you were brought up on the streets." We both sniggered.

"Well, Keane and I were out having dinner." I smiled. "Gui walked in." I frowned. He was by himself and looked like he had the weight of the world on his shoulders so we asked him to join us."

I crossed my arms. "Ah God help him," I said. "Poor Gui."

"So, we chatted about this and that and then of course he mentioned you. He was pissed off that you were ignoring his texts and calls. He went on and on. Well, my blood was boiling and I couldn't keep my mouth shut. I said he had a bloody cheek trying to have his cake and eat it. He looked at me in shock, asking what the hell was that supposed to mean. I asked him if he was for fucking real, that he had another baby on the way and needed to cop on. To leave you the fuck alone and get his priorities straight and stop being a sleaze bag! He was flabbergasted, they both were. You should have seen their faces. They kept looking from one to the other, like I'd lost my marbles."

I noticed she kept looking towards the door, guilt was written all over her face.

"Evee, how the fuck did you get here? I know it wasn't on your broom." She walked to the door and opened it. "Evee, I swear to God, he better not be out there. I'm not messing, I'll murder you."

"C'mon Mrs Murphy." Mam kissed my cheek and fixed my hair as best as she could.

"He's out there isn't he Mam?"

"Your father and I have spoken to him. Seems like a lovely chap. You never mentioned how handsome he was. Please listen to him, darling."

"Well, can you at least pass me a mirror and my make-up bag?"

"You're about to have a baby, you're glowing."

"Bag NOW and do not let him in until I do damage control. Sweet Mother of Jesus," I cried, looking in the mirror. "Seriously Mam, I look like shite, the state of me. Why didn't you tell me."

"I'm quite sure he's seen you without makeup or clothes!"
"MAM!"
"You could look like Mrs Kelly down the road and he still wouldn't care."

"Mammy, you're terrible, it's not her fault she drank herself blotto because her husband is a gobshite." There was nothing I could do to fix what was looking back at me in the mirror, except brush my hair. I sighed. "Okay, let's get this over with." I groan in pain as another contraction hits my body. My brows and eyes wince and I let out a scream. "Oh Jesus, that's the worst so far."

"Are you sure you won't have any pain relief? It's not too late."

"I'm quite sure what's about to walk through the door will take my mind off it."

"Yes, he's a bit of alright," she winked. She kissed me again and opened the door. My heart was pounding in my chest. He's here. He knows. Fuck!

"Rhyleeeeeee."
"Oh my God Lan." I burst into tears as she carefully climbed up beside me and gave me the biggest hug. "Am I seeing things? You're really here," I sobbed. "I've missed you so much. Look how big you've grown."

"I've missed you so much too Rhylee. Why did you leave me?"

Holy fuck, what do I tell her. What does she know? She knows I'm about to pop one out, otherwise she would have thrown herself at me.

"I'm so happy you're here sweetheart." I kissed the top of her head as she lay awkwardly on my chest. The door opened again but it wasn't him. "Daiyu, I don't believe it." More tears. "Rhylee, you're glowing. I'm so happy to be here for this."

"Daiyu, I'm so sorry. It broke my heart leaving like that without saying goodbye to you and Lan."

"Dear Rhylee, I would have done the same thing under those circumstances. That woman is pitiful! Let's not waste precious time talking about her."

"Well, I'm in shock that you're all here. Any more surprises out there?"

"Gui said he was flying over in the private jet and asked if anyone else wanted to come. Genny wanted so much to come but Wwan is not well. Keane and Gui are waiting patiently outside."

"Oh God, I'm not sure I can handle it."

"It seems to me, you are one of the strongest women I know. Will I let him in now?" I nodded.

"Suppose so."

"Lan, give Rhylee a kiss, carefully now."

"But I don't want to go," she cried.

"Gui and Rhylee need to talk. Don't worry, you'll see her again."

"I don't believe you. You said that every time and I didn't."

"Lan darling, I'm not going anywhere. Neither are you. You can come back when I've spoken to Gui. Okay." She nodded. "Are you having a boy or a girl," she asked.

"I don't know, it's a surprise."

"I'd like a baby brother." My eyes widened.

"Let's go Lan and try some Irish tea. Bet it's not as good as ours."

She gently rubbed my tummy and whispered, "See you soon little brother." Daiyu and I looked at each other in disbelief. Lan skipped out the door and I swear to God, I thought I heard her say, "Daddy, I'm getting a baby brother!" My heart was hammering. I sniffed my underarms. A little funky, nothing I could do now.

He's here, he's here, he's actually here!

EPILOGUE

I sat there, nervous as fuck when he strode in, hot as sin and I never felt as plain and frumpy in all my life, guaranteed he left a trail of love-struck nurses. His t-shirt was stretched tightly across his chest and strained around his muscular arms. His eyes held mine and there it is, the electricity charging between us. We both stayed still but I couldn't stop my heart from beating right out of my chest. He's so fucking gorgeous, it's just not fair. He sat on the bed and said nothing for a moment and just stared at my tummy. Fucking hell. I could feel sweat beading on my forehead.

"They say the first thing you should do when you find out your girlfriend is pregnant is to show her support, because she's probably even more scared than you are."

"Isn't that why you went and got her a juice," I murmured.

He hesitated for a moment. "I got her juice because she said she was on antibiotics."

"Wait, what. That's not true."

He took my hand and circled the back of it with his thumb. "You hugged her and said it was the best news ever."

"I did because she said she'd met someone. The relief I felt when I heard those words. She lied to both of us. Evee I'm so sorry you had to go through this on your own, but I'm here now." He tenderly brushed a strand of hair behind my ear. "God, I've missed you."

"And what about Jingfei and the baby? It's not a choice. You don't get to choose who you'll play baby daddy with. I won't be part of a love triangle."

"She's not pregnant!"

"What?"

"The first I heard about becoming a father was when Evee told me the other day. And why you left. My stomach was turning, trying to figure out why. I was afraid in case it was something I did to hurt you. I can't imagine what was going on in your head and I'm so sorry. When I finally calmed down, I confronted her. She was shocked I'd found out because she'd gotten away with it for so long. She saw us rejoin the party and knew what we had been doing and was overcome with jealousy."

"Jealousy is a very ugly thing. It's like a disease and she's riddled with it. It's there all the time like a bad friend. It was my constant companion whenever I thought of the two of you together."

"I'm so sorry. She had to think quickly of a way to get rid of you. So, she played on your high morals saying she was pregnant knowing you'd do the right thing and leave."

"Nasty bitch!"

"I've told her I want nothing more to do with her and have signed over my share of our company to Keane."

I gasped in pain. "Oww!"

"Will I get the doctor?"

"It's okay. Ow. Ow. Ow!"

"Rhylee, please tell me what to do?"

"I'm fine. Do you want to feel our baby kick?"

"Our baby. Can I?" I nodded. His smile was so big I wanted to cry. I took his hand and placed it on my tummy and giggle nervously.

"Oh my God, I felt that. Holy crap, that's amazing. Does it hurt? Do you know what you're having?"

"No, it will be a surprise. And yes, I won't lie, it hurts like hell."

"Rhylee, I'm not just going to say things because I think you might want to hear them. I want you to know that I would have chosen you every time."

"What if she had been pregnant though?"

"I'd never turn my back on my child. I know you wouldn't want me to either."

"Definitely not."

"This is the best thing that has ever happened to me. From the very first moment I saw you, I knew you were my soulmate. You're etched on my heart like a tattoo."

"I didn't think you believed in stuff like that?"

"I never have, until that fateful day I met you. The thought of not having you or our baby in my life feels like my heart would break into a million pieces. Not having you there made me realise what I was missing. I'm such a fucking dick for not listening to what my heart and gut were trying to tell me all along."

I bit my lip, suppressing a smile. "Wait, did you say girlfriend?" I bury my face in my hands and sob my heart out. "Please don't cry," he begged. I shook my head, but the tears wouldn't stop coming. He held me as I sobbed uncontrollably. "Rhylee, I want the fairytale ending. I want happily ever after in our future. I've already got your parent's blessing. He climbed off the bed and got down on one knee. He stared into my eyes. His full lips curved into a smile as he dug into his pocket and pulled out a red box. My mouth dropped open in shock and I couldn't stop the frightful sobs retching from my body. You wouldn't think they were happy tears.

"Rhylee Murphy, please will you marry this dickhead?" His voice was dark and velvety. I half laughed and half sobbed as tears coursed down my face. I pull myself together and wipe my face with the sheet.

"Wait, you're asking me to … to … marry you," I stammered.

He opened the Cartier box to reveal an emerald-cut blue diamond surrounded by brilliant white diamonds with baguettes flanking each side.

"Holy shit," I shrieked with excitement, "It's ginormous."

"Not the first time you've said that," he laughed, wiggling his eyebrows.

"Oh God, don't remind me. Thinking of that makes me want to cross my legs but I can't. Is that a blue diamond?"

"Yes, a rare diamond for a rare beauty."

"Ah stop."

"So, will you?"

"Oh my God yes. Is this really happening?" I pinched myself. "Ouch." He placed the ring on my finger. "I can't believe it fits. My hands are like balloons."

"Mom said to get a size up, just in case. I'll have it resized later." Standing he gently caresses my cheek, the back of his knuckle sliding over my mouth.

"I've missed these lips, Mrs Rhylee Lee." I giggled. "For the first time in my life, I've found someone I can trust with my heart. I never thought that would happen."

"Don't, I'm going to bawl again." His large hand reached out to tip my head back. He groaned against my lips as his hands cupped my face. The kiss is soft and tender, then hungry until I scream, "Get the feckin doctor," into his mouth.

He stopped at the door as I try hard to control my breathing. "I've adopted Lan by the way." He smiles and it takes my breath away.

"You did?" Pant pant. "Oh my God, that's fucking amazing." I clenched my jaw.

"Are you sure there's no family waiting for her somewhere?"

"She was a street child. My people did a comprehensive search of the streets and they found no family."

"How."

"I'm a billionaire, that's what we do."

"Argh. Please get the doctor. Aaaaahhh!" I hear him telling everyone outside, "She said yes," to screams and rapturous applause.

A half-hour later after pushing an eight-and-a-half-pound little human out of my body I sobbed uncontrollably holding our beautiful son. Being maternal, I handled it like a pro and he was already wrapped up tightly like a chicken wrap. The nurse walked in and asked me to put him on my boob. I was a little embarrassed at first.

"Wow, clever boy. Look at him latching on and it's only his first time."

"Like father, like son," I giggled.

"He's so beautiful," Gui sobbed. And has your golden hair too."

"Oh my God, you're crying?"

"I know. I don't think I've ever cried. I just can't believe it. I'm overwhelmed with happiness just looking at him."

"His name is Mason if that's okay. After your dad." Tears fell from his eyes. Then he kissed me like I was a goddess. "What about your father, won't he be upset?"

"I had already made up my mind if it was a boy. Dad understands and wants the next one to be called Patrick. Even if it's a girl," I giggled."

"Thank you. It means so much and mom will be over the moon. Would you mind if I send her a photo of you both. Honestly, though, how are you?" His voice is gentle and caring.

"Ecstatic. The doctors gave me a five percent chance of getting pregnant because I have Endometriosis. So, as you can imagine, I would have endured any amount of pain for this little guy."

"Fuck, you are amazing."

"What about you Daddy? Having a newborn is life changing."

"So is getting engaged. Two things I never thought were going to be a part of my life. Marriage and parenthood."

"Has it dawned on you yet that this is your life from now on? You can't ask for a refund at the kiddie store."

"It's just dawned on me that I'm a father, responsible for two little humans, engaged to an angel and could have easily fucked it all up. Who cares about sleep? We'll figure it out together. I love you, Rhylee Murphy."

"Thank you," I say, resting my hands on his chest. "For what?"

"I love you is something I never thought I'd hear you say."

He runs a hand through his hair. "I was afraid. Fuck! I've said it. A grown-ass man like me, admitting he's afraid. I got used to pushing people away. That's all I knew. It became the norm and I was happy with it. I thought I was. They all had expiry dates. They just didn't know when they'd expire. Some lasted longer than others." He shook his head in disbelief. "To think I've wasted so much precious time. I've missed all your hospital appointments and should have been there to look after you. You went through it all alone and I'm so, so sorry."

I swallow hard, keeping my hands on his chest. "It's not your fault. I should have told you. I kept something precious from you and it was so wrong. Our little family has so much to look forward to."

He cupped my face and took my lips in his and kissed me for the longest time. "You know the moment I saw you, I was blown away. Innocently sitting there and oblivious to the effect you had on me. When our eyes locked, I felt all the air leave my body and I had to remind myself to breathe. I fought my feelings for you every minute of every day. I've experienced some life-affirming moments in my life, but the best one of all is right now. You can't imagine the intensity of happiness I'm feeling at this moment. I've wandered for far too long. Lost until you saved me. I've found myself. Something I thought I didn't deserve."

Any doubts or insecurities I had melted away. I threw my arms around him and we clung to each other as I cried into his chest. "Wow, who knew you were such a romantic?"

He pulled back to look into my eyes. "It's been there all along, you just peeled back the layers. Did you miss me? I'm sure you didn't have a minute to think about me."

"Well, you'd be wrong. I thought about you constantly and some nights I cried myself to sleep. It made me sick to think you were tied to her when it should have been me. I thought about you every day.

6.15 Gui is getting up.
6.25 Gui is at the gym.
8.00 Gui is driving to work.
8.20 Gui is at his desk.
1.00 Gui is having lunch. I wonder what he ate.
5.00 Gui finishes work.
5.15 Gui is driving home.
6.00 Gui walks through the front door.

I was losing my mind until I found out I was pregnant. Only for this little miracle, I would have continued functioning like an empty shell."

He leans in closer and gently presses a kiss to my lips. My body is screaming, more. "You eventually gave up though. You stopped trying." I whispered.

"I know. I felt like I was turning into a stalker. So I took a break, only because I was thinking about you too much. Didn't work though because I was still thinking about you," he laughed. "I will never leave you again. You showed me I was someone's, someone. I thank you for that. I realised, if you change nothing, then nothing will change."

The sincerity in his voice brought tears to my eyes. Again! "Will you stop," I giggled, "All this crying is making my eyes burn. And I'm sure I still look like shit." "You look beautiful."

Knock, knock.

"I suppose we should let them in now."

"Can I ask you something first?"

"Of course. Anything wifey." He popped his head around the door. Can you just give us a few minutes guys?" He sat back down and balanced his big frame on the edge of the bed. "Why did you change the plans for the London house?"

He leaned over and kissed our son's head.

"I wanted to include an indoor pool for Lan. She's practically a duck, never out of the water." I sighed in relief and rested my head on his shoulder.

"Why?"

"Ah, just Jingfei and her lies, she's just so full of it. It's disgusting what she's done."

A frown creased his brow. "Don't let it upset you anymore. I don't want to hear about that insane woman ever again. She's been dealt with. Okay!"

"Yes, Sir." Colour rushed to my cheeks as his eyes held mine as he just stared. A sexy smile worked its way across his face revealing his perfect dimples. His eyebrow rises in surprise.

"Do you know what you're doing?"

"Yes, Sir, I do." His eyes lit up in excitement as he drew in a deep breath.

"Fuck." A knowing smile crosses his face.

"I can't wait for the day to have you naked in the playroom." He said, giving me the best come fuck me look.

"Soon… Sir. When we get back home," I purred. He inhaled sharply.

"It's on the market and there's already a buyer interested in it. We can look for something here instead."

"In Ireland?" I gasped.

"Yeah, I'm sure you'd like to be around your family for a while. Ireland is just as good, if not better to have another office. The tax incentives are very appealing. We can stay between here and China if you like. I honestly don't mind which country it is as long as I'm with you."

Tears blur my vision. "I'd like that very much Mr Lee." His eyes drop to my lips and then my breasts and I feel an ache down below.

"Your tits are fucking huge."

"Mr Lee behave," I giggled. He laughed out loud. I can't wait to strip you naked and make you mine." I raised a brow. "I mean make you, my wife." He blew out a heavy breath. "My blue balls need sorting though."

I burst out laughing. My mind takes me back to how hard he was the last time we were together. Fuck's sake, I've just given birth and I'm horny as fuck. He's unlike any man I've ever known. My man. I smile. "What are you thinking about?" He asked.

I blush. I didn't think he'd notice being flushed and covered in a veil of sweat. "Nothing," I fake a smile.

"Rhylee Lee, it's written all over your face." Bloody hell! A knowing smile crosses his face. "I'm going to cry. You called me Rhylee Lee."

"Stop changing the subject." I try to stare him down.

It's no good, we both burst into laughter.

"I'd say I'm hornier than you," I whispered. He bent and whispered in my ear.

"Why are you whispering?"

I giggled. "I don't want our son to hear us talking about sex."

"Well, he's going to hear us when I get you home. Do you know how fucking hard you make me? My blue balls are almost black," he grimaced. "You wanna see?"

"Oh my God stop," I burst out laughing. He grabbed my hand and placed it over his huge bulge. "Oh," I gasped. I felt it pulsing and I went bright red. He looked at me with a dirty smile across his face. "I need you to suck my cock."

"You're so bold, Mr Lee."

"Worth a try." He lifted my hand and holds it to his chest. "We are going to have such a wonderful life, Rhylee. Now fucking kiss me." I kissed him gently as my hands ran through his hair and teased my tongue into his mouth. "Fucking hell, I'll blow if we don't stop," he growled, pulling away.

I smirked. "I think we should let them in before you lose control," I said, shaking my head with a grin. "On second thoughts. Lan should meet her baby brother first."

"You're quite right Mrs Lee."

Lan is unsure what to do when she walks in. "Say hello to your baby brother, Mason," I say. Gui lifts her onto the bed and she kisses my cheek and then Mason's.

My eyes well up as I look at my beautiful family. Then at the massive diamond on my finger and smiled the goofiest smile ever. "Thank you," I whispered.

"For what?" He asked.

"For giving me my fairytale." He looked lovingly at me and my heart fluttered.

"It's me who should be thanking you. Once in a lifetime, you meet someone special who chooses you and changes everything. I love you more than you'll ever know and I'll tell you every day."

"I love you and love that I'm getting my 'Happily ever after' with you."

Milton Keynes UK
Ingram Content Group UK Ltd.
UKHW040837160724
445389UK00001B/37